HIGHLAND LOVE

"You know what?" Catie whispered, experiencing her first surge of feminine prowess.

"What, love?" His voice sounded husky.

"I've always wondered what Scotsmen wore under their kilts."

Silence.

She let her hand slide up to his beard, back down his neck to his shoulder, then over his chest, exploring and wandering leisurely. "In fact, I find I'm wondering that very thing right now."

"Catie, darling, a wee bit further up my thigh with your hand and you'll be knowing what's under my kilt." He drew in a shuddery breath and looked down at her, somber-eyed. "I'm thinking you're wanting to prove to yourself that I'm wanting to make love with you, lass. Am I thinking right on this?"

"Maybe."

"You're needing loving, Catie, I'm knowing that. But, lass, I canna give it to ye unless it's *my* loving you're needing."

DANGEROUS GAMES   (0-7860-0270-0, $4.99)
by Amanda Scott

When Nicholas Barrington, eldest son of the Earl of Ul-
combe, first met Melissa Seacort, the desperation he
sensed beneath her well-bred beauty haunted him. He
didn't realize how desperate Melissa really was . . . until
he found her again at a Newmarket gambling club—being auctioned off by her father to the highest bidder. So,
Nick bought himself a wife. With a villain hot on their
heels, and a fortune and their lives at stake, they would
gamble everything on the most dangerous game of all:
love.

A TOUCH OF PARADISE   (0-7860-0271-9, $4.99)
by Alexa Smart

As a confidence man and scam runner in 1880s America,
Malcolm Northrup has amassed a fortune. Now, posing
as the eminent Sir John Abbot—scholar, and possible
discoverer of the lost continent of Atlantis—he's taking
his act on the road with a lecture tour, seeking funds for
a scientific experiment he has no intention of making.
But scholar Halia Davenport is determined to accompany
Malcolm on his "expedition" . . . even if she must kidnap
him!

One

Scotland, 1990

Laird Harold Cameron lay dead.

His widow, Letty, crossed the ice-crusted ridge and took her proper place. Despite the treacherous weather, the clan helicopter executed a perfect honorary *fly-by*. Its whirling props beat at the air, droning in her ears and pulsing in her temples. When it disappeared over the ridge into a wall of fog, Letty braced herself then looked down on her beloved Harry's rain-swept coffin. Pain, sharp and swift, seized her heart. Rainbow spots blinded her eyes. Her head swam, and the ground rushed up to greet her.

Carry me, she prayed. This time she couldn't walk alone. She shut her eyes and began the litany, seeking solace where so often she had found it in the past.

When she finished and felt brave enough to face what would come, she opened her eyes, but she didn't dare to glance at the five distinct groups of mourners, or to her side at her grandson, James. Though for different reasons, their haunted expressions would be the same, would only add to her agony.

A tightness spread through her chest. She stiffened against it. Burying her husband of half a century had her feeling every day of her seventy years. Empty. Angry that Harry had left her. And frightened. So very frightened. . . .

To some, her fear alone would have justified killing the

Cameron. She couldn't change that sinful fact, though it did console her to know that no man, no matter how noble or just he deemed his reasons, would openly admit that shameful truth. James had long since seen to that.

A twinge of pride for her sole heir eased the hurt that Harry's loss held on her heart. Feeling sturdier, she risked a glance at her grandson. His expression as dark as the foul winter sky, he lifted his chin until all she could see was its underside. The freezing rain quickly soaked his beard, darkening it to the color of dried blood. He looked down, worry and fear for her clouding his eyes, then stretched out his hand and dropped a fistful of crushed heather into the hole he'd chiseled into the frozen ground—the gaping hole that now held his grandfather's coffin.

Her Harry's coffin.

Oh God! Her love, her best friend, was dead!

Pain speared through her heart. Ice-cold fear crept into her bones. Shivering, she forced her arms to stay at her sides and not to cross her chest in supplication. She couldn't cry. She wouldn't. Not now and not here. Never here.

Her clan, the three neighboring ones, the villagers and James—all would expect her to face this God-awful tragedy with courage and dignity, with spirit. But the sad truth was, her spirit was sorely flagging, and she just didn't know if she had the strength to pull herself up alone.

It had only been a year—one scant year, for God's sake—since she'd buried her sole son and his wife. One scant year since she'd watched James lower their coffins into the ground on this same barren ridge.

The old pain joined the new and surged through her chest. How much heartache could one soul bear? How much pain could one small, insignificant woman withstand without losing her mind? It wasn't right for a woman to outlive her children. It wasn't . . . right.

The tears in her heart slid up her throat, choking her,

burning the backs of her eyes and stinging her nose. She fought them, and looked away.

Buried under nature's winter wrath, the Highland ridge looked stark, as bleak as the empty eyes of the Cameron mourners. Just like before. But neither empty eyes nor demons from hell could have kept James Cameron from his duties then, and they wouldn't now. Praise God, James was strong enough to see to his duties no matter how crushing his pain. Steeped in tradition, he had allowed no other man to shovel the sacred earth; he had buried his parents himself. And as Harry's sole heir and the new Cameron laird, James alone would bury his grandfather. It was fitting. Proper. And, God forgive her for her weakness, it was comforting.

A puffin trilled a mournful tune and James's knuckles bleached white. She couldn't bear seeing that. He had loved his grandfather so. Why had Harry had to die? *Why?*

Squinting against threatening tears and blowing rain, she glanced over at Father MacDuff, the old priest who had become her spiritual advisor and confidant over forty years ago. He too was steeped in tradition, droning on in the old Gaelic language, committing Harry's soul to God as if this were the twelfth century rather than the twentieth. Aye, there was good in tradition. Familiarity. Safety. Stability. . . .

Her old friend met her gaze. She saw his unease; saw it, and worried that it might be just. Maybe she *had* lost her grip on reality. Did the insane know the moment insanity struck them? Did they? Or were they filled with doubts, or even blissfully ignorant that they'd slipped over the edge into madness?

The cold fear in her grew stronger, weakening her knees. Shivering, she crossed her chest with her arms and again looked away.

One by one the Camerons stepped forward to drop rose petals on Harry's coffin. Harry had hated roses. Too many thorns, he'd said. But he had loved their scent . . . her rose water scent. She closed her eyes and again felt Harry nuzzling her neck, growling his pleasure, nipping at her skin as he had fifty years ago. As he had a week ago. She drew in a deep breath, shuttered thoughts that he would never hold her again, then opened her eyes. Since only petals fell, she didn't stop the Cameron mourners. Her Harry would carry her scent with him through eternity; her scent, and her heart.

Celwyn, the Cameron maid, stepped forward and dropped her yellow petals, her sob lifting her shoulders. She'd wrung her hands in her coat until it had crumpled the fabric. Her sister, Bronwyn, stood stone-faced at Celwyn's side, giving her the evil eye for being emotional. Letty paused to again thank God James hadn't married *that* woman, then looked back at Celwyn. She had loved Harry, too.

A tender hitch knotted in Letty's chest. Celwyn's spreading gossip of Cameron affairs in the village had annoyed Letty and, even now, she would be miffed, but to her way of thinking, James's people needed to know their laird could be gentle. That truth had surprised them, to be sure—probably as much if not more than her own breaking down.

Celwyn glanced up, and Letty saw the worry in her eyes. Heat surged to Letty's face, and she shifted her feet. Her toes had gone numb and were stinging. A blessed state, being numb, but so elusive in times of tragedy.

She supposed she shouldn't have tried to explain Catherine Morgan to Celwyn. The lass was just too young. Only with age can a body accept that things go on in this world which defy rational explanation. Only with age comes the presence of mind, and the serenity to accept all one doesn't understand.

Harry would've understood. Even with his mother's inferior English blood, he would have understood. Her Harry had been an exceptional, superior man.

The Camerons continued their trek past Harry's coffin, their footsteps crackling loudly, turning the crusted ice into muddy slush that would freeze again long before nightfall. Staring at the wet pine box littered with red, white, and yellow rose petals, Letty again suffered the lonely ache, the emptiness of losing Harry.

Especially now. Now, when she most needed him to guide her through this terrifying dilemma. Dear, dear Harry. What would he have her do?

She looked up at James. His expression had grown masked. Harry would have her tell James. Their grandson was strong but not, thank God, as ruthless as the first Cameron laird was said to have been over nine hundred years ago: a laird whose name her James shared.

She sighed. Aye, Harry would have her tell James, have her do the one thing she could not do. The risks were too high, and she had too little left to lose.

Celwyn was back in place with the Camerons and again wringing her hands. Letty fought back a sob of regret. *Oh, Harry. Talking to her was such a mistake. Yet I'd had to talk to someone. Finding that diary, learning the woman who'd written it had traveled from this time to that of the first Cameron laird, learning she'd become a Cameron ancestor and that I had brought her to Cameron . . . Well, who wouldn't have been stunned? Who wouldn't need to talk with someone?*

Letty stared at his coffin, mystified. *It can't be true, can it? How could it be true?* Shaking, she squeezed her eyes closed to shut out the possibility. *I don't even know a Catherine Morgan. But did you, Harry?*

Again Letty searched her mind, drifted back through fifty years of introductions and acquaintances, and again she failed to place any Morgan other than her old friend, Annie. Annie, who had never married and couldn't possibly have a daughter or a granddaughter named Catherine.

Oh, Harry. What am I to do? What will happen if what the diary claims proves true? What will happen to James, to all Camerons, if this Catherine Morgan shouldn't come to Cameron? If she shouldn't go back and become an ancestor?

The same dark fears that had sent Letty reeling the night she'd first found and read the diary threatened her now. Summoning every ounce of courage she could muster, she fought them. There'd been a spectacle that night, but there would *not* be a spectacle at her Harry's funeral.

I know the fault for that was mine. Why, oh why, did I claim finding the diary a miracle? If only I'd kept it to myself, then Celwyn wouldn't have heard it—or repeated it in the village. More importantly, James wouldn't have heard it. Oh, I know he overreacted in true Cameron tradition. Worrying. And I know it's my fault he ruined the chapel door with his shoulder. Letty squeezed her eyes shut, then shot Harry's coffin an apologetic look. *But the truth is that the whole ordeal surprised me. Surely you understand that. But I would have calmed down on my own . . . eventually. And if you'd been here with me where you belong instead of in that damn box, then I wouldn't have had to deal with it alone. So the fault is yours too.*

Was it really? Harry hadn't *wanted* to die. Letty fidgeted, remorseful. Snow crunched under her feet. *I'm sorry, dear. It's just that this is so hard to fathom, and James . . . Well, you were right about James. He does need a wife to soothe his soul. I know, you said so at least a thousand times. But I still say that losing a bit of his stubbornness first wouldn't hurt. He definitely gets that from your side of the family, darling, and it's such a trial.*

She sighed and looked at James from under her lashes. Tenderness welled. *Aye, he has a stubborn streak as wide as Kirkland Dam, and a temper as foul and fierce as a Highland winter. Not so fierce as yours. . . . Well, maybe it is as fierce as yours, but the night I found the diary, James was gentle. He cradled me in his arms as if I were as fragile and tender as a spanking-new bairn. He'll make a fine father, if we can ever get him to marry. He's a proud man, our James, and getting him to recant his vow not to marry won't be easy. But even if he does, if what that diary says proves true, then him marrying won't happen unless I do the right thing about this Catherine Morgan business. How could he? Oh God, Harry. What if I make a mistake? What if I—*

James touched her arm.

Letty swallowed a gasp and looked around. The Camerons were all back in place. The Kirkland clansmen stepped forward, their heads bare to the stinging rain and icy wind, their laird conspicuously absent.

"Hot-headed and lusty," Harry had said of the Kirklands fifty years ago. It was true then, and true now. Though their men weren't as lusty as Cameron men, of course.

She stared at the kilt of the man leading them; the Kirkland's second. Where was their laird? Why hadn't he come to Harry's funeral? How dare he *not* come to Harry's funeral.

No matter. Dipping her chin, she dropped her gaze to the crusty ice. No matter. Harry would meet his Maker without the Kirkland just fine. And he'd agree it was Catherine Morgan who mattered now. For James's sake, Catherine Morgan was all that mattered now.

When the last of the Kirklands returned to their group, Colin Ferguson, the youngest of the four lairds, stepped forward. "My sympathy, Lady Cameron," he said, then sprinkled a spray of soil over Harry's coffin.

How like Colin to know Harry loved the land more than what grew in it. Scotland. How Harry had loved Scotland.

Seeing pity in Colin's eyes, Letty nodded to reassure him all was well, knowing perfectly well it wasn't. Her Cameron pride intact, she then looked on to the Fergusons passing Harry's coffin single-file, their looks and expressions mimicking their young laird's.

The wind gusted and the MacPherson laird stepped forward, his billowing black coat dripping rain, his expression equally sleety. James stepped closer to her, and Letty narrowed her gaze on the big laird. The MacPherson clenched his jaw, glared at her, and then tossed snow onto Harry.

Letty nearly smiled. She didn't, of course—they were enemies—but she could have. If the MacPherson did anything the least bit kind for any Cameron, Harry would haunt the man—and MacPherson knew it. Yet he had come to bid Harry a final farewell. This time her respectful nod was genuine. Given grudgingly, but genuine.

The laird nodded back, then walked on, no doubt to tell more gossip.

So far he'd done little damage but Letty still stared daggers into his back; it was expected. Some in the village had hotly defended her. They firmly believed living with Harold Cameron could do awful things to a woman's mind. Others denied she'd been affected at all. To them, being devout as Lady Cameron surely was, she'd never succumb to such a mortal sin as insanity. As if the insane had any choice in the matter! Still others pitied her. Spirited or no, it was clear as day to them that her grief had overcome her God-given sense. Grief had soured her lust for living.

Soured *her* lust for living? If he'd been in it and not spiriting his way to heaven, Harry would've rolled over in his grave laughing at that one. But if he thought it true, he'd scorch her ears with his lectures on the Scot's duty to embrace life, on her to follow the traditions he'd held dear.

And though it rankled, she had to admit that, on hearing the gossip, a few of the villagers had preened. The old hag finally had shown her true colors. Hadn't they warned against her pious lies for years?

Letty glared at the MacPhersons. Thank God those ugly rumors had come from them, the senseless twits, and everyone knew the Camerons had been feuding with the MacPhersons for nine hundred years.

What had started that feud, anyway? Letty cocked her head.

Harry would remember. Harry remembered everything about Cameron history.

But Harry was . . . gone.

A sob rose in her throat. She swallowed it back down. Just a few more minutes and this would be over. She could do it. She could talk with Harry some more, do her duty, follow tradition and hold up for just a few minutes more. Harry would expect—no, Harry would demand her to hold up. She'd given him her word.

A MacPherson clansman strutted by and lifted his nose over Harry's grave. Letty didn't dare check to see how James had taken that snub, but still she gripped his arm to keep him in place. There would be no bloodletting brawl at her Harry's funeral. Afterward would be soon enough for James to box the upstart's ears.

Behind the clans, the villagers huddled under a sea of black umbrellas, waiting patiently for their turn to parade past Harry's coffin. They'd come to the funeral knowing the service would be a lengthy one. The old Cameron, they would say, had done too much that required forgiveness; so much that even the devout Lady Cameron's pleas for his salvation would fall on deaf ears, and Harold Cameron's soul would be spirited straight to hell.

They were wrong, of course. Letty sniffled. Her Harry was surely already tucked away, safe and snug in heaven, going on about his duties there. But she forgave them. After all, they had been deceived.

The villagers came forward. Letty gave each of them a respectful nod. It was not for the Cameron that they had braved the brutal storm, but for her. She knew that, and she loved them for it. The laird had been feared. But for reasons she'd never fully understood, the villagers and the clan members had given her their love. It was a gift she considered precious. So very precious.

Still she wasn't naïve, or unaware of their pitiful tales. Since Harry's death, rumors about her had swept through Cameron Village like a life-eating fire, belching dark secrets and family skeletons burned bare-bone clean. They knew that after she'd seen Harry dead she'd locked herself in the chapel for three full days and nights. They knew that James, God love his heart, had allowed no one in the castle to intrude on her grief. And they knew that Celwyn, the young Cameron maid, had sworn hand on the Bible to Father MacDuff that she'd heard Letty screeching her thanks to God for the miracle that would spare her grandson's life.

Uncertain it was a miracle, Letty squeezed James's arm. He covered her hand with his, and gave her a gentle pat. She stared at his fingers, blunt and strong and raw from the cold and wind. Yes, Harry would have her tell James about Catherine Morgan's diary. But whether or not finding that book had been a miracle, Letty couldn't tell James. He was a Cameron down to the marrow of his bones, and no Cameron would allow Catherine Morgan to endanger her life by going back to the first laird, as the diary said she had. For James's own safety, Letty couldn't tell him. Lacing her fingers with his, she looked up at her grandson. For her own selfishness, she couldn't tell him. She already had buried too many of those she loved. James was all she had left now. She couldn't lose him, too. Harry was . . . gone.

Dear, dear Harry. God, but she missed him. She swallowed back a sob, stiffened against the gnawing pain, thrust out her chin, then scanned the mourners with their now watchful eyes. So they had come. The defenders, the pitiers, and the MacPhersons had joined the merely curious and the few devoted mourners at Harold Cameron's funeral. Harry would have expected them. And, though Letty would have preferred that only those who'd loved Harry had come, she understood why the others had felt they must attend his funeral.

They were on a mission.

Each wanted to see for himself whose hushed whispers proved true.

Each wanted to see for himself if Lady Cameron indeed had lost her mind.

Their uncertainty terrified her. Because, truthfully, she herself wasn't sure.

* * *

I'm watching you, Letty Cameron. Aye, you've put on a brave front but, a moment ago, fear shadowed your eyes and it's bleached your face deathly white. You know everyone sees that you're struggling, yet you can't make it go away. You're wallowing in misery and fear—and I'm savoring every moment of it.

My my, I never imagined such an intense reaction from you. You look so frail and beaten that even the fat, old priest is trembling, fearful his precious Letty will soon join the Cameron in the grave. And you will—if I wish it.

I've seen MacDuff's terror before. The fool trusts everyone. That flaw has made him vulnerable for a long time. Even before he became a priest, when the good Father MacDuff was just plain Gregor Forbes, he was as easy to lead as a lamb to slaughter. Fitting that even his name isn't of his own choosing, eh? "MacDuff" comes with the collar, Letty. It's an honorary tribute to his twelfth-century predecessor, the first Cameron priest. You didn't know I knew that, did you?

There's a lot you don't realize I know. But what matters is that by whatever name he's called, this MacDuff should've known better than to cross himself—twice no less—when the coroner decreed the Cameron's death due to natural causes. Of all things. Absurd, eh, Letty? Harold Cameron dying of natural causes?

God, but I hate stupid people. And that coroner is as stupid as MacDuff. I heard MacDuff myself, later that same day atop Kirkland Dam, tell the Kirkland—the Kirkland, for God's sake—it would take a miracle to keep you alive. And that asinine remark started all the dangerous speculation. Had Harold Cameron died in his sleep without a whimper? Or had he been murdered?

MacDuff will answer for the trouble he's caused. His loose tongue has put me through hell for a week. His hell will last longer, and be more painful. Aye, that I promise. For now, all's well that ends well. The old Cameron's coffin is in the ground, and you, his proud old woman, after burying your son and his wife just a year ago with courage and not a tear, now stand slumped against James, weeping like a wounded child.

I heard you carrying on like a wild woman about that diary you found in the chapel, too. Unfortunately, you made sense only to the demons in your mind. I couldn't find the damn thing that night, but I'll find it soon. I must know what in it has affected you so magnificently.

In the meantime, my obstacles are crumbling. Oh, I know I have to be careful, especially of James. The new Cameron laird looks wooden, aye, but he is in pain. Admirable that even devastated, he stands tall and wears his red-and-black tartan plaid proudly, by God, though it's rain-soaked and limp. I wonder, Would he love his colors nearly so much if he knew I'd used them to kill his parents?

Amusing that mere water effected their fall, and it will effect his. Then I'll reclaim everything stolen from me. It's my destiny, eh, Letty?

Aye, proceeding with my plans will take cunning—the new laird is nobody's fool—but then, neither am I. I've succeeded before, and I will again.

The priest has finally finished. For that, even I give thanks. My danger again has passed. Harold Cameron is dead and buried. Soon you will leave my beloved Scotland for an "extended rest" in America. And the new Cameron will be left alone to suffer his grief. Grief that will blind him, until it's too late.

Just look at him, Letty. Even the mist rises for the arrogant bastard, enveloping him in a frosty gray shroud. 'Tis fitting, because he's at my mercy. He doesn't yet realize it, of course, but he will. And when the Kirkland is discovered, James's debt to me will double. You see, I alone will believe him innocent of attacking the Kirkland laird. But then, I alone will know who committed that attack. Clever of me to deliberately confuse everyone, eh?

I should celebrate my mischief. Aye, I should. Here at your Harry's grave, I'll whisper the words I've wanted to speak for so long: "Beware, James Cameron. Today you're a mighty laird, but by the end of the next Festival of the Brides, everything you love or value will either be mine, or dead."

I can't help but to laugh, Letty. He doesn't know I've made the vow, much less that I can keep it. But I can. I can do anything I wish, and I've proven it.

Harold Cameron is dead.

And for the third time, I've gotten away with murder.

Two

Letty Cameron sniffed. The two huge collies flanking her grandson were wet, and smelled it. Between that and James's roaring her head felt near ready to explode.

Disgusted with the lot of them, she tugged a hot pink floppy hat down on her ears. "Do lower your voice, James. I'm not deaf yet. Though if you keep shouting—"

"If shouting you deaf would keep you at home, I'm thinking it'd be the thing to do." He paced the great hall, his anger evident in his steps.

"Well, it won't." She glared at him. At times the man could try the patience of a saint. "And you can just quit your snarls. They're worse than Zeus and Cricket's."

The pounding at her temples had her shushing herself. "I'm going to America, and I won't hear another word about it."

"Damn it, Letty, you're being unreasonable."

That statement earned him a second glare, then slowed her down. This trip would seem unreasonable to James. He'd no idea *why* she was going. Her heartstrings suffered a wild jerk. He looked so worried.

She walked over to him. Cricket and Zeus flanked their master, growling. She stared at the dogs, daring them to move, and held them pinned until they hushed. "Cowards," she said, knowing they were anything but. If anyone else tried getting as close to James, Cricket and Zeus would go straight for the throat.

"Letty."

Reaching up, she patted James's bearded jaw. "Don't bother, love."

He narrowed his brows in question.

"Don't bother beating yourself to death with *if onlys*. If Harry were here, I'd still be going."

James covered her hand with his, pressing her palm flat on his tufted jaw. His voice grew tender. "I'm worried about you. It's been less than a month. . . ."

"I'm fine." Hoping she sounded reassuring, she forced a brittle smile. If her grandson knew the reason for her trip to New Orleans, he'd have her straitjacketed and locked up. Which was exactly why she'd not told him. That, and because if she failed . . . no, she wouldn't fail. She didn't dare fail. Their very lives depended on her success.

Her hand began to tremble, then to shake. She stepped away so he wouldn't feel it.

Father MacDuff rushed into the hall, huffing as if he'd just finished a marathon run and tugging his ample self out of his overcoat. Cricket and Zeus, Letty noted with disgust, ignored him. "Gregor, what's got you in such an uproar?"

"I was afraid I'd missed you." He tugged at his sleeve, but couldn't get it off.

Letty helped the poor dear. Coming from the cold into the warm hall had his glasses fogged and his skin the color of ice. "Well, you didn't. You really shouldn't rush around so. We're too old for that nonsense anymore."

"My thoughts exactly." Pacing by the rocker, James gave it a solid whack. "Maybe you can talk some sense into her, Father. She's got no business rushing off to America. Not now. She's not even out of mourning." James looked at her hot pink outfit and grimaced.

Letty stiffened. "If I mourned more than a week for Harry, he'd haunt me to my grave, and you know it. Harry hated me in black. He hated anyone in mourning, and I won't do what I know my Harry despised. Now you stop this nonsense, James. It's been years since I've seen Annie Morgan. I've said I'm going, and I *am* going."

The throb at her temple grew stronger. She resisted the urge to rub it. James wouldn't miss that telling sign. "Besides, you know your grandfather hated traveling. I couldn't get him to Edinburgh, much less out of Scotland, and I'm wanting to see my friend."

"But you don't even know Annie anymore," James said. "It's been years."

"Forty-two, since I've seen her. But we've corresponded." Letty let James see her impatience. "It's high time I saw her again. Forty-two years is being patient enough, don't you think?"

James clenched his jaw and stepped forward. "What I'm thinking, is that what I'm thinking doesn't much matter."

"Now, children," Father MacDuff intervened, his glasses finally clearing. "James, your grandmother is right. When you get our age, you need the comfort of familiar people—especially during times of stress and tragedy."

James folded his arms over his chest. "I'm familiar."

"So is Annie," Letty said, dismissing James's frown. "I would remind you, young man, I'm your grandmother, not your daughter. Though if you don't get busy soon, you'll—"

"Don't start on that again." He gave her a warning look that she completely ignored, then let out a sigh that heaved his shoulders. "All right. All right, go."

"Thank you." She lifted her chin. "I shall."

"But I'm calling you once a week to make sure you're safe."

Despite his wagging a finger at her, she knew the argument was over. She'd won. Still, it had taken her three days. At times, James could be a stubborn cuss. That definitely came from Harry's side of the family. His English mother had been more stubborn than the patch of summer weeds in the hedge maze. It'd taken years of devoted wifely work to break Harry of that flaw. Well, honesty forced Letty to admit, to weaken it, anyway. Darling as he'd been, poor Harry never had overcome the trait.

She would agree to the calls only because if she didn't, James would start the arguing all over again and her paining head demanded the reprieve. "You have my permission to call every Saturday."

James bent down, kissed her cheek, lingered for a long moment, and then whispered, ever so softly, "I love you, Letty."

If she failed, she'd never again hear him say those words. She'd never again feel the touch of his cheek pressing against her face. She forced the words out past a constriction of fear in her throat. "I love you, James."

Before the tears came, she stepped back and sucked in a breath. "Go on now. Take the dogs for a run to the stream. That always soothes your temper."

"I'm wanting to see you off."

She shook her head. "I want a private word with Father MacDuff."

James gave her a curt nod. "All right. But I don't like this. Why do you have to go to America? Why can't you do your grieving in Scotland? Your friend could come here, I'm thinking."

"For God's sake, James, stop." Totally out of patience, she pulled herself up to her full five-two. "I'll grieve where I choose, and I *choose* New Orleans. Now, not another word—and I mean it." She'd said and meant it at least twenty times in the past three days. Maybe this time, he'd listen.

Father MacDuff clasped James's shoulder. "She'll be fine, James. I'd think you'd better spend your worrying on Annie and the people in New Orleans." The priest tucked his chin and looked at James over the top rim of his glasses. "They've not encountered our Letty for some years, if you'll remember."

"But Annie's fickle," James protested.

"Annie's my friend," Letty said in a near shout. "Don't you be insulting her."

James didn't back down. "I didn't say she was a bad person, I said she was fickle." He shrugged. "Truth is truth."

He had her there. Letty lifted her chin. "She's not fickle."

He crossed his arms over his chest and stared down at her with one of his best we-both-know-better looks.

Infuriated, Letty sniffed. "She's just a wee bit eccentric."

"Excuse me?"

Narrowing her eyes, Letty shouted. "She's eccentric. Eccentric, James. But Annie is not fickle."

James gave her a cool smile, walked to the castle door, then pulled it open. Looking back over his shoulder at her, he sighed. "I give up. But the first Saturday you neglect to answer my call, I'm coming to get you. And no crazy stunts while you're there. You're a Cameron, I would remind you."

"Yes, James." She had to bite her lip to keep from smiling. He was back to using the *c* word again. That proved it beyond all doubt. At least he considered *her* sane.

"I'm serious, Grandmother."

Grandmother? Oh my, he was serious. "I see that you are. What I don't see is why you're raising such a fuss. I'll be back before Christmas. A scant month is all we're talking about here." She slid him a pitying look. "Oh. Oh, my. I hadn't considered it, but I suppose you'll be terribly lonely while I'm gone, having no wife to keep you company."

He opened his mouth, no doubt to roar, then without uttering a sound closed it again, snapped his fingers for the dogs to come, then left the castle.

Letty celebrated with a satisfied sigh. She'd known that would shut him up.

"Has he been like that all week?" Gregor busied his hands, wiping his glasses.

"Worse. Today was pretty mild, actually." She paused to frown. "If you keep rubbing so hard, you'll have your lenses as thin as paper."

Suspecting she knew why he was nervous, she walked over to the buttery, disappeared behind the screen for a moment, then re-emerged with two snifters of brandy. Her nerves could use a strong shot and, if his actions were telling, so could Gregor's. The man was awfully pale, and he kept clutching at his stomach. "Are you ill?"

"Nay, I'm fine." He took the offered glass with a grateful nod. "You're sure about going through with this?"

She wasn't sure of anything. But by her reckoning she had no choice. "Aye."

He lifted his glass. "Then, Godspeed, lass."

"God willing." She tapped her glass to his.

The sip burned going down her throat. She'd have to bring up the subject. Left to Gregor, they'd still be standing here skirting the issue on New Year's Day. "Did you read it?"

"Aye, I read it." He pulled the battered diary from his jacket then passed it to her. "And the test results agree. The parchment and ink are genuine twelfth-century."

Letty closed her eyes and let the news sink in. She'd known it, of course. But knowing it and hearing her beliefs confirmed as truth were two different things.

"And I, um, apologize for . . ."

Hearing discomfort in his voice, she opened her eyes. "For thinking I'd snapped my crackers?"

He nodded, and her heart thundered. "So you do believe it's a miracle?" she asked.

"I'm not sure what to think, lass." He sat down on the rose silk settee. "Had this happened to anyone else—"

"But it didn't. It happened to me."

"Aye." His eyes rounded. "Whether it's a miracle or not, I don't know. But I do believe you found Catherine Morgan's diary for a reason. What that reason is, only the good Lord knows for sure."

Letty sat down beside him. "You don't seem to be having much trouble accepting that this Catherine Morgan traveled back in time."

"I'm not sure she did." His gaze grew earnest. "But I'm open to the possibility. Who am I to judge what can or can't happen?" He pinched the bridge of his nose. "Besides, theories about a soul living through many lives are too common to dismiss without due consideration."

"But reincarnation isn't what we're discussing here, Gregor. This is about a woman living now who somehow went back to then."

"And wrote a diary linking herself to both times." He grasped Letty's hand. "Aye, I know. But consider it, Letty. If we believed in only what we could physically sense, we'd be lacking more than faith, now wouldn't we?"

The fire in the grate snapped. A spray of sparks shot up the chimney. "I suppose."

"We can't touch time, yet it exists. We can't touch love, yet we both know it too is real. And what of tenderness or compassion, of grief, or faith itself?" Rubbing the back of her hand, his fingers gentle yet strong and reassuring, he smiled. "I guess what I'm saying, lass, is that anything is possible. Aye, even this Catherine Morgan woman traveling through time."

Tears clogged Letty's throat, burned the backs of her eyes, and set her nostrils to stinging. For a long moment they just looked at each other, two old and trusting friends. A tear slid down onto her cheek. "I didn't realize just how much I needed to hear you say that."

"I know." He brushed the pad of his thumb over her smooth cheek and cleared his throat. "Faith's my business, lass."

"Thank you for believing in me, and for having those tests done on the diary—and for not telling James and getting him worried."

"I love you, Letty."

"I love you, too, Gregor." She gave his arm an affectionate squeeze, then stood up. "Well, I'd better get going."

"Will you go to Annie's right away?"

Letty nodded. "She's expecting me. And that's where the diary says I found Catherine Morgan."

He set his brandy snifter on an old oak table and frowned. "You don't know what will happen to her here. Have you considered that?"

Fear gripped Letty's stomach. She covered it with her hand. "I've thought about it. It seems logical that if she's living in another time, she'll not at the same time be living in this one." Letty turned her head and swiped at a tear. "But if she doesn't go back, then James will die—or cease to exist."

Gregor touched her shoulder, turned her toward him. "What are you saying, lass?"

"It's simple logic." She lifted a hand. "Catherine Morgan said in her diary she went back in time and married James Cameron. Their children—"

"Sweet Mary!" Gregor crossed himself. "James is their direct descendant!"

"Precisely." Letty grabbed the priest's hand. "And if Catherine Morgan doesn't go back, then she won't marry the first Cameron laird, and she won't have his children. Without those children, my darling Harry's ancestors won't ever be born, so—"

"Your grandson James, the current Cameron laird, will not exist," Gregor finished for her. "Sweet Mary." He crossed himself again.

Hadn't this occurred to Gregor? That Letty's life too would be different because her beloved Harry never would have been born? Intolerable, that. "For pity's sake, Gregor." Letty hissed and pulled his arm down. "You'll have your arthritis flaring up. And I might be adding that for a man who feels fine, you surely look peaked."

"I am fine, lass, and we've certainly got more pressing matters to attend to at present than my paltry stomach irritation." He stilled. "You accept this—about the diary?"

"I'm working on it. It's not easy to accept."

"The diary is authentic, Letty. It's a proven fact that it was written in 1100. And your deductive reasoning on the Cameron lineage, I'm sorry to say, makes sense." He rubbed his neck. "What we haven't proven is whether or not this Catherine Morgan was . . . sane." His face flushed red.

"At Harry's funeral you were questioning my sanity," Letty reminded him.

"I confess I was concerned, but I hadn't read the diary then."

Letty pinned her oldest, dearest friend with the same stare she'd used on James's dogs. "And now?"

"I believe, as you so eloquently put it, your crackers are unsnapped."

Enormously relieved, Letty breathed easier. "Catherine Morgan was sane too, though I'm sure she faced her share of *doubting Thomases* back in 1100—not the least of whom, I expect, was the Cameron laird she married."

Gregor retrieved the brandy snifter and clenched it until his knuckles went white. "How do you know?"

Letty debated not telling him. He'd doubted her. But, she reminded herself, she'd had more than a few doubts of her own.

She walked to the wall and looked up at the portrait of the first Cameron laird. That James was a huge man. Sitting atop a gleaming black stallion, he wore only the Cameron plaid and black boots—the clean-shaven, spitting image of her grandson.

A shiver raced up her spine. She turned to answer Gregor. "I know because I went to the archives and looked at the old records. We have them from back then, you know. Since King Edgar made James laird in 1100, every Cameron marriage, birth, and death has been recorded there."

"And you found Catherine Morgan's name mentioned?"

"I found that a Catherine married James in 1100 at the Festival of the Brides feast."

"Sweet Mary." Father MacDuff swallowed, causing his

Adam's apple to bob. "When had she arrived? From where?"

Taking it as a good sign that he'd not crossed himself again, Letty replied. "The records say she came from the mist the first night of the festival."

"Came from the mist?"

Letty shrugged. "I guess there was a frustrated poet in the family tree."

Her old friend quirked a brow. "Was the festival in June back then?"

Again Letty nodded. "Translated to the Gregorian calendar, it's the same. Two days, beginning June twenty-fourth." She set down her brandy on a little oak table then retrieved her purse from the settee. "The way I see it, I've got until then to find this Catherine Morgan and get her back here."

"What if she refuses to come?" He blinked, then blinked again. "If you tell her this—"

"She'll think I'm crazy. I know." Letty narrowed her eyes, hardened her voice. "Which is why I'm not going to tell her—or James. And neither are you."

"But—"

"No," Letty insisted. "Don't you see? If James learns any of this, he *will* believe it—I've no doubt about that. But he'll stop Catherine Morgan from meeting her destiny. He'd never risk her coming to harm."

Father MacDuff lowered his gaze. "Maybe he's supposed to stop her."

Letty looked up.

"Maybe that's why you found the diary."

"No. No, the diary says she went back," Letty contradicted him, wishing she felt as certain as she sounded. "If it were just my life involved, I wouldn't risk hers either." Letty paused, considered telling Gregor her plans. She couldn't stop Catherine Morgan from facing her future, but Letty could see to it that the woman didn't face fate alone. However, Gregor was back to looking worried again, so she decided she'd best keep her plans to herself. "I see no choice in this. Without the Camerons, the villagers don't stand a chance."

"Robert Kirkland and his godforsaken dam."

"Aye." Letty decided she might as well reveal the last of the possible proverbial nails in Catherine Morgan's coffin. And in Letty's own. She'd outlived her child and her husband. She could not, *would not,* outlive her only grandchild as well. "When I was going through the records, I learned something important about Kirkland Loch."

"Oh?" Gregor raised his brandy snifter to his lips.

"Until that same feast where Catherine Morgan met and married James, that loch belonged to Clan Cameron."

MacDuff sputtered brandy. "How—? How—?" He tried again, but got no further.

"I don't know how it changed hands." Letty gave him a few good whacks between the shoulder blades. "But I'd be willing to bet Catherine Morgan had something to do with it."

"You're breaking my back," he gasped.

"Sorry." Letty tilted her head and looked at him, still bent double. "There is another factor we've not considered."

Gregor straightened up and his face lost a bit of its flush. "I'm almost afraid to ask."

"No more so than I am to suggest it. What if Catherine Morgan goes back as she's written, but while she's there, she somehow changes history?"

He slanted Letty a look heavy with reprimand. "Fate is fate. What will be will be—anyway."

Letty narrowed her gaze. "Are you sure?"

He hesitated. "No. I'm sorry to say, I'm not."

"Neither am I." Letty slung her hot pink purse over her shoulder. "But I'm thinking that's where faith steps in."

"What?"

Letty rolled her gaze heavenward and rushed through a quick prayer for patience. "Faith, Gregor. You know—your business. Surely God wouldn't have let me find Catherine Morgan's diary to hurt her. And if she changes history, well, I'm thinking maybe God wants it changed. Why else would I have found the diary?"

Gregor shook his head. "You'd better go. You're making sense."

"I take exception to that."

"I know, lass. But be kind, mmm? I'm wearing the collar. I'm supposed to be giving, not getting, spiritual reassurance."

Letty grunted her feelings on that remark. "Really, Gregor. You are human, after all, and even a priest's soul needs a booster shot once in a while."

Catherine Morgan fingered the gold medallion at her neck and looked at the two elderly women sitting across the coffee table from her. Never in her twenty-two years had she seen more conspiratorial looks pass between two people in such a short time.

Personally, before Letty had arrived in New Orleans four days ago, Catherine had thought her godmother's friend a little flaky. But now she wasn't sure. Her reasons had nothing to do with Letty's age, though. Any woman who dared to wear a zebra stripe jumpsuit with neon orange knee-boots had to be a little touched. Yet she seemed friendly—not that Catherine expected a woman wearing such bold clothes to be timid—and she had the most beautiful green eyes, even if at times they did look haunted.

"Have you decided, then, Letty?" Annie, thin and just as eccentric as Letty, sipped her tea. Steam rose from the delicate cup.

"Aye." Letty scrolled her gaze to Catherine. "Your godmother tells me you're looking for a job."

Catherine reluctantly nodded. Fresh out of college, she needed a job she could begin building her career on: one that put her history major to use, and one that wouldn't embarrass her fiancé, Andrew. Oh, he swore her acting as a companion to her godmother didn't embarrass him, but Catherine knew better. The problem was that "history" jobs were as elusive as Andrew's approval.

"Are you interested in history, Catherine?" Letty nibbled at a cheese puff. "Scottish history, to be precise."

Catherine's heart started a low, thrumming beat, but she kept her excitement hidden. She'd always loved Scottish history, been fascinated by it. "Yes."

Now what was wrong with her throat? She'd quacked like a duck. Andrew would have been mortified.

"Good." Letty glanced at Annie. When her godmother nodded, Letty looked back at Catherine. "It so happens I have nearly a thousand years of family records that need organizing. Everything from ledgers to personal diaries." She tilted her head. "Do you keep a diary, dear?"

"Mmm, no. I don't."

"Oh." Letty smacked her lips. "Well, when my Harry was alive and I had a question about Cameron history, I'd just ask him. My Harry knew his history. My grandson, James, does too, but he's so busy, rushing around all of the time, and him with no wife to make him slow down. . . . Well, never mind about James. You'll meet him soon enough. Anyway, now that my Harry's gone, I find myself grappling. And I don't mind telling you, my dear, nine hundred years of unorganized Cameron history requires a great deal of grappling."

So did keeping up with Letty's conversation. Catherine felt dizzy. Not only did Letty's distinct brogue make following her monologue difficult, but Catherine's ability to concentrate had gone kaput. The prospect of immersing herself in a job she'd love had her mind racing and her spirit soaring.

Easing her hand to her thigh, she covertly pinched herself. When she felt the sting, she couldn't help but smile. She hadn't died and gone to Heaven. But for being on Earth, she'd come close. "I'd love that."

"Wonderful!" Letty smiled and her eyes lost that haunted look. "We'll leave for Scotland on the first of December. That'll give us five days to get you ready—"

"Scotland?" Catherine's heart sank. "I can't go to Scotland."

"Why not?" Annie asked, her brown eyes challenging.

Catherine had to think for a second. "Because of Andrew. I'm engaged, Annie. I can't just take off for another country without even consulting my fiancé."

Annie rolled her gaze. "You're not married to him yet, dear heart. I don't see why you need his approval to do the least little thing."

Annie didn't like Andrew, but did she have to flaunt her disapproval in front of Letty? Catherine's face burned. "Accepting a job in a foreign country isn't the least little thing."

"But it is something you've always wanted to do. Why not do it now?"

Letty pressed a stilling hand to Annie's forearm, then spoke to Catherine. "I would love to have you, dear. James would be equally welcoming, I'm sure. Annie says you have a deep respect for history and that's vitally important to James and me. We are Camerons, I would remind you."

"Thank you, but—"

"This arrangement would be perfect for both of us. Why don't you talk to Andrew?" Letty sat back and crossed her legs. "In fact, why not invite him to come along?"

"Really?" Her hope flared again, then just as quickly died. "Oh, no. Andrew wouldn't. He'd never leave the law firm unsupervised for more than a few days."

Letty worried her lip. "I'll tell you what. Let's prepare to go on the first of December as planned. If Andrew wants to come along, fine. If not, he and Annie surely can join you for the holidays. That's only three weeks. Then afterward, we'll come back to the States for a while."

"That'll work." Annie gave Catherine a broad smile. "Oh, Catherine, I do so want you to do this. You might never again have the chance." She stretched to refill her teacup. "Even Andrew shouldn't begrudge you three paltry weeks."

"No, he shouldn't." Catherine stood up, excited and worried. She'd defended Andrew, but she wasn't at all sure of his reaction. "I'll go call him."

Letty watched Catherine go. A beautiful woman, Harry's ancestor was. Long blond hair and eyes the color of heather. James loves heather. But why did the lass smother her emotions? She'd wanted to jump for joy—it had shone in her eyes—yet she'd held herself in check. It wasn't natural. Not natural at all.

"Well, what do you think?"

Letty wheeled her gaze to Annie. Bars of sunlight streaked through the window and across the hardwood floor near her feet. "About what?"

Annie frowned. "My godchild."

"I think what I've thought for four days. She's lovely."

"You're quite right. She is." Annie sighed and reached for another cheese puff. "You know of course that Andrew will pitch a fit about this trip to Scotland."

"Mmm, I suspected he might."

"He runs her ragged," Annie complained. "It's always what *he* wants."

"Why does she put up with it? She's surely had her share of male attention, she's beautiful."

"No, she's not—had her fair share of male attention, I mean." Annie frowned. "Andrew claimed her before her parents died. Engaged four years, you know."

"Four years? I don't believe it." Letty firmly set her cup to its saucer. The fine china chinked. "Catherine's clearly an innocent."

"Yes, she is." Annie sniffed and tucked a wiry strand of gray hair back into the bun at her nape. "And if *that* doesn't prove something's wrong with Andrew, then nothing will."

"Mmm." Letty pressed a fingertip to her cheek. "If not her, then what's he after?"

"The law firm," Annie bluntly admitted. "He worked for her father."

The sun eased behind a cloud and the room darkened, fading the bars of light on the floor to shadows. Letty grimaced. "And when Jason died, Andrew took over, since he was engaged to Catherine."

"Exactly." Annie reached over to the table lamp and gave its pull chain a firm yank.

Well remembering those ill feelings from James's relationship with Bronwyn, Letty snorted. "That sorry shepherd."

Annie agreed with an emphatic nod. "But try telling that to Catherine."

Letty lifted a brow. "Stubborn?"

"As a mule." Annie grabbed a cheese puff from the plate. "And worse, she's convinced she loves him."

That did pose a problem. Letty fought the knots filling her stomach. Catherine Morgan had to go back with her—preferably, without Andrew. "So when is their wedding supposed to be?"

"June twenty-fourth."

A shiver shot up Letty's spine. "Dear God, the first day of the festival."

"Excuse me?" Annie reached for yet another cheese puff.

"I said, you're going to make yourself sick, eating all that cheese. Milk products are awfully hard to digest, you know."

"Fiddle on my digestive system, Letty Cameron. I need your help. We've got to stop my goddaughter from marrying Andrew. He'll ruin her life."

"Settle down, dear." Letty reassured her friend. "I don't think that's going to be a problem."

"It has been a problem. Andrew's changed Catherine. She used to wear her hair loose and free, and she never wore the drab browns she wears all the time now. Pastels, that's what my Catherine used to wear—inside and out." Warming to her subject, Annie slid forward on her chair. "And Catherine used to laugh, too, Letty. Really laugh, straight from her heart." Annie's worry and bitterness seeped into her voice. "But then Andrew, the prig, convinced her to tamp her 'exuberant spirit.' "

"She's been trying to please him, but she'll soon tire of that."

"She hasn't tired of it in four years."

Letty harrumphed. "My James hasn't been seeing to it that she did tire of it for four years, either." Annie gaped, but Letty calmly sipped at her tea, then added, "If everything you've told me is true, then Catherine hasn't really wanted anything Andrew didn't want—until now."

"I guess you could be right."

"Of course, I am." Letty sipped from her cup. The tangy tea felt good in her throat. "Catherine's a smart woman, she'll come around."

Annie started to reach to the plate of cookies beside the cheese puffs, but she looked at Letty, then drew back her hand. "I just hope she comes around *before* the wedding."

"Oh, I'd bet on that. When I leave here Saturday, your goddaughter will be going with me, Annie—and she'll not be marrying Andrew on June twenty-fourth."

"I wouldn't be too sure. You don't know Andrew. Don't underestimate him. He'll twist Catherine around until she thinks *not* going is her idea."

"Don't underestimate *Catherine*. There's a reason she's always wanted to go to Scotland. Some powerful reason. And I'm betting it's more powerful than Andrew. . . ." Letty reached for the phone.

"What are you doing?"

Letty gave Annie a conspirator's wink. "I'm calling the powerful reason."

Annie scrunched up her face. "What?"

The receiver at her ear, Letty rolled her gaze heavenward. "I'm calling James, dear."

Annie's confusion faded to a slow smile. "Ah, James."

In her private suite, Catherine twisted the phone cord around her finger and listened.

"Absolutely not," Andrew said. "It's five weeks until Christmas, and you haven't even finished our shopping."

"But this is Scotland, Andrew. Letty's family has a castle in the Highlands."

"Please, don't shout." His heavy sigh cracked static through the receiver. "Look, it's impossible. My family's expecting me—both of us—for Christmas. We've made plans for New Year's Eve."

Catherine swallowed her disappointment. Why couldn't he bend a little? He knew this was important to her. "We can go to the New Year's party at The Clarion next year. Please, Andrew." She hated the pleading she heard in her own voice.

"We simply can't. I have year-end reports to take care of, too."

He hadn't said it, but the implication was there. If she knew how to do those reports and did them instead of wasting her time with history, then he would have more time for her. She swallowed a sharp remark that would have accomplished nothing but to convince him he'd made a mistake in choosing her as his future wife. She hated legal paperwork. But to go to Scotland . . . "I'll do them."

Andrew laughed. "That's funny, darling."

She squeezed her eyes shut. "What's funny?"

"You're a historian. You're not qualified to do my reports."

She clenched her jaw so tight it ached. She could tell him the reports were hers. She *was* qualified, just uninterested, and it was *her* firm. But she wouldn't say any of those things. She wanted his approval—and she wanted him to give in. Ticking him off wouldn't accomplish either objective, so she settled for the simple truth. "I want to go, Andrew."

He didn't answer.

"Andrew?"

"I heard you. I'm sorry to disappoint you, but I live in the real world, Catherine. I have responsibilities. I can't flit off to a foreign country just because you have a whim. Now, you're going to have to be adult about this."

Be adult? She *was* an adult. Hadn't he noticed that she'd grown up? When was the last time he'd really looked at her?

"A whim?"

"Now, darling, you know what I mean. For God's sake don't cry. You know it makes your eyes puffy for days, and we have a client dinner on Saturday."

Another one. Andrew worked hard to keep the firm successful. She should try to be more understanding. She had promised her father . . .

A background buzz preceded Andrew's impatient sigh. "I've got another call. Look, I'm sorry about Scotland, but maybe we can go over for an anniversary or something, some time. I'll make it up to you. I promise."

Any words but those and she could have remained civil. How many times in their four years had she heard his *"I promise?"* Forty? A hundred? He'd been giving and breaking his word so long, he probably didn't even realize how worthless his promises were anymore. But he would know. She had to be honest. This was Andrew: the man she meant to share her life with, to marry. The man she loved. And she'd had it!

She drew in a deep breath for courage then, for the first time, defied her fiancé. "I'm going to Scotland on Saturday, Andrew. If you want to come at Christmas, Annie will tell you where I am. If not, then I'll be back after the New Year."

Her hand grew clammy against the plastic receiver. She'd spoken slowly to give him time to adjust.

He didn't. "Don't issue ultimatums. I won't stand for them."

"I didn't." She defended herself. "You told me what you were going to do, now I've told you what I'm going to do. That's not issuing ultimatums, it's communicating."

"Don't instruct me, either."

She didn't say it, but she thought that he was the one who needed to act like an adult. Yet maybe he was right. Maybe she'd gone too far.

Oh God, what if he broke their engagement?

When would she ever learn to temper her exuberant spirit? Andrew hated emotional displays; she knew that. A sinking feeling racked her stomach. He probably would cancel their marriage. But this was Scotland. *Scotland!*

"I'll pick you up at eight on Saturday. Wear something discreet, hmm? And not that black thing with the back out. And your contacts. You should get rid of those tortoiseshell-frame glasses, Catherine. Maybe something in a solid color. Brown, I think."

Her visions of Scotland were fading. No. No, she wouldn't let them. Not yet. "Andrew, I want to ask you something."

"Quickly, darling. I've another call waiting."

He always had another call waiting, another commitment that rated higher than her on his priority list. Still, the woman in her had to know. Since overhearing Annie and Letty's opinions on Catherine and Andrew's relationship, curiosity had infiltrated into what before then she'd just accepted. "Do you find me attractive?"

"Catherine, please. Your timing is—"

"Do you?"

"We're engaged, aren't we?"

"Do you, Andrew?" Why was she persisting? She knew she was courting disaster.

"Yes."

Slumping back against her pillows in relief, she prodded on. "Then why haven't you made love with me?"

"Don't be base, darling. It's beneath you."

"Don't you want to make love with me?"

"Catherine, please."

Her patience snapped. "Damn it, Andrew, we've been engaged for four years and you've never attempted more than a few halfhearted kisses. I think I have a right to know why."

"There is more to marriage than lust and sex."

His chilling tone made her shiver. "But shouldn't those things be a part of it?"

"Not in a Huntley marriage."

"Well, what *is* in a Huntley marriage?"

"Position, social standing—"

"Money?"

He didn't answer.

Her chin started quivering, tapping against the phone. "Do I appeal to you sexually, Andrew?"

More silence.

"I asked you a question."

"I don't want to discuss this. There's no need—"

"There *is* need. If I'm going to spend the next fifty years or so in bed with you, Andrew, there's every need. Do I appeal to you sexually?"

"No. I'm sorry, Catherine, but I don't find you particularly stimulating."

She couldn't breathe. The diamond ring on her hand felt so heavy. She jerked it off, put it down on her bedside table, then stared at it. Why didn't her heart hurt?

Numb, she decided. She was numb—all over.

"Catherine, this doesn't change anything. We'll have a good marriage."

"Annie was right all along."

"Excuse me?"

Catherine drew in a deep breath and looked away from the ring she'd once been so proud to wear. "It's not important."

"Good." He let out a nervous laugh. "Everything will be fine. You'll see. Incidentally, I changed the china pattern you selected at Carrington's. Much too garish, darling."

"It's white with an opaque iris. How can that be garish?" Catherine squeezed her eyes shut. *Please, God. Please, tell me china doesn't come in brown.*

"You'll like the one I chose. Promise. I'll pick you up at eight on Saturday."

He hadn't heard a word. But this time she refused to back down. She was through backing down. "I won't be here, I'll be in Scotland—with, or without you."

"I'm not going and neither are you. Now stop this, Catherine. I've got work to do."

She cringed at the anger in his voice, but she held her ground. "I am going, Andrew. You're welcome to come." She'd said it because he was still her fiancé, but whether or not she'd meant it would take her a while to sort out. "I know you're busy now, so I won't keep you from your work any longer. Let me know what you decide."

"What's gotten into you? Catherine? Catherine, don't you dare hang up that phone!"

Quietly, she lowered the receiver to its cradle. There was only so much she could or would do—even for her father.

James stood atop Kirkland Dam and looked down on the murky water. It seemed to grow more polluted every day. He let fly a string of curses that had Zeus and Cricket taking off for the shore.

Why in hell wouldn't Robert Kirkland listen to reason? He had to breach the dam so fresh water could flow through, and that's all there was to it. The problem wouldn't be cured, but it would reduce the immediate environmental impact and give the four lairds time to cure whatever was causing the problem. Kirkland wasn't an idiot fool who couldn't see that they had a serious problem. He *was* their problem. He respected money, not nature, and the electricity generated by his dam converted into lots of money—and unfortunately, into lots of dead fish.

Cricket's barking caught James's ear, and he looked from the three black lumps on the shore to his collie. "Zeus!" His heart raced. "Get away from that water!"

The dog loped up the shore, then crossed the moor. Cricket followed.

James frowned. The water had to be unsafe, regardless of what the Kirkland's tests showed. Nothing could look that bad and be healthy, and if the villagers didn't stop eating the damned fish and drinking the loch water, they'd be unhealthy as well. But old wives' tales die hard, and the villagers still believed the water had mystical healing powers. Worse, they believed Kirkland's damn test results.

Scanning the shoreline, James saw another lump, and grimaced. He walked across the dam, then down the slope. Squatting, he spread apart the dead grass. Another dead puffin—without a mark on it.

"Damn it." James clenched his hands into fists. If Kirkland was right and the water was safe, then why the hell was everything dying?

Having no answer, James drew himself up, walked off Kirkland's land, then back onto Cameron soil. It was time he ordered a few tests of his own—by someone *he* trusted.

My my, Cameron, I've never seen your face this naked or raw or vulnerable. Few know that in their feared laird lives a dreamer. But I know. That's my weapon to use against you. To make your dreams nightmares.

You're in a fine rage, aren't you now? Positively reeking of determination. Aye, you'll confront the Kirkland soon.

For a time, I feared his inept men would dawdle too long and not find him alive. Thankfully, he clings to life as tenaciously as you do.

So my attack was successful and has served its purpose well. You see, your heather was found on the unconscious Kirkland's chest. Naturally, all the clans blame you for his injury. Clever of me, eh—to use your heather?

Aye, you'll confront him soon. And when you do, then my work truly will begin.

Though much remains to be done, in the end, you will fall, Cameron. By God, you will. You damned me, and you must repay.

My demand?

Your life.

My dream?

To strip you bare and see you rot in hell.

Three

Catherine stopped in her tracks.

The phone rang again.

Why couldn't she move? It might be Andrew. Maybe he'd changed his mind. It *had* to be Andrew. Who else would call her at three in the morning?

In a flurry of motion, she juggled the box of tissues and grabbed up the portable phone. The lump in her throat felt like a swelling sponge. "Hello."

"Catherine Morgan?"

Hope died. She didn't recognize the man's voice, but it wasn't Andrew's. "Yes? Who's calling?"

"My name is James Cameron. I'm Letty's grandson."

Allowing her shoulders to slump, Catherine shuffled across her suite from her bed back to the piano, sat down on the bench, and plopped the tissue box down beside her. Then she tensed. It was three in the morning. This had to be bad news. "Is something wrong, Mr. Cameron?"

"Not a very pleasant greeting—even for an American," he admonished her. "I'm calling to ask about my grandmother."

Catherine sniffed and wiped an errant tear from her eye. "An ambassador, I'm not." She gave the piano keys a swipe with the tear-soaked tissue. Dull notes thunked sound into the silent night. "Especially at three in the morning."

"Ah, that explains it then."

"Explains what?" Catherine frowned. At conversing, he was as ditsy as his grandmother.

"Letty's been extolling your virtues. She says you're a sweet and gentle lass, but you don't sound much of either, I'm thinking. Though, considering the time—I'm sorry I forgot about the time change, lass—I suppose it's understandable. Yet when a man is worrying about his kin, I would remind you, a body could be a wee bit more patient with him."

Clenching her jaw, Catherine counted to ten, then counted again, to keep from letting him have it. "Your grandmother is doing fine, Mr. Cameron. If you want to talk to her though, I'll have to give you another number."

"It's three in the morning and she's not there?"

Oh, brother. Just what she needed. A raging Scotsman. "Actually, she isn't. You've somehow gotten the number to my private suite. Letty's staying with Annie in the main part of the house. I'd offer to go get her, but there are three flights of stairs."

"Well, why did she give me your number, I'm asking?"

Catherine wouldn't do it. She wouldn't yell. She cooled her voice and hoped his phone ear froze solid. "You'll have to ask her that."

"Ah, I'm understanding what she's about."

Glad one of them did, Catherine waited for him to end the call. She was really in no mood for this. Why hadn't Andrew called back? A nervous twitter attacked her stomach. Maybe he wouldn't call. No, even if Annie and Letty were right, he'd call. He wanted the firm, didn't he? But in that case, did she want him?

"Since I have you, Catherine, I'm asking, has Letty been grief-stricken? She thinks she can't grieve at home—her image, you understand—but it's not been long since Harry died, and I know she's hurting."

Empathy washed away her anger. Catherine understood hurting. Losing her parents and now this with Andrew. "She really does seem fine, Mr. Cameron. She and Annie have kept busy with what Annie calls her civic duties."

"Call me Jamie, lass." He cleared his throat. "Would you mind me calling you of an evening about her? Letty's not, um, understanding about my worrying. But I am worried, Catherine. Losing Harry was hard on her."

It had been hard on Jamie, too. Catherine could hear that it had in his voice. He didn't sound comfortable, asking for the favor, either. But his concern for his family had outweighed his own preferences. She liked that. "No, I don't mind."

"So tell me about yourself, Catherine Morgan." He sounded relieved, and determined. "Who are you, lass?"

Catherine almost snickered. She'd been asking herself that same question all afternoon and half the night. Was she engaged? Single and unattached? Was she unstimulating, or . . . ? She shunned the thought. The hurt was too fresh, too painful. "I'm just Catherine Morgan. No one special."

"Ah, you wouldn't be jesting me now, would you? If you'll recall, my kin's in your care."

"No, I'm not jesting."

"Letty says you're Annie's goddaughter and her companion."

Here it comes, she thought. The put-down for being a companion in the twentieth century. Couldn't anyone appreciate the fact that she enjoyed her job? That it gave her the freedom to pursue her interest in history? She squeezed her eyes shut. The answer to that was clear. Andrew and his friends were always saying she'd been born centuries too late. But she wasn't going to take the put-down anymore. Not one time more. "Yes, I am."

"A noble profession, I'm thinking, caring for our elders. Especially with them being, um, a wee bit eccentric. Tell me more, Catherine."

Noble? She closed her gaping jaw and tried to gather her scattered wits. "I don't know what to say."

"You could start with being American. Nay, on second thought, a body ought not to flaunt their flaws."

"Flaws?" The man *was* as ditsy as his grandmother—but interesting, in a strange way.

"Aye. Scots are superior, lass. 'Tis a well-known fact."

Boy, he was laying it on thick, accentuating his brogue. "In Scotland maybe. But certainly not here." Why were butterflies swarming in her stomach?

"There's no need to get riled, Catie. You can't help where you were born."

"Lord, you're charming." What happened to Catherine? Where had Catie come from?

"Ah, a woman of taste."

She couldn't resist. "An American." She smiled in spite of herself.

"An American, aye, but one with the good sense of a Scot. Maybe we could convert you, I'm thinking."

"I've done all the converting I intend to do, Mr. Cameron." Her heart felt ready to rocket out of her chest. "But maybe you'd consider . . ."

"Nay, lass." He chuckled. "I'm a Scotsman head to heel."

She smiled into the receiver. "The way I hear it, Harry had an English mother."

"Aye, he did." Jamie let out a sigh. "But we've forgiven him for that."

"Since he couldn't help the way he was born?" She gave herself a pat on the back for tossing his words back at him.

"Harry was a victim of his genes. But there's hope for you, lass. Convert to Scots, and ease your ails."

Only a call from Andrew—an altered Andrew—could ease her ails. "My ails and my genes are American."

"Unless you convert. Then, we'll forgive you. Think about it overnight. You'd make a hell of a Scot, Catie," Jamie went on. "I'll call for your answer tomorrow."

"Tomorrow? You're not across the street, you know."

"True, but it's not often I get to talk to an American with the voice of an angel. Most Yanks screech."

Catherine laughed, she couldn't help herself. "Letty should've warned me you're a Highland Romeo."

"Romeo was a one-woman man, I would remind you. He never strayed from his Juliet."

What did Jamie mean by that? That he did stray, or that he too was a one-woman man? She cocked her head and looked at the receiver.

"Which brings to mind your engagement. Sir Andrew, is it?"

Just how much had Letty told him about her? "Andrew Huntley," she said. Why did she want to tell Jamie she wasn't sure if she was *still* engaged? "He's an attorney."

"Oh, God. Two flaws," Jamie muttered. "All I can say, Catie lass, is you've a lot of wifely work ahead of you. But at least you're off to a good start."

His mind was a maze. An intriguing maze. "I am?"

"Aye." He dropped his voice to a husky whisper. "You answered the phone sounding sexy. Puts a man in the frame of mind for agreeing with you, lass."

Sexy? Her heart tripped over its own beat. Her voice sounded *sexy?* She had to get off the phone. "Good night, Mr. Cameron," she said in a stiff tone.

"Jamie," he corrected her and dropped the pitch of his voice. "I like the way you make it sound. Besides, we're going to be talking to each other far too often for being formal."

"Is that a threat or a promise?" Now her blasted heartbeat seemed suspended. What was wrong with her?

"A promise," he purred in that soft, husky brogue.

Relief flooded her. Promises she could handle. Men didn't keep them. Hadn't Andrew proven that? "Great. Good night, Jamie."

"Catie?"

"Yes?"

"I always keep my promises, lass. It's Scots tradition."

Had he read her mind? She swallowed hard. "Good night, James."

"Sweet dreams, Catie."

True to his word, Jamie called every night. Catherine looked at the wall clock. Every morning actually, at precisely three. But she didn't mind. Jamie made her laugh. For that, Catherine felt grateful—and suspicious. Had Letty told him about Andrew's formal defection?

At two-fifty, Catherine began clock-watching and pacing the hardwood floor of her suite. When ten minutes later the phone rang, she grabbed the receiver as if it were a lifeline. "Jamie?" Her voice cracked.

"You sound upset, Catie."

The concern in his voice had a fresh surge of tears threatening her. She swallowed them back. "A bit."

"Can I help, lass?"

Too tender! "Maybe later."

"I'm thinking I should speak to Letty—"

"To spy on me?"

"Aye."

He didn't sound at all repentant. "I'll tell you myself . . . later." Well, hell. Now she was weepy-eyed again. She swiped at her eyes and snatched up the tissue box.

"All right."

Static crackled on the otherwise silent phone, and Catherine realized he was waiting for her to choose their topic. "Letty and Annie are out for the night. Oh, sorry. Letty told you yesterday she and Annie would be at the protest overnight, didn't she?"

"Ah, the wee Louisiana deer." He feigned a totally transparent sigh. "I'd forgotten. Are the little tyrants for or against, I'm asking?"

In spite of her explicit decision not to, Catherine smiled.

James Cameron could make the devil smile, and he was a lot stronger than her. Especially tonight. "The little tyrants are eccentric sweethearts, as you well know." Letty and Annie had been very supportive today. "And, on this issue, they're *for* controlled hunting on the reservation, and *against* the 'wee Louisiana deer' starving to death."

"A worthy cause, I'm thinking."

Catherine looked up at his photo, framed in a shiny oval and perched atop the piano. Letty had put it there that afternoon. After Andrew's call, she and Annie had put Catherine to bed with hot tea and loads of pampering. A woman needs familiar things around her at a time like this, or so Letty had said.

Looking at Jamie's picture, Catherine thought Letty might just be right. His titian-colored hair hung long on his neck, and his full beard emphasized the strength in his jaw. Jamie Cameron looked much too rugged to be called handsome, and much too rustic not to appeal. His thick slashes of auburn brows and prominent cheekbones removed any doubt that he was a formidable, compelling man. One worthy of respect. And he had the most beautiful green eyes Catherine had ever seen. Transparent and honest. Yet, looking into their depths, she felt, more than saw, secrets. Secrets as distorting as depression glass.

Compelling, yes, and intriguing. But Jamie was not suave and sophisticated. She sighed wistfully. He was not Andrew.

A sharp ache filled her chest.

"Catie? Lass, are you still there?"

He sounded worried, and a little impatient. Just as his grandmother had been that afternoon. Catherine slid off the piano bench, bringing the tissue box and the photo of Jamie with her, and stumbled her way to her bed. "I'm here." She plopped down, sank deep into the mattress.

"For a moment, I thought your Sir Andrew had spirited you away on his trusted steed."

His words formed the image in her mind, and the back

of her nose started stinging. She twitched it, and blinked hard to fight against more tears. Letty, the interfering, but well-meaning tyrant, had told Jamie everything. Why didn't that surprise Catherine? If she weren't feeling so low, she'd be angry. But Jamie's sweet brogue lured, and she needed to talk with someone safe. Annie and Letty were too darned biased. They both disliked Andrew, and made no bones about it.

Gripping the receiver, Catherine's palm grew damp. She scooted up to her pillows then curled her knees to her chest. "My white knight left without me, Jamie." Pain, deep and aching, poured through her. She stiffened against it, against feeling so vulnerable—and against Jamie's possible response. He might think she needed leaving.

"Wonderful!" Jamie exclaimed. "By damn, that's the best news I've heard today!"

Catherine frowned and gave the phone receiver a good glare. "I said, he *left* me, James Cameron. Are we having a problem with slang translation here?"

"Nay, I understood you proper, lass."

She shook her head. Maybe they'd had another translation foul-up anyway. She tried another tactic. "We won't be getting married on June twenty-fourth."

"Well now, darling," Jamie said in a tone that would do the Grim Reaper proud. "Since he's left you, I would think you wouldn't be marrying him at all."

"I won't be." Admitting it out loud made the break-up real and so . . . final. The sharp pain dulled to a lonely, empty ache.

"Good," Jamie said, sounding pleased. "Then you've no need to rush back to America. You're free to stay here for the festival."

He cleared his throat and his voice took on a reprimanding edge. "I had considered it a wee slight for you to schedule your wedding during my festival, lass. But since you've sent Sir Andrew packing—"

She'd sent *Andrew* packing? "But I didn't even know you then."

"A slight," Jamie insisted, as arrogant as sunshine during a crisis. "Pure and simple."

"James Cameron, you're as sympathetic as a stone." Catherine let her frustration flood her voice. "As bad as your grandmother."

"It's in the genes," he confessed. "We're Scots, I would remind you. We hold to tradition." He paused, and for some reason she pictured him loosening his shirt collar at his throat. "But if you're set on marrying, I could replace your errant Sir Andrew, I'm thinking. You've only to say the word, lass."

Shock pumped through her, then settled. He was teasing. Of course, he was teasing. Leave it to Jamie to suggest the outrageous, the ridiculous, the unthinkable!

She uncurled then slid up on the sheets until her back rested against the headboard. What would he do if she accepted? She should. Just to see what happened. A laugh gurgled in her throat. He'd backpedal so fast he'd wind up in China. But he wouldn't squirm. Not Jamie. "You've never even seen me. What kind of man proposes to a woman he's never seen?"

"One who appreciates a woman's sexy voice."

Her heartbeat did a little skip. She pressed her hand to her chest. "Do you propose to every woman you think has a sexy voice?"

"Nay, truth is truth, and I've been dead set against marrying. But propositioning . . .Well now, that's a different matter."

He was lying. She didn't know how she knew it, but she did. "I could be a dog."

"A dog?" James growled from deep in his throat. "Tell me where to find him, Catie. I'll kill the bastard!"

Why was he angry? "Jamie, what's wrong with you?"

"Sir Andrew's got you so mixed up you're not even recalling your species, and you're asking what's wrong with *me?*"

She should've known. "It's a slang expression," she explained. "Being a dog is being ugly."

"That's worse. The fool's insulted you *and* man's best friend."

Cricket and Zeus. Catherine smiled. Letty had warned Catherine about the collies so she wouldn't be surprised on seeing them. "He did not. I said, I could be a dog. You might not like the way I look."

He scoffed, brushing that comment aside as he would a pesky fly. "I'm sure looking at you won't set me to screaming."

"You're incorrigible." Chilled, Catherine wiggled her toes and tucked her legs up under the covers. "And I might add, not at all knightly."

"I'm not a knight." He gave her an affronted sniff. "I'm a laird."

"Chivalrous," she corrected herself. "I meant chivalrous." She jerked the quilt up to her chin. "You're not at all chivalrous, James Cameron."

"You expect a man to be chivalrous when he's dying of loneliness?"

Catherine laughed in his ear and brushed her hair back from her face. God, but it felt good to relax while talking to a man. Especially to Jamie. She never knew what to expect. And no matter what she said, he didn't seem the least bit shocked, or irritated.

"I'll bet a month's salary you've got women falling at your feet." She glanced at his photo. A bet she couldn't lose. James Cameron was a bona fide hunk. Not her type—too rugged for her tastes—but a man any woman could appreciate.

"It's not a rug I'm wanting, Catie, but a warm, loving woman. These Highland winters are long and dark and cold, perfect for snuggling up by the fire and getting . . . warm."

His seductive suggestion sent a stellar flush rippling through her, and her voice softened. "Incorrigible."

"Starving," he whispered huskily in his thick brogue, rolling the *r* in a way that set her heart to thumping.

Her cheeks burned hot. She set his photo down on the pillow beside her. She and Jamie both knew he hadn't meant food, and she had enjoyed—enjoyed!—hearing him talking to her that way. Had she lost her mind? She loved Andrew.

And he'd dumped her.

She licked at her dry lips, certain this was one time when seeming obtuse would be to her advantage. "Is Celwyn refusing to cook again today?" Jamie had complained last night about her serving him sandwiches. "I told you to be more diplomatic."

"I am diplomatic."

"No, Jamie. A diplomat doesn't tell his maid her dinner tastes like spring grass."

"I like spring grass."

Catherine smiled into the receiver. "Cows eat grass, dear. Not humans."

"Chewing on a tender blade helps a man with his thinking, I'm saying."

"Worrying."

"What?"

"It helps a man with his worrying." She fluffed her pillow, then again leaned back.

"Then, too," he agreed. "You know, Catie Morgan, for an American, you're an understanding lass."

"We Americans are a very caring people. Not at all bloodthirsty."

"Are you saying Scots are bloodthirsty?"

"You must admit, Jamie, there's been a lot of bloodletting in Scotland's history."

"What do you know of Scotland's history?"

"A great deal. I did an independent study on it in college."

"You've a degree in history?"

"Don't sound so surprised."

"I'm not surprised you hold a degree, lass. I'm surprised you're that interested in Scotland."

Hearing a rumble through the phone, she frowned. "Why are the dogs growling?"

"Nay, it's not the dogs. It's my stomach. Celwyn's off at her sister Bronwyn's until Letty comes home. She's single, too, you know."

"And it wouldn't seem proper for her to stay at the castle unchaperoned?" Bronwyn. Bronwyn. Catherine was sure that during their very first conversation Letty had mentioned that name. But not that she was Celwyn's sister.

"Celwyn's reputation is worthy of consideration, even if it is damn inconvenient."

He sounded piqued. But having his honor questioned would pique Jamie. "So you're starving, hmm?"

" 'Tis the sorry truth, I am. Neglect, it is, I'm thinking. Letty ought to worry about her kin dropping from weakness instead of the wee deer."

"Poor baby. Do you think you'll survive?"

"I'm doubting it."

"Maybe you should quit pouting long enough to stick your nose out of your castle. There's a new invention that's truly amazing. I think it'll cure your ails."

"Oh?" He sounded suspicious.

Catherine smiled. "It's called a can opener, dear. You punch through a can with this contraption, wind it by its ingenious crank, and *voilà!* Instant food." She spotted a piece of lint on the quilt and plucked it off. "After you've mastered that, you can tackle heating the stuff."

"You don't say?"

"I do say," she teased. "There's a remarkable appliance in the modern world kitchen called a stove. But, I think you'd best master the basics first. In the kitchen, being a babe can be dangerous."

"I'm no babe, darling. Though if you'd a compassionate

bone in your body, you'd come rescue me right away. I'm needing feeding, love, not instructing."

Love. Feeding. Warm sparks of awareness flared through her body and settled low in her belly. Jamie's complaints about her giving him instructions sure were a lot different than Andrew's. She pressed her hand to her stomach. "A suggestive rascal too, I see." Her face had to be fire red. Why did she talk so loosely with Jamie?

"If it'll get you to my castle, I'll do more than suggest." She gasped.

Jamie laughed, warm and throaty. "I'll behave, lass, but I won't apologize. I meant every word. I do want you to come, Catie. Letty's a wee bit old to be traveling alone, I'm thinking. She is seventy, you know, and slowing down. Aye, it's time she gave up all-night protests and settled into her rocker on the castle landing."

Catherine guffawed. "Your grandmother wouldn't touch a rocking chair unless it had rocket launchers instead of rails. Neither would Annie. We should all be so 'slow.' "

"Catie, you're a mere lass. It'll be years before you're half Letty's age, I would say."

She swallowed a chuckle. He was as subtle as mud. "Are you asking my age, James Cameron?"

"Sly, eh?" A smile lurked in his voice.

"As a sledgehammer." The phone receiver grew warm in her hand. She switched to hold it with her other one.

"A man who's offered to marry a woman ought to be knowing her age, I'm saying. I'll tell you mine."

"You're twenty-six," she stated. "And I'm twenty-two."

"I knew you were interested in me!" A loud slapping sound came over the phone, as if he'd whacked his thigh. "Checked with Letty, didn't you? Go on now, lass, confess. 'Twill only hurt a minute."

Catherine rubbed her own thigh. "I believe Letty mentioned it." His would be different, harder and covered with silky hair. Her fingertips tingled. She jerked her hand back and stared at her leg as if it were a strange object suddenly sprouted. "She talks about you constantly."

"By damn, I knew it!"

"To Annie," Catherine added quickly.

"Ah, you're lying sweet Catie. But I forgive you. You're a Yank, after all." Before she could think of a sharp retort, he let out an arousing little growl and went on. "Letty talks to me about you, too."

He dropped his voice, caressed his words with that sexy Scottish brogue of his. "You've long, blond hair. I've a partiality to blond hair. Especially silky, blond hair. Did you know that?"

"Mmm, no, I didn't." Why did her throat feel so thick?

"Well, I do." He let out a sigh that she swore ruffled the fine hairs on her neck, then continued. "You've eyes as lovely as my heather, I hear. And lush, firm——"

Realizing she was sliding down on the mattress, Catherine jerked upright. "That's enough, you Highland Romeo."

Jamie laughed deeply. "Ah, Catie. I want to meet you. It's hard work for a man to steal a woman's heart over the phone."

Hard, but not impossible. In the time Letty had been here, Catherine had talked to Jamie at least once a night. Those days didn't number many, that was true, but they numbered enough. The tiny piece of her heart—that one corner Andrew had left untouched—Jamie had claimed, in a way. Sexy, but safe. Friendly and fun. Caring and . . . liberating. That's how she saw their relationship. Evidently, he did too.

"Catie, kindly attend. I said, I want your heart, love. You could answer. Unless . . . Are you overwhelmed with gratitude?"

Love. She couldn't muster a snappy retort. Fingers of sadness had clenched around her heart. "You don't want my heart, Jamie." The truth in that had her reaching for a fresh tissue. Andrew didn't either. Four years and—*poof!* He's sorry. He'd thought about their conversation and decided she'd been right. He deserved a wife he found stimulating.

Stimulating. What an innocuous word. Anger boiled inside her. Why hadn't he just spit out the God-awful truth? He'd alluded to the damning words often enough. Why hadn't he described his feelings about her in plain, simple language?

Frigid.

Failure.

Femme fatale flop.

A fine list of credits, she thought, plucking at the nubby quilt top. Disgusting.

"Catie?"

She squeezed her eyes shut. "Yes, Jamie." Damn, she was going to cry again. *Rally,* she told herself. *Rally!*

His tone deepened, and his tenderness crept to her. "Did he truly hurt you, lass?"

Oh God. Tears trickled down her cheeks and the lump in her throat seemed to swell twice its size and block her windpipe. "Hurt? Yes. Devastate? No. Deflate? Definitely."

"Did the fool say why?"

She heard Jamie's surprise, his anger, too. And something else she couldn't quite peg. But whatever it was, it felt good. "I can't lie to you, Jamie. I wish I could." She paused to draw a deep breath to disguise a sob. "Can we just not talk about it yet?"

A long moment passed, then he said softly, "You're needing a shoulder, I'm thinking." He muffled a curse at the dogs to stop their growling, then kept his voice hard. "By damn, Catie. I want that shoulder to be mine."

A tightness spread through her chest and her tears fell freely. She couldn't stop them. She tried, but she just couldn't stop them.

It was the shock. And the hurt. A woman couldn't get over loving a man or get used to the break-up of a four-year engagement in a piddling afternoon. Oh, she knew herself well enough to realize that once she did get over the shock she'd be spitting mad—even if Andrew had landed her ego a death blow.

At least Jamie sounded righteously indignant on her behalf. That helped a little. Feeling better, she reached for a fresh tissue and dabbed at her eyes, hoping she reached the mad stage before she singlehandedly upped the value of Kleenex Corporation's stock.

"Catie, are you still there?"

He sounded unsure of himself. Surprising. He didn't seem the kind of man who often felt insecure. "I'm sorry." She let out a brittle little laugh that she knew wouldn't fool him. "I'm not handling this very well, am I?"

"You're doing fine," he said. "You've no need to be strong with me, darling. Go ahead and have a good jog."

Jog? She frowned and searched her mind. "Do you mean jag? As in, a good crying jag?"

"Jog. Jag. If you Yanks would have a wee bit more respect and stop slaughtering the King's English—"

Catherine gazed heavenward and cut in. "I'm devastated here, Jamie." She purposely huffed into the receiver to be sure he didn't miss it. "The last thing I need is to argue the inferior Scot with the superior American, okay?"

He laughed.

The rotten, awful man! "Jamie," she warned. "I'm getting annoyed. You're supposed to comfort me, damn it!"

"I'm sorry, lass. I know from experience how much this sort of thing can hurt. But you're a strong woman, I would remind you."

"Well, I don't feel strong. I hurt like hell." She sniffed. "And I'd lay odds you were the dumper, not the dumpee."

"Why do you think I hide out in my Highlands?" He asked, ignoring her subtle question. "I'll tell you, lass, my sheep are much easier to get along with than a temperamental woman."

"You hide, you barbaric beast, because you love the Highlands. And because you're protecting poor womankind from the stress. Only so much of a good thing can be tolerated, and you know it. One look, and like flies, we drop at your feet."

"You have a thing for rugs, lass. No man wants a woman he can walk on. Aye, I'd settle for one woman, I'm thinking. But, nay, not at my feet. Still, you do my soul good, pretending I could have such an effect on a bonny lass."

Thoughts of where he would want his woman had her heart knocking against her ribs. "Not your soul," she argued. "I'm good for your ego. And I don't think it needs stroking."

"Everyone's ego needs stroking."

A lilt eased into his voice, but there was something else there, too. Concern maybe?

"When you come to Scotland, I'll stroke yours."

"Jamie!" Her face felt scorched. And sure that had been his intention, she forced her voice calm—calmer, anyway. "I'm sure you would—and well." Unfortunately, she was only half-kidding, and that rattled her. "But I'm slinking back to lick my wounds. I think I'll leave you men alone for a good, long while."

"You're being unfair, Catherine Morgan." He clicked his tongue to the roof of his mouth in reprimand. "Condemning mankind for the actions of one fool."

She lowered the receiver from her ear. This conversation hurt. But she didn't want to hang up. Not yet. As usual, Jamie was making her feel better. She shifted the topic. "How did the shearing go?"

"We shear in May, lass. 'Tis December." He cleared his throat. "Notice I'm being chivalrous, Catie, letting you change the subject."

"I noticed."

"You're welcome, darling." There was a tender smile in his tone. "Now, as I was saying, the wool's gone through the mill and been sold."

Catherine laughed. "I'm seeing a flock of naked sheep."

Jamie let out a very masculine growl. "I'm seeing a single naked woman."

"James!" What was the man trying to do, give her a heart attack?

"It's your fault," he said, as if he believed it. "You've got a sexy laugh, lass. It's husky and warming."

"Knock it off, Romeo." She tried to sound irritated, but couldn't. He had this strange effect on her.

"Catie?" All traces of humor faded from his voice. "You're going to refuse to come, aren't you? At the last minute, you're going to change your mind."

She looked at the lampshade, at the soft amber light pooling on the table around its shiny brass base. She'd packed and unpacked fifty times today. But Jamie's knowing didn't surprise her. He seemed linked to her ebbs and flows. "I'm lousy company."

"I'll make you feel better, lass."

He would. He had already. But something in his tone—that same something she'd heard earlier—warned there was more to this kindness than a mercy mission to get Catherine Morgan glued together again. "What's wrong?"

He hesitated for a long minute. "The truth is . . . I need your body."

A hot flash of shock then desire streaked through her and shot to her thighs. "James!"

"Mmm, sorry. Poorly put, I'm thinking." He paused to regroup, then went on. "What I'm meaning is—" He cleared his throat, sending a muffled crackling through the phone. "By damn, Catie. I mean just what I said. I *need* your body—here, with me, at the festival."

Catherine frowned into the receiver. Jamie clearly felt uncomfortable. Not upset, but embarrassed. Letty had said Bronwyn really had done a number on Jamie. He might flirt and tease, but no woman since Brownwyn had gotten close to him. He'd even sworn off marriage. That meant . . . Oh, boy. "Why do you need me there?"

"Actually, I need you before then," Jamie hedged. "Father MacDuff is ill."

Ditsy. And darned hard to follow. "Who's Father Mac-Duff?"

"He's Letty's best friend. If she loses him after just losing Harry . . ."

"I see."

"Aye, I think you're beginning to. It does grate at a man to be needing a woman and have her neglecting to answer him, lass, in case you aren't knowing."

"I'm thinking, not neglecting," she said. Jamie *needed* her. And that, Catherine concluded, pegged the problem. Jamie needed her, and he didn't want to need anyone.

She sat up, shifted on the pillows, and waited until the clock quit chiming before going on. Four o'clock. They'd been talking an hour already? "I know this isn't a proposition, Jamie, so exactly what is it?"

She could have asked herself why she felt a pang of disappointment that he hadn't propositioned her. But she already knew the answer. She was not stimulating. So why was she feeling increasingly aware of Jamie, increasingly attracted to him? Because, she told herself, he *was* stimulating. And because she'd lost her mind.

That had to be the reason. Crying over Andrew. Lusting for Jamie—a man she'd never seen face to face. She paused a second to consider that. Maybe it was just feeling wanted she was lusting after. Yes, that seemed more likely. She'd never been prone to flighty affections. Besides, Jamie was too rough, too rustic for her tastes.

Jamie ended her contemplation. "I'm fearing 'tis clear as a cloudy day I'm being about this, Catie. But truth is truth, and I do need you." He heaved a sigh that shuddered across the Atlantic Ocean and through her. "And this time, nay, I'm not proposing."

He'd substituted words again. "Propositioning," she corrected.

"That either."

She raised a questioning brow at the receiver. Had he intentionally switched from proposition to propose? No, he couldn't have. Jamie had said himself he wasn't the marrying kind. But then that meant— Oh God, he was in trouble!

Catherine jerked up. "What's wrong, Jamie?"

"First, love, calm down."

"I'm calm," she lied. She felt many conflicting emotions, but calm wasn't among them.

"I'm wanting you to know, Catie lass, that had you not told me you'd split the blanket with Sir Andrew, I'd not be asking you for this favor."

She plopped back, rested her head on the pillow. "Jamie, this is America. Andrew is not a sir, and we didn't have a blanket to split. I didn't live with the man."

"But since you have tossed him out on his foolish elbow," he went on as if she hadn't interrupted, "I do need your help with a nagging matter."

If his words got any stiffer they could make the trip from Scotland to New Orleans without benefit of Ma Bell. Still, a little of her tension eased. This matter wasn't pressing or worrisome to Jamie. It was nagging.

She pursed her lips. Bronwyn. It had to involve her. Strong, bitter feelings rose up, surprising Catherine. She'd never even met Jamie's former lover. But considering she'd never met Jamie, either, and her feelings for him were both strong and favorable, she supposed she shouldn't feel surprised.

"Shoot," she said.

"Nay, Catie." He grunted, clearly exasperated. "I'm not wanting to shoot anyone."

Catherine rolled her gaze heavenward. "American slang," she explained, settling in for a long chat. This was going to be one of *those* conversations. Jamie's phone bill for the month would rival the national debt. "I meant, go ahead."

"Ah. That's good, I'm thinking." His expelled breath

hissed over the phone line. "It's Bronwyn," he said, confirming Catherine's suspicions. "She's stirring up trouble with my neighbors again."

A swift shaft of anger arrowed through Catherine; one she hadn't expected. "I thought you two 'split the blanket' last summer."

"Aye, we did. But she's wanting to split more than the blanket, Catie. She's wanting to split my land."

"A love spat." Catherine smiled. "Scotland style."

"Now don't be getting floppy, Catie."

She resisted laughing at his stern reprimand. "I think you mean flippy."

"Isn't that what I said?"

"No."

"Damn it, Catie, I don't love the woman. Now let me get on with my begging before it chokes me."

"Watch your temper, Jamie, dear." Oddly relieved that he didn't love Bronwyn, Catie swallowed hard. "Beggars should be humble. It's what—"

"Do you know how it tries a man's patience to beg a woman who's giving him a schoolmarm's lecture? 'Tis degrading, I'm thinking."

Asking her for help was degrading? Funny, she twitched her nose, he didn't sound degraded. Or humbled. He sounded arrogant. "Mmm." She dropped the tissue box onto the carpet.

"You could pretend to be feeling a wee bit of sympathy, love."

He'd said it again. *Love.* It didn't mean anything, of course. So why did her bed suddenly feel ten degrees warmer?

Tossing back the edge of the quilt, she stretched and turned the lamp off, biting a smile from her lips. "Sorry, none to spare. I'm nursing a broken heart here, remember?"

"Nay, you're not. 'Tis merely bruised." He dropped his

voice to a husky rasp, warm and inviting. "And I've offered to fix it, I would remind you."

The tenderness in his voice brought a tear to her eye. She brushed at it and wondered if she invested in Kleenex Corporation stock if she could be cited for inside information. She *knew* they'd be showing a profit this quarter. Why couldn't she get herself off this emotional roller coaster? She'd let Andrew lead her around for a while, but not without a reason, and she'd never been a weepy, wimpy woman. "Since you've offered to marry me, I suppose I should help you."

"Does that mean you want to marry me, then?"

What was that in his voice? Hope? It was! But was it hope that she would accept his whimsical proposal, or that she'd refuse it? Either way, she gave him the only answer she could give him. "No, though I thank you for offering to be my knight in shining armor."

"I'm no knight, lass. I've told you that before."

"Laird, then," she corrected. "I meant laird. But count your blessings, dear. If I accepted, I'd have your armor rusted solid in no time flat."

"I'll risk it."

The air evaporated from her lungs. "Enough, Jamie. No more teasing on wanting or being wanted, okay? Andrew snipped my wings pretty close. I need a little time for them to grow back."

He hesitated, then grunted. "We're allies, lass. There for each other. You want a friend? I'll be your friend. You want a husband? I'll be your husband. You want a lover? Well, sweet Catie, any time."

The temperature in her bedroom spiked from warm to hot. She tossed the quilt onto the floor then rolled to the other side of the bed to cooler sheets. The man was a torch! She ought to accept. Just to see James Cameron sputter, she ought to say yes. He wouldn't squirm, no, but him sputtering might be a sight worth seeing. "Are there laws against suggestive intercontinental phone calls?"

"Suggestive?" He grunted. "I wasn't suggesting anything, Catie. I was merely expounding on our alliance so you'd know exactly where I stand. Ah, but you're not ready, are you, darling? Well, no worry. Here's what I'm thinking we should do. I'll help you get over missing Sir Andrew, and you help me diffuse Bronwyn the Terrible. Scots and American. Me and you. Allies."

Before he could get off on an international tangent—with Scots being the superior, naturally—Catherine cut in. "How exactly can this ally help?"

"Come to me, Catie. Cushion me from Bronwyn's pranks."

"What's she doing?" Jamie asking for this kind of help? Letty would faint, fall right out of her combat boots.

"I have a wee stream." His voice grew dreamy. "A beautiful wee stream that's the closest place to Heaven on Earth."

He paused and heaved a sigh that had her shivering.

"My stream empties into Kirkland Loch, and Kirkland Loch has a dam that's owned by one of my three neighbors. That neighbor is saying the loch water is safe, but it's not."

"For their sheep?" Catherine asked. Jamie owned a large flock and, she supposed, his neighbors did, too.

"Nay, love. Sheep go for long periods of time without water. We've ample rain for them."

"Safe for what, then?"

"My people. The dam generates electricity, but it also pollutes the water because that water can't flow freely. The loch is damn near stagnant."

Though she didn't understand why that was bad, Jamie's curses removed any doubt but that he thought it awful. How should she respond to that? "Oh."

"Oh?" he roared. "Oh? I'm talking about the ruination of the eco-balance of the loch here, Catherine. You could be a wee bit more outraged, I'm thinking."

If James Cameron didn't want a dam in the loch, she felt sure there wouldn't be one—at least, not for long. She smiled at the phone and forced an anger she didn't feel into her voice. "The rotten grubs. How dare they? Just who in the name of Sam Hill do your neighbors think they are to even consider ruining the—" Blast and damn. On a roll, and she'd forgotten what he'd said. "The—"

"Eco-balance, love," he finished for her, the smile back in his voice.

"How dare they consider ruining the eco-balance of *your* stream!" Far from an activist like Jamie's grandmother, Catherine still hated seeing anything—the air, the land, or the sea—abused. And had she for a moment thought Jamie serious, her outrage would have been sincere. But in just days, she'd come to know James Cameron well. Not by sight, but heart-to-heart. Their talks had been much more telling of the man than years of physically being with Andrew had been. "Give me the names of these environmental terrorists. We'll set them on their foolish elbows!"

"That's my lass." He sounded pleased. "First, there's Duncan MacPherson. Crafty, but women seem daft about him."

Jamie meant crazy. Close enough, she supposed. "A dishonest hunk." Another Andrew. Enough said. "Okay, go on."

"Colin Ferguson. He's a good sort, Catie. Young and gentle as a lamb. But Bronwyn's latched onto him and muddled poor Colin's mind, I'm thinking."

Catherine picked up Jamie's photo again. She couldn't see it in the dark, but she pressed the cool metal frame against her chest anyway. "Can a woman do that to a man—muddle his mind?"

"Bronwyn chooses her moments, love."

He'd said it again. Catherine could almost feel Jamie's blushing, and deliberately goaded him. "Her moments?"

"In the, er, you know."

How darling. James Cameron, who usually cut right to

the heart of matters, was talking around the subject. "In the what?"

He heaved a sigh that could uproot a pine. "In the bedroom, Catherine. She chooses her moments in the bedroom. There, are you satisfied?"

"Yes." Catherine swallowed a laugh. Getting Jamie on the defensive didn't happen often. But when it did, it was delightful. Still, that it had been over a woman surprised Catherine. She'd now seen it all.

James Cameron, as eccentric as his grandmother in his own way, iron-willed and stubborn and of volatile temperament, was embarrassed.

She sighed. How very darling.

"Then there's Robert Kirkland."

Jamie's voice had grown tight, laced with a strange grit that made her shudder. She looked up at the ceiling in the darkness and imagined his beautiful green eyes, remote, hard. That image bothered her.

"I believe you'd call him a viper in the grass."

"A snake," she weakly corrected. Why were her insides shaky?

"Whatever! He's bad, Catie. By damn, that's what's important. If allowed, Robert Kirkland would destroy the entire Grampians."

Bad? The Grampians? She didn't think now was a good time to tell Jamie that, currently in America, bad was good and most Americans would think the Grampians were some senior citizen's group, if not someone's grandparents. Few, she'd wager, would think them a range of mountains. "What exactly do you want me to do?"

"Don't change your mind. Come to Scotland. Stay with me for the festival." He paused for a long moment. "I need you, Catie."

He needed her. Andrew had tossed her aside. He hadn't wanted her. But Jamie wanted *and* needed her. Regardless of his reasoning, Jamie had made her feel good, less like a reject. And the plea in his voice tugged hard at her heart-strings, a plea she had no will or desire to refuse. He was a proud man. Asking her hadn't been easy for him. "The festival starts on the twenty-fourth of June, right?"

"Aye."

"Letty wants to come back to the States after the holidays."

"We need the time to plan our strategy. Besides, she'll not want to leave until MacDuff recovers." Jamie blew out a sigh. "Don't pass that along—about MacDuff being unwell, Catie. Letty will worry herself sick until she sees the man firsthand."

"What's wrong with him?"

"The doctor isn't sure. Seems he's going down every day. Stomach cramps, sweating, vomiting. It's like a case of the flu that just keeps getting worse."

"How long has this been going on?"

"Since Harry's funeral. The good father was overly fond of Harry."

She heard pride in Jamie's voice and felt his worry for his priest. "They were friends a long time. Grief, maybe?"

"I expect. That can cause all sorts of physical symptoms. He might be feeling a wee bit guilty, too. He's been in love with Letty for years, though he'd never admit that or do anything to break his vows. Gregor MacDuff is an honorable man."

"I'm sure he is," Catie agreed. "And I'm sure he loved Harry, too."

"Aye, he did that."

Catherine bit her lip. "You should tell Letty, Jamie. If my best friend were ill, I'd want to know."

"Aw, Catie. You know how she gets, lass."

"That's why *you* have to tell her."

"Compromise?"

"Terms?"

"We tell her together. There's safety in numbers, I would remind you."

"True," Catherine said. "But this is personal. Why don't you discuss it with her, and then I'll decide about staying on in Scotland."

"Nay, let's settle it now. Letty can't hold out against the both of us—about returning to the States, I'm meaning."

That soft rolling brogue again. Husky. Sexy. Catherine closed her eyes and savored hearing it. The steady ticking of the clock across the room faded. Jamie's collies growling a ruckus on his end of the line grew sharp. She felt confused, battered, and so tired.

"Catie?"

"I'll talk to her with you if you'll compromise on my coming?"

"Terms?"

Oh God. Oh God. The last of her control crumbled and tears spilled down her face. *Need me, for me. Tell me I'm pretty. Tell me you need to touch me. Lie to me, Jamie!* She fought against whimpering. Too much had happened for one day. "Before Letty gets home in her camouflage gear and her neon orange hunting vest—" Catherine paused to swallow a knot of tears lodged in her throat. "Sing to me, Jamie."

"Poor Catie, you're still needing a wee bit of soothing, I'm thinking."

"Aye, Jamie," she said, borrowing his Scots *yes* and indulging in a delicate little sniff. "I'm needing soothing."

" 'Til I can comfort you in my arms, then."

The clock chimed five just as Jamie began to sing in his rich, full-throated tenor. Catherine swore the soulful sounds could soothe the beast in anyone—even her. Even tonight. The evening Andrew officially had ended their engagement.

She closed her eyes and let Jamie's sweet notes bathe her, let them seep deep inside to rinse the hurt from her heart. And, silently, she thanked him. He had made her laugh. Had talked her through nights that would have been long and lonely. Now he was drying her tears, soothing her.

And this too, felt good.

Singing to her? The mighty Cameron?

My, my, aren't you something? Sitting there with your eyes closed, your face all flushed from the fire, singing to this Catherine Morgan you dare to call Catie. I've never seen you show such gentleness as you do with this woman, Cameron. You're so sincere!

You think you're alone in the castle, don't you? Well, you aren't. You should listen to your dogs, man. They've warned you that I'm here. I'm always here, watching you.

They're saying in the village that Letty will return come morn. Is it true? Is she bringing her friend's goddaughter, Catherine Morgan to Cameron?

Not answering, eh? Well, sing on, then. Sing on, and I will search for the diary. While you haven't heard Catherine Morgan's name before, I have. The night Letty cried it out in the chapel. Exciting night, that.

But no more exciting than now. You, the mighty Cameron laird so feared by the villagers, singing . . . a love song.

What an unexpected stroke of luck! I'll seize it, of course, to further my plans. Tomorrow I'll see you with your sweet Catie, and then I'll know if you love or value her. Then I'll know if she too must die.

Four

Through the helicopter window, Catherine saw him.

Huge and brawny and dressed in *full Highland fig,* he stood alone on the isolated moor, looking as if he'd stepped off the pages of *National Geographic* to inspire images of a historical realist, a rustic giant just barbaric enough to capture a country, or a woman's heart.

He held his jacket over his arm. His black shirt stretched snug across the widest set of shoulders she'd ever seen, his throat was bare, and the deep vee gap at the placket of his shirt exposed a healthy expanse of hairy chest. Her mouth went dry, her breathing shallowed to puffed wisps, and she lowered her gaze to his red and black kilt, to his bare knees and boots.

Boots? With a kilt? She blinked and checked again. Boots. Worn but polished glossy, and red socks dangling black tassels, hugging his calves near his knees.

The wind whipped at his russet hair, overly long and glinting burnished gold in the afternoon sun. Wishing she could see his eyes, she pressed her nose to the cold window. But while he was close enough to cast a strong, masculine impression, he was too far away to see distinctly.

"Ah." Letty shouted to be heard above the whirling props. "I guess there's no need to introduce James."

"He's beautiful," Catherine said, then grimaced. She'd thought it, but she hadn't meant to say it.

"Aye, he is that." Letty slid Catherine a satisfied smile,

then crunched down on a peanut-butter cracker. "In body and in spirit."

The helicopter set down on a concrete pad with a jarring thud. It was too late now to back out of coming. Catherine was here, in Scotland. Finally.

Though aware of the barren moor, the woods beyond it, and the castle's honey-colored towers stretching skyward behind Jamie, she couldn't seem to focus on anything except him. Why was that? He wasn't her type. His whole manner reeked of barbaric antics, not in the least bit suave or sophisticated, which is what always had attracted her to men. His hair was too long, he was too big—every inch of six-five—and he had a wicked grimace on his face that scared her right out of her socks.

Yet there was still something . . . captivating about James Cameron. But what? Worrying her lower lip with her teeth, she tried to figure that out, but failed to peg it. Hell, maybe it wasn't him. Maybe it was just this thin Highland air.

She looked at him again, let her gaze drift slowly down from his head to the tips of his boots. Her chest went tight, her breathing nearly stopped, and her stomach fluttered. Then her muscles clenched. No, it was definitely him. And why was he grimacing?

God, but she was nervous . . . and regretting their loose-tongued conversations. Not even her father, who had reprimanded her as regularly as he'd shaved, had seemed so unapproachable. There was just no telling what Jamie thought of her. He probably regretted being so open with her too, now that they were meeting face-to-face and sharing his castle.

How should she greet him? A handshake seemed ridiculous. The man had sung to soothe her, after all. A hug? No, he might think that too personal. A nod? Too indifferent. Panic seized her stomach. *How then?*

Cricket and Zeus ran from the stone castle steps across the barren ground, and then flanked Jamie, dropping to their hind-ends, alert, ears perked, ready to greet or to mutilate on their master's command.

A pang of fear shot through her chest but, just as it took hold, Jamie bent down to say something to one of the dogs, and she glimpsed what he was holding behind his back. Her fear drained away, and her heart melted. The rustic giant looked formidable, yes, as grim-faced as death, but he clenched a sprig of fresh heather in his hand. How very darling.

"Well," Letty said. "Are we going to sit here and stare at him all day, or get out of this flying tub so you can meet the man?"

"Sorry." Catherine smiled self-consciously, grabbed her purse, then ducked to step out of the helicopter. The spinning props kicked up a strong, chilly wind. On the concrete pad, she turned and offered Letty a hand. "Hold on to your cap."

Safely down, Letty gave Catherine's arm a pat. "Don't fret, dear. Unless James tells them to, the dogs won't bite."

Catherine glanced at them, then at Jamie. It wasn't the statue-like collies parked on their haunches that had her worrying. The beasts looked more friendly than their statue-like master. *He* hadn't loosened a muscle. "Jamie looks like he might."

"Bah!" Tugging on the hem of her lime green sweater, Letty stilled and then slid Catherine an inquisitive look. "Did you say, *Jamie?*"

Catherine nodded. "That's what he told me to call him."

"Ah, I see." Her eyes twinkling, Letty smoothed her skirt. "He isn't as fearsome as he looks, dear. He was worried you wouldn't come. James is a lamb. Why else would he phone you every night for the past week?"

He didn't look like a lamb. He looked as mean as sin. Of course, his grandmother wouldn't see him that way. "Five days," Catherine automatically corrected.

"Five days, then." Letty lifted a superior brow.

Catherine shrugged. If she were looking at the teasing,

sensual man who had charmed her with his banter and soothed her with his songs, she could agree with Letty. But this nearly bare-chested giant appeared far different from the Jamie she knew. On the phone, he'd been warm and intimate—Jamie. But in the flesh, James Cameron seemed remote and cold. She fingered the medallion at her neck. Maybe if she knew what was on his mind, she could reconcile the two. Was he glad she was here? Sorry he'd invited her? Wishing she'd refused to come despite his insistence that she should? What was he thinking . . . ?

She was the most beautiful woman he had ever seen.

James specifically directed the thought to go away three times, yet it still stuck like glue. Evidently, it would take a wee bit of time to get used to her looks. Annoying, that—and provoking. Why shouldn't he become the barbaric beast she'd accused him of being? It made perfect sense. Aye, he could drag her into his castle and make passionate love to her until she couldn't remember Sir Andrew's name, much less that she was loving the man.

A tempting strategy, sure as certain. But one posing three distinct problems. One, they'd have to get out of bed sometime. He swept her head to heel with his gaze, and inwardly shuddered. Though with her sweet curves that could take a good long while. Two, Catie would retaliate. She'd likely make him wish he'd never heard the words "barbaric beast" much less tried to take up the actions of one. The sprite had spirit; there was no doubt about that. And third—and most confounding—he damn well couldn't move. His feet felt planted. How the devil had looking at the woman rooted him in the ground?

He deepened his frown and added a sigh. It was Catie's fault he was having these feelings. He'd expected her sexy voice and that warming laugh of hers to drive him insane. But he hadn't expected she'd be beautiful. From their talks, he'd known she was beautiful inside, and, aye, Letty had remarked on Catie's being bonny at least a dozen times. But Letty thought scraggly sheep, red cows, and swamp rats were bonny. Her beholder's eye couldn't be trusted.

Yet she'd hit center-target this time. The darling woman whose contradictory philosophies and sweet and sexy voice had intrigued the hell out of him, had the audacity to further tempt him by housing all her enticing confusion and spirit in the body of a muse. Damn her for that.

He'd known she had long blond hair. He hadn't known that sun-kissed, her hair would gleam as golden as the moor in high summer, or that wind-tossed and caressing her face, it would give her the mussed look of a woman freshly loved.

And her eyes. God help him, he hadn't expected her eyes. Every bit as enchanting as his heather. Though the look in them wasn't soft and slumberous, as he'd imagined. But then Catie wasn't as he'd imagined. She was standing on the moor looking wary and uncertain, not lying in his arms, naked and satiated.

Desire slammed into his stomach, hot and hard. So did anger. The urge to beat Sir Andrew to within an inch of his life hit James like a sledge. *Unstimulating?* How could any man in his right mind find Catie Morgan unstimulating?

James couldn't fathom it. Yet, according to Letty, that's what the man had told Catie. And that was why she was hurting.

Hell, James's body grew taut, if Catie were any more *unstimulating,* he'd be making love with her right here among the stones and brush. With Lady Luck's smile, he might be able to hold off until they reached the upper bailey courtyard's rose garden or its hedge maze. But even with his superior Scots self-discipline, he couldn't imagine waiting beyond that. It'd be asking the impossible of a mere mortal, and he was a realistic man.

Aye, he'd suspected it all along, but now he had proof.

Andrew Huntley was a soft-headed fool. An inferior Englishman with the passion and perception of a dead stump.

Catie thought she needed time to ease her Sir Andrew ails, but, nay, what the woman needed was proper loving—in and out of bed. James stiffened his shoulders. No worry, then. She was his ally, and he'd be giving her all she needed.

Trembling and trying to look brave, the lass walked toward him, her arm linked with Letty's. Knowing the importance of quickly learning an ally's strengths and weaknesses, he kept his expression mask-hard to test her mettle. His size alone daunted most women, setting them to fidgeting or flinching, and he was curious to see how Catie would fare.

She held his gaze a full thirty seconds, then gave him the sexiest slow blink.

A trickle of pleasure ribboned through him and curled around his heart. Aye, he'd chosen well. Catie needed loving, but she'd make a good ally. And he meant for her to know it—starting now.

When they stopped before him, Jamie looked from one woman to the other. Letty was smiling; Catherine, worrying her lower lip with her teeth. She'd been troubled about coming, all right. She'd eaten streaks in her lipstick. Letty looked like a tiny parrot in her green sweater, knee boots, and matching baseball cap. Catherine looked cool and sophisticated in soft cream slacks that clung to her hips and a soft fuzzy sweater that did serious damage to his libido. He glanced down to her loafer-shod feet and nearly smiled. His ally was a highbrow.

"Well, *Jamie,* aren't you going to welcome me home?"

He looked from Catie's feet to Letty's twinkling eyes and again had to smother a smile. The little tyrant had guessed his plans and, with one word, she had approved them.

He bent down, dodged the bill of her cap, then pressed a kiss to her soft cheek. "Welcome home, Letty."

Straightening up, he looked down at Catherine. She seemed shy and nervous. The shy part surprised him, they'd been open and intimate on the phone; the nervous part, he ignored. She'd get over that soon enough—once he'd given her a proper greeting.

"Are you all right?" Now why had he asked her that?

She dipped her head and stared at his boots. Sunlight streaked her hair gold and cast a shadow on the tip of her chin. "Yes, Jamie."

"I'm going on to the house." Letty inhaled deeply. "My, but it's grand to be home."

James forced himself to look away from Catherine long enough to warn his grandmother. "Father MacDuff is waiting in the hall. He's no been well, Letty."

"Mmm, missing me and Harry, I expect." Walking toward the castle, she looked back over her shoulder, a glint of mischief in her eyes. "Aren't you going to give Catherine a traditional Scots greeting?"

Without waiting for an answer, Letty whistled. Cricket and Zeus took off after her. Catie watched Letty until she climbed the stone steps and disappeared behind the heavy oak door. He bided his time. This greeting, he wanted private.

When Catie turned her attention to him—to his chest, actually—he forced the frown from his face and the hardness from his voice. She'd managed better than most. "Welcome to Scotland, Catie." He offered her the flowers. "And to my home."

She took the heather, her hand so delicately boned he half-feared brushing it with his fingertips would break it. She was tiny, much smaller than he had pictured her in his mind—a scant five-two. He towered over her, but instead of feeling powerful and strong, he felt oafish, cumbersome.

Tilting her head a bit, she looked up at him, but she didn't smile. "Thank you, Jamie."

Sadness clouded her eyes. He didn't like it. The wind caught a strand of her hair, whipping it across her face. He gently smoothed it back. The backs of his fingers grazed her cool cheek and it grew rosy. Her skin felt so soft, so fragile. As fragile as her bruised spirit.

An unfamiliar tenderness spread through his chest. He didn't like it, either. He meant for her to realize she was a warming woman, aye, but not by risking his own heart.

Gazing at her lips, he saw the pink tip of her tongue between her teeth. He caught himself leaning forward, heard himself letting out a longing groan. Then his sweet Catie was on tiptoes, pressing a chaste kiss into his beard.

Reminding himself not to rush her, he gave her a sweet peck of a greeting. He had to move slowly. Catie believed she was nursing a broken heart. James felt sure that after a four-year engagement, Sir Andrew had become just a bad habit. But truth is truth, and bad habits are the most difficult to break.

She pulled back, and James forced himself to pull his mouth from her cheek. When he opened his eyes, she gave him an angel's smile, and his heart slammed against his ribs. She looked so soft, smelled and sounded so soft.

His resolutions scattered like untended sheep. One second he stood beside her; the next, he folded his sweet Catie in his arms.

He'd surprised her. But soon he decided he liked Catie surprised. She curled her arms around his neck and buried her face in his shoulder, setting off little explosions in his loins that seemed to grow stronger in the bursting.

God help him, she felt soft, too. Feeling her tremble, he drew her tighter, flush against his chest, and claimed her lips. She touched the bare skin at his nape, at his throat, and breathed a sigh that sent him spiraling. His good intentions withered, but the taste of her, the sweet taste of her was worth any repayment she might demand.

Forcing his lips from hers, he rubbed his nose against her soft neck. Though it was the dead of winter and icy-cold, she smelled of sunshine and spring grass and heather: all his favorite things. Her breath warming the chill from his cheek, he trailed her jaw until his lips hovered hers. "Ah, Catie. You came," he whispered huskily and, unable to resist, he again claimed her lips.

He meant only to taste her, to show her she'd pleased him, but sweet and responsive, she curled her arms tighter around his neck and welcomed him. Her unrestrained breasts flattened against his chest, their tips pebble hard, and sighing his pleasure against her lips, he deepened their kiss. Her fingers kneaded at his nape, and wanting her to know he liked what she was doing to him, he spread his fingers on her back and let them drift up between her sweater and her silky camisole, lingering, gently caressing each tiny vertebra from her waist to her nape. Delicate. Aye, and so sweet.

She nibbled at his lower lip. He grunted and flattened his palm, rubbed little circles on the smooth silk. The fabric bunched and glided over her skin and a vision of her filled his mind. Catie, taunting him, standing before him with that wisp of lace sweeping the swell of her breasts, that length of sheer silk skimming her ribs. Catie, coming to him, sliding against his bare chest and whispering tender love words in his ear. Catie. His sweet Catie.

He murmured his longing and nudged at her lips. When she opened her mouth, he thrust his tongue deep. Their lips crushed together, their warring tongues mated, warm and wet and seeking.

She wanted him. The knowing gnawed at him like an aching tooth. Not making love with her right then was the second hardest thing he'd ever had to do. The first had been to not interfere with her engagement to Sir Andrew.

Sir Andrew!

Too fast. James was pushing her too hard, too fast. Catie would welcome him, aye, with her body, but with her mind and heart she'd regret welcoming him later. And, between them, he wanted no regrets.

His knees weak, his body hard, he forced himself to pull back. A sexy whimper of protest, low and from the back of her throat, had him throbbing, shuddering . . . and considering his phone efforts a success.

He'd proven all he'd needed to prove for now. Catie saw him as an ally, aye, but also as a stimulated man.

And, by damn, he was stimulated. He couldn't speak, and if her trembling was any sign, neither could Catie. So for a long moment, he just held her.

Her fingers curling in his beard, she nuzzled his neck and breathed deeply. "I'll say this for Scotland, Jamie. Its greetings beat the socks off an American handshake."

He let out a low growl and nipped at the underside of her chin. "Aye, 'tis the Scots' superior nature. We're a lusty, passionate people. But 'tis good to know you Americans can be depended on for a proper response."

She drew back to frown at him for that biased comment, her face flushed, her eyes stormy. But their hips met, and her frown faded. "Jamie?"

He held off a smile, though he had to work at it. She might sound uncertain, but she looked like a delicious treat needing and wanting savoring. Very pleased, he rubbed their noses. "Aye, lass?"

Worrying her lip, she unlaced her hands from his neck, and gave his beard a gentle stroke. "You can put me down now."

The cool wind stung his neck. Put her down? James paused and took stock. A jolt of surprise streaked through him. When in hell had he picked her up?

From the broken chapel door, Letty saw Gregor sitting on the first wooden bench, near the altar. Two candles burned, sending light flickering into the small, shadowy room. She walked up the center aisle. The closer she got to him the more hesitant her steps became. His shoulders were slumped. Gregor Forbes didn't slump his shoulders. Not ever. Not even when Harry had died.

She sat down beside him, her worry now full-blown. "Hello, Gregor."

He looked at her, and she nearly gasped. His vivid blue eyes were dull, sunken, and his skin had turned the color of paste. "What in heaven's name is wrong with you, dear?"

"I don't know, lass." He grimaced, loosening his clerical collar at his throat. "I get worse day by day."

She clasped his hand. His fingers were swollen thick, his nails a chalky white. "What does Patrick say?"

"Our good doctor can find nothing." Her old friend shook his head. "I've been taking vitamins and antibiotics—I've even taken to drinking a glass of warm milk before bed—but nothing seems to help."

Perplexing. Clearly *something* was wrong. "Harry vowed warm milk would keep a body from suffering cramps."

Gregor frowned and rubbed his stomach. "I hate to dispute your Harry, Letty, but milk doesn't stop cramping, or a queasy stomach, or anything else I've been suffering."

Letty sent him a solid frown. "If the milk is making you feel worse then, for pity's sake, dear, stop drinking it."

He wrinkled his forehead and squeezed her hand. "I didn't say the milk was making me feel worse."

He hadn't? She would have sworn down to her bones she'd heard him say that very thing. Mmm, divine intervention? Possibly. He was a priest, and they were in the chapel. Where else might one be more apt to be intervened upon by divinity? She patted Gregor's hand. "Stop drinking it, anyway, mmm?"

"I don't want to hurt the girls' feelings," he said. "Bronwyn suggested I take the drink, and Celwyn's been so thoughtful, preparing and carrying it to me. They'll think me ungrateful."

"Feed it to the philodendron in your chamber." Letty shrugged. "The girls will never know the difference, and maybe your stomach will heal. Milk is awfully hard to digest at our age, dear."

That comment earned her a disgusted look that promised a penance of an extra novena. "You're instructing a priest to practice deceit?"

"Deceit? Would I suggest such a thing?" She slid him a worried look. "Still, it's your stomach, Gregor, and plants too do need feeding."

"Aye."

"Well?"

"All right." He huffed and rubbed his ample, round belly. "I'll feed the plant."

Letty held up a finger. "And say not a word."

"Why?"

She hadn't a clue. "Because I asked you not to."

"Oh." He looked as unsure as she felt about what to make of that. "Not a word then—unless specifically asked," he agreed. "I'll no be lying to my kin."

Acid poured into her stomach.

Catherine pressed her palm against her belly and walked toward the castle. At the opening in the upper bailey wall, she frowned. Her physical reaction to Jamie had her confused and embarrassed. Her cheeks felt as hot as glowing embers and her insides still hadn't quit shaking. She'd never been kissed like that in her life. She'd never kissed a man like that in her life, either.

One thing was sure. Jamie certainly didn't kiss like Andrew. There was nothing restrained, or silent, or controlled about James Cameron. From the first moment his lips had touched hers, he had consumed. She again felt the rush of heat, the fluid and flowing feelings. Jamie had made sounds, too. Deep and husky, passionate sounds that told her how much he enjoyed kissing her. And his hands, so big and tender and arousing, had trembled with wanting to touch her.

Suddenly light-headed, she blinked, then blinked again.

Oh yes, Jamie clearly had been out of control. For the first time ever, so had she. And she'd liked it.

But it worried her. Never before had she been indiscreet. Never before had she not cared who might be watching. With Andrew, even the simplest kiss had been orchestrated. Each of them knew what was expected, and what wasn't. With Jamie, she had no idea what to expect. She didn't understand the rules. That was invigorating and exciting. Fun. And scary.

She hadn't expected his deep tongue thrusts, his melding of their hips, his thoroughly possessive hold. And she certainly hadn't expected that the feel of his beard against her face and hands would cause such a flood of lust in her. Her body responded to him like something wild, something love-starved. She supposed she was love-starved, but she couldn't believe she'd shown that to him. Yet, he hadn't seemed to mind. Odd, but he'd actually seemed to like it.

Like it? No, Jamie's kiss hadn't been that tame. It'd been feral, savage, wanton. She felt her lips curl. It'd been wonderful.

Had she lost her mind? A woman couldn't be in love with one man and her body respond so overwhelmingly to another. Could it?

She looked at Jamie and that hot flood of craving washed through her again. Well, hell. She frowned. It could.

Jamie linked their arms. "What do you think of my castle, lass?"

Catherine studied the mammoth structure breaking the smooth skyline. Two round towers flanked a stone center the color of heated butter. Something shiny in its rough-hewn walls caught the sunlight and glittered like sparklers on a fourth of July night. And high atop the towers, the banners she'd seen from the helicopter flapped in the cold wind. His castle looked like something out of a fairy tale.

A surge of pleasure rippled through her and she wanted

to kiss Jamie again. She'd fit in here. The real Catherine Morgan would fit.

"You've not answered me, lass." Jamie stopped on the first of five long steps that led to the castle door.

Why shouldn't she indulge in the things *she* wanted? Trying to please everyone else hadn't done her any good. Love had gotten her a broken heart and classified as not stimulating. Maybe lust was right for her. She'd have to think about that. Lust never had been her style. But then, her style had gotten her onto this emotional roller coaster in the first place. Maybe a good dose of lust would trip the brakes.

"Catie." Jamie sighed his impatience. "You're ignoring me, I'm thinking."

She smiled and patted his arm. "No, I'm not. *I* was thinking. What did you ask?"

He gave her a little snort and a big frown. "Do you like my damn castle is what I'm wanting to know."

An hour ago, she would've thought it a neglected relic. But now, she looked at it differently—through her own eyes. Not Andrew's. Not her parents'. But her own. And what she saw of the castle, of its upper bailey courtyard with its hedge maze and rose garden, and through the gap in the stone wall to the open moor, she liked. The rugged terrain tugged hard at a longing cord that seemed natural, as much a part of her as her umbilical cord once had been.

She looked up at Jamie and squinted against the sun. "It's lacking."

"Lacking?" His deep voice boomed.

She pointed up at the banners. "I see the Scottish flag— darling lion—and your Gaelic Cameron banner. . . . Are those arrows on it?"

"Aye," he said in a brittle voice. "Five of them, bound together—united."

"Mmm." She looked down from the flags to him. "Lacking."

"Catie," he said, his jaw clenched. "Finding a man's castle

lacking isn't likely to arouse much affection in his Scots heart, in case you aren't knowing."

She gave him an affronted sniff. "Ignoring a woman's heritage isn't particularly endearing to an American, either. Where's Old Glory?"

His jaw gaped. "I'll no fly a Yank flag from me tower."

"You'd have me reside in your castle clear through the festival without one hospitable gesture to remind me of home?"

He narrowed his eyes. "You're trying to blackmail me, sweet Catie lass. I dinna like it."

Dinna? Don't, she mentally translated. "That's diplomacy, dear, not blackmail." She smiled sweetly. "Blackmail's insisting. I'm asking."

Jamie held her shoulders and planted a kiss to her lips that had her legs wobbling. "I'll fly your flag, I'm thinking," he said softly, then turned his voice hard, "when the rafters fall!"

She laughed in his face. "You will."

"I'll not before then." He frowned and thrust out his chin.

Stubborn and proud. She liked that. "All right," she conceded. "Not today, you ungrateful, inhospitable lout, but one day. I have to say though, you're already testing the bounds of our alliance."

He snorted, apparently not in the least bit concerned. "So, otherwise, do you like my damn castle?"

She smiled. "I love your castle."

"Are you sure?" He gave her a wary look she adored. "It took you a long time to decide."

"There's something special about it. Something almost mystical. Something . . ." Unable to specifically describe that something in concrete terms, or even to grasp it, she shook her head.

Jamie opened the door and gave her a smile that had her heartbeat tripping. "I know, lass."

He sounded as if he did know exactly. She smiled back

and entered the castle's wide foyer. The great hall's tile floor was etched in a pattern of rushes and, stepping onto it, Catherine half-expected the branches to crunch as real rushes had under Jamie's ancestor's feet centuries ago. Soft candlelight eased the shadows from the room, flickering amber light from iron holders on the wall, from a great chandelier centered overhead, and from a huge stone fireplace with a crackling fire in its grate. She smelled the wood burning, heard the hiss of moisture seeping from the logs to the flames. A mix of heavy leather and thick, slab benches surrounded six wooden tables. And a rocking chair, the biggest she'd ever seen, was near the hearth, beside a little mahogany table. Seeing the phone on it, she turned to Jamie. "You sat there when you called me."

"Aye."

She'd come home. The feeling welled. Jamie's home wasn't fancy or filled with expensive antiques like Andrew's. It wasn't cold and distancing. It was an old, odd mix of armor and soft pillows inside a huge hall with ceilings twenty feet high, walls of brown polished stone striped with heavy wooden beams, and centuries of pure warmth and comfort. It felt like home.

Shunning the warm, good feeling, she chastised herself. It was home. Jamie's home. But it was *not* her home. In six months she'd be back in New Orleans. Back in her sterile suite at Annie's. And back in her missing Andrew mode.

She stepped over to the hearth and let the heat from the fire warm her hands and her face. But she had six months. Andrew wouldn't intrude here. She'd been given a reprieve, and she intended to enjoy it. When she returned home again and had to deal with Andrew and the law firm, then would be soon enough to begin mourning losing him in her personal life. She looked back at the gentle giant studying her so thoughtfully and a flash of fear scattered inside her. If she did opt for lust with him, she might just be mourning Jamie a little then, too.

He stepped closer, firelight softening his hard features. "I thought you could rest a bit, then we could take to the moor. I'm wanting you to see my stream."

Catherine smiled. Jamie, too, was nervous. Why hadn't she realized that earlier? And why did his being nervous bother her so much? She stepped forward, reached up, and tweaked his nose. "I could use a wee bit of rest, I'm thinking."

Laughing, he scooped her up in his arms. She thumped against his chest and swore she'd hit a brick wall. To steady herself, she latched onto his shoulders and pressed her cheek against his beard. She could've purred. She didn't understand that. She'd always hated beards. But before today she'd never before felt a man's beard graze her skin. As Jamie would say, it was warming. This lust business was looking better than love all the time.

"Ah, Catie lass. We'll make a Scot of you yet."

He squeezed her and she snuggled. The tip of her nose was cold, she brushed it with Jamie's. "Or maybe I'll convert you. You'd make a fine Yank. Of course, you'd have to cover up your knees."

"You'd have me give up me kilt?" He pretended an indignation she considered half-real.

"A pity—you have sexy kneecaps—but, yep, you'd have to ditch the kilt. Americans would swear you were wearing a woman's skirt."

His jaw fell slack. "Nay, they'd no ask me to toss me kilt in a ditch!"

She nodded that they would.

"A woman's skirt, ye say?"

Again she nodded.

"Impossible!" He snorted. "The kilt is a most manly garment."

"Not in America." Ditching the kilt was a lie, of course. And they both well knew it. James Cameron was as untamed as his Highland lands; masculine and all man—and his kilt fit his image beautifully.

His eyes smoldered. "You'd best get your rest now, Catie."

A tremor in his voice conspired with a look in his eyes to tell her he wouldn't mind joining her. That she fleetingly considered letting him had her swearing at herself again. If his hands on her back would loosen a little and she could put some distance between them, then maybe she could ignore his hard body telling her he wouldn't mind at all—and her own telling her it wouldn't mind, either. He was purposely seducing her to bolster her ego; she knew it, but she reveled in the new feelings, anyway.

She touched his face, let her fingers explore his full beard. It was soft. Why had she thought it would feel bristly? Wiry? Enchanted, she rubbed his silky whiskers. The heat from the fire warmed his skin, and its light shadowed his neck behind the lobe of his ear. She touched that spot, then let her thumb stray over his jaw to sweep along his cheekbone. "You have freckles on your nose, Jamie."

"You don't," he said gruffly.

"I like your beard."

"Aye, 'tis manly."

Even his arrogance was charming. She touched the tiny lines fanning the skin beneath his eyes and imagined him squinting against the glare from the sun. "I like your eyes, too."

"I like your sexy voice. It's . . . warming."

Lord, but this Highland air was thin. She felt ready to faint. That was a ridiculous notion, of course. Catherine Morgan had never fainted in her life. Reassured, she licked her lips and brushed his beard with the back of her hand. Warmth seeped to her limbs and her voice grew softer, deeper. "Is it proper in Scotland to tell a man you like the way he kisses?"

"Aye," he whispered huskily. "Honesty is always proper."

She nearly smiled. Never would it occur to James Cameron that a woman wouldn't like his kisses. "And is it proper for a laird to tell a woman he's kissed that he liked kissing her?"

"If he did like it, aye, 'tis proper."

"Oh." So did he like kissing her, or didn't he?

"Oh?"

She shrugged and raked her lower lip with her teeth. "Just, oh." Her cheeks burned hot. She shouldn't have asked. Had she really needed the added disappointment? "I brought you a present."

"Keep it." When she looked up at him, he added, "I'll take another kiss."

"You liked it?" Well, hell. She sounded shocked.

"Nay." His expression looked as hard as stone.

"But then why—" Her frown eased to a smile. "Ah, yes, you did. You liked it. But you didn't like liking it. Is that it?"

"Nay, I'll not lie to you, lass. I didn't like it one wee bit."

"Oh." She shouldn't feel disappointed, but she did.

"I felt it," he switched from English to Scots, *"aw frae the bein."*

Fidgeting with his collar, she gave him a questioning look.

"All from the bone," he translated.

He hated her kiss down to his bones? She sighed her frustration and, stroking his beard, looked into his eyes. Beautiful, deep emeralds filled with secrets. "You're not being diplomatic again. Are you trying to create an international incident?"

"With my ally?" He lifted his brows. "Nay, what I'm trying to do is to control my starving."

He did like her kiss, but he didn't want to like it. That *was* it. And he felt both from the bone. Poor Jamie. He was as afflicted as she in the love and relationship departments. However, he wouldn't appreciate that truth being pointed out to him. Obtuse definitely rated advantageous here. She cupped his chin in her hand. "Mmm, Celwyn's still in the village."

"She's on her way home now."

Confused by the disgust in his voice, Catherine tilted her head. "Don't you want Celwyn here?"

He gave Catie a flat look. "Bronwyn the Terrible's coming with her—for the holidays."

"Ah, I see."

"Nay, I'm thinking you don't. Not yet, anyway. But you will."

That Catie couldn't help but look forward to seeing. What kind of woman stimulated Jamie? "Do you want to see your present?"

"Later," he growled.

She pinched and tugged on his beard. "I'm keeping it until Christmas, then—to teach you diplomacy."

He laughed. "There are things I'd like to teach you too, Catie."

Her body flushed hot and she swallowed hard. "Romeo."

"Aye." His eyes twinkled. "But I'm considering flopping over a new loaf."

"Turning over a new leaf?" she asked.

He gave her a cranky look. "Whatever."

"What new leaf?"

"Barbaric beast." He squeezed her tighter and nipped at her neck. "That's much more appealing than the timid self I'm showing you."

"You—timid?"

"Aye." He lifted his chin. "And I don't mind saying I'm feeling a wee bit slighted at your slow notice, lass. Even a Yank should be observing a manner so chivalrous."

He really believed he was timid. She almost smiled. "Barbaric beast suits. You're big."

"You're not. But you're . . . warming."

If she didn't stop this right now, she'd wind up making love with James Cameron, and that—no matter what her body wanted—would be wrong for both of them "Um, Jamie, I can't rest—at least, not yet."

Worry joined the naked desire in his eyes. "Why not?"

A gentle feuding happened inside her. She loved another man. She craved this man. Accepting that she'd left her good sense on the other side of the Atlantic, she smiled. "Because I'm dangling."

He creased his brow with his frowning. "Dangling?"

She nodded.

Jamie hesitated, then her meaning registered and his displeasure flitted across his face in a near snarl. " 'Tis your own fault."

"My fault?"

He set her to the floor then backed away so quickly she nearly toppled. "Aye, you make me forget myself."

A common problem between them. Catherine dipped her chin to hide her smile and to savor the physical evidence of his reaction to her. He hadn't pretended to soothe her wounded ego. He wanted her. When Jamie had held her, she'd felt the hardness at his hips, the physical proof his desire had been honest. A rush of alien feelings raged in her. She wanted to shout her joy, to explore each of the feelings. But her logic insisted she beat a hasty retreat.

Jamie cleared his throat. "I'll show you to your chamber."

He didn't seem at all embarrassed. In fact, he moved his body full in front of her so she'd be sure to notice his arousal. Keeping her tone light was difficult. What, if anything, was James Cameron wearing under that kilt?

Her heart lodged in her throat. "Lead the way, Sir James."

He took the second stair step, then paused and looked back at her. "Don't call me that, lass."

"Ah, laird. I meant laird." She tilted her head and looked up at him. His gaze was hot, knocking the breath right out of her. "Laird's exactly what I was thinking," she mumbled. "Laird."

"Nay, that's not why." He touched her face with a gentle

fingertip. His voice grew thick. "A woman shouldn't be so formal with a man she's just seduced."

"Seduced!" Her jaw fell slack. She snapped it closed. "I didn't," she nearly shouted. "Did I?"

"Aye, you did."

"I didn't." She couldn't have. She hadn't been able to get Andrew's attention, and Jamie looked a hundred times more virile. He had to be teasing.

He rolled his gaze heavenward. "Seduced. Pure and simple."

"Really?" She felt herself smile and smacked it from her lips.

"Aye, I said so, didn't I?"

"Well, yes, but—"

"I'm not taking it kindly, Catie, your questioning my honor. I'm a Cameron, lass. My word is as solid as God's will."

Feeling anything but sorry, she apologized.

He nodded his acceptance and the light overhead played on his chin and chest. "Fine. I'll not demand repayment, as is custom. You're a Yank, after all."

"Repayment?" She studied the banister's sheen and picked up the faint scent of lemon oil. Well tended. Jamie clearly loved his home.

"Aye. I'm laird, lass. Descended from the medieval warlords. Any who offend me have to repay to allay my anger—"

"And if they don't?"

"They suffer my wrath."

"Oh." She smiled at him, not at all afraid of his wrath. "So I've seduced you then, but you aren't angry."

"I'm miffed," he countered, giving her a disgruntled look. "Having seduced me—and doing it so sweetly, I might be adding—your using my title, be it the right one or no, makes me feel . . . cheap."

She nearly stumbled from the step. "What?"

Jamie steadied her. "Only women can feel cheap, you're thinking. Nay, don't be denying it, I can see the truth in your eyes. But now how would I be feeling, I'm asking, if I gave myself to you? You'd not respect me come morn. You'd use me then toss me out with the relish."

"Relish?"

"You ken my meaning," he said impatiently. "The refuse."

"Rubbish?"

"Whatever! The point is, Catie lass, I'd be lying on my foolish elbow and you'd be off seducing your next conquest."

"That's the most ridiculous bunch of 'relish' I've ever heard. You're ditsy, James Cameron. Totally and completely ditsy."

"What I am is warmed. Pure and simple, love. And the fault for that is yours."

"Mine?" Her heart was going to stop. Just any second, it would positively stop.

"Aye." He lifted his chin. "You talk like an angel and kiss like a witch. I'm a mere mortal, I would remind you."

"A witch?" She gave him a good glare. "Are you insulting me? I have a very dear friend who's a witch, so I wouldn't really think you were, but the tone of your voice—"

"Ah, I know what you're about. It'll do you no good to pretend innocence now. You've gotten a spell from your friend and you're hexing me." He nodded emphatically, then grunted. "I can't really blame you, Catie love, but now that I'm knowing for fact you're hexing me, and since you're a Yank, it's only right that I warn you. If you take advantage of me while I'm suffering my weakened condition, you'll bear the full responsibility for whatever happens."

"Your weakened condition?" she bellowed her indignation and gripped the banister hard. The man looked totally serious. "You are the most—"

"Aye, darling." He slid her a wicked smile and tweaked

her nose. "The most. But . . ." He cocked his head as if perplexed. "Are you cold, lass? You're shaking."

He knew darn good and well she was irritated, not cold. And clearly he expected her to scream at him. She wouldn't give him the satisfaction, by damn. She wiggled her brows at him. "I'm just cold enough to warm your Scots blood."

"A hexing witch." His eyes twinkled. "Pure and simple."

She stared, bemused. "Barbaric beast."

"Oh, I'm wishing." He let out a longing sigh. "But that'll have to wait." He curled a big arm around her waist, then hauled her to his side. "Come on now, else you'll have no time for a nap before dinner." He led her up the winding stairs. "I lit a fire in your chamber, so it should be comfortable. There's no electricity. I'm against it."

"Because of Kirkland's dam?"

"Aye." He motioned with his hand. "Those hair things you do will have to be done by nature."

She gave him an unsteady look. "You don't have *any* electricity?"

Turning right into the hallway, he laughed at her shock. "Nary a watt. What's wrong, love? Is life without beyond a Yank's comprehension?"

"Frankly, yes." She lifted her chin. "But I'll manage. We Americans are made of stern stuff."

"Aye, appealing stern stuff." They turned off the main hall, into a second one that was dimly lit and carpeted. At the second door, Jamie stopped and gave her a formal little bow. "Your chamber, lass."

"Quaint. Chamber, not room." She twitched her nose at him. "Where's Letty's chamber?"

He grunted and pointed left. "Just around the corner."

It was a long way to any corner. Catherine narrowed her gaze. "And yours?"

Those slashed brows of his knitted. "Next door."

"To whom?"

"To you."

The gentle feuding in her stomach grew to a full-scale war. This lust stuff was powerful. "I see."

His gaze grew hot. "Aye, I'm thinking you're beginning to."

The little hairs on the back of her neck rose. The gentle giant looked and sounded just a little too pleased. A hot moistness rushed to her thighs and she settled her gaze at his throat. "Jamie, you will be a gentleman, won't you?"

"Nay, lass," he said in a voice laced with mock regret. "I'm sorry to have to say it, but truth is truth and I'll not."

Snapping her head up, she saw a devilish twinkle in his eye.

"We leave being gentlemanly to the inferior English. We Scots have hotter blood."

"Barbaric beast." Catherine stepped into her chamber, then shut the door. Leaning back against the slick lemon-oiled wood, she heard Jamie's muffled laughter.

This time, she didn't bite the smile from her lips, but reveled in it.

Good God, you gave her heather!

Oh, the symbol was lost on the Yank, but it was not lost on me. Lonesomeness? The mighty Cameron lonely? Ridiculous!

But you do value the Yank. Amazing, that. Unless you've given up sex. Aye, that has to be it. She definitely lacks experience. Anyone could see that in the way she touched your beard. Her fingertips fairly shouted discovery.

Odd, but so did yours. You were so . . . tender. None of your legendary raw power or untempered passion. And yet, for the absence of all that, you did appear ready to take her there, on the moor. . . .

I'm thinking you feel more than lust for the Yank, and I should kill her now. Before the first blush of romance fades and you tire of her sexual ineptitude. Yet killing her right away might be premature. It was her name Letty called out in the chapel. . . .

In a few days, surely no more than a few days, I'll find the diary. Maybe by then you'll realize you love the Yank. You knowing would make the killing so much sweeter. She'll die slowly, of course. It's only right for her to suffer greatly for your sins.

For now, I'll enjoy making you both fearful for her life. Mmm, what do you most adore, Cameron, eh? Beauty, I'd say. Aye, beauty is perfect.

I'll cut your sweet Catie's face.

You will be devastated.

By God, I can hardly wait.

Five

She was being kissed.

Drifting in the luscious netherworld between sleep and wakefulness, Catie groaned and pulled her hands to his face. Soft tufts of silky beard tickled her palms and the smell of cedar grew pleasantly stronger. Jamie . . .

"Jamie!" She gasped and shrank back on the pillow, wide awake.

Chuckling, the gentle giant pecked a kiss to her forehead. "Wake up, lass, and quit your snoring."

"I don't snore." Catherine grabbed for the patchwork quilt, but couldn't reach it. He stood in the way, fingering a lacy sachet of potpourri that had been on the washstand in the corner. As the smells of heather mingled with his cedar, there she lay: trapped in bed wearing a skimpy camisole and lacy panties she'd bought eons ago and had just worked up the nerve to wear, and not another stitch. Where was a good earthquake when a body needed swallowing up?

She glared at him. His eyes twinkled, the rotten man, and his smirk made it evident he expected her to kick up a royal fuss. She wanted to—oh, how she wanted to—but she wouldn't do it. She just wouldn't. But she had to retaliate by doing something.

From under her lashes, she risked another glance. Still smirking, the lout. What he needed was a good dose of his own medicine. But was she woman enough to give it to him?

Why not give it a shot? What more could she lose? He already knew she was a *femme fatale* flop. Since his expectations wouldn't be too high, maybe she'd knock him off-center just enough to get her revenge.

She slid off the bed. The braided rug felt cool under her feet, though the fire in the grate had the room warm and toasty. Almost hot. Mmm, the fire? Or the heat in Jamie's gaze? He squeezed the sachet and backed up a step to avoid her sliding into him. Little bits of crushed potpourri sprinkled to the floor. He didn't seem to notice, and that brought her a little satisfaction, but she wanted more.

Raising her arms, she stretched, letting out a liquid moan, and watched him from beneath lids lowered to half-mast. His eyes glazed. Better. But not good enough.

She stepped closer, until their bodies brushed, then looked up at him. Firelight danced across his beard. "I like the way you wake me, Jamie." Her voice still sleep-soft, husky, she tiptoed and kissed the underside of his chin. "Thank you."

He didn't say anything, but his Adam's apple bobbed three times. Maybe he couldn't say anything. No, he was a lusty Scot. She'd just surprised him a little, but he'd soon recover. Unless she kept him off balance. "Jamie?"

He clenched his jaw and gave her a tight little nod that easily could have snapped his stiff neck. The poor sachet was squashed. She leaned back, flattened her hands on his chest, then pressed her hips against his thighs. "Is something wrong?"

He looked down, his eyes the stormy green of the gulf during a hurricane. "Nay, everything is fine."

Gauging by his expression, things were about as fine as he said the loch water was healthy. Any sudden moves and his jaw surely would crack. "You smell nice," she said, developing a fondness for his scent. "Like cedar and spring grass." She stroked his shirt front. "Have you been worrying?"

"I'm fine."

He didn't look fine. He looked rattled, and that worried her. "You're being timid, then?"

"Aye, timid." He tossed the sachet over to the washstand. It landed inside the empty bowl.

She drifted a light fingertip over his silky beard. "Would you like it if sometime I awakened you—returned the favor?" Without waiting for an answer, she pointed to the third door in her chamber, the one she suspected led to his room. "Is that how you came in here?"

Jamie nodded. Fire shadows hid the look in his eyes.

"So, would you?"

Silence.

"Jamie?"

Sweat dotted his forehead. "Get dressed, Catie. I'm wanting you—" his eyes grew somber, and his hand at her waist kneaded her bare flesh "—to see my stream."

His brogue had grown thicker, sexier. Lightheaded, she pegged the reason: thin Highland air. It wasn't the air at all, of course, but she needed the lie to keep this relationship in perspective. If she let him, James Cameron would steal all of her heart and walk right over her. But she wouldn't let him. She'd suffered her fair share of stompings and had no intention of suffering anymore of them.

Logs snapped in the grate and a spray of sparks burned bright, fizzled, and then died, leaving the flames and their warm glow. "You didn't answer my question, dear. Would you like it if I returned the favor?"

"Aye, I'd like it." He frowned, dropped his hands to his sides, and moved to the door. Hand on the knob, he paused, his expression deadpan earnest. "Catie?"

"Yes?"

"I'm thinking when you come to me, you'd best plan on staying a long while."

Every muscle in her body contracted at once.

He went on into the hallway then softly closed the door. She stared at the sheening wood for an unblinking second, afraid to try to move, then hurried to the washbowl, stubbing her toe on its leg. Pain shot through her foot and up to her knee. Grimacing, she moved the crushed sachet to the ledge, poured the water, then splashed her hot cheeks. The man was a torch!

Why hadn't he teased her back? He didn't really want her. She was a *femme fatale* flop, for pity's sake. True, around him she didn't feel much like a flop but that didn't mean anything. Or did it?

No, he couldn't really want her. Of course, he couldn't. Could he?

Water dripping from her chin to her chest, she stared at the closed door. Anyone could fall in lust, she supposed. Especially a man who'd sworn off marriage. Lust was nothing like love. Love hurt. But lust . . . invigorated. He could maybe be in lust with her. He'd been shut in here for a long time and, compared to no woman, any woman would look good. Even a flop.

"Hurry up, Catie." Jamie called out from the hallway.

She snapped to and hurried to the closet, skimmed past three outfits—all pencil slim, brown and conservative—then pulled out a soft, pale blue dress with billowy sleeves and a scooped neck. Its hanger thunked on the floor. She toed it back into the closet, tugged on the dress, then slung low on her hips a gold chain belt that jingled with her every move. Hearing it tinkle, she looked at herself in the mirror. This was the real Catherine Morgan. And she couldn't wait to see Jamie's reaction to her.

She spun around. The skirt swished against her calves, and she abruptly stopped. Andrew had hated this dress. What if Jamie did, too?

"Wait a second." She gave herself a stern lecture. She was through trying to please men. All men. She thought of her father, of his dying wish, and the flush of guilt that had become her second nature washed through her. How she'd hungered for his approval, wanting only for him to be proud of her, to love her. But he hadn't. She wasn't conservative, reserved, sophisticated. She was too spirited, too loose with her emotions. And where he'd left off faulting her, Andrew had picked up, carried the torch. So often the actions of the two men blended in her mind.

She reached to the chain around her neck and fingered the medallion her father had given her. She'd tried being what they thought she should be, and she'd been miserable. Now, she wanted to please herself, to be herself, and not what either of them thought she should be. She wanted to again find the real Catie Morgan, knew she needed to find her or, later on, she'd look back and regret. She didn't want to look back and regret.

Her father had lived his life. Andrew was living his. And the time had come for Catie Morgan to live her life. Her life, her way.

She'd given it to them.

Now, she was taking it back.

Catie let the feeling of being in control of herself settle, then turned away from the mirror and opened the door.

Jamie stood just outside in the wide hallway. Her stomach fluttered and suddenly she wasn't so sure she wanted to risk seeing disapproval in his eyes. He was the only man who hadn't wanted to change her, and the thought of seeing condemnation for her in him hurt. Avoiding it, she let her gaze slide down his tartaned length to the hardwood floor.

He didn't say anything.

Why didn't he say *something*?

Her stomach did a little flip. She cursed it, and herself. She'd just been through this and had sworn off this nonsense. Defiant, she stiffened, snapped her head back, and looked up at him.

His eyes had glazed.

The fear in her melted. The darling man didn't have to say anything, after all.

"Well, ally." She stepped out and closed the door. "I'm ready to see your stream."

A little smile crinkled the skin near his eyes, as he draped a cloak woven in the same colors of his kilt around her shoulders. It was a heavy thing, lined with sheepskin and warm from him holding it.

"You'll get chilled, love. The wind's free on the moor."

Love. He'd said it again. Why didn't it grate at her ears? Why did it sound so good? It could be his brogue, or it could be that, in their case, love was lust. That seemed more likely. "I thought there would be ice on the ground."

"There will be, come morn." He lifted the hood, tilted her face toward the window at the end of the hall, then tucked in her hair. "Several inches."

"Of ice?"

"Nay, lass, of snow." He tied a silky black ribbon at her neck to secure the hood. "The ice comes later."

He had the most gentle hands. "Oh."

"Ready?" The smile lurking in his eyes still didn't reach his mouth.

Her insides soft and woozy, she wanted to kiss him again. What was wrong with her? Had to be raging hormones. That fit with lust not love. Looking at Andrew certainly never had made her feel like this, but every time she looked at Jamie . . .

"Catie?"

"What? Oh. Oh, yes." She'd been staring at him like a dazed idiot. From the curl at the corner of his lip, it had amused him, too. "I'm ready."

He clasped her hand and led the way.

Halfway down the stairs, she glanced over the banister, and stopped. On the far wall below hung a painting of Jamie. Seated astride a gleaming black horse, rearing and pawing the air, Jamie held a menacing sword blade lifted to the sleety gray sky, his expression fierce, his muscles rippled. The raw power in the man and the beast captivated her.

"Jamie," she whispered, hearing a tremble in her voice. "It's . . . magnificent."

He stopped on the step at her side and circled an arm around her waist. "That's James, the first Cameron laird. I'm told we favor, but I don't see it."

She glanced at Jamie and caught the twinkle in his eyes. "If James had your beard, you could be twins."

"Nay, Catie." He gently squeezed her side and gave her an affronted grunt. "I'm much better looking than James."

Biting back a laugh, she adjusted the hood's ribbon at her throat.

"What, I'm asking, are you finding so amusing?"

"Your modesty, dear." Traces of laughter lingered in her voice anyway. "No doubt you're more modest than James, too."

"No doubt. I am being timid, I would remind you." He glanced at the portrait. "Still, James was a good laird. Ruthless."

The man wouldn't know timid if it waylaid him, yet he sincerely believed he did. "To a degree, I suppose James had to be ruthless. He lived in harsher times."

"Aye, he did. Had James been soft, his people would have died. In the twelfth century, men were—"

"Bloodthirsty," she interjected.

"Aye, they were indeed." He shifted his weight and the stair creaked.

"That wasn't a compliment, Jamie."

"It wasn't?"

She gave him a firm negative nod.

His expression hardened. "An insult?"

"I'm afraid so. But one that's been earned."

"You're talking about insulting my kin, lass. I'm no forgetting you're a Yank, but here, a man doesn't take that offense kindly. Wars have been fought for less."

"Ah, Cameron pride."

He lifted his chin. "Aye."

"Well, it was rude to admit it, even if it's true. I'd repay, but I don't want to make you feel . . . cheap." She wiggled her brows, linked their arms, then went on down the steps.

Jamie came along without uttering so much as a syllable. Another lesson learned, Catie thought. Stun the man, and keep him stunned. Her blood warmed and she secretly smiled. This little lesson in diplomacy she meant to teach him could be fun.

They crossed the rush-tile entry, then stepped outside the castle door. Cold air hit her full in the face, darn near swiping her breath, but, within minutes, she was breathing deeply, feeling invigorated. To the left of the castle landing near the hedge maze, a huge black horse pawed the ground. His muscles flexing had his shiny coat gleaming blue-black in the fading sunlight. "Yours?" she asked Jamie.

He nodded.

Catherine swallowed hard, praying he wasn't, and fearing he was, planning on riding that monster beast to his stream. "Um, are you going to ride now?"

Again Jamie nodded.

A sinking feeling seized her stomach. "And you expect me to ride, too?"

She watched for a third nod, but instead Jamie whistled. The dogs came tearing around the corner of the castle and the horse trotted over, skimming an evergreen and setting its leaves to rustling.

"Come, Catie." Jamie tugged Catherine down the steps.

She pulled back. "I don't know about this, Jamie. I've never been on a horse before. He looks so . . . big." The monster looked huge, every bit as dangerous as the beast in the painting. "Can't we walk instead?"

"Ah, I'm seeing what you're about. You're fearing Thunder."

"I am not," she lied. "I'd just rather walk."

"You are, darling," he insisted. "But there's no need to

be embarrassed with me. Your being faint-hearted doesn't surprise me at all. Yanks are notorious—"

"Faint-hearted?" The wind caught her hems, swirled her cloak and dress. She slapped them against her thighs. "Yank—er, Americans are not cowards, James Cameron. If anything, we're stout-hearted." She poked his chest with a warning fingertip. "And don't you dare dispute me on that."

He laughed. "You're trying to lie to me, sweet Catie, but your fair skin won't be letting you get away with it. I'd take offense, but I'm knowing—"

"I am not afraid, James Cameron."

"Fine."

"Fine." She let her huffed chest relax.

"Prove it." The wind tussling his hair, Jamie lifted a brow, turned, then grabbed Thunder's reins. "Come ride with me."

Spit. Spit, spit, spit. Catie risked a covert glance at the monster beast. It rolled its big black eyes and let out a snort that had her shaking in her shoes and fighting the urge to run. And Jamie stood there smirking, the awful man. She couldn't let him think she was a coward; he'd drive her up the wall with his Scots superiority remarks.

She stiffened her spine. Just how much could dogs and horses differ, anyway? She held out her hand to let the horse get a good whiff of her scent and hoped to heaven the beast didn't bite her fingers off.

When it didn't, she leaned close to its head, and whispered. "Please, don't make me look bad, Thunder. I've got the courage of an entire country at stake here."

The beast snorted . . . but he didn't bite. Taking that as a good sign, she stroked its nose and was pleasantly surprised. "Why, you're as soft as velvet, Thunder."

He rewarded her, nuzzling her hand, and Catie smiled. "What a sweetheart, you are."

"Don't be insulting my horse." Jamie checked Thunder's saddle. "He's no sweetheart, he's a stallion."

"I was praising him."

"Insult. Pure and simple." Jamie adjusted the bit, securing it. "A soft sweetheart is nothing to be calling the Cameron's stallion."

"Don't listen to him, Thunder."

The horse whinnied. His flesh quivered and his breath fogged the cold air. "What do you think, Cricket? Zeus?" Catie glanced at the collies. "Should I go for it?"

The collies barked. "It's unanimous, then." Her stomach sinking, she wheeled her gaze to Jamie. "I'll ride, but if your beast tosses me on my foolish elbow, James Cameron, I'm holding you responsible."

He looked at her over Thunder's back, his eyes steady. "Trust me."

She stared at him for a long, unblinking moment. Oh, but he asked for a lot. Yet, when looking into Jamie's eyes, what woman could refuse him? Catching herself too late to deny she'd nodded, she again silently cursed the thin Highland air. Her brain had to be suffering oxygen deprivation. That was the only possible explanation for her losing her sense every time she looked at the man.

He clasped her waist, then lifted her onto Thunder's back. "He'll no hurt ye, lass."

Jamie was emotional again. Every time he got emotional, his brogue deepened and he used more Scottish words. She liked that telling habit. She also liked that her trusting him pleased him.

"You'll be fine." He mounted behind her, settling her between his thighs.

She held up her hands, unsure where to put them. "I trust you. Didn't I say I did?"

"Actually, nay, ye didn't."

"I'm on this beast's back, aren't I? Would I get up here if I didn't trust you?" She looked down to the dirt, then groaned. "Oh God, the ground looks so far away." She was going to die. To fall off this beast and break her stupid neck. "What do I do with my damn hands?"

His chest rumbled against her back. Laughing? She was terrified and the man was laughing? She shot him a withering glare. "I asked you where to put my hands, James."

He slapped them onto his rock-hard thighs.

She nearly fell out of the saddle. Fighting a serious attack of nerves, she snorted darn near as loud as Thunder had. "I said I trust you and I do. So stop showing your backside, you ungrate—"

Jamie kissed her quiet.

She kissed him back.

When he lifted his head, she sighed her content and slumped back against his chest.

"You children don't linger," Letty shouted. "Dinner will be ready in an hour."

Catherine darted a look at the castle landing, her face already burning fire hot. Letty stood there and, of all times, she wasn't alone. A squat, round priest with a shock of white hair and the pallor of a man who'd been ill stood at her side. He had to be Father MacDuff, and she'd made one devil of a first impression. Jamie would be furious. Catherine squelched a groan.

"Father," Jamie shouted. "Have you met my darling, Catie?"

Her ears would ring for a month. Thunder did a little sidestep, and she clamped down on Jamie's thighs. He tightened his arm around her ribs.

"A pleasure, lass." The old priest's wrinkled face split into a smile.

His darling, Catie? Jamie wasn't angry. Because that made her ridiculously happy, she smiled back at the priest. "Hello, Father. I hope you're feeling better."

Before he could answer, Jamie dug his heels into Thunder's flanks. With a healthy shiver, the horse took off—and Catherine understood instantly how the beast had earned his name. The sound of his hooves pounding the ground remarkably resembled thunder.

Letty watched them go. "She trusts him, Gregor."

"Aye, it appears she does."

Letty elbowed his ribs a gentle jab. "He's crazy about her, too. I told you he would be."

"Aye, you did." Gregor frowned and rubbed at his neck. "They seem to suit, I agree."

"Well, why the long face, then?" The man clearly worried over something. She clicked her tongue to the roof of her mouth. "Did you change your mind and drink the milk before bed?"

"Nay." He looked away.

"Well, what's wrong, then? I would think you'd be happy for James."

"I am, lass. Bronwyn hurt the laird, I'm knowing that. But I canna help but wonder how James will feel when the lassie . . . leaves."

Letty laced her arms through his. "I've already thought of that, and I think I have the matter resolved."

"Oh?"

"Gregor." Letty slid him a reprimanding look. "I know you didn't think for a second I'd let Catherine go back to 1100 alone."

"You're sending— Sweet Mary, Letty, you canna." Gregor's eyes stretched wide and he lifted his hand.

"Of course, I can." Letty snagged his arm and pulled it down. "Now don't start crossing yourself and worrying our Maker with nagging matters we can handle perfectly well ourselves. He'll be busy soon enough with Cameron troubles." She shook her head. "And you're a priest, Gregor Forbes. Where's your faith?"

"Faith?" He gave her a shrewd look that had her flushing.

"Well, faith and a wee touch of cunning."

"So that's why you asked about history changing." He gasped. "You planned this all along!"

"Planned what?" She blinked, wide-eyed.

"Don't you pretend with me, little lassie. I know ye too well."

"Aye, you do. Which means you should have known my belief that our Maker helps those who help themselves." She turned to hide her smile and walked into the castle.

"Aye, I should have known. Sweet Mary." Gregor crossed himself then followed Letty inside.

"Could you stop this beast, James Cameron?" Catherine leaned back and tried to look up at him. "My teeth are jarred loose, my stomach's stuck somewhere in my backbone, and I can't see squat that isn't jiggling."

Jamie smiled. "I've told you to relax. Your back's stiffer than a rooted pine."

Was he nuts? Relax? No one staring death in the face relaxed. "I *am* relaxed."

Finally, Jamie drew back on the reins. When Thunder stopped near a clump of firs, Jamie lifted Catie, then turned her around to face him. "What are you doing?" she asked, fighting the hem of her cloak, tangling around her legs.

He set her on his thighs and, nose to nose, smiled at her. "I'm going to help you relax."

The look in his eyes was sheer devilment. A blowing russet leaf caught on his sleeve. She plucked it off and let it fall to the ground. "Not like this, you aren't."

"Aye, darling, I am," he whispered and claimed her lips.

She raised her hands to his tweed jacket to push him away, but somehow—she wasn't sure exactly how it happened— her ambling fingers wound up inside his jacket stroking his chest. Then he began a slow, rolling action that pressed their bodies intimately close and she completely forgot her opposition to straddling James Cameron's hips. That flood of strange honeyed-feelings flowed through her, and she tried shoving back, but his grunted protest and his hand firmly pressing down on her lower back had her stilling, relaxing against him . . . and deepening their kiss.

Long minutes later, *he* pulled away. "Ah, that's better."

Her heart thudding against his chest, she nodded her agreement and gave him a slow blink. She couldn't talk if her life depended on it.

The slow, rolling motion didn't stop. Her sensitivities gravitated to where their bodies met. She glanced down at the tall grass, bending to the wind. The horse was moving, causing the gentle rocking that had her senses inflamed. Drawing in a deep breath, she leaned forward and rested her head against Jamie's chest, perfectly content.

"That's my lass," he murmured, closing his arm around her.

She smiled. She wasn't unstimulating. No, not at all; not to Jamie. His body was gloriously hard. "You know what?" she whispered, experiencing her first full surge of feminine prowess.

"What, love?" His voice sounded husky thick, sexy.

She started to squelch her question, then thought better of it. Glancing at a limb overhead, she grabbed a brown leaf, pinched it off, and watched it tumble from her fingertips to the leaf-strewn ground. "I've always wondered what Scotsmen wore under their kilts."

Silence.

When the wind tossed the leaf and it disappeared among the grass and gnarled tree roots, she let her hand slide up to his beard, back down his neck to his shoulder, then over his chest to his ribs, exploring and wandering leisurely. The man was huge, and hard all over. "In fact, I find I'm wondering that very thing right now."

"Um, Catie darling, a wee bit further up my thigh with your hand, I would warn you, and you'll be knowing what's under my kilt."

"You feel good." He did. Like sun-warmed velvet over metal. But she hadn't meant to say it.

He drew in a shuddery breath and pulled back on the reins. When Thunder stopped, Jamie looked down at her, somber-eyed, fixed and hard-expressioned. "I'm thinking you're wanting to prove to yourself that I'm wanting to make love with you, lass. Am I thinking right on this?"

Off in the distance, Cricket and Zeus raised a ruckus Jamie totally ignored. "Maybe." Just as serious, she looked up at him. "Are you still in your weakened condition?"

"Aye, I am." He looked deeper into her eyes, and his own gaze grew tender and pleading. "Touch me, Catie."

"You're asking me to take advantage of you?" The hair on his bare thigh set her fingertips to tingling, the rough wool of his kilt scratched the back of her hand.

"I'm being chivalrous, lass," he whispered. "It's clear you aren't knowing what you do to me, and I'm thinking maybe you should. I'm understanding your needs, and my own. Truth is truth, sweet Catie, and I'm needing your touch."

She rubbed the underside of his kilt between her finger and thumb, the back of her hand brushing his thigh. "Do you want to be my lover, Jamie?"

He didn't answer, just caressed her with his magnificent green-eyed gaze.

A simple "yes" was all she asked for, but she didn't get it.

Disappointment spiked through her chest, settled bitterly in her heart. Why had she asked? Why couldn't she have just enjoyed the moment without making a fool of herself? She lowered her gaze to his chest. "I'm sorry. Asking you that wasn't fair." Why did she have to be so damn stupid? Hadn't she learned her lesson with Andrew? She was probably the oldest virgin in Scotland. What man as virile as Jamie would want to make love to an ancient virgin? What lusty Scot would want a virgin Yank? "I had no right."

"You had every right."

The dogs ran circles around something, fussing. She lifted

her gaze to Jamie. He didn't appear angry, he appeared worried. What should she make of that?

"It's not you, darling, but the timing that's wrong," he explained. "You're wounded, I'm thinking, and wanting affection. Trouble is, you're wanting any man's affection, and not particularly mine."

That opinion mirrored her own about him. Jamie was a Highland Romeo, a barbaric Scot, rustic and virile and needy. But about her was he also right?

She worried her lip. The love versus lust dilemma. Again. "Letty told you what Andrew said, didn't she?" If Thunder meant to kill her on this ride, Catie hoped he'd do it now.

"Aye, she told me." Jamie stroked her jaw with the pad of his thumb. "I'm wanting to hear you say Andrew was wrong, Catie."

She wanted to say it, but how could she? He wasn't wrong. He was right. Her eyes stung. She blinked and looked down at Jamie's knee. Thunder neighed and the soulful trill of an unseen bird filled the silence a full minute before she could summon enough voice to answer. "I wish I could, but—"

"By damn, you believe him." Jamie grasped her shoulders as if he meant to shake her.

"Why shouldn't I?" Catie thrust her chin. "We were engaged four years—four long years, Jamie—and not once did Andrew ever kiss me like you have."

Jamie grunted. "Well, of course he didn't."

She frowned and shot him a questioning look.

"The man's English, love. He lacks a Scot's passion."

"God, but you're arrogant." She let out a sigh that reeked of frustration.

"Thank you, lass." He smiled.

He took *that* as a compliment? Set back on her heels, she clenched her jaw. "It was an insult, James. Believe it or not, people other than Scots can feel passionate."

"Aye, don't I know it?" He grinned, entirely too pleased with himself. "You're feeling pretty passionate right now."

"I am not." She shifted back on his thighs, hoping distance would hide the truth.

"Aye, you're lying again, love. But I'm knowing what you're about, I'm thinking. You're trying to prick my good nature so I'll force you to repay."

"You don't have a good nature, you oversized lout." She deepened her frown, then let her stiff shoulders crumble. "Look, Jamie. I know you're seducing me to feed my ego, and I appreciate the thought, but—"

"I'm not." He cupped her face in his hands and dropped his voice to a whisper. "You're no unstimulating, Catie."

The truth shone in his eyes. It knocked the fight right out of her, wrenched her heart, left her feeling fragile and vulnerable. "Please, don't lie to me about this, okay?"

Jamie's voice turned hard. "Just this once, I mean to prove my word to you, lass, but dinna demand it of me again. I've been timid with you because you're a Yank, but I'm warning you, darling, I'm a fierce-tempered laird. Your questioning my word insults me and, in future, the costs to you of allaying my anger will be great."

Jamie cupped his fingers around the backs of hers and slid her hand up his long muscular thigh. On contact with his bare hips, she gasped in a ragged lung of heavily scented pine, and jerked back.

The sun slipped through the trees and dappled her face. He clenched his jaw again and brought her hand firmly against him. Seeing worry light in her eyes, he softened his expression and swallowed back a chuckle. His darling Catie wouldn't find favor in him being amused just now. "Nay, love," he said to reassure her. "It doesn't hurt like you're thinking."

She looked doubtful, but kept her silence. She was learning. He moved his hand to skim her side, imagining the feel of her skin beneath her clothes. Her hand remained on him, and he offered her an encouraging nod.

Timidly, she began to touch him with just her fingertips. When her touch became a caress, he nearly fell off his horse. He knew he should talk to her to soothe her fears, but just how he'd manage that, he didn't know. Holding his own thoughts seemed damn near impossible. Catie had gentle hands, aye, but the feelings those hands aroused were anything but gentle. "I'm meaning no offense, darling, but didn't you ever—"

"Oh, I know all about sex," she said, her voice far too soft to inspire belief. "Just not, um, on a practical level."

She touched a particularly sensitive spot, and lingered. "That feels good, love." He allowed himself a grunt of pleasure and closed his eyes for a brief second to savor. Then what she'd said hit him. "Ye *never* touched Sir Andrew?"

"It's not my fault, Jamie," she insisted, clearly defensive. "He would've fainted and fallen over dead."

What kind of man took his woman to bed and refused her the right to touch him? "Inferior . . . Englishman. . . ." Jamie finally managed.

She grew more bold, curling her fingers, cupping her palm. His chest heaving, Jamie engaged in an internal war. Catie needed loving. He wanted to love her, but it was too soon. She didn't want him. She wanted to punish Andrew, to prove to herself she was a stimulating woman. "I . . . see."

Lifting her chin high enough to park a teacup on it, she squeezed him. "Not yet. But you're beginning to."

Shock stunned then pumped through him. It couldn't be true. She'd been engaged four years.

Oh God. Four years, aye, to a dead stump of an Englishman. Jamie swallowed hard, did his damnedest to keep his voice level. "Catie lass, are you telling me you're a virgin?"

She stared at him a full minute, then nodded once.

"Sweet Ch—" Why hadn't he known? Why hadn't he

realized she'd never touched a man *before* feeling her touch? It was her fault. Aye, it was. Her kisses left his head spinning. What man with a spinning head could think proper? A virgin. A virgin. By damn, this problem was even more serious than he'd realized.

Catie frowned. "I thought Letty told you."

"Nay. Not that. She never whispered word one about that." Catie was building up to something. He could almost see the wheels turning in her mind. Her face looked ready to flame, and he didn't want her embarrassed with him. "Don't worry, lass. I won't hold it against you. I once was a virgin myself."

"That," she said in unison with her sweet strokes of pleasure, "was no doubt a very long time ago."

"Aye, it was." He grunted, then shouted at the dogs. "Cricket, drop that limb." Damn dog. Jamie'd be picking splinters out of its mouth for a week.

Catie stilled her hand. She wanted to make love with him, so why shouldn't she? They were both adults, free to consent or refuse. Both in lust. So why not? The trouble was, exactly how did a woman go about asking a man to make love with her? Subtly?

She pondered on it for a second, then decided. No, she'd ask him straight out. Stunning Jamie was the best way to handle him, wasn't it? It'd worked well before.

The wind whipped her hair over her face. She smoothed it back. "Jamie?"

"Mmm?"

"I've been thinking."

He gave her a worried look and a halted, "Aye."

Ignoring it, she ploughed on. "I'd like for you to remedy that little flaw for me, if you wouldn't mind, please."

"What?" The veins in his neck bulged.

It'd been hard enough to say once, but she cleared her throat, priming it, and began to repeat. "I said, I—"

"I heard what you said, lass."

"Would you stop shouting?"

"Shouting is exactly what I need to be doing, I'm thinking."

"I don't like it—and you're upsetting Thunder." She gave the fidgeting horse a gentle pat. "He doesn't mean to roar, Thunder. I guess I've surprised him."

"If you're saying what I think you're saying, aye, you have done that."

She continued talking to the beast—the non-speaking one. "I know getting rid of my flaw won't be the most pleasant task for an experienced man, Thunder, but he is supposed to be my ally. The prospect of doing an ally a kindness shouldn't set the man to shouting, now should it?"

Weak-stomached and afraid to chance a look at Jamie, she turned her gaze on the dogs. "What do you think, Cricket? Do you have to ask Zeus to—"

"Zeus," Jamie bellowed, "is the female, Catherine."

He'd used her full name—a bad sign if ever there was one. Maybe stunning him wasn't such a good idea, after all. "But Zeus is a man's name."

"You're questioning my honor again."

"Not your honor, James, only your decision to name a female Zeus." She swatted at his thigh. "Is it asking so much for you to teach me how to be stimulating? I know I'm lousy at it, but blast it, you aren't and, if Scots are as lusty and have the hot blood you say they do, then you could do it and probably not even notice I'm lacking."

"Not notice? Woman, are you dense? How could any man not notice?" He held up a hand. "Nay, dinna answer that. This whole matter is foolish because I've just proven to you that you *are* stimulating."

Thunder neighed. Evidently he didn't care for Jamie's sharp tone either. "You've just proven that under your kilt you're as naked as a newborn, and you've proven you respond to touch. But you have *not* proven that *I'm* stimulating." She scooted as far away from him as she could without falling out of the saddle. "If you don't want to make love with me, damn it, just say so. But you'll be admitting that all you told me on the phone was a lie, James Cameron. Just nonsense you said because you were an ocean away."

He narrowed his eyes to pinheads, clenched his jaw so tightly she fully expected to hear its bone crack. "Admit it. You lied, Jamie. You're not any more eager to take me to bed than Andrew was, now are you?"

Jamie didn't answer, just kept his expression grim and his body as rigid as a metal rod.

She slid him a solid frown and held it so he wouldn't miss it. "You're not being the best ally, dear. I ask you for one little favor, and—"

"Christ Almighty, woman. Even in the name of diplomacy, a virgin shouldn't go around asking a man to make love with her."

"Why not? Men ask women all the time."

"This has nothing to do with double standards, so don't you be acting as if it does." He sighed then shook his head. "I've been too timid, I'm thinking. Aye, too timid, and too damn chivalrous."

"I've been a virgin twenty-two years, James, I know what they should and shouldn't do." Did the man take her for a fool? "And I haven't asked *a man,* I've asked you." She let her shoulders slump and her head loll back. "Blast it, Jamie, it's time. I'm too old to be a virgin, anymore."

"Age is no reason—" he began, then his expression grew black as night. "What the hell am I if not a man, I'm asking?"

"Good grief, are you going to start on that honor business again? It wasn't personal, just a—"

"You've neutered me, and I'm not supposed to take it as a personal offense?"

He was in a foul mood. If the veins on his neck bulged any further, he'd likely have a stroke. "I didn't mean to offend you."

"Well, what *did* you mean? Because truth is truth, lassie, and offend me is exactly what you've done."

"You sure are touchy. Totally charming." She plucked a sliver of lint from his thigh then flicked it onto the ground. "You'd think I'd asked you to do something awful."

"Aye, that's precisely what I'm thinking you've done." He looked away, muttering. "A crazy Yank who doesn't have the God-given sense to know a kilt isn't a woman's skirt still ought to know a man takes offense to being neutered."

She snagged his chin with a fingertip and swiveled his head back toward hers so she could frown at him. "You've got a nasty temper, James Cameron. If I asked, I'll bet a lot of men would be pleased to make love with me."

"You'll no be doing that, Catherine Morgan," he said through his teeth. "And that's a promise."

"Then you do it," she shouted, resisting the urge to stomp his booted foot, still snug in the stirrup. "You're my ally, damn it. Didn't you say you'd provide whatever I needed?"

"Aye, I did, but—"

"Uh-uh. No buts. You said it, and I'm holding you to your word." She nodded to let him know she meant it. "You said you'd be my friend, my husband, or my lover. Any time, you said. Well, it's time, Jamie, and Scots don't lie, right? I need for you to make love with me, and I fully expect you to keep your word."

"Woman, you're making me daft. Stop giving me that Yank look and stare your daggers at my damn stream."

He didn't look daft. He looked ready to commit murder. Maybe she should let him stew for awhile.

She swept her gaze down his stream. Foamy, white water washed over the smooth, brown rocks. Tall pines shot up from the sloping shore, sun-dappling the snowy ground beneath them. Hearing the water rush and the wind rustle through the crisp leaves, she pressed her hand to her chest. "Oh, Jamie. It's beautiful."

"Aye, it is."

"What's that?" she asked, pointing to a moving white lump on the far shore.

Jamie squinted. "Ah, that's a puffin."

"A what?"

"A puffin," he repeated. "A wee bird."

"He's darling."

"Damn it, Catie. Darling birds, soft sweetheart stallions—me kilt a woman's skirt." He shook his head. "Are you bent on insulting everything in Scotland?"

Thunder sidestepped. Catie tightened her grip on Jamie's thighs. "You consider everything I've done an insult?" Oh, he'd best be careful. He was awfully close to falling into a trap.

"Damn near."

She stroked his thigh and murmured in her best sexy voice. "Then I'll repay." She nodded. "And I promise to respect you come morn, and to not make you feel . . . cheap."

He muttered something nasty under his breath. "Hold on, you hexing witch. I'm thinking it's time to show you the loch."

Jamie snapped the reins and Catie smiled to herself. It was time, all right. Time to run. But amazingly it was Jamie who wasn't ready for loving. He needed her, and he didn't want to need anyone. He liked her kisses, and he didn't want to like them. He liked her touching him too, and he positively hated all that made him feel. Ah, James Cameron wanted to make love with her, but he didn't want to find himself loving her as well, and that pegged the problem.

Feeling gregariously good-natured, now that she'd sorted the matter, she decided she'd just have to help him along in his opinion. James Cameron might be ditsy, but he was also darned sexy. He'd be a perfect lover. And, at sometime during this ride, she had decided. Acquiring him as her lover was item one on the real Catie Morgan's things-to-do list.

Turning around to face him, she wrapped her arms around

his neck, slid up on his thighs, then wiggled her backside
to settle in. Honest to Pete, the man's legs were harder than
rocks. "Is it far, Jamie?"

With a groan, he reached around her to hold the reins.
"Nay, but it'll seem like miles."

Was he worrying about the loch again? She tilted her
head. "Maybe you should grab a sprig of grass to chew on."

He raised his brows.

"You're wor- . . . thinking," she corrected herself, not
wanting to get him riled up again.

"There is no spring grass. 'Tis December, I would remind
you. And I'm no thinking, I'm worrying, pure and simple.
And I'm feeling cheap." He gave her a pitiful look. "It's not
every day a virgin asks me to make love with her while she's
loving another man, lass. 'Tis degrading, I'm thinking. Especially considering the bastard's English. Aye, there's the
rub. 'Tis worse than degrading, 'tis—"

Catie kissed him quiet.

When he started his deep-tongued thrusts, she met him
eagerly, swirled their tongues and caressed his chest and
shoulders.

Too soon, he pulled back and whispered on a shuddering
sigh, "You're no playing fair."

Because she wasn't, she nuzzled his neck. Lord, but he
smelled wonderful. Skin-warmed cedar and hungry man; a
heady mix. "I didn't know playing fair was a prerequisite.
Men proposition women all the time. You told me that yourself on the phone. Remember?"

"Catie," he warned. "You're trying my patience, love."

"Come on, Jamie. Do you really think I'm that naïve?"
She bent low then tucked a fingertip at his boot top. "You
can bet your tassels Andrew wasn't celibate the entire time
I spent stuck in that convent he called a college. I strongly
suspect he hasn't been celibate since I've been home, either.
He might not have a Scot's passion, but he's not dead, Jamie,

and if he's ever been kissed like you kissed me, then I know he's been loving someone, and it sure hasn't been me."

Thunder quivered. Jamie paused to whisper a soothing word or two. "You're needing loving, Catie, I'm knowing that. But, lass, I canna give it to ye unless it's *my* loving you're needing. You're a virgin, I would remind you."

He was emotional. His burr had thickened and he'd used more Scots dialect. For all his intimate experience, the darling man didn't know spit. "There's no need to fret over the matter, dear. Sexual intercourse is just a combination of physical reactions. Who your partner is doesn't mat—"

Jamie clamped a hand over her mouth. "Dinna say it. Dinna dare say it. Do you hear me, woman?" When he looked as if he could talk without blasting her ears, he brushed down her neck to her breast, then fondled it. "Making love is physical, aye, Catherine. Any man's touch can pucker your nipple. Any man." He softened his voice. "But loving is spiritual too, lass. When you're loving the right person—one you love before, during, and after the loving—then, there's little physical about it and nothing in the world like it." He forced the softness from his voice. "But with the wrong partner, you might as well dunk yourself in an icy loch. Either will give your heart and soul equal pleasure."

A sharp gust of wind cut right through her, and she shivered. She scooted closer as if to steal some of Jamie's warmth. "But the physical release—"

"Is completely different." He curled his arms around her, blocking the chill. "One's satisfying and warming, the other leaves you cold and your soul longing."

She frowned. "Are you sure about this, Jamie? I've read a lot of books about this and none of them say—"

Books. Lord, help him. "Do you feel the same kissing me and kissing Sir Andrew?"

"Oh, no. It's different."

Jamie frowned. Did she mean it was better or worse? His kisses had to be better. Sir Andrew was English. His kisses likely warmed her about as much as soppy milk toast. "There you have my point," Jamie said, feeling very pleased with himself. "Now you've no reason to doubt my honor again."

Thunder fidgeted. Catie turned around and, to keep her from falling on her cute arse, Jamie helped her settle back against his chest. She gave Thunder's neck a gentle pat and envy slammed through the beast's master. Jamie wanted a little pat himself.

"Oh my God."

Jamie followed her gaze. His stomach curled. "Aye. This is the loch, Catie."

"The water is . . . *black.*"

"Aye."

"It stinks."

"Rotting vegetation," Jamie explained. The first shades of twilight had the loch looking even darker and gloomier than it did in the bright light of day. "Everything is dying."

She looked back at him and he saw his despair mirrored in her eyes. "Show me the dam," she said, anger shaking her voice.

Jamie spurred Thunder. The moment she'd seen the pollution, Catie had gone as rigid as when she'd first mounted Thunder. Near the dam, he pulled back on the reins and stopped.

She bunched up the folds of her cloak. "Help me down, Jamie."

He dismounted, lifted her over the saddle and then down to the ground. "Now you see my worries."

"It's awful." She began pacing a path along the rock-strewn shore. "Disgraceful. Mucky!" She stopped near a clump of weeds and crossed her chest with her arms. "What are you doing about this?"

"I've sent Iain to Edinburgh with samples for testing."

"This pit hasn't been tested?"

"Pit?"

She nodded.

"Nay, Catie," he said. " 'Tis not a pit, 'tis a loch." He squinted and searched his mind. "Lake. Yanks call it a lake."

Her eyes squeezed shut and her lips moved, as if she were praying for patience. Warming, that, and very unusual. She had no fear of him, or of making him angry.

"I was asking if the water has been tested before now?"

She seemed genuinely interested. Intense, too. "Aye, but not by my own man. The Kirkland had the tests done, as it's his dam."

"The greedy laird." Catie grimaced. "Well, what do his tests show is wrong with the water?"

"Nothing."

Catie propped her hand on her hip, her whole manner reeking outrage. "Are we having a translation problem, here?" She pointed to the water. "Any fool can see that something God-awful is wrong with that loch, James Cameron."

"Nay, I understood you proper, lass. And I know something is wrong. That's why I sent Iain to Edinburgh with the samples."

"Who's Iain?"

"My second."

She cocked her head. "Your second what?"

Jamie shrugged. "My second. If I die before fathering a son, Iain becomes laird of Clan Cameron."

"Oh, Iain's a Cameron, then."

She sounded relieved. Jamie almost smiled at that. "Aye, a distant cousin."

"Good." She rubbed the tip of her nose. It was red from the cold. "He can be trusted, then."

Jamie pulled himself up to his full height, crossed his chest with his arms, then glared down at her. "Now would I be sending a man I couldn't trust, Catie Morgan?"

She stepped forward and stroked his beard, not at all intimidated. "I wasn't questioning your honor, dear."

"Oh?" It sure as certain felt that way from where he stood.

Stretching on tiptoes, she brushed a kiss to the soft spot at his throat. "No, I wasn't. I was just getting it straight in my own mind, is all."

"I see."

"No, you don't." She looked back at the dam, paced a few steps, stopped, visually measured, then turned to him. "Why don't we just breach the damn thing? It's earthen. It wouldn't be that hard to do."

He almost smiled. A Scottish reaction, if ever there was one. He caught her up in his arms. "The dam isn't mine, Catie. Scots don't just trespass onto neighboring lands."

"Bull. They have for centuries," she countered, catching his shoulders and wrapping her arms around his neck.

"They got their feet cut off for their trouble, too."

She rolled her gaze heavenward. "An archaic, barbaric penalty. The Kirkland wouldn't dare try to cut off your feet."

"Nay, but he might yours. You're Yank, I would remind you."

She sneered. "Put me down."

He did, and she backed away, studied the loch, then looked back at him, a glint of determination flinting in her eyes. "One foot or both?"

Good God, she was weighing the matter. He mounted Thunder. "Get over here." He pointed to the stony ground beside Thunder.

"You haven't answered my question." She gave him an innocent look. "And why are you shouting?"

"Damn it, woman, are you *sure* you're not Scots?"

"American," she said. "To the bone."

He grunted to let her know what he thought of that remark. Yet he couldn't help but admire her spirit—and her stubbornness. She was a feisty, bossy bit of a woman. Fine traits. Rare, but fine.

She brushed at a fly buzzing near her shoulder. "I've been thinking."

"Oh God."

"I heard that."

"I meant for you to hear it." He held her stare. She hadn't moved.

"Well, don't you want to know what about?"

Resigned that the woman wasn't going to move until she'd had her say, he nodded.

"Before I came to Scotland, you said you'd marry me."

"Aye." Even God, Jamie was sure, was wondering what outrageous remark she'd come up with next. "Are you wanting to wed, then?"

"I wasn't finished."

"I'm a laird, Catherine. You should be a wee bit more respectful."

"You're not my laird," she countered, her jaw setting in that stubborn fix.

"I wouldn't be reminding me that you're not one of my clan just now, lass. I'm not a man known for being partial to Yanks, and I'm even less partial to insolence."

"We're allies," she reminded him, not moving an inch. "And I've offered to repay you for any insults."

Had the woman no sense? She had no fear. More than pleasant, that. But a wee bit of sense would—

"I don't recall agreeing to any terms or conditions. You didn't request a compromise on the terms of our alliance. You said you'd marry me. You said you'd be my friend." She walked closer and stood next to Thunder's heaving belly. "And you said you'd be my lover . . . anytime."

"Aye, I did." She had him on that. "But that was before I knew you were a vir—"

"You didn't set any conditions." She clasped his thigh and boldly slid her hand under his kilt. He jumped a full two inches out of his saddle. "Were you teasing me, James Cameron?"

"Nay, darling. But—"

"Were you deliberately misleading me, then?"

"I'm Scots, Catherine." He frowned to let her know she'd insulted him—again.

"And?" She inched her hand higher, curled her fingers around him, then squeezed.

He swallowed a groan. "And Scots don't do . . . that."

"Do what?"

Damn if he could remember. "Whatever!" He jerked his leg and cleared his throat. "Get up here."

"How?"

He reached down and hauled her up. "You're hexing me, woman, and I'm telling ye I dinna care for the feel of it."

A stab of hurt speared through her heart and Catie bit down on her lip. There it was. Pure and simple, as Jamie himself would say. He just didn't care for the feelings—or for her touch. She could see that plainly now. Jamie really was irritated. Well, hell. Here came the weepies again. She could start her own blasted waterworks company. "I'm sorry. I thought you could—"

She felt his chin at her shoulder. "Could what, love?"

Did he have to choose now to get that compassionate tone in his voice? How could she give him the standard "nothing" response when the man sounded so compassionate and caring? "I thought you could soothe me."

"By making love with you?"

She nodded, staring at a twisted twig on the ground.

"Poor Catie." He rubbed her arm, shoulder to elbow. "Sir Andrew truly hurt your womanly pride, didn't he?"

Her chin quivered. "He broke my heart, too."

"Nay, love. Believe me, he didn't."

"He did."

Jamie smiled. "Kay-oh. But it'll heal."

"Okay," she corrected him, then sighed her defeat. "It won't heal, Jamie. I'm flawed for life. I thought for a while today I could become my old self again, but I was wrong."

Her voice pitched high. "I don't even appeal to you, for God's sake."

"Before I take offense, I would ask what you're meaning by that remark."

"Well, hell, look at yourself, Jamie. If I can't stimulate you, I'm a lost cause." Now she was sobbing again. Dumb and disgusting.

One of the dogs sniffed at the ground near the shore. "Cricket!" Catie sniffled and wiped her eyes on the hem of Jamie's kilt. "Get your buns away from that water!"

What now were Cricket's buns? He wondered, but didn't ask. "I know you're upset, lass, and you probably don't realize you're causing a draft, but I'm surely feeling the cold."

She dropped his kilt and felt her face heat.

"You didn't mean to neuter me again, either," he said.

"Neuter you?" She knitted her brows, clearly perplexed. "I meant that you're sexy. You do reek of being sexy, Jamie. I was praising you."

He brushed a wet spot from her cheek. Reeked of being sexy. He liked that. "I'm thinking you're confused, love. Your deflated, womanly ego is warring with your aroused, feminine spirit. Give them time to come to terms, mmm?"

"Laird Cameron."

The male voice boomed from across the dam. A man stood there, on Kirkland soil.

"Aye." Jamie shouted to him, then whispered to her. "Look at the water, Catie."

"What?" His hold at her waist grew tighter and she shushed.

"The Kirkland says to tell ye he's got the results of the second run of samples on the water."

"And?"

"Just like before," the man said. " 'Tis safe."

Jamie let fly a stream of curses that scorched Catie's ears. It didn't matter one bit that they were bellowed in Gaelic—a curse was a curse, recognizable in any language.

"Damn it, Daniel." Jamie switched to English. "Do you see that—that mucky, I'm asking? Or are you telling me Kirklands are daft *and* blind?"

"Nay, I'm telling you neither. I'm seeing it, Laird."

The verbal battle continued. Catie sat straight as a sword, her gaze glued to the water Jamie cursed and her mouth firmly shut. Her ribs ached from his tight hold, but even if it killed her, she'd not whisper a word. Not a syllable. By God, she'd not even breathe. No way was she diverting the outraged Scot's attention to her. Let Daniel, the man being cursed as the Kirkland's lackey, deal with Jamie's temper. He'd been the fool who'd gotten Jamie in this mood, after all.

"I'll be passing yer warnings on to me laird, Cameron." Daniel's voice grew hard. "And don't be thinking the Kirklands too thick-skulled to know ye attacked our laird. We found yer calling card, but it didn't do ye any good. The Kirkland still willna be breaching his dam!"

Jamie's nod shook Catie so hard she swore she'd rattle for a week. Shocked by Daniel's false accusation, she darted a covert glance at the young man. He spurred his horse and took off, kicking up a clumped spray of muck. "Blasted sorry shepherd," she muttered, borrowing Letty's standard phrase about Andrew.

"What did you say?"

She turned so Jamie could see her frown. "I called Daniel a sorry shepherd."

Jamie's laugh took her by surprise and rattled her just as much as his nod. She smiled back and settled on his thighs. "I've been thinking."

"Saints preserve us."

"I'm ignoring that. This Kirkland needs a lesson or two in diplomacy, Jamie. How dare he make accusations against you?"

"How do you know I didn't attack the Kirkland?"

"You're Scots."

"Aye?" He frowned his confusion.

"If you had attacked the man, you wouldn't need to leave a calling card behind to let them know it. You'd have *told* them, pure and simple."

"Aye, I suppose I would have."

"American insight. A superior trait," she said. "So what do you think? Should we teach the Kirkland a lesson in diplomacy?"

"I'll no have you breaching the man's dam, Catherine."

"Why not?" She shrugged. "And don't mention my feet. He wouldn't dare."

"He'd try, and I'd have to kill him."

She clicked her tongue to the roof of her mouth. "These are the 1990s, for crying out loud. People don't go around cutting off trespassers' feet or killing people."

"Not officially, but, aye, it happens."

She looked back and opened her mouth to challenge him, but the gleam in his eye warned her that he expected it, so she snapped her jaw shut without uttering a word.

He lifted an arrogant brow. "You're basing your opinion on your college books, lass, not on actual living in the Highlands. Scots value respect more than anything else. To violate a man's holdings is one of the worst insults that can be done to him. It implies the trespasser is the stronger, that the holder isn't capable of defending what's his."

"But I thought the royals were nothing more than titles now. When Scots became British—"

"Bite your tongue, woman," he said in a voice more stony than the rocky ground they crossed. "No Scot will ever consider himself British."

"You *are* British, Jamie," she insisted. "Check your passport."

"Words scribbled on a piece of paper canna change what's etched in a man's heart, Catie. Scots are Scots, and that's that. Here, we hold to the old ways." He spurred Thunder into a full gallop.

Catherine's backside ached, assuring her she'd sit gingerly for a week. She gritted her teeth and vowed she'd not complain even if she couldn't sit for a month. She'd attacked Jamie where he was most vulnerable, and for that she should suffer his fit of temper.

Soon she grunted a groan with each jarring thump. Her backside stung like fire. The man's thighs should be registered as lethal weapons. She held on for dear life and squeezed her eyes shut.

When she thought she surely would die, she cursed her weakness and whimpered. "Jamie."

He immediately slowed down. "Are ye all right, lass?"

"Yes." She had to force the word to come out sounding civil. A blistering curse marched on the very tip of her tongue.

"Say *aye,* Catie. At present, hearing yer Yank *yes* grates on me ears."

It did grate. She could hear it in his voice. His brogue had grown so thick she could almost slice it. He was emotional again. She'd humor him through his snit. Women have been soothing men's tempers for centuries. "Aye, Jamie." She nuzzled him for good measure.

"Thank ye, lass."

She glanced back at him and saw the underside of his chin. He looked down and his eyes were fiery bright. Her heart lodged in her throat. Jamie was truly upset. "Help me turn around."

He lifted and twisted her to face him so fast she hardly felt the move. The face of death couldn't look more grim than her ally's. She stroked his beard. "Oh, Jamie."

" 'Tis his property, aye, but seeing the loch looking so poorly and hearing that bastard vowing all's well . . ." Jamie heaved a sigh and a shudder. "I'm needing a wee bit of soothing, Catie."

"Aye, you are." She snuggled closer and cuddled him. Her cloak draped over his knees, enclosing them in a warm cocoon. "Are you very angry, dear? You look angry, but you don't sound angry."

"Until Iain returns, my hands are tied. But, aye, I'm angry."

"Oh." She pressed her lips to his cool neck and felt his thrumming pulse. He was angry all right, but diversion might help. She curled her fingers in his beard. "Well, since you're already in a black mood, tell me why you and Bronwyn the Terrible split the blanket."

His hand on her back pressed hard, pulling her flat against his chest. "She betrayed me with the MacPherson."

"The dishonest hunk women are daft about?"

"Nay, he's not a hunk of anything, lass. The MacPherson is a man. A laird, pure and simple."

Jamie was a laird and there was nothing simple about him. "Slang," she said. "A hunk is someone good-looking. A man women admire."

"Ah, I see. Aye, then. Women consider the puny laird a hunk."

Catie chuckled. To Jamie most giants looked puny. "Why did she betray you?"

"Why does the sun come up in the morn and set at night?"

"Remember diplomacy," she warned, then before he could squawk, she went on. "What did Bronwyn say?"

"She was sharing MacPherson's blanket. That's what she said."

His pain seeped to Catie. A tight band cinched around her heart. "You loved her."

"Nay, but at the time I thought I did. I was in love with her, though." He glanced down at Catie's upturned face, his hair windblown, his eyes tender. "There is a difference, in case you aren't knowing."

He had that instructor tone in his voice again and his breath warmed her face. She spoke her thoughts. "Did kissing her make you feel the same way that kissing me does?"

"Nay."

That he wasn't happy about that was blatantly clear. She couldn't have expected it would feel the same. James Cameron wasn't in love with her. He didn't love her, either. He was in lust, and that was emotionally safer. Yet Catie couldn't stave off a feeling of disappointment. "Oh." She worried her lip and fingered the hair at his nape. "Andrew didn't love me, either, Jamie."

"I know." He gave her a reassuring squeeze. "But he was lacking, lass, even for an Englishman." Jamie dipped his chin and kissed her crown to soften the blow of his disclosure. "You would have devoted yourself to your wifely duties and made the man a finer wife than he deserves."

"Yes, I would have," she insisted, hearing and hating the pout in her tone. Uncertainty crept in. "Wouldn't I?"

Jamie smiled above her head. His Catie was needing reassurance from the toenails up, but her spirit was answering his call to the colors. A few more days of him blowing hot and cold and he'd have her wings grown back *and* flapping the Highland Fling. "I said so, didn't I?"

"Aye, you did." She smiled against his chest, then pulled back and looked up. She wrinkled her brow and tapped her lip. "Mmm."

"What?"

"You're needing kissing, James Cameron."

He lifted his brows. "I am?"

"Aye." She thrust out her stubborn chin.

He had to work at it to hide his smile. "You're the one who's needing kissing, I'm thinking."

"Is that a fact?"

She stared at him for the longest time, nary a drop reluctant to hold his gaze. He liked that. It was an experience he hadn't enjoyed often. Most women feared him. But not his sweet Catie. "Aye, that's a fact."

She narrowed her eyes and leaned forward. Was the lass going to bite him?

"You're right." Catie rubbed their noses. "I said, I like your kisses, Jamie." This time, she claimed his lips.

Before his head started spinning, Jamie indulged in one last coherent thought: Somewhere in Catie's family history there'd damn well been a string of Scots.

Kiss her, Cameron. Go on, enjoy her chaste touch—while you can.

You astride Thunder, your sweet Catie astride you. Are you inside her now? The cloak makes it impossible to know sure as certain, but I wager you're not. Even wearing your colors, she's still a milk-blooded Yank.

Yet, I'll give the devil her due: she has a wee bit of spirit. Her reaction to the loch amused me. A tiny bag of bones, so scrawny a man could count her ribs, and yet she dared to show you her temper. If you tapped her, you'd kill her. Doesn't she understand your power?

Nay, 'tis clear she doesn't. But it doesn't matter. Soon enough, she'll be dead.

You see, I've decided to give you a gift, Cameron: Guilt.

I'm going to wait until after you take her, to kill your sweet Catie. From the look of you, I won't wait long. We've talked of appreciating beautiful women often and, because we have, I'm amazed the Yank fires your blood. But knowing she does, fires mine. So, if a night in your bed doesn't kill her, then I'll murder her myself. Of course, I'll no be kindlier in the killing, and you'll feel no less guilty. It'll be your fault the Yank dies. And you'll knowing it is my gift.

Mmm, I suppose I should give Daniel a gift, too. Secretly, of course. He made substituting the water samples so very easy—both times.

Six

"You're my ally. I've decided you'll be the one, James Cameron, and that's that." Loosening the ribbon at the throat of her cloak, Catie entered the castle. What was all the excited chatter in the hall about?

Dressed from head to toe in neon yellow, Letty walked into the entry. "What have you decided?"

"Nothing important," Catie said quickly, feeling her face flush. Good grief, all she needed was Letty on her side and Catie'd be a virgin until she was ninety.

"Nothing important?" Jamie muttered a curse, slammed the castle's door, then strode to Catie's side. "The hell it isn't important." He jerked a thumb toward Letty. "Tell her what you're about. A good woman's lecture is what you're needing on the matter, I'm thinking."

Catie flashed Letty a smile, and gave Jamie's ribs a solid pinch and a whispered warning. "This is private, Jamie, between us. I'll thank you to kindly shut up. If you don't, damn it, I'll demand you repay."

"Me?" He tossed his jacket toward the brass stand beside the door. "You can't do that."

"Why the devil not?" She lifted his jacket from the floor, then snagged it on the stand's nearest hook.

"Because you're not Scottish."

"I'm in Scotland."

"Aye." He took the cloak from her hand then hooked it beside his jacket.

The stand swayed from the force, and she steadied it. "I'm residing in a Scot's castle, aren't I?"

"Aye, you know you are—"

"And haven't I worn Cameron colors nearly all afternoon?"

"Aye, you have, but—"

"And haven't I offered to make—" She stopped midsentence. A warning look lit in Jamie's eyes that fairly screamed she was pushing him too far, so she changed course. "Because I said so, dear."

He rolled his gaze toward the rafters. "You're saying so doesn't mean squat here, Catie Morgan." He wagged a finger at her. "You'll no be directing me on Scots matters. I would remind you that *I* am laird here."

Catie shot him a very unladylike glare and added a whispered and equally unladylike warning. "There's only one way you'll earn the right to discuss what I might and might not direct, James Cameron. So unless you're ready to put up, shut up—dear." She finished with an angelic smile.

"Children," Letty interrupted in her most matronly tone. "I can appreciate that you've hit a rock on the path to your alliance, but can your bickering wait? We've nagging trouble here."

"What's wrong, Letty?" Jamie asked.

Nagging trouble? That had a familiar ring to it. Jamie had turned to his grandmother, but he also had clasped Catie's hand in his firm grip. He wasn't through roaring yet. She indulged in a secret smile. She kind of liked him roaring. Did he do everything with as much passion? Working his flock? Riding Thunder? Making love . . . ?

The three raised voices from the hall grew louder by the heartbeat.

"What the blazes is going on in my hall?" he asked in a shout that had Catie's ears ringing.

"Stop your bellowing, James." Letty gave him a sharp look. "Celwyn and Bronwyn are back, and they're telling

Gregor something about MacPherson." Letty waved an impatient hand. "With one trying to outshout the other, I can't make heads or heels of the mess except to say that there's trouble."

Jamie strode into the hall, tugging Catie with him. She grimaced. Two women were indeed shouting at poor Father MacDuff, who seemed nothing if not at his wit's end. They talked so fast, wedging streams of words in between rapid breaths, that the poor man looked about to lose his head, pivoting it to look from woman to woman to keep up with the speaker. Bronwyn. Celwyn. Bronwyn. Celwyn. Bronwyn. Celwyn. . . .

Not brave enough just yet to check out Jamie's ex-lover, Catie flitted her gaze over Celwyn. Slender, about twenty, Celwyn had black hair and soft blue eyes. The word sweet came to mind, and stayed. Poor thing looked distressed, though, wringing her hands so much she had them red from the rubbing.

Bronwyn's shouting grabbed Catie's attention, but her thick brogue made it impossible to figure out what she was saying. Dressed in exotic purple silk, she looked beautiful . . . and tall. Catie sighed. Of course, Bronwyn would be both. And far from having Catie's own pale coloring, Bronwyn's skin appeared vibrant: a perfect face, framed by jet black hair that tumbled in soft, perfect curls down her perfect back, and perfect, piercing blue eyes that at the moment flashed perfect anger. She even moved like a sleek and sultry cat. One pacing a short path on a shorter chain. Well, hell. No doubt she could muddle a man's mind in bed. Andrew wouldn't call *her* unstimulating; Catie would bet her glasses on that. The woman oozed sex appeal.

"That's enough!" Jamie shouted.

Celwyn shrieked. Bronwyn looked at Jamie as if he'd lost his mind. And Father MacDuff slumped, clearly relieved and saying, "Bless you, Laird."

"Catie," Jamie said. "This is Celwyn."

The woman offered Catie a shy smile. "Hello."

Bronwyn stepped forward, her high heels clicking on the tile floor. "James, MacPherson—"

Jamie cut in, his tone harsh with a reprimanding edge. "Isn't doing anything now that hasn't been done in the nine hundred years the MacPhersons and Camerons have been feuding, Bronwyn. Certainly nothing more important than acknowledging your laird's lady."

"Your *lady?*" Bronwyn asked, not sparing Catie so much as a cursory glance. "I . . . see."

Everyone around here said that they saw, but Catie had serious doubts about how much any of them really did see. When Bronwyn raked a cool glance over Catie, the resentment churning in her stomach at being snubbed progressed right on to anger. No wonder Jamie wanted help with her.

"Hello," Catie said in a brittle voice, giving Jamie's former lover a brisk nod.

"Hello." Bronwyn flicked Catie a dismissing glance, then turned back to Jamie. "Can you give the Yank a history lesson later, Laird? We have important clan matters to discuss."

"Mind your tongue, Bronwyn," Jamie warned in a lethally quiet tone that had the tiny hairs on Catie's neck rising.

"Bronwyn," Father MacDuff interceded. "Act kindlier, if you please. Catherine is a guest in your laird's home."

"You'd be wise to listen to the priest," Jamie added, his tone not softening one whit more than the stranglehold he held on her hand.

Only by the grace of God did Catie refrain from wincing. Jamie's grip was tighter than the pinch of a good set of pliers. She had to do something. The tension was thicker than Bronwyn's brogue. And over what? Catie didn't give a flying fig if Bronwyn *ever* spoke to her. Why did it seem so important to the men?

"Excuse me." Bronwyn slid Jamie a coy smile.

He stepped toward her, trying to shake loose Catie's hand. She held fast and tugged him back, seeing the very second Bronwyn realized she'd gone too far. "Sorry, love," she said. "I'm out of sorts because MacPherson is bottling and selling the loch water in Edinburgh again."

"Aye, I'm aware of that." Jamie narrowed his eyes and laced his fingers with Catie's. "Just as I'm aware that word of the second water sample results is spreading through the village."

Bronwyn lifted an arrogant brow, but she wasn't looking at Jamie's face. Her gaze seemed locked on watching Jamie's thumb rub the back of Catie's hand. "Are you aware that when Celwyn and I passed through, the villagers were drawing water from the loch?"

"Why on earth would anyone touch that water?" Catie asked before catching herself.

Jamie turned to look at her, the hardness fading from his eyes. "The villagers believe the water has healing powers."

Bronwyn gasped. "You're discussing Scottish matters with a Yank?"

Jamie leveled Bronwyn with a blistering look. "Leave my hall."

Catie's knees wobbled and she thanked God Jamie wasn't looking in her direction.

Shrugging, Bronwyn turned to go, her dress brushing her calves. The crinkling sound seemed amplified in the silence.

"Bronwyn," Jamie said.

Catie covered their laced fingers with her other hand. "No, Jamie," she whispered to keep the others from hearing. "You'll only make the matter worse."

Bronwyn stopped and looked over the slope of her shoulder back at him. "Aye?"

"You will never again be rude to anyone in my castle. Especially not to my lady. Do you understand me?"

"Yes, Laird." She turned her gaze on Catie. "I am sorry,

Catherine. I didn't realize that you were more than just James's latest *lady.*"

The emphasis Bronwyn had put on the word grated at Catie's ears and made her want to cringe. How dare Bronwyn attempt to make Catie feel inferior? Dirty? Anger swirled deep in her belly, but she kept her voice calm, nonthreatening. "Now that you are aware, I'm sure you'll be civil, won't you?"

"If you're still his woman in a week, then we'll see."

"Bronwyn, I warn you—"

"That's reasonable," Catie interrupted, far more worried by Jamie's near-whisper than by his shouts. "I'll be here much longer than a week. That's a promise."

Bronwyn smiled like a sly cat. "We'll see."

Jamie narrowed his eyes. "Because I respect Father MacDuff, I will forgive your insult, Bronwyn. But I warn you, one more ill word or action, and you'll be punished."

If looks could kill, Catie would be a goner. A shiver ran up her spine and she glanced from Bronwyn to Jamie. "Punished?"

He didn't answer, just held Bronwyn pinned with his unblinking glare.

"Banned," Letty said, stepping to Catie's side.

"Jamie, no!" Catie gasped. "You can't ban—"

He did turn his gaze on her then, and she wished he hadn't. He looked about a half a blink from murder.

"You will not direct me in clan matters, Catherine."

"But—"

Letty shot Catie a warning look that had her hushing and nodding. "Of course not, dear."

Father MacDuff looked ready to keel over. He busied his hands wiping his glasses. Letty strode over to Bronwyn and whispered something that turned Jamie's ex-lover's face as red as Celwyn's hands. Celwyn herself looked like a frightened deer that expected a lethal blow just any second.

Catie sighed. That woman was in dire need of a friend.

She smiled at Celwyn, offering reassurance and decided a private chat with Bronwyn the Terrible was definitely in order. Judging by her glare, her becoming civil was impossible, but Catie would make the effort, anyway. Then if she failed, she could despise Jamie's ex-lover with a clear conscience and the proper conviction instead of with jealousy.

Letty and Bronwyn walked toward the kitchen. Father MacDuff and Celwyn followed, leaving Catie and Jamie alone in the hall. "For a first meet, that wasn't too bad."

"Nay, it could've been worse."

"Jamie, would you have banished her?"

"Aye, I would. No one will treat you unkindly in my castle, Catie."

Deeply touched, she smiled. "You're a good man, Jamie."

"Aye, darling. I am."

"Arrogant, too." His stomach growled and Catie patted it. "Is it time for dinner, dear?"

"Aye," he murmured, the tightness leaving his voice. "I'm starved."

"Mmm," Catie whispered. "Me, too."

He bent close to her ear. "For food, Catie Morgan."

She looked up at him, feeling decidedly mischievous. "To each his own, James Cameron." She let out a deliberate sigh. "But I have to say, as allies go, you are one sorely lacking laird."

"One day, woman, you're going to push me too far," he warned. There was heat in his eyes, but no anger.

"God, I hope so."

Just after dawn, Jamie mounted Thunder and rode to Kirkland's castle. Before he found Camerons at odds with the MacPhersons *and* the Kirklands, Jamie had to set matters straight on the Kirkland's attack.

He crossed the wooden bridge leading to the motte, Thunder's hooves clacking on its planks. The water in the moat below looked ink black. Frustrated, Jamie scanned outward over Kirkland lands—and saw not a soul. Why hadn't someone approached him?

Alerted by the oddity, he rode on through the lower and upper baileys, still unnoticed. Had Kirkland come to Cameron, he would have been intercepted by Jamie's men as soon as he'd crossed onto Cameron lands. Yet Jamie rode past the shearing shed, the cottages, and the old tannery, and he saw not the first sign of life. Nothing stirred but the chill wind and the leaves on the evergreens.

At the back of the castle, Jamie halted Thunder. In short order, he identified the Kirkland's chamber window then shimmied up the stones to it. He paused on the wide ledge to listen for sounds of guards, but heard nothing, so he looked through the dusty glass.

Kirkland lay stretched out abed. Bronwyn slept cuddled to his side. Seeing her there lessened Jamie's worry. If the Kirkland had been seriously injured, he never would have entertained Bronwyn last night.

Smiling, Jamie tapped on the dusty window.

Kirkland roused and opened his eyes. He looked Jamie's way, frowned, then hauled himself out of bed, stark naked, and opened the window. "What the hell are ye doing here, Cameron?"

"We need to talk." Jamie sat down on the window ledge. "If you've got the energy."

Kirkland rubbed his belly and blocked Jamie's view of the naked Bronwyn, sprawled on the bed. "You're a sorry bastard, coming here at the crack of dawn."

"Aye, don't I know it." Jamie crossed his hands over his chest. "Sorry, I might be for waking you, but I didn't attack you at the dam."

He stared at Jamie for a long moment, then nodded. "Since I dinna see for certain, I'm willing to give ye the benefit of doubt. Kirklands won't demand repayment, but I'll no breach me dam, either."

"I'm not asking for benefit of doubt," Jamie countered. "I'm saying, I didn't do it."

When Robert looked away, Jamie followed his gaze, out across the bailey wall. Not a Kirkland in sight. Again, he thought that odd. "Someone left thistle on my woman's pillow, Robert." Jamie slid the other laird a cool look. "I'm no blaming a Kirkland for it, but if I learn one found his way to her chamber, I'll be back."

Kirkland lifted his brows, leaned against the window jam. "I dinna order yer woman visited. I've been a wee bit busy." He jerked a thumb toward Bronwyn. "Is yer woman knowing?"

"Nay." Jamie couldn't tell Catie, she was delicate. The lass would be terrified that a man had stated his intention to harm her in her own chamber. Jamie would find out who and settle the issue with the bastard. Afterward, he'd tell Catie.

"Ah, I see."

"Nay, you don't." Jamie gave Robert a sincere look. "My woman is beautiful . . . and chaste. Any man touching her—"

"Will die. Aye, I understand." Robert scratched his stubbly chin. "Ye know I'm as partial to beauty as ye are, James. But I'd no be settling my differences with ye by marking yer woman with the thistle."

"Nay, you wouldn't. And I wouldn't be settling my differences with you by attacking you blind, either."

Robert frowned. "I don't suppose ye would. Ye would've killed me face to face, not clapped a shovel to the back of me skull."

"If killing you had been my intention, aye, face to face." Jamie sent him a level look. "So if you're not marking my woman with the thistle, and I'm not attacking you, then who's responsible?"

"I'd say that's what we're needing to find out. I'll get back with ye."

Jamie nodded and curled his fingers around the stone

ledge. Kirkland closed the window, crawled back into bed, then nudged Bronwyn awake.

"Injured, hell." Jamie chuckled and scaled the stony wall down to Thunder's back.

On the ride home, he saw not one Kirkland. And, for some reason, Bronwyn's remarks about the MacPherson's selling loch water in Edinburgh kept coming to his mind. Now what was he to make of that? More importantly, if not the Kirkland, then who'd marked Catie with the thistle, putting it on her pillow?

Letty grabbed a handful of almond shells from the basket dangling at her wrist then spread them near the bare-winter bush. She called out to Celwyn from the far end of the rose garden. "Put just a few near the base, dear. Too many, and the roses won't bloom this spring."

Celwyn waved and began dropping shells from her own basket.

Hearing footsteps crunch in the slush the sunlight had made of the snow, Letty turned and smiled. "Good morning, Gregor."

"Morning." He wiped his glasses on his coat lapel and looked out toward the ridge. "Letty, walk with me."

"What's troubling you, dear?"

He didn't look at her. "I've a need to talk something over with Harry. A worrisome problem, I fear."

Worrisome? Frowning, Letty called out to Celwyn. "We're going to visit with Harry. Be back in a while."

Celwyn nodded and waved.

Letty set her basket down on the ground and clasped Gregor's arm. "What worrisome problem?" She headed for the ridge, mindful of her step. In patches, the snow was slick. "You said you were better. Are you—"

"Nay, lass." He patted her hand and squinted against the sun. "I am better."

On the barren ridge, they stopped beside Harry's grave. Letty looked down at his headstone and sighed. Lord, but she missed him.

"I'll have your vow to keep secret what I'm about to tell ye, lass."

Letty looked at Gregor, her uneasiness growing to full-blown worry. "You have it." His strange behavior had her stomach knotting. "What is it?"

"I am better, Letty." He looked down at her, sadness and fear haunting his eyes. "But the philodendron died."

"What?" She pressed her hand to her heart.

"I poured the milk on it night before last and again last night, just as we agreed," he said. "This morning, the plant was dead."

"Oh God."

"It had to be something in the milk." He squeezed his eyes shut for a second, then reopened them. "And I fear one of my girls put that something there."

"Celwyn or Bronwyn?" Letty frowned. "Impossible." Feeling more certain, she insisted. "That's ridiculous, Gregor. They're Camerons."

He lifted his brows in question and scraped a bit of ice from Harry's headstone. "Who else could have done it?"

"Gregor look at me." When he looked up, his chin quivered and the sadness in his eyes broke Letty's heart. Few things in life hurt as deeply as betrayal. And, though she fought it, in a tiny corner of her mind she wondered if maybe one of the girls also had put the thistle on Catie's pillow. "Who do you suspect?"

"I don't know. And until I do, I'll not hear a word said about this to anyone."

Letty protested. "We should tell James."

Gregor stood up. "He'd ban them both."

"Aye, he'd have no choice," Letty said with a sigh. "Very well, we'll not mention this for now. But do be careful, Gregor." Tears burned her eyes and she blinked hard. "God help me, I can't lose you, too. I've buried too many I love already."

"You'll no bury me, lass." Gregor put a comforting arm around her shoulder. "There, there, dry your tears now and tell me how Catie's faring."

Letty swallowed her emotions. "She's fine. James jerked her out of the archives last night. She was still hard at work at midnight. I think he was feeling neglected."

"Ah, she's a fine woman. The laird couldn't want for one better."

"She is," Letty agreed. "It worries me that she was threatened in her own chamber—she doesn't know, of course. I found the thistle and took it straight to James." Letty winced.

"Upset, eh?"

"Raging. I thought I'd have to tie him up to keep him here 'til dawn." Letty heaved a sigh. "The diary, the thistle, and now you with the plant. I canna believe such goings-on are happening at Cameron."

Deep lines of worry etched Gregor's face. "Why doesn't Catie know?"

Letty sensed his dread in asking the question and set out to ease his mind. "James forbid me to tell her. You know how fiercely protective he can be."

"A prank?" Gregor asked, hope in his voice. "She's done no one here harm."

"At first, I thought it might be, but with this plant business, now I'm not so sure." Letty frowned. "I don't mind telling you, Gregor, I'm worried."

Grief etched deep the lines in his face. "It rattles me to the bone, thinking one of my girls is trying to kill me, Letty.''

"I know, my dear." She turned toward him and folded the priest in a motherly embrace. When he buried his face in her shoulder, she felt his shaking. The urge to comfort him was so strong, but having no words that could comfort, she just held her dearest friend close, and wept with him.

* * *

It's been a long day, and many suspicious looks have passed between those in your castle, Cameron. But now the day is done, and you're tucked safe in your bed—or in your sweet Catie's—and I am out here in the freezing snow, sweating from my efforts. God, but these wooden casks are cumbersome. Before I'm done here, my hands will be raw, but it'll be worthwhile come morn, when you're greeted by more floating fish.

I'm a wee bit disappointed in you for accepting so easily that MacPhersons bottled and sold the water. Harold wouldn't have done that. He'd give even his enemy the benefit of doubt.

I've never known you to be so careless, Cameron. But, I expect I know the reason. 'Tis that scrawny Yank. Aye, 'tis her, all right. Otherwise you would have recalled that Kirklands are the greedy ones, not MacPhersons. I shouldn't fault you; the deceit was brilliant. Having the men wear MacPherson colors to do their black deeds . . .

My, wouldn't it just gall you to know I'd arranged it? You'd never believe me capable. But I am capable, Cameron. Your parents learned that. So did Harold. And before I'm done, you'll learn it, too.

There, the final splash. I'm done. I hate it that this job is over. Yet, as they say, there's no rest for the weary. Or is that the wicked? No matter. Either way, I've more work to do this night. Before dawn, I'll have given you your gift.

I will have slashed your sweet Catie's face.

Seven

The smell of loch muck grew stronger and stronger.

Roused from a deep sleep, Catie kept her eyes closed, snuggled down under the heavy quilts, and sniffed.

A floorboard creaked.

Someone was in her room.

She jerked upright, toppling her glasses from her nose. They hit the floor with a sickening clack. Bent on giving James Cameron hell for sneaking into her chamber in the dead of night, she looked up. Above her head, moonlight glinted on a streaking silver blade. Gasping, she lifted her arm to deflect a downward thrust.

The blade struck her arm and sliced deep.

"Oh, God." Pain swept through her, swift and strong. "What are you doing? What the hell are you doing?"

Eerie moonlight streaked through the shadows. Above her, the blade glinted menacingly, arced for a second stab. Her heart knocking against her ribs, Catie screamed and rolled out of bed.

The attacker stepped into a path of dim light. Masked and dressed in black, he let out a blood-curdling whisper. "Running, Yank? My, my, you're a coward."

Was the attacker a man or a woman? Catie couldn't be sure. In a quick glance, she measured the distance to Jamie's chamber door. She could make it. The attacker just stood there, rocking back and forth on the balls of his feet.

When he rocked back, Catie ran. Two steps from the door,

the attacker grabbed her wounded arm and jerked her back. Pain bolted through her arm, spread through her chest. She couldn't breathe. Nausea rolled over her in waves. She balled her fist then slammed it into the attacker's middle, banging her hip against the washstand.

His breath swooshed out and he bent double.

"Jamie!" Catie screamed, lashing out again at the attacker. "Jamie!"

The attacker clipped Catie's chin with a punishing right. Reeling, she stumbled back, hit her shoulder on the fireplace stone, then fell to the floor. Footsteps scuffled close by. She tried to get up, but slipped back down in her own blood. A sharp kick rammed a boot into her spine. Pain bolted through her back, and she couldn't seem to move. Her arm throbbed, her stomach heaved, the iron smell of her blood tortured her nose, and her muscles ignored her commands. She couldn't fight anymore. In a cold sweat, she closed her eyes to block out the blinding spots, drew her knees to her chest, and suffered the punishing kicks to her back, her side, her thigh. "For God's sake, Jamie!" In her mind she screamed, but she heard only a whimper of sound.

"Jamie won't be coming, sweet Catie." The attacker laughed throatily. "He can't hear your call from Bronwyn's chamber."

A man? Gruff and deep, was the voice a man's? He had to be a man. No woman was that strong.

He was going to kill her.

Her survival instincts rallied. She buried the pain and, from the corner of her eye, watched for an opening. When the attacker raised his foot, she grabbed it and then shoved. Pain spiked through her shoulders, down her arm, and through her back. The man fell backward, and the knife hit the floor and clanged. Where in hell had it landed?

Wasting precious seconds searching, she gave up and scrambled to her feet. "Jamie!" Oh God, why had she locked the door? She fumbled with the knob.

"Catie?"

Jamie. She slumped against the door. He was coming. He wasn't with Bronwyn. The attacker had lied. "Help me, Jamie."

"Move over, lass! Do you hear me? Move away from the door!"

Catie rolled against the wall. Hearing the attacker running for the hallway, she lunged at him, snagged the loose fabric at his back. He jerked away, jarring her shoulder. Fresh pain gushed through her with the force of a geyser, and suffering yet another wave of nausea, she staggered, clutching at her arm and crying out against the pain. It couldn't hurt more if it'd been severed. Blood oozing out between her fingers made her hand sticky, had her head swimming. She tried to grab onto something solid but found only air, and more spots crowded the old; she could see nothing.

"Catie!"

A hard thud slammed against the door between their chambers. She stumbled blindly toward it. Another heavy thud, then a crack, and the door flew open, slammed back against the stone wall. Light from his chamber spilled into her room, and then Jamie was there.

He saw the blood and turned ashen. "Good God, lass, what's happened?"

So happy to see him she wanted to cry, she opened her mouth to answer, but words wouldn't come. The pain was so strong. So blindingly strong. "Jamie," she finally managed to whisper. And satisfied with her accomplishment, for the first time in her life, Catie Morgan allowed herself to faint.

The musty smell of the archives comforted her and Catie breathed in deeply. Normalcy, from sights to scents to sounds, held great appeal to her, and had since last night's attack. Would her insides ever stop shaking?

For the umpteenth time that afternoon, she adjusted the arm sling looped around her neck. The blasted knot at her nape was driving her crazy, irritating her neck.

Boxes stuffed with papers, ledgers, and folders lined the walls and misshapen stacks of yet more documents had been crammed into every conceivable space. She'd separated everything by century. Now she'd move on to decades, then to years. When that was done, then she'd start seeing what was there.

In the center of the dimly lit attic was a huge and very old wooden desk. Mahogany bookshelves formed neat rows on both sides of it, and behind it. Those shelves were the only well-tended things in the entire archives. Spines straight, the books were in perfect order. What books were there, only the person who had cared for them knew; there wasn't a catalogue. At least, Catie hadn't found one yet.

She leaned over the old wooden desk and added creating a catalogue to her quickly expanding list. If she worked twenty-four hours a day until the Festival of the Brides in June, she'd still not be done going through all of the records.

"What the hell are you doing out of bed?"

Catie spun toward the door, her good hand flying to her chest. "For crying out loud, Jamie. Would you stop sneaking up on me? You almost gave me a heart attack."

His feet spread apart, he crossed his chest with his arms. His elbows bumped both sides of the doorway and the top of his head barely cleared the opening. "I asked you a question, love."

"I couldn't stand it anymore, Jamie. I was bored stiff." She shrugged, sending a searing pain streaking through her arm. She hissed in a breath and fought against a wince. If Jamie saw it, he'd have a bloody stroke at her being up here, working.

"I'm wanting you in bed." His voice sounded as hard as his arm muscles looked.

It'd be wise to get him on the defensive. From his grim

expression, the sooner, the better. She warbled her brows at him. "Sorry. My offer was good yesterday, but you shot it down."

"I've shot nothing, lass . . . yet. But if you're not back in that bed—"

"No."

"No?" He stepped into the archives and snapped the door shut. "You've seven stitches in your wing, Catie Morgan."

"I know that."

"You should be abed, recouping. You're delicate, lass."

"I'm petite, not delicate. And I'm fine."

"You passed out cold."

"I did not." She tossed the pen onto the legal pad.

He dipped his chin and stared.

"It was just a little faint." She shook her head and lifted her chin. "And if I'd known what a bloody fit you'd throw over just a little faint, I wouldn't have done it."

When he neared the desk, she warned him, "Watch out for Cricket's tail."

Jamie stopped and looked down. The tail in question began a friendly thump against the hardwood floor. "What, I'm asking, is my dog doing in your archives?"

Her archives? Jamie joined her at the desk. "Cricket's decided he likes me."

Jamie's jaw fell slack. She gave him an offended grunt to let him know what she thought about that rudeness. "It's true."

"My dogs don't like anyone but me."

"Arrogant. To the bone."

"Don't be thinking your compliments can change the subject, lass."

Compliment? Good grief. "Cricket does like me," Catie countered. "Watch." She made tiny kissing noises and tapped her skirted knee. "Come here, Cricket honey."

"Honey? By damn, now you're insulting my dog." Jamie

raked an impatient hand through his hair. "Is nothing sacred to you, woman?"

"Charming, Jamie. Totally charming." Cricket came and sat at her feet, then raised his nose and waited for her pat. She bent over. "Good boy," she said, unable to keep her pleasure from her voice. "You're an angel."

Cricket gave her hand a wet lick, fingers to wrist.

"If I hadn't seen it myself, I wouldn't believe it."

Catie looked up at Jamie. "Cricket's liking me is clearly a case of my American superiority, James," she said in her best haughty tone. "We Americans are very likable people."

"Come here." He held out his hand.

Cricket didn't growl, but he stepped between them. Catie walked around his rump, then looked up at Jamie. "Yes?"

"Kiss me."

"What?"

"Kiss me, Catie."

She caught his waist with her good hand and stretched to reach his lips. He didn't bend an inch. He didn't look at her, either. She sighed her frustration. "You'll have to help me out here, dear. You're a little taller than I am." She praised herself for stating that truth so civilly. The top of her head barely reached the underside of the giant's arm, for God's sake.

"Mind your wing, love," he said.

She grabbed his shirt front and jerked him into a decent bend, then planted an angry smack to his lips. The man was still staring at the dog. "What in blazes are you doing?"

"Yell at me."

"It'll be a pleasure. You're acting like a nut!"

Cricket growled and shoved his nose between their thighs.

Jamie lifted her, bumping her arm. She grunted at the pain that caused.

Cricket barked, then barked again, working himself into a fine fidget. His nails clicked on the planked floor as if he were tap dancing.

Jamie looked pleased. "Kiss me again, Catie."

Tempted to bite the fool out of him, Catie kissed his lips. Cricket threw a bloody fit, barking and growling, snarling and showing his teeth. Catie drew back and shushed him. "You're being rude, Cricket honey. If you don't hush, I'll never get the man in the proper frame of mind to cure my flaw."

"Which one?" Jamie asked with a grunt. "You've quite a list of flaws for choosing, I'm thinking."

Cricket didn't even slow down. He was kicking up a royal fuss. Catie gave the dog a glare and snapped her fingers. "Stop!"

The dog quit, mid-yap, and dropped back onto his haunches.

"I'll be damned."

"You surely will, James Cameron. In case you haven't noticed, you've quite a list of flaws yourself."

"Nay, lass. I'm meaning about Cricket."

Catie frowned. The man was ditsy, and that was that. What didn't he like about her, anyway—besides her calling his animals sweet names? "What about Cricket?"

Jamie smiled. "Do you know, Catie lass, I've had Cricket and Zeus for four years—since they were pups?"

"Well, no, I didn't, but—"

"And do you know that they still growl at Letty when she gets too close to me?"

"They don't." Did he think she'd believe *anything*?

"Aye, they do. Cricket sees Iain every day. But once he tapped my shoulder to gain my attention and Cricket went after the man."

"Really, Jamie." He was joking, being outrageous again. "Cricket wouldn't hurt a flea."

"Aye, he would, I'm saying. Cricket went straight for Iain's throat."

Jamie wasn't joking! "Good grief. Was Iain hurt?"

"Nay." Jamie looked from Cricket to Catie. "But if I

hadn't called him off, I'm thinking, Iain would be buried on the ridge with my kin."

"Cricket?" Her doubt came across in her tone. Catie looked at the dog. "But he's so sweet-tempered."

"Damn it, Catie! The dog's paid you a fine honor, and you insult him for it?"

She gave Jamie a disgusted look. "I was praising him, James Cameron. Why do you take any tenderness as a blasted insult? I'm going to tell you something, dear. If I had meant to insult you—or your birds, or your horse, or your dog—you'd damn well know it."

"Slap me."

"What?" The man had slipped over the edge.

"Damn it, Catherine, slap me!"

She gave his cheek a solid whack.

Cricket didn't move. He watched. But he didn't move.

Jamie smiled and gave her a quick kiss. "Aye, just as I thought."

"Your mind is warped."

"Nay, darling. 'Tis clear as a straight path, I'm thinking." His eyes twinkled. "Cricket's given you his loyalty, which means he'll protect you with his life."

She snorted. "Well, don't you try slapping me to prove your theory. I'd land back in America. You don't realize your strength sometimes, Jamie."

A worried look lifted his eyes. "Am I hurting you?"

"Aye." She brushed their noses and whispered against his cheek. "Your refusing to cure my flaw is causing me great pain."

"Are you hungry, lass?"

She mimicked his rolling *r* and responded. "Starving."

He gave her a long, loving kiss. One that stole her breath and what little sense she'd mustered since her midnight encounter with the attacker.

When Jamie lifted his head, his eyes were stormy. "That'll have to do until your wing's healed," he whispered in a husky burr that had her tingling. "Then, I'm thinking, we'll both feast."

She worried her lip and gave him a slow blink. "Will loving me be a feast for you?"

Jamie paused. A warm tingle shimmied through his throat and spread through his chest. Uncertainty was there in her eyes, aye, but so was the spark he'd been hoping to see. He answered honestly, feeling as if he'd been run through the heart with a double-edged sword. "I'm thinking, it might."

Catie smiled and stroked his beard. He loved the feel of her hands on his face. Warming. *Aw frae the bein.* Cricket's tail thumped the floor.

"If you'll stay with me, I'll go back to bed now, Jamie."

She was still shaken by last night's attack. Maybe he should move her to another chamber. The thistle, then the attack. Aye, maybe he should move her into his chamber. "Cricket won't let anyone come near you, lass. You'll be safe."

"I'm not a coward," she said in a flat tone that dared him to disagree. "I fought first, then fainted—and only because I chose to faint."

"Nay, you're no coward." He set her down on the floor then walked to the door. "There, are you satisfied?"

"More or less." She twisted her lips.

"More or less will do for now. Come along."

"Oh, all right." She walked past him with Cricket dogging her heels.

Jamie snuffed out the candles, then closed the door behind him. "From now on when you're in the archives working, you'll wear your glasses, love. The lighting's poor and that puts too much strain on your eyes."

She stiffened. Did the man know *everything?* "I don't remember telling you I wore glasses."

"You didn't."

"Then, how?"

He tweaked her nose. "You squint."

"I do not."

"Aye, you do." Laughter lingered in his voice. "Don't get floppy, Catie. I like your squinting."

"Flippy, Jamie," she corrected him, thinking a little praise would go a long way toward settling her nerves. "I don't squint, of course. But if I did, would you really like it?"

"Aye, darling. It puts a man in the frame of mind of doing . . . things."

Her heart began a thrumming beat. "What kind of . . . things?"

"Warming things." He scooped her up in his arms and growled into her neck.

Laughing, she slapped at his chest. "You're a crazy barbarian, James Cameron."

He got a wicked gleam in his eye. "Starving for a Yank witch can make a man crazed."

Catie stilled in his arms, her good hand squeezing his shoulder. "What—What did you say?"

The teasing left his voice and his burr grew deep and husky. "I said, I'm wanting to love you, woman."

Catie couldn't breathe. Her darned heart seemed suspended mid-beat. And those eyes! She looked deeply into them and, feeling withered, she slumped against his broad chest. He wasn't teasing, or shoring up her bruised feminine ego. He really wanted her.

"Close your jaw, love. I'll behave 'til your wing's healed."

Was he teasing, after all? She shot him a suspicious look. He was . . . maybe. Blast and damn the man. He was on-again, off-again so darn much he had her dizzy. "You'll change your mind a dozen times between now and then," she predicted. "And don't lie to me. My glasses do not look sexy. They make me look dopey."

"Dopey?"

"Dumpy. Dippy. Like a geek."

"A what?"

"An idiot, James. Like an idiot."

Finally, recognition lit in his eyes. "Nay, love. They make you look smart . . . and sexy."

"They don't." Her hope that they did was clear in her voice. If a lusty Scot like James Cameron said glasses made a woman look sexy, then she had to believe it, didn't she?

"Aye, they do. Damned sexy." He lowered his voice. "I've seen you wearing them, Catie."

"When?" She didn't believe him for a second. She'd been careful about that. Being unstimulating was hard enough without adding looking dopey to it.

"In your chamber last night. You fell asleep with them on your nose."

She had! "What are you doing creeping around my chamber in the middle of the night, James Cameron?"

"Watching you sleep."

That disclosure took the wind right out of her sails. She blinked hard. "Oh."

"And you know what, Catie?"

"Mmm?" Noises were definitely easier to manage than words. The look in Jamie's eyes had her insides soft and woozy again. How did he do that?

"Just looking at you with your glasses on made me hard."

She gasped. "James!"

"It did, I'm saying," he firmly insisted. "I had to lock your door."

"It was already locked."

"Nay, it doesn't lock from your side."

"You locked me in?"

"I locked me out," he countered. "You were too tempting."

She cocked her head. "Then why couldn't you get in when I was attacked?"

"I mislaid the key." He swept a fingertip down the slope of her nose. "Your glasses were right there. So sexy, Catie. I wanted to crawl into bed with you and make love 'til dawn."

"I want you to stop this." He was determined to have her blush to death. Or to die of a heart attack—before he cured her flaw. But if what he said was true, she almost would consider dying worth it.

"I had to take three icy showers, darling. Three."

"Jamie," she complained, her gaze glued to his neck. His cedar scent had her own throat thick. "You're embarrassing me."

"I'm making you hot."

"You're not!" He was, but she needed the lie.

"Yes, I am. You're wanting me, Catie love. Go on, confess. 'Twill only hurt a minute."

It would hurt forever, especially when he laughed in her face. She gathered her courage and told the truth—more or less. "I've already said I want you. But you are not making me . . . that."

"Hot, Catie. And, aye, I am. Your nipples are hard, your breathing is too, and you're blushing the prettiest shade of red I ever saw. Ah, you are. You're hot." He looked pleased with himself about that. "But I forgive you for your sweet lying, lass. After all, you are a—"

"If you say because I'm a Yank, I'll deck you, so help me, James Cameron." Why didn't the man put her down on the steps so she could put a little space between them?

"Nay, love. I wasn't going to say that." He gave her a puzzled look. "Why would a woman want to make her man into a ship's floor, I'm asking?"

Her man? Catie swallowed hard. "Slang," she whispered, "for punch."

He shook his head. "A ship's floor and a fruit drink?"

"Hit, Jamie," she said from between her teeth. "Deck and punch mean hit."

"Ah." His expression cleared. "You're such a sweet liar, lass. Spirited, too."

Her voice stayed tight. "I don't appreciate your insults, dear."

"I was praising you, love."

"For lying?"

"For your spirit."

That surprised her. Her father and Andrew had condemned her spirit, yet Jamie praised that trait? "Oh." Damn the man. He wouldn't even let her work up a good fit of temper. Why couldn't he do what she expected him to—just once? "Well, what were you going to say?"

"That when a woman's hot and wanting her man's loving—"

"Would you please stop saying *that?*" Her face had to have gone from red to purple. She could feel the fire. Damn this thin Highland air. And she hadn't denied that Jamie was her man, either. Good grief, he'd still be laughing at her in his grave.

"Truth is truth, Catie. You *are* hot. And I'm going to make you hotter."

If he did, she'd burn straight to ash. A sizzling heap of smoldering ash. "Is that a threat or a promise?" *Please. Please,* let it be a promise. Men don't keep promises. Her father hadn't. Andrew hadn't. But . . .

God help her, she was going to faint again. Jamie *had* kept his promise. He'd called, hadn't he? "No, don't answer that." She gave him a pitiful look. "Would you just take me to my chamber now. I've been dangling over these steps far too long."

Jamie took the stairs two at a time down to the second floor. "I wish you'd refrain from using that word dangle, Catie. I dinna like it."

"The reason you don't like it is because when *I'm* dangling, *you're* forgetting yourself."

"I'm not." He gave her a look that said he expected no disagreement.

She tweaked his beard. "Yes, you are."

"You're talking Yank again."

"I *am* a Yank."

"Nay, I've decided you're not—and don't be arguing with me about that or I might change my mind and leave you flawed, after all. I'm laird here, and I've decided that inside your beautiful chest beats the heart of a Scot. And that's that, Catie Morgan."

She smiled. She couldn't help it. Coming from Jamie, her being a Scot was the highest compliment. She'd always admired Scots. A hardy, fiercely loyal people. Damn good kissers, too. "Aye, Jamie."

He harrumphed. "And don't you be ayeing me so sweetly."

"Don't you know your own opinions?" She gave him a good frown. "You just said for me not to argue with you, and when I agree, then you want me to argue. Just what do you want, James Cameron?"

"What I'm wanting is to make love with you, lass. And you're not able, so be kind and cease your chatter."

That was the one. The ultimate shock. She pressed her hand over her chest and waited for her heart to rupture, but it didn't happen. Instead, little bubbles of joy burst warmth like sunshine deep inside her. "Yes, Jamie."

He darted her a warning look. "You're doing it again."

She laughed in his face. "I'm sorry, dear. I couldn't resist." She rubbed his beard. "But I accept full responsibility. And when the time comes, I'll accept the fault for your fall from grace, too."

"Witch."

"Mmm, barbaric beast," she murmured and nuzzled his neck. Even to her, it sounded like an endearment.

Inside her chamber, he set her down. "God, but I wish. You don't know how bad I'm wishing." He backed out into the hall and snapped his fingers. "Cricket, guard."

The dog padded across the floor and sat at Catie's feet. Jamie gave her a stern look. "And don't be hexing my dog anymore, Catie Morgan."

Wishing she were a witch so she could hex him, she

crossed her heart. "I promise I won't hex anything—except you."

Muttering something nasty about God's warped sense of humor in granting women the ability to hex the good intentions right out of a man, he drew the door shut.

Laughing, Catie fell backward, onto the bed.

"Damn it, Cricket, you're trying my patience!" Standing atop the red quilt in the middle of her four-poster bed, Catie wagged a warning finger at the collie.

The beast just sniffed, and glared right back at her.

"James Cameron!" she screamed at the top of her lungs.

Zeus got through the open door first. When Jamie walked in, Catie was groaning, "Good grief, not another dog."

Jamie shot her a puzzled look. He'd heard her bellowing as soon as he'd cleared the top stair. "Catie? Darling, why are you standing on your bed? Is this one of your weird Yank customs?"

"We don't have any weird customs."

"I beg to differ with—"

"Why did it take you so long to get here?" She crossed her chest with her arms. "I've been calling a solid hour."

"I'm here now, lass. What's wrong?"

She pointed an accusing finger at Cricket. "That—that beast is what's wrong."

Jamie looked at the dog. Cricket wagged his tail and growled a whine. "What did he do?"

Catie settled her good hand on her hip, hiking her skirt up to mid-thigh. "He won't let me out of this bed, is what he's done. 'Guard,' you said. But you didn't tell the mutt that *I* wasn't the one he was to keep pinned!"

Jamie cocked his head and gave her a blank look.

Thoroughly miffed, her chest heaving, she plopped down on the bed and sat Indian-style, then ticked off items on her fingers. "I've tried sweet-talking. I've tried praising. I've tried ordering, directing, and even begging. But no matter what I do, that damn dog won't let me out of this bed, much less out of this chamber!"

"You're shouting, love," Jamie pointed out, trying hard not to laugh. She was in a fine rage and it was fact that she wouldn't appreciate him seeing humor in the situation.

"If you don't get me out of here, I'm going to do more than shout. I'm gonna kill something!"

"Now, lass, don't be mad at Cricket," he said, thinking to cajole her. "He's only trying to protect—"

"I am not mad at Cricket, you barbaric beast. It's you I'm ready to whack in the head. Cricket's just following orders. *You* gave them."

Jamie sat down beside her on the bed. "Well, I thought you needed to stay put." He rested a hand on her thigh.

She swatted it off. "Stay put?"

He laced their fingers, and softened his voice. "Aye. Patrick said you should rest, I would remind you. He gave you a healthy sedative last night, Catie."

"Hush about the doctor or I'll stuff a sock in your mouth, James Cameron. I'm not sick. I'm fine."

"You aren't sounding fine."

"I'm frustrated to the gills, Jamie."

"Why?"

"You know exactly why, so quit pretending. Mostly I resent a dog forcing me to stay in this blasted bed." She pulled her hand free, then slapped the mattress.

"You're throwing a temper tantrum, is what you're doing."

"I have been treed in this bed for hours!"

Treed. Another new word. Hadn't the woman learned any of the King's English? "Aye, you have, darling. But now I have offered to be 'treed' with you," he reminded her, hoping that whatever 'treed' meant his agreeing with her would defuse her anger. "Let me see where Cricket bit you."

She smacked her lips and looked at him as if he'd lost his mind. "Cricket didn't bite me, Jamie."

He knew Cricket hadn't; the dog had given her his loyalty. But with her cheeks flushed and her nostrils flaring, Catie looked so bonny, Jamie decided he might just keep her annoyed. "Well, how exactly did he *force* you to stay abed, then?"

She plucked at the quilt and muttered a curse on his head. Darling, that. He considered kissing the meanness out of her, then decided to annoy her a bit more first. Leaning toward her, he lowered his voice. "I asked you a question, lass."

Her sigh ruffled the quilt.

"Catie?"

She glared up at him. "He licked me, Jamie. Every time I moved to the edge of the bed, Cricket licked me until I backed up."

She shot the dog a withering look that had Cricket whining and slinking across the floor. Even Zeus snorted.

Jamie choked on a laugh threatening his throat. "I see."

"Well, he did."

"Aye, I'm believing you, lass." He nodded to prove he meant it, and wondered if he'd ever stop feeling dazzled by her eyes. "By damn, licks from such a fierce beast can be lethal."

"Don't you make fun of me."

Lord, she was breathtaking when she was miffed. Aye, he might just keep her that way. Rosy-cheeked and fiery-eyed. Mindful of her wing, he caught her in his arms and pushed her back on the bed. "I'm not making fun, Catie Morgan, I'm trying to make you see that if you'd gotten up, Cricket wouldn't have harmed you."

"Well, I didn't know that then, okay?"

Daylight streaked in through the window and slanted across the bed. He stroked her silky hair. Splayed on her

pillow, it shimmered gold highlights. "Well, now you do."
Jamie gave her a peck of a kiss.

Her nostrils flaring, she slapped at his shoulder. "You told
me that story about Cricket and Iain on purpose—to scare
me."

"Aye, but it is true." She was learning his ways. He kissed
her temple to let her know that pleased him.

She curled her arm around his neck. "I should demand
repayment. You're as sympathetic as a stone, Jamie Cameron."

"True, darling. But my Yank witch has a fondness for
rocks, I'm thinking."

"Does she now?" Catie tugged on his beard. "I'm thinking that at present, she doesn't like you one little bit. Not a
pebble's worth. And what are you thinking about that?"

"I'm thinking she's lying . . . and she's wanting kissing
again," he said. Her eyes twinkled, looking as beautiful as
early morning dew on his heather. "And I'm thinking that
after my lady's tussle with the licking beast, I should be
chivalrous and give her what she's wanting . . . to soothe
her." He kissed a lingering path down the slope of her neck.
"Are you needing soothing, love?"

"That depends." She sniffed. "Is soothing the same as
repayment?"

"In this case, aye." He lied with a clear conscious and a
good heart. If he hadn't, he would spend the next hour calming Catie down. The lass did have a fine temper.

Her chest rose and brushed against his. "Then, aye, Jamie,
I'm needing soothing. 'Tis been a trying afternoon."

She'd mimicked his burr, and had made a decent effort
of it, too. Pleased, Jamie murmured against her throat, "Ah,
I do love a woman who knows what she's needing."

He kissed her sweet lips and gently wound his arm around
to her back. Their chests met, and she sighed her content.
Urging her lips apart, he darted his tongue into her welcoming mouth. Her tongue met his, warm and wet, and she

whimpered the sexiest little moan from the back of her throat. He drew her closer then rolled onto his back, pulling her on top of him and, when she stretched out full-length and settled in, breasts to chest, hips to hips, he thought he'd died and gone to heaven.

She nibbled at his lips, her fingers in his beard, her breath hot and sweet on his face. "I want you, Jamie, as repayment."

He looked into her stormy eyes, knowing his own were somber. "There's only room for the two of us in this bed, Catie. Sir Andrew—"

"Doesn't come into this." The pulse at her throat throbbed. "I want you."

"Why?"

Her emotions flitted across her face. You make me feel things. Warm, wonderful things that I've never felt before. With you, I feel sexy, desirable, lovable. Do you realize how much a woman needs to feel those things?"

He cupped her face in his hands. She didn't need to hear him say that she was those things; she needed to be shown. But if his ally wanted the words as well as the actions, then he'd be giving them to her. "You are sexy and desirable and lovable to me, Catie. You're all those things and . . . more."

He thrust his tongue deep into her mouth, curled his arms and cupped her bottom in his big hands. Sensations exploded, rocking his body. His sweet Catie was arching her enticing hips and rocking against him, stroking his calf with her bare toes—so sexy, that—and whispering warm, loving words of longing that ignited more fires in his already burning body . . . and in his heart.

"Well, children, I'm glad you're strengthening the weak spot in your relationship," Letty said from the doorway.

Catie went rigid. Jamie groaned, cursed himself for not closing the door, and rolled Catie onto her back, using his body as a shield. "Letty, your timing is God-awful."

"Aye, I see that it is." The little tyrant was smiling. "But

I thought you'd want to know that Iain's back. In fact, he's right here." She linked arms with the red-faced giant and together they filled the doorway.

Catie groaned like the dying. Cricket started a deep-throated growl and Zeus joined him. Not daring to look down at Catie, Jamie gave her a reassuring pat and ordered the dogs to hush. Then he greeted his second. "Hello, Iain."

"Afternoon, Laird."

Just that, and the man's voice held laughter. Catie covered her face with her hands. By damn, she was redder than the quilt.

Iain cleared his throat. "You haven't introduced me to Catie, I'm thinking."

Jamie bit a smile from his lips. "Catie, this is my second, Iain. Iain, my lady, Catie Morgan."

"This is not an afternoon tea, James Cameron," Catie whispered on a groan. "Get them out of here."

"Mind your manners, love," he said, kissing her forehead. "Say hello to Iain."

She groaned, deeper and buried her face against his chest, then stuck up a finger, bent it, and muttered a shaky "Hi."

Jamie gave her rump a solid pinch.

She jerked up and whacked his arm. "Damn it, that hurt."

Letty gasped. Seconds later, she frowned. "Cricket didn't attack."

Jamie shrugged. "Catie's hexed him."

"I wish you'd stop saying that, Jamie. I'm not a witch, for crying out loud."

That scolding brought with it a glare he'd not soon be forgetting. "When you recover, lass, you do it with gump-tion, I'm thinking. But I'll no have you embarrassed about loving me—not even if you glare your daggers 'til nightfall."

Letty and Iain came into the room and stood on opposite sides of the bed. Cricket got between Catie and Letty and Zeus inched between Jamie and Iain, but neither dog inter-fered.

Her face as red as fire, Catie looked Letty straight in the eye. "Cricket treed me. Jamie was helping me up."

"I see."

Catie muffled a groan. For once, Letty saw, all right. "More or less."

"I understand." Iain's blue eyes twinkled merrily. "I was just this morning talking—as I was trudging along in the ice storm on me way back from Edinburgh—that if I were the laird's lady, and if his monster dog 'treed' me abed, I'd just punish the laird for it by treeing him abed for a while." Iain nodded, shaking his shaggy head. "That's exactly what I was thinking this very morn."

Catie gave him a grateful smile. "That's just what I myself thought, Iain. I guess great minds travel in pairs." She tilted her head. "Tell me. On your journey, did you happen to pass a blarney stone?"

"Aye, 'tis a fact, I did." He nodded, letting her know he meant to go along with her nonsense. "But that was after."

"Ah." Catie smiled.

"I've been known to 'tree' my Harry a time or two," Letty added. "An unpleasant task, to be sure, but necessary on occasion to remind a man that his woman has spirit."

Jamie nearly split his side laughing. That earned him another healthy backhanded whack to the chest. Ignoring the pesky sting, he swung his arm around Catie's shoulder and pulled her to his side. "That's my lady, all right. Spirited. She could use a pinch more of the trait, but I'm thinking I'll cure that flaw. 'Tis my duty to my ally."

"Your ally?" Letty's eyes sparkled. "Aye, I'm sure you'll cure her flaws—in about nine centuries or so, give or take a decade or nine."

Jamie frowned. "What the hell does that mean?"

Catie smiled. "It'll means it never happen, dear."

Iain cut in. "I hate to dampen your fine mood, Laird. But we've important clan matters to discuss."

"I know about the water samples, Iain."

Catie's flat tone dared Iain to challenge her right to hear the results. That amused Jamie. The woman had converted to Scots and she didn't even know it. Eventually, he'd inform her, of course. Maybe he should thank Bronwyn for pricking Catie's temper on the matter. Nay, he wouldn't. Bronwyn was keeping herself busy enough these days with the Kirkland and the MacPherson. Next, she'd probably be sleeping with Colin Ferguson, God help the man. Then she'd have sampled all the lairds.

Iain glanced over, and Jamie granted him permission to speak in a nod Catie wouldn't see or discern.

"The loch is contaminated."

"Aye, but with what?" Jamie asked.

"Cyanide." Iain's eyes lost their twinkle. He was worried. Pure and simple.

Jamie grimaced. "How bad is it?"

"The report says heavy concentrations." Iain swallowed hard. "To reach such a level, someone has to be purposely dumping the cyanide into the loch, Laird—that's what the report says."

"Oh God," Letty said. "The villagers!"

"Don't worry." Catie squeezed Letty's hand. "Jamie will take care of it."

Her faith in him surprised Jamie, but it pleased him, too. She learned quickly. "Iain, ask the other lairds to meet me at Kirkland Dam. And get word to the village. Have Father MacDuff help."

"What should I do, Jamie?" Catie asked.

"You'll no be going out in the storm, lass. You'll catch the fever."

"I'm not delicate."

"Nay, love. But you've stitches, I would remind you."

She gave him a disgusted look that he found enchanting.

"I'm off, then," Iain said and headed toward the door.

Letty walked out with Iain. She paused at the door and looked back. "It'll take a good two hours for Iain to summon the lairds." Letty glanced at Jamie, then turned her shrewd gaze back to Catie. "From the looks of him, I'd say James could use a little more treeing, if you ken my meaning." She locked the chamber door, then pulled it shut.

Jamie absently stared at the quilt. Catie leaned back against the four-poster's headboard and tugged Jamie with her. He rested against her good shoulder and covered her legs with his. "Jamie, do you always hold conversations with your grandmother and your second while you're in bed with your ally?"

"I've never had an ally before, nor a woman in my chambers, for that matter."

Her heartbeat sped. "Oh?"

"You're surprised, eh?"

"I suppose." What had Bronwyn been to him then, besides a lover? Catie rubbed a lock of his hair between her fingers. 'Who do you think is doing this—to the loch, I mean?"

"I don't know, lass. The Kirkland has many enemies—he's as greedy as sin."

"MacPherson?" she suggested. "He's feuding with you and he knows how you feel about the loch."

"Nay," Jamie said, then reconsidered. "Probably not. He's feuding with Camerons, not Kirklands. He'd have damaged my stream, I would say."

"What about the other laird? Ferguson, was it?" She rubbed a bit more of his hair between her fingers. A curl locked around her finger, and she decided his hair wasn't too long, after all.

"Aye, Colin Ferguson. But he's a fair man, he'd not endanger the villagers."

"He might." Catie waited until Jamie looked up at her then continued. "You said Bronwyn had latched onto him and she could muddle a man's mind. Maybe she's muddled Ferguson's mind."

"She has. But she isn't capable of vicious muddling, only

conniving. She'd no hurt the villagers, either. Bronwyn's loose with her loving, but she cares for her country and people."

"Mmm." The light had faded dim. Catie looked over at the window. Snowflakes clung to the glass. The fire burning in the grate crackled. "I must say, you're taking this pretty well. I thought you'd be ranting and raving."

"I'm no surprised as much as relieved. Now that we know what the problem is, we can resolve it."

"Right." She let out a delicate snort. "Without so much as one lusty yell? Who do you think you're kidding?"

He smiled. "I'll yell, later." He closed his eyes and brushed the side of her breast with his cheek. "Right now, I'm of a mind to purr."

"You like me stroking you, hmm?"

"Aye, it feels good." He rubbed little circles on her shoulder and grazed the swell of her breast with his thumb.

She gave him a smile he didn't see. "May I ask you something?"

"Aye." His thumb grew bolder, seeking her nipple.

She savored a pleasant little shiver. "How did Harry die?"

"In his sleep," Jamie said, his voice growing hazy. "One morn he just didn't wake up."

"He must have been quite a man. Letty still loves him very much."

"Aye, he was that."

Jamie's fingers joined his thumb on her breast. He had big hands, wonderfully firm fingers, blunt nails, but a gentle touch. Amazing. . . . She didn't want him to stop. Maybe if she kept his mind occupied, he wouldn't notice what he was doing. She stroked his scalp with slow sweeps of her fingertips and brushed a curl from his ear. "What happened to your parents?"

"They drowned in the loch last winter."

"Were they swimming?" She rubbed his forehead with her thumb.

"Aye."

She frowned and traced the shell of his ear with her fingertip. "The water must have been freezing cold then."

" 'Twas. They suffered cramps, the coroner figured." Jamie snuggled closer, until his chest was firmly against her side and his breath warmed her neck. "Talk to me about something else, Catie."

"What do you want to talk about?" He smelled of man and cedar; warm and wonderful.

He sighed and the heave of his chest nearly knocked her off the bed. But she held tight and didn't say a word. She couldn't. Jamie finally had stopped his torture and had worked his fingers inside her blouse. Another inch and he'd . . .

"Tell me you like feeling me touch you." He cupped her bare breast in his hand.

She groaned, her back clearing the bed a good two inches. Her nipple peaked against his palm and her throat muscles constricted. She closed her eyes and breathed in deeply, awed that her body could be so sensitive to touch. "I like it, Jamie."

He shifted his weight 'til they could see eye to eye. "Look at me, Catie. I'm wanting you to know who's loving you."

Puzzled, Catie met his gaze. "I know."

Was he jealous of Andrew? Insecure? She thought about it and decided he wasn't either. Jamie's arrogance wouldn't tolerate any competition and that pegged the reason for his demand.

Holding her gaze, he slid his hand under her skirt then up the length of her thigh. Clamoring for breath, she curled her fingers and squeezed his shoulder. "Jamie, I don't have on a slip."

"Aye, darling. I'm knowing." His expression more determined than it had been on the moor, he skimmed over her panties, pressed his palm flat on her stomach, then spread his fingers.

Her muscles quivered. His touch was deliberate, far from a gentle caress, but not harsh or punishing. Jamie did need reassuring. He needed to know that Andrew wasn't in bed with them. But how did she give that reassurance? If she mentioned Andrew, Jamie might . . . stop.

He rubbed her abdomen and cupped his hand between her thighs. "Who's loving you, Catie?"

His hand burned her through the lace. She arched her hips and answered: "You are, Jamie."

Grunting his approval, he covered her mouth with his. He licked at her lips with sweeps of his tongue, flexed his fingers, and explored the elastic at her legs. When his fingers slipped beneath to her bare skin, she suffered a shock of pleasure and gasped. She hadn't expected the surge of honey-feelings to gravitate to his fingertips, and she wanted him to experience that sensation, too. "Jamie," she whispered, feeling breathless. "I want to touch you."

He let out a sexy groan and inched the lace down over her hips. "When you're well, love. You're a wee slip of an injured witch, but I'm still a mere mortal."

She caressed his throat with the tip of her nose. "I'm feeling . . . strange things, Jamie. It almost hurts."

His lips curved in a slow smile against her lips, and he drew a lazy circle with his fingertip. "You're hot for me, love."

She caught his lower lip with her teeth and gently bit down, her sweet little body arching. He kissed her hard, let her feel the fury of his passion, and raised her desire to fever pitch.

When she was panting as raggedly as he, she began murmuring sweet, stilted words of wanting between rapid-fire kisses to wherever her lips happened to touch. He growled his pleasure and thrust his tongue deep into her mouth, his finger deep into her warm sheath. He hissed in a breath and delighted in a shudder. She was so tight. Her muscles spasmed, her body jerked. Rejoicing with her, so did his.

She cried out and clung to him, her fingers digging into his arms. He nearly came. His heart thundered a wild beat, his head reeled, too full of aroused sensations. He stretched his fingers and, when she began moving against his hand, he worked to bring her pleasure. She was so responsive. His merest touch had her shuddering, opening to him, and he basked in the fury of her passion.

"Ah, sweet Catie," he whispered on a moan. "Who's loving you, woman?" Her chest heaved, her beautiful breasts rising and falling, and between them he could hear the thundering of her heart. He took her peaked nipple into his mouth and suckled.

She lifted off the bed and cried out. "Too tender!"

"You're needing soothing, love," he whispered between gasps. "Soothing." He watched her face, her delicate, beautiful face, experiencing the magic of desire. Her sensual gyrations and erotic sounds, so warming, so close to climax. He increased the rhythm, pushed his tongue deep into her mouth and mirrored his wild thrusts. She stiffened, rode the crest of passion's wave, and tumbled into delicious spasms that he felt clear to his soul.

He held her for long minutes, calming her with gentle strokes and whispering his own loving words, words his sweet Catie needed to hear as much as he needed to say them. Her spasms weakened to wee tremors deep inside her, then slowly eased, and she stilled. He kissed her long and hard, telling her she'd pleased him. "Who's loving you, Catie?"

"You are," she whispered. "Come inside me, Jamie. I want to feel you."

"Nay, love. Now's not the time."

"Why?" Her cheeks grew as rosy as they had when she'd come to him. "Andrew—"

He pressed a fingertip against her lips. "Shh, don't. When we're loving, we'll talk of no others. Not in our bed, Catie." He kissed the corner of her mouth, the dip in her chin. "The simple truth is that two hours in your arms won't satisfy the need in me." He wondered if forever would be long enough. "You're too . . . warming."

Jamie heard her swallow. He half-expected her to ask if that was a threat or a promise, but the woman surprised him yet again.

"You're probably right. You're a lusty laird." She kissed his fingertip at her lip and her expression grew serious. "I love the way you make me feel. You're a good ally, Jamie."

He liked Catie's surprises, and smiled to let her know it. "I'm a Scot."

"Aye, you awful man." She smiled back, not looking at all displeased, then licked her lips. "Show me, Jamie. I want to know what it's like."

"What are you wanting to know, lass?"

"What you feel when you're loving me." She gave him that slow blink that set him to blaze.

He shuddered. When he could, he answered on a ragged sigh. "I'm feeling hexed. That's what I'm feeling, sweet Catie."

"And you like it."

She hadn't asked. She'd already learned his thoughts about that. "Aye, I do, woman," he answered, anyway. "You're definitely a witch."

"Your Yank witch," she said, and gave him a long, loving kiss.

Jamie pressed his hand against her stomach and wondered what their grandchildren would say about her still hexing him fifty years from now. He tilted back his head to receive her kisses to his throat. Aye, in fifty years or so, he just might have gotten used to being hexed.

Word is streaking like lightning through the village, and tempers are running high. My mischief is coming to light.

I have to say, your Yank surprised me, Cameron. Unlike you, I rarely underestimate my enemy, but she fought harder than I expected. I wanted to scar her face to feed your guilt and instead wounded her arm. A pity, but it will do for now, especially as you've learned about the cyanide in the loch. Soon you'll meet with the lairds and demand the dam be breached. Best not, Cameron. You'll be doing more damage than you can imagine.

For now, go on and attend your duties. We all know you are ever dutiful. Your Yank is ripe. Take her soon, eh? I'm a wee bit anxious to see her headstone on the ridge near Harold's.

Guilt is such a warming gift. Aye, you'll wear it well. And to keep it strong, I'll feed that guilt, just as soon as I find the diary. I know in my bones it holds a valuable key.

I'll be watching you atop Kirkland Dam, but know this: Whatever happens there, in the end, you will do as I wish. My destiny will again be mine.

On your knees, you'll beg me for mercy, Cameron. But you'll find none.

I'll damn you to the same fate you damned me.

Eight

The four giant lairds stood atop Kirkland Dam, squared-off and engaged in a fierce verbal battle.

At present, three of the lairds were shouting at Jamie. But feeling good-natured because his alliance with Catie was moving along at a good clip—and because his complaints about the loch finally had been proven as fact—he let them. Until the lairds vented a fair amount of steam, no one would be listening much, anyway.

If Catie saw them, she'd likely vow only bloodthirsty Scots could work up such a rage over a piddling pit of water, even though she'd mustered a worthy rage over the matter herself. *One foot or both,* she'd asked. Darling, that. Inside, he smiled. She'd worn her anger like the old warlords had worn their shields, and her temper had sliced every whit as sharp as one of their battle swords. Aye, the woman was showing the makings of a damn fine Scot.

She'd find it telling too, that the lairds had positioned themselves atop the dam nearest their own lands.

Robert Kirkland stood dead center, his cold dark looks seemingly intensified by his black, deep purple, and drab green tartan: Exactly what one would expect from a laird whose clan motto is "wary is life." Colin Ferguson stood to the southwest, holding his gray stallion's rein , his brown hair whipping back and forth in the brisk wind, his gaze pivoting between Jamie and Kirkland in obvious confusion. Unfortunate, that. Duncan MacPherson, leathery-skinned and considered handsome by some, and as the dishonest hunk by Catie, stood to Jamie's southeast, giving him a sleety glare. MacPherson's red plaid looked bold against the snow, made the circles under his eyes appear even deeper.

Bronwyn must be giving her men little rest. Both Kirkland and MacPherson looked bone-tired. She was a lusty woman, Jamie would give her that. A creative lover, aye, but lacking. Aside from lust, she shared not a whit of emotion. When the sex was over, everything was over. Was that why she'd never touched the need to be tender and gentle and protective in him? Probably not. Only Catie had touched those needs in him, and they hadn't yet made love.

Aye, Catie touched him, and she'd find their positions on the dam telling. He could almost hear her. *You men are territorial fools.* She'd bellow her curse, naturally, and she'd swear the flaw blinded them.

She was probably right.

The Kirkland's booming voice claimed Jamie's attention. "I've had two separate testings done to please you, Cameron. Both stated the water is safe."

Jamie kept his expression as stony and cold as the ice-crusted ground on which he stood and silently cursed Kirkland for staining his soul black with greed. "You're holding an accurate report in your hands, Robert."

Kirkland narrowed his eyes. "Are you suggesting the reports I have are inaccurate."

"Aye, I am." Jamie nodded toward the water. " 'Tis black as ink and it stinks like the shearing barn in high summer. Can you deny it?"

"I've no need to deny anything. My reports prove the water is fine."

Jamie clenched his jaw. Kirkland had sent Daniel with the second test results to rub salt in Jamie's wounds, because Jamie had dared to dispute the first tests. But now he had proof. And it would be Kirkland who suffered the salty sting—him, and the villagers who depended on the water.

"Ignore all three reports, if it'll make you feel better," Jamie suggested. "Just look at the evidence before your eyes. Go on, look! Then tell me there's nothing wrong."

Duncan MacPherson lifted his scathing gaze from the report. "Cyanide?" He tossed the papers onto the icy ground. "Bah, I'm no believing it."

Jamie crossed his chest with his arms, planted his feet apart in the traditional warlord stance. The lairds fell silent and Jamie's lethally soft voice carried on the chill wind. "Are you calling me a liar, MacPherson?"

Colin shifted on his feet and gave his whinnying horse a soothing pat on the flank. "I'm sure Duncan only means the report comes as a shock, James."

Jamie held MacPherson pinned with his gaze. Colin was trying to keep peace—to stop a bloody altercation, actually—but whether or not one occurred didn't depend on him. It depended on MacPherson's next words.

Kirkland strode a short path atop the dam. "Hell, James. Everyone knows a MacPherson would rather side with the devil than with a Cameron."

"Aye," Colin agreed. "Ever since the Forbes matter, MacPhersons have been best at holding a grudge."

Duncan's leathery-skinned face split in a grin. " 'Tis good of ye to notice."

Strutting fool, Jamie thought. Before the focus shifted from the issue, he intervened. "This isn't a question of the Forbes and Cameron feud with the MacPhersons. That happened over nine hundred years ago."

"Kin is kin, Cameron." MacPherson shrugged.

" 'Tis your kin, too, who'll be dying," Jamie reminded him. "Your land is southeast of Cameron, aye, but you too have kin residing in the village."

Colin stepped forward, his eyes mirroring his inner conflict—a deadly flaw in a laird.

"None of us want our people to die, James," Colin said.

"So you accept my test results."

The youngest laird raked a telling hand through his hair and let out a snort of pure frustration Jamie well appreciated. "I don't know whose tests to believe," Colin answered honestly. "They're all authentic."

"And the water itself?" Jamie lifted a questioning brow. "What authentic bits of business do your eyes tell you about the water itself, Colin?"

Already red from the cold, the laird's face turned redder. Kirkland moved to Colin's side. "Cameron always has opposed my dam, Ferguson. Even he canna deny that."

"I'm no denying it," Jamie assured him. "Truth is truth. Opposed I am, and always have been."

"You refuse to come out of the dark ages." Kirkland waved an impatient hand. "You still allow no electricity at Cameron. None of us are forgetting that."

"That's true," MacPherson interjected, nodding his affirmation at Colin.

"No MacPherson has stepped inside Cameron castle since the time of the first James Cameron," Jamie reminded MacPherson. "How might you be knowing what is or isn't there?"

"Your views are plain among the villagers."

"Ah, so the laird of Clan MacPherson relies on gossip for his information now, does he?"

MacPherson narrowed his eyes, and the dark circles beneath them flattened to thick black slashes. "Have a care yer dinna push me too far, Cameron."

"Evidently, I've no pushed you far enough. You're still burying your head in the sand and denying the truth right before your eyes. But I'd no bury my head in that water, if I were you. I doubt a MacPherson could survive the dunking."

"Well, Colin?" Kirkland shifted on his feet. "MacPherson has made his position clear, and so have I. Everyone in Scotland knows Cameron's opposed. What say you? Where stand Fergusons on this matter?"

"I dinna want anyone dead, but I'm no convinced which results to believe. My eyes tell me something is killing the fish and the birds. On the way here, I saw a dead puffin and an entire school of trout, belly-up, in the loch. Though the bird bore no mark, I canna dismiss that the water could have killed it. And something surely killed the fish." The young laird lifted his chin. "I see but one fair stand for the Fergusons. I'm reserving judgment 'til I have me own tests run."

Had their positions been reversed, Colin's would have been Jamie's precise reaction to the dilemma. Siding with Camerons, and against Kirklands, would net the Fergusons a formidable enemy. Siding with Kirklands and MacPhersons would have alienated Camerons. Requiring his own report, Colin had acted honorably and spared his clan everyone's wrath—for now.

"Fine." Kirkland walked back to the center of the dam, a satisfied gleam in his eye.

When Colin looked at Jamie, he nodded his agreement to another five or six days of frustration. Why did everyone trust a piece of paper more than their own eyes?

MacPherson grunted. "Fine. I'll be having me own tests done, too. We agree, then. Until the Ferguson gets his results and I get mine, there'll be naught mentioned on the matter in the village."

Jamie had expected that reaction, and he'd planned for it. "The villagers are already aware of my results."

The other three lairds gave him a simultaneous groan he well understood.

MacPherson added a glare holding nine hundred years of hatred. "Leave it to a Cameron to have my hall stuffed to the rafters with complaints."

Jamie slid Duncan a grim smile. "I've done nothing to you that I haven't done to myself. All of our halls will be full."

"That's true, Duncan," Colin interceded. "And James had

no choice but to spread word through the village. If we kept silent, our clans could suffer. Nay, James had no choice."

Jamie accepted Colin's support as his due. Though he appreciated it, he didn't thank Colin. To do so would have insulted the young laird's judgment, would have implied that Colin's decision had been based on friendship with Camerons and not on what was best for Fergusons.

The Kirkland wasn't so accommodating. His snarl could compete with Cricket's. "The clans are in no more danger today than they were yesterday," he said.

His annoyance rooted in lost dollars. Jamie knew that, and shifted the topic to more important matters. "I've heard," he interrupted the Kirkland mid-curse and glared at MacPherson, "someone's selling loch water in Edinburgh again. I'm sure the sales will stop until the safety of the water is determined."

"Cease your glares, Cameron." MacPherson narrowed his eyes. "I'm no selling any water. It once belonged to a Cameron, I would remind you. I know it's tainted, though I'm doubting it's with cyanide."

MacPherson hadn't flinched. But he had made a valid point. Still, if MacPherson could make money on something that could even be remotely considered Cameron property, he would. The man had more gall than sense if he thought Jamie believed him. MacPhersons clung to the old ways, and the old ways were feuding ones with the Camerons. Duncan would sell the water or anything else to gain even an indirect edge against the Camerons.

Kirkland had worked himself into a righteous lather. "You Camerons have been trying to get your hands back on Kirkland Loch since 1100. It was given willingly then and, by God, it'll remain in Kirkland hands forevermore—with its dam intact!"

Jamie deliberately softened his voice, but kept its chill. "How much is the electricity the dam generates worth to you Kirkland?"

"Ask the villagers what it's worth to them!" Robert Kirkland roared. "For heat? For cooking their food? Go on, ask them its value."

Jamie stepped forward. "Your water will soon be killing them, man. The dead don't answer questions."

"Bah!" MacPherson added a disgusted grunt, then gained his mount. "This isn't getting us anywhere."

Kirkland and Colin took to their horses as well. Jamie didn't move. "For God's sake, open your eyes. The fish are dying. The birds eating the tainted fish are dying. And if you don't breach that bloody dam so fresh water can filter through that stagnant pit, then the villagers—all of our people, yours and mine—will die, too. Is that what you're wanting?"

" 'Tis a loch, not a pit, James," Kirkland said, then muttered, "Damn Yank talk from a Highland laird. God spare us." He rode off without a backward glance.

Colin didn't. "I want to do the right thing, James."

"I know." And he did. Colin might be the youngest laird, but he weighed the elders' opinions valuable, and he was trying to be fair. Jamie couldn't fault the man for that.

"James, did you attack Kirkland?"

"Nay. Did you attack my ally?" Jamie whistled for Thunder.

"Your ally?" Surprise riddled Colin's voice. "I wasn't knowing you had a woman, much less an ally."

"She was also marked with the thistle in her chamber a few nights ago." Thunder neighed at his elbow, letting Jamie know he'd arrived.

"Good Lord." Colin's Adam's apple bobbed. "Did she see—"

"Nay," Jamie said. "She knows none of it. Letty removed it from Catie's pillow long before she awakened."

"I'll ask around and see what I can find out. Your men are on this, I'm sure."

"Aye." Jamie shared a look with Colin that the lairds both understood. Guarding the woman without her knowing she was being guarded made the duty difficult. Jamie claiming a Yank as his ally made the duty even more complicated.

Colin's horse snorted and tossed his head. His master gave his neck a calming pat. "I'll get back to you with the test results. And if I hear anything about your woman, I'll send word right away."

Jamie nodded.

When Colin had gone, Jamie again studied the loch. A heavy grey mist lay low over the water, but the blackness beneath it still mocked him. The icy wind carried a telltale crunch from the little wood on Cameron land. Jamie scanned the tall pines. Splinters of weak, winter sun penetrated the mist and flickered golden glimmers on the melting snow, giving it a mystical, magical look. He thought of Catie. His sweet Catie. And the need to talk to her, to share his frustration, hit him like a stallion's kick to the stomach.

He mounted Thunder, then rode home.

He's stopped drinking the milk.

MacDuff knows something is wrong, or he'd be dead. Instead, he's growing stronger, and his glances of late have been wary and unsure. Suspicious. Aye, he knows.

You both have me vexed, Cameron, failing to behave as you should—as you normally would. How did you manage to keep your unholy temper in check? You should have browbeaten Kirkland into breaching the dam. Why didn't you? And then to have you look right at me and not see me . . . Aye, it was a close brush with death. If the sun hadn't glared off that icy branch, you might have discovered me—and my secret with me. Imagine. Dying unavenged because of shifting numb feet. My, my, how tragic that would have been!

A bit more study on explosives and Catherine Morgan will be dead. That will cause you great suffering. Then soon thereafter things will be as they were meant to be.

Your neighbors, allies and enemies, disappointed you too,

eh, Cameron? Your tests proved your assertions, yet they fell on deaf ears. What you failed to understand is that the others ignored the truth because ignoring it is more comfortable. To acknowledge the truth brings with it a responsibility to act, to do something to change things, eh? Lairds do not embrace change. Not when it costs them their comfort.

I can't find too much fault there, as I enjoy comfort, too. Our means of gaining comfort are just . . . different. Mine will come in my revenge. The best part of it is that you will shoulder the blame for all my mischief. And only one person will believe you innocent, Cameron. The guilty one who will watch you beaten down until, alienated and alone, you die.

Me.

Nine

"Me?" Catherine clutched at her medallion.

"Aye, you." Letty lifted her chin. "I've seen you abed with my grandson, Catherine. Along with the laird's pleasures come his responsibilities." The little tyrant narrowed her eyes. "Or are you telling me your intentions toward my James aren't honorable?" Letty tut-tutted. "Oh, Annie won't like hearing about this."

Her intentions honorable? "What?" Catherine screeched, then lifted a hand to shush Letty. The hall was full of angry clansmen, and she'd rather Letty didn't repeat her remark. Honest to Pete, these Scots were strange. Wasn't it enough that the incident had embarrassed ten years off her life then? Did she have to pay again now? No way could she look at Letty. Or at Father MacDuff, who stood beside her.

He coughed behind his hand until his face turned purple.

Catie slid him a begging look, but the twinkle in his gaze told her there'd be no help from him, coming her way.

The men's shouts changed from angry to near-riot. Catie glanced back through the entry opening at them and saw a sea of Cameron colors and raised fists. Good God, how did Letty expect Catie to deal with them? She had her hands full with one raging Scotsman. She slid Letty her best forlorn look. "I'm American. They'll chew me up and spit me out."

"Bah!" Letty waved that notion off. "They're Scots Catherine, not cannibals."

"But Jamie might not want me inter—"

"If he returns and finds you've let his clan tear down his hall, James will be thinking you're a sorry shepherd."

Father MacDuff nodded his agreement. "Letty's right about that, lass. James is fiercely protective of his castle."

Catie gave them both a good frown. "You two are hanging me out to dry here."

"Nay." Father MacDuff gave her shoulder a fatherly pat. "We'll no be doing that."

"We'll be doing all we can to help you in your duties, Catherine," Letty assured her in her best haughty tone.

"My *duties?*"

"Aye." Letty thrust out her chin. "Until your Jamie can return to see to their needs himself, soothing his clan is your duty, dear."

Catie folded her arms over her chest. "I'm not his wife, Letty."

"Nay, you're far more important to him. You're to be his ally."

"An ally is more important than a wife?" Catie frowned her confusion.

"Catherine Morgan, are you saying you agreed to become James's ally without knowing what it means?"

"He didn't exactly ask me." Catie worried her lip. "He sort of just announced it."

Letty wrinkled her nose at MacDuff. "They're clearly still trudging up the rocky path, Gregor."

"Aye." He nodded. "Settling into the terms of an alliance often takes a wee bit of time."

They clearly didn't know Catie and Jamie were already allies. Why hadn't Jamie told them? And what should Catie make of the fact that he hadn't? She sure wasn't going to feel insecure about it, or waste a moment thinking he was ashamed for her. He probably just hadn't gotten around to it yet.

By God that's all it had better be. Well, hell. What if he

was ashamed of her? No, he wasn't. He just couldn't be. Could he?

"I'm thinking I should explain the way of it, Letty," Gregor said, looking down at the little tyrant over his glasses. "Maybe it'll help smooth the path."

Letty nodded her agreement.

"In the Highlands," Father MacDuff explained, "a laird must consider what is best for his clan in choosing his wife. But an ally is a freely chosen partner."

"Good God, are you saying he loves me?" Catie bellowed. Impossible. He declared their alliance before he'd even seen her.

Letty lifted a superior brow. "I'm saying, if you aren't knowing the answer to that, you've no business being abed with my grandson, is what I'm saying." She heaved a sigh. "Nay, Annie surely won't be pleased."

A loud crash came from the hall.

"Maybe later would be a better time to discuss this, hmm?" Father MacDuff's suggestion came with a series of little coughs and raised bushy brows.

Letty nodded hard enough to snap her neck. "Aye."

"Wait! I thought you were going to help me." Catherine let them see her panic.

"We are, lass," he assured her.

Catie slumped in relief. "Thank God."

"Precisely." Letty hooked the priest's arm, then turned toward the chapel. "We'll be praying for you, Catherine. You'd best get in there before they break anything else. James is a wee bit touchy about his possessions, too."

Celwyn rushed in from the hall, wringing her hands in her skirt. "Sweet heavens, Catie, what are ye going to do?"

The woman looked ready to faint. Catie felt like fainting herself, but there wasn't space enough on the floor to fall that was unoccupied by angry Camerons. She searched her mind and worried her lip. "Get them something to eat," she decided. "And coffee. Hot coffee, Celwyn."

Catie smoothed her taupe skirt and straightened her shoulders. "They're cold and angry. If we keep their mouths full and their hands busy, then maybe they won't yell so much or break anything else."

Celwyn nodded.

"And for God's sake, smile. That'll throw them for a loop." On seeing Celwyn's blank look, Catie translated. "It'll confuse them." She shrugged. "When your victim is smiling at you and stuffing you full of hot coffee and food, it's hard to commit murder."

The worry slipped from Celwyn's eyes. Her smile became genuine. "Ah."

"Good, ah." Catie pushed at Celwyn's shoulder, shoving her toward the kitchen. "Hurry now."

How did she get into this fix? Unsure, she pasted on a smile that she felt sure more closely resembled Cricket's snarl. Compared to the one she intended to lay on James Cameron—when he ever got home—this snarl would do as a smile just fine.

Spotting the cloak she'd worn riding, she yanked it from the stand. The barbarians likely would be slower to kill one of their own. Draping it over her shoulders, she walked into the hall, her back straight, her knees weaker than spit. One glance at their faces, and she whispered a silent prayer for the courage to die with dignity—at least, to not whimper when they killed her.

She fixed her gaze on Jamie's rocker near the fireplace, walked straight to it, and latched onto a spindle for support. Then she waited for them to quiet down. She wouldn't yell to gain their attention. No way. She was saving all her temper for James Cameron's head. How could he leave her in a fix like this?

She visually scanned the crowd. Thirty red-faced clansmen, all big as giants, glared down at her, their faces animated in angry shouts. Inside she cringed, but outwardly she did her damnedest to look serene. And she waited . . .

and waited. Didn't the uncivilized fools know they were sup-posed to shut up?

Minutes later, she accepted that they clearly didn't. And her calm was ineffective. With luck, her next attempt to re-store order would work better. If it didn't, she'd just faint, she decided. She was a Yank. They wouldn't be surprised by the weakness.

Condemning herself as a wimpy coward for even thinking of fainting, she squeezed her eyes shut. Lord, but she was shaking. Had she ever in her life been this nervous? She considered all the things she intended to shout at Jamie if—*please God!*—he ever got his buns back to this castle. Then she worked up a good bellow, swallowed it, opened her eyes and stared daggers at the older man standing front and cen-ter, shouting curses on Jamie's head.

That made her mad. She could curse Jamie; he was her ally. But for his own clansmen to curse him, well, blast and damn, how dare they? She pointed at the man. "Take off those Cameron colors."

"What?" the angry man roared.

"You're standing in your laird's hall, dishonoring him and his colors. I'll not have it. Now you take them off right now."

"I'm a Cameron down to me bones, lassie, and don't you be saying I ain't."

"You ain't." She held his glare, though every bone in her body warned her to run for her life. "No Cameron worth his salt would condemn his laird for warning his clan of danger. I'm saying, a true Cameron would have the sense to know his laird was only doing his duty, and he'd sure as spit not condemn his laird for that."

The man's look grew dark as pitch.

Bracing for the eruption, she crossed her chest with her arms and spread her feet, adopting Jamie's stubborn stance. It'd always made her want to find the nearest rock and dive under it.

"Thomas." A crusty old man beside the one she'd insulted snorted. "Are ye letting a wisp of a Yank challenge yer honor?"

Thomas didn't answer, just held her glare, his mouth set in a grim line nearly as fierce as Jamie's. She'd gotten his attention, all right. Now what exactly did she do with it?

The staring match continued until others began falling quiet. Soon, a dropped pin would have echoed. Catie broke out in a cold sweat. "Thomas," she said in a sweet, soft voice. "I would remind you that your laird doesn't use electricity from Kirkland's dam, or water from his loch." The men in back strutted toward the front. Moving in for the kill?

Don't think of it. Press on. "Your laird isn't acting on this issue for his own safety, he's protecting you. It's your laird's duty to protect you, isn't it? We both know it is, and yet here you stand—all of you—condemning him for doing his duty." She shook her head. "How can you condemn him for protecting you?"

A man with thick beefy fingers stepped forward. "What we're condemning, lassie, is having no heat. My kin is cold."

"If you use the water, laddie, you won't need any heat. You'll be dead." She let out an impatient sigh she meant for them all to see. "Cyanide doesn't discriminate. It kills everyone. Do you want your kin dead?"

That spurred a heated response.

Thomas lifted a hand, and restored quiet. "The lassie has a valid point."

Catie studied him. It might be her imagination, but he almost seemed pleasant now.

"I've a question," Thomas said. "Ye wear Cameron colors. Who are ye, lass?"

"She's a Cameron ally." Jamie's voice rumbled from the back entrance through the hall. The clansmen parted a path and he walked through, his expression jet black, his jaw clenched so hard that the muscles in his cheeks twitched.

Catie cringed. She was in for it now. With his expression, she had no doubt she'd been right. Her meddling in his affairs was not 'a pleasing thing' to the man. She'd tried to tell Letty, but would the little tyrant listen? *Noooo*.

"Whose ally, I'm asking?" This from beefy-fingers.

Jamie swept the room with his gaze, his expression not softening or warming a bit. "Mine."

That disclosure put a healthy buzz in the hall. Catie rolled her gaze heavenward and saw James Cameron's painting on the wall. *Ruthless. He'd had to be or his people never would have survived.* She looked back at Jamie. Is that what he was doing? Insuring her survival?

"What's her name, Laird? We canna go 'round calling her yer ally."

"Catie."

Catie was Jamie's special name for her, an endearment she liked hearing only from him. She started to correct him, to tell the men her name was Catherine, but Jamie didn't look like he'd appreciate it, so she kept quiet.

Celwyn came in and began serving sandwiches from a big tray. Catie walked over to the buttery and lifted the coffee tray, then followed in Celwyn's footsteps.

When she offered Thomas a cup, he looked at her strangely. "You're the laird's ally, yet you serve his men?"

Catie glanced Jamie's way, but he didn't say a word or offer any silent instructions. Typical. Hang her out to dry. "You're a Cameron," she told Thomas, hoping to hell she wasn't breaking some little odd Scottish tradition Jamie just happened to forget mentioning. "Jamie's your laird and he has specific duties to you. As his ally, so do I." At least, according to Letty, that's how things worked here. Hopefully, Catie hadn't made a major mistake. Letty had been in one of her more eccentric moods this morning.

Bronwyn entered the hall. Cricket cut a path between the men, stopped beside Catie, then promptly bared his teeth at

Thomas. The man backed up so fast he spilled hot coffee down his chest.

"Cricket," Catie admonished the dog and dabbed at the spill. "Look what you've done. Tell Thomas you're sorry."

Cricket stepped forward, his tail tucked between his legs.

"Keep that beastie away from me, lass. I heared what he done to Iain."

"Show your bravery, Scot," she whispered. "Cricket, come along and apologize."

The dog stopped at Thomas's feet and let out a single bark.

"Thank you very much," Catie said. "Now go to the fire."

When Cricket plopped down by the fireplace and Jamie dropped into his rocker, shaking his head and sighing like a man dying, she supposed he was mad at her again. He was. He was muttering. What the devil had she done wrong this time?

Someone grabbed her wrist.

Thomas let go of her arm and backed up. "Yer dabbing off me hide, lassie."

"I'm sorry, Thomas," she whispered. "Truth is, I'm worried. Jamie's angry with me."

"Nay, he's shocked." The old man ventured his opinion. "Cricket is feared throughout the village. James can pull off the beastie's ears, but it heeds no one else."

"Of course, he does."

"Never has."

Damn Scots. You have to prove everything to them. "Cricket honey, come."

The dog was at her side in a flash. She patted his ears, rubbed her face in his scruff. Cricket stood statue still. She gave first one ear a gentle tug, then the other. "See, he's no beast, he's an angel."

The wary men looked at Cricket, then at her.

"He's hexed," Jamie explained.

The dubious looks ceased. Hexed, it seemed, everyone accepted.

She wanted to set him straight, but he looked ready to spit nails. Maybe she'd better get away from him for a little while—just long enough for him to get over being miffed with her for interfering in his clan's business. It would be the considerate thing to do, and scratching an itchy temper was stupid in any country. Aye, she'd get away from him—as a kindness. He certainly wouldn't think her a coward. Not after she'd defended him before his clan. She'd hide out in her chamber until he calmed down, then she'd straighten him out. That's just what she'd do. She cast him a measuring look. Three or four days should do it. Five days, max.

She turned for the stairs. Before she cleared the bottom step, he grabbed her arm. Cricket growled low and deep from his throat. Catie shushed him with a warning finger pressed against her silent mouth. Thankfully, he listened. "Yes, Jamie." She smiled at him. "Did you want something, dear?"

"Aye." He hauled her to his side. "Where's Letty?"

"She's in the chapel praying right this very minute," Catie said, hoping that mentioning his Maker would prick Jamie's conscience.

It didn't. His grimace turned to a full-fledged frown. "Where are you going?"

"Up to the archives. I have work of my own to do too, you know." Maybe now the man would give her the gratitude she'd earned for keeping his home intact.

He didn't. "Why are you leaving my hall?"

She lowered her voice and bent close so only he could hear. "Your men are staring at me as if I'm a ghost, Jamie." Why hadn't he noticed that on his own, damn it?

"Aye. In a way, you are."

First a witch and now a ghost? Not a trace of teasing lit in his eyes. Actually, they seemed somber. "I'm not a ghost, Jamie."

"Nay, I didn't mean that."

"You're being about as clear as mud—again."

"After Bronwyn, I vowed I'd never marry."

"Yes?" That came as no surprise. Letty had warned Catie that since Bronwyn, no woman had gotten close to Jamie. Evidently, no woman ever would again. That insight carried a flood of disappointment. Catie squelched it. "And?" she prompted, urging him to continue explaining.

"I've told my clan you belong to me."

What did she make of that? Clearly they were having a translation problem. But later, when they were alone, would be soon enough to figure it out. "Oh."

"They're shocked." His expression softened. "You handled them well, lass."

Why did she feel like melting into a little puddle? "If you're pleased, then why don't you introduce me to your men? I'd like to know more than Thomas's name, Jamie."

"No."

"Why not?" She asked the question, but she already knew the answer. He was not pleased. Jamie was ashamed of her. That made *her* angry. And it hurt. "I defended you to them and you repay me like this?"

His eyes twinkled, the bewitching, green-eyed barbarian. Thank heaven he didn't realize the effect he had on her.

"Aye," he whispered, his burr taking on that husky tone that turned her woozy-headed.

She shook it to clear her thoughts. "I'm going to the archives, then." Damn if she'd stay where she wasn't wanted. So he really was ashamed of her. So what?

Well, hell. He wanted to sleep with her, but he didn't like her enough to introduce her to his clan, just enough to claim her like he would his dog, his horse, or his castle. Lousy laird. Blast and damn. Now her eyes were burning and she couldn't blink fast enough to keep a tear from falling. She coughed to cover a sob. Jamie let go of her arm and she started up the steps.

"Catie."

She turned around.

He crooked a finger at her.

She started to ignore him—the man deserved to be ignored for his lack of gratitude—but from the corner of her eye she saw Thomas watching them with avid interest. Jamie might well be ashamed of her, but she'd not shame him.

That decision made her feel better. The ditsy lout probably had changed his mind. She headed back down the stairs. Of course, he'd changed his mind. He'd thought about it and seen that he'd behaved shamefully.

They met at the bottom of the steps. The look in his eyes had her heartbeat tripping over itself. Warm.

"Are you going to the archives now, lass?"

She'd just told him she was. She added deaf as a stone to her growing list of his faults and considered giving his ears a good scorching. Maybe that'd improve his hearing. But then she remembered Jamie had an abundance of pride. He was Scots. He couldn't just say he was sorry. Still, in his way, he was apologizing. Feeling vindicated, she nodded.

He touched her cheek. "Remember your glasses, love."

Well, it wasn't much, but considering Jamie was Jamie, she ought to be happy for what she'd gotten. He swept her cheek with the pad of his thumb. He might be a lousy laird and an ungrateful lout, but he had wonderful hands. "Aye, Jamie."

She turned and started back up the steps, then what he'd done hit her. Her temper rose faster than her feet. She stopped and looked back down at him. He still stood there, the rustic giant with twinkling eyes, staring right up at her as if he were innocent.

Determined, she marched right back down to the bottom step and crooked her finger at him. "Jamie."

He stepped closer and lifted his brows. She curled her arms around his neck and whispered. "You're not getting away with it. I demand repayment. Now."

"Now?"

"Aye. And you can quit your glaring. I saved your hall. You owe me, and I mean to collect." In case he decided to argue, she added, "And that's that." Before he could object, she leaned forward and planted a Class-A kiss to his mouth. His lips were warm, but his nape was still cold from being outside. She began rubbing it and felt his arms circle her back.

The whoops and ribald laughter coming from the men penetrated her hazed mind. She thought she might just die on the spot from sheer embarrassment, and tried to pull back. Jamie wouldn't let her. No, the awful man would make her live. He lifted her in his arms and thrust his tongue deep into her mouth. Then, she couldn't think at all.

"I'm saying, love, *that*," he placed her back on the step, "is that."

She slumped against the banister and just looked at him. He was the one who was supposed to be learning a lesson here, aye, but the man was such a good kisser. She looked at the giant, head to heel, as he liked to say. He was handsome and big and hard . . . all over. And why hadn't she ever noticed that even if his hair was a shade too long, it suited him. Barbaric. A beautiful barbaric beast. . . .

Jamie smiled. "Aren't you on your way to the archives, love?"

"Mmm?"

"The archives," he repeated. "Aren't you on your way?"

She jerked upright. "Oh. Yes. Yes, that's exactly where I'm going." She fled up the steps, certain her face would at any second burst into flame.

His laughter followed her. "Remember your glasses."

She looked back at him. The look he gave her reminded her of what he'd said about her in glasses. More specifically, of what seeing her in glasses had done to him. Hard. Heat surged from her face down her middle to her thighs. She turned and walked slowly up the steps. When she rounded the corner, she slumped against the wall and smiled. To be ornery, she might just wear her glasses all the time.

Jamie left the chapel. In the hall, he saw Colin, standing in the entryway and talking with Celwyn. "Are you two off for a ride?"

"Nay," Colin said, tuning toward Jamie. "I came to see you."

The worry in Colin's eyes was clear. Celwyn was wringing her hands. She, too, had noticed. "The test results?" Jamie asked.

Colin nodded. A bead of sweat rolled down the side of his face. "I'm sorry to say it is, James. Both MacPherson's and mine. I wanted to tell you myself that they agree with the Kirkland's. The water is safe."

Jamie grimaced and stared at the young laird. "Colin, can you look at the loch and honestly say you feel it's safe?"

He shook his head. "I'm no sure what to think. My logic says one thing, but my heart another."

Colin looked up and Jamie saw the conflict in his eyes.

Bronwyn walked into the entry from the kitchen, brushed between Celwyn and Colin and linked her arm with his. "You know what they say about hearts, Colin?

He looked down at her. "What?"

She slid him a wicked smile, "To ignore the heart, lest you become its fool."

Jamie frowned. Celwyn turned and went into the hall. She looked . . . hurt. Now why would the lass be looking hurt?

"I'm going for a ride on the moor." Bronwyn fingered a button on Colin's shirtfront. "Would you like to join me?"

Jamie nearly groaned. Bronwyn didn't ride the moor. She rode to the little wood near the stream for her afternoon rendezvous.

"Aye, I would."

Without even saying good-bye, Colin turned and he and

Bronwyn walked out of the castle. She'd have him worn-out in less than a week, Jamie predicted. Ferguson was a good man, but unseasoned. And, Jamie figured, Colin would need more stamina and finesse than his years and temperament could provide to keep up with Bronwyn Forbes. Jamie smiled. If nothing else, the man was in for a learning experience he'd not soon forget.

Catie straightened up and looked around the candlelit archives. Finally all of the ledgers, diaries, and household account books had been separated into centuries and further into decades. So had the miscellaneous documents that no one thus far had deemed worthy of folders. And she had completed one card for each book on the shelves. Later, she'd make a subject file. Right now, she was eager to dig in and examine the documents.

The decision on where to start had been easy. Eleven hundred: the beginning of Cameron time.

She pulled the box marked 1100 over to the desk, then plopped down in her chair. Cricket squealed. Catie nearly fell on the floor. "Sorry, angel." She checked his tail then gave him a few pats. "You've been so quiet, I forgot you were here."

Cricket gave her hand a wet lick.

She yelled toward the door. "It's okay, Thomas. I just stepped on Cricket's tail."

He didn't answer. Must be engrossed in his reading. Knowing he was posted outside her door, just in case, made her forget her aversion to being guarded. Not that Jamie had given her any choice in the matter. He certainly was protective. She might just like that.

After adjusting her glasses on her nose, she took the first bound item from the box: a diary written by Catherine Forbes in 1100.

On reading the first sentence, Catie plunged into the past. . . .

> *God, help me die bravely.*
> *This is the worst night of my life.*
> *At the Festival of the Brides feast, King Edgar made James Cameron laird of the Forbes clan. The first thing the God-awful man did as laird was to rename the clan Cameron; the loch, Cameron Loch. My father was publicly humiliated, paraded before all the clans and exposed as a traitor. That woman, that awful woman they say came from the mist, named him. And then, God spare his soul, Father confessed.*
> *Because he had shamed the Cameron by making it appear as if he and not my father had betrayed Scotland and King Edgar, the King has given me to the new laird. I am "repayment for royal doubt of the Cameron's loyalty." He shall surely kill me dead."*
> *May God have mercy and let me die quickly.*

Cricket's low growl startled Catie. She snapped her gaze, and welcomed relief. "Jamie." Why did the man insist on sneaking up on her?

"If my own dog bites me, Catie Morgan, 'tis a black mood I'll be in, I'm thinking."

"He won't." She patted her chair arm. "Stop, Cricket honey."

Jamie gave her a thoroughly disgusted look. "Cricket *honey?*"

"What?" She leaned back and adjusted her glasses.

Jamie sat down on the corner of the desk. "You're corrupting my dog."

"I'm teaching him American ways, not corrupting him."

"I dinna like it. He's Scots."

"He's converting."

"The hell he is. I'll no be having any of that, Catie. I dinna care for it."

She shrugged not at all worried. "You don't like me either, so I don't suppose it much matters."

"Now why would you be thinking that, I'm asking?"

He sounded surprised, but he wasn't fooling her. Not for a second. "My first clue was when you refused to introduce me to your people. That really was rude of you, Jamie, and not at all diplomatic, especially considering I'd just defended you to them."

"Of course you did." He looked genuinely puzzled.

She narrowed her eyes. "Don't you even realize you've offended me?"

"I've not." He hotly denied it.

He scowled at her too, which didn't do much to calm her temper. "Aye, you have."

"I said, I've not, lass." He wagged a finger at her. "Now don't be disputing me on the matter of my own intentions or—"

She dropped Catherine Forbes's diary back into the box. "If you so much as whisper one word about repayment, I'll sock you in the nose, James Cameron."

"Dinna threaten a Scotsman, Catie."

She smiled and patted his beard as she had Cricket's scruff. "I'm not threatening, dear, I'm promising."

Jamie stood up. When she looked up at him, he forced his voice civil. "I've told my clan you're mine, woman. How, I'm asking, can even a Yank take that as an insult?"

"This Yank would remind you that she isn't your dog, your horse, or your rug. She isn't your property."

The lass was working herself up into a proper tantrum, pure and simple. But why? He frowned, then reasoned through the problem. "Ah, I know what you're about."

"You're acting ditsy, Jamie, and you don't know spit."

"You've been up here, pondering on Sir Andrew, haven't

you?" Jamie grunted. "Damn it, Catie, I thought we'd gotten past that sorry, inferior Englishman."

"What?" She shook her head. "How in blazes did Andrew get into this? It's you—"

"That's precisely what I'm wanting to know." Jamie leaned forward, across the desk. "Has he come into this?"

Not two inches from his face, she shouted, "No!"

A proper tantrum, all right. God, but he loved irritating her. She was so easy to annoy. A scant hundred-ten pounds of bossy, opinionated, stubborn, illogical woman. Perfect. And his. "If Sir Andrew isn't involved in this, then why are you forgetting what you are to me?"

That question earned him a glare he'd be feeling for a week. "I'm supposed to be your ally," she said, "but I know now I'm not."

"Aye, you damn sure are."

"No, if I were, you wouldn't be ashamed of me."

"Ashamed of you?" He couldn't help bellowing. She'd stunned him. Again.

"You wouldn't introduce me."

"I didn't want a brawl on my hands." He thought he'd done well. Very civil. She'd asked and he'd simply said no. He'd not raised so much as an eyebrow, much less his voice.

"Why on earth would you have a brawl on your hands?" she asked, looking skeptical and irked. "Are you teasing me again? Or are we having another translation problem?"

On hearing hope in her voice that they were victims of foul communication, he frowned. "I'm no teasing," he said. What was there to misunderstand?

She settled her hands on her hips. "Do you know the word *ashamed*, Jamie?"

"Aye."

"Well, explain yourself, damn it."

Her voice trembled. Her chin quivered, too. Aye, she was close to tears. But why? What had he done this time?

"You don't get it, do you?"

He gave her a negative nod, afraid he'd say the wrong thing and send her off on a long crying jog. He wasn't of a mind to be singing half the night again, soothing her.

"Why wouldn't you introduce me to your clansmen? I'm going to be here a long time, Jamie. I want to feel like I belong, not like an interloper."

Ah, peace was finally in sight. And if he had to embellish the truth a wee bit, well, her ego could use the shove. Nay, he wouldn't lie to her. He'd just take the truth back a couple of centuries. "Had you smiled at one man and not at all the rest, he would have challenged me for you, lass. Then I would have had to fight. I didn't think you'd care to have men brawling in the hall."

She stumbled backward. "What?"

He caught her arm and steadied her, wondering how in hell a woman could stumble while standing perfectly still on solid ground. An inferior sense of balance, he supposed. "It's true, lass." He nodded to let her know he meant it. "Men outnumber women here. You're forgetting that, I'm thinking."

"Bloodthirsty barbarians." She whacked the desk.

Cricket ran for cover. Jamie considered joining him, but the kneehole space under the desk was too damned small.

"You didn't even thank me for taking up for you."

"But you're my ally. When a man has to thank his ally for defending his honor, it's become a sorry day, I'm thinking."

"And you might have mentioned this quirky tradition of yours about smiling at people before now. Is it the same for looking at them? Is that why you told me not to look at Daniel that day at the dam?"

"Aye." The woman didn't understand spit. She thought he was ashamed of her. *Ashamed of her?* She'd defended Cameron, for Christ's sake. How could he not be proud?

Tugging at her arm, he hauled her down the stairs, then into the dark hall. Near the fireplace, he sat down in his rocker, then lifted her onto his lap. She settled with a thunk that had him grunting. For long minutes, he just held her, rocking slowly, gazing into the fire, and rubbing her back with long, sweeping strokes.

When she quit huffing, he decided she'd calmed down enough for him to explain the way of things. "Catie lass, I've not been fair to you, I'm thinking. You came to Cameron as my ally, but you've no idea what that means. When a man takes a woman as his ally, he trusts her to always be on his side. And he trusts her to know that he will always be on her side. Right or wrong. Skinned or on the hoof."

He paused, but she didn't say anything, so he supposed she had no questions thus far. "When a man and woman become allies, there's no need or reason for either of them to be thanking the other. When a man does something good, he knows his ally is pleased. And when a woman does something good, she knows she's pleased her ally."

"If he doesn't tell her and she doesn't tell him, then *how* do they know?"

The fire was gone from her voice. Jamie pressed his lips to the top of her head to let her know that pleased him.

Catie looked up at him. "Never mind. I think you just made your point. You're pleased I'm not angry anymore."

"Aye." Finally, peace at hand. "There's a bond between us, Catie. I feel it, and I know you do, too. That's how it is between allies."

"Aye, I feel it." She snuggled down and buried her face at his chest. "It's like a marriage, isn't it, Jamie?"

He didn't think so. A marriage could be bad or good between a man and woman, depending on the reasons they'd married. An alliance was stronger. Definitely better. But Catie sounded pleased and he didn't want her crying again, so he didn't dispute her. Besides, she was stroking his beard. And if it caused no injury he'd swear black was white to avoid giving her reason to stop that. "Of a fashion."

"I think I like being your ally."

Could a man die from the pleasure of a woman's hands touching his face? "Of course you do, darling."

She let out a delicate little snort. "Arrogant barbarian."

She wiggled her backside and settled in for a good, long rock, which suited him just fine. He could sit here forever, a happy man. His sweet Catie curled on his lap and rubbing his beard, him holding her in his arms, and them dreaming into the fire. Nay, a man could want little more on a cold Highland night.

"I love that painting of James," she said, sighing contentedly and caressing his chest. "It's powerful."

"Aye." His tone came out more brisk than he'd intended. He kissed the top of her head to soften it even though he felt jealous and a wee bit miffed. "Only a Yank could be more attracted to a man and a horse on a bit of canvas than to the man rocking her in his arms."

The trying woman smiled.

He slid his hand to her nape. The fire had warmed her back and stirred her sweet scent. He breathed in deeply and savored.

"I found out today that Clan Cameron used to be Clan Forbes."

"Aye, it was. Until King Edgar caught the Forbes betraying Scotland and the Crown." Jamie's sigh ruffled the tiny hairs on her nape. He soothed her skin there with a gentle rub. "One Forbes is much like another. Let's talk about something else, Catie. I'm weary—"

"What do you mean? About the Forbes?"

He knew from experience that the only way to stop her questions was to answer them. "Bronwyn the Terrible," he explained. Unable to resist the temptation, he kissed the soft flesh behind Catie's ear. That spot had been taunting him for a full five minutes. He'd done well in being so patient. Her little shudder rocked him to the core.

"Is Bronwyn a Forbes?"

"Aye." He growled from deep in his throat. "You smell good, Catie. Like heather and spring grass."

He felt her smile against his chest. The lass remembered his fondness for both. Aye, she was learning his ways.

"Then Celwyn is a Forbes, too."

"Aye, they're sisters, if you'll recall." Would the stubborn witch ever quit hexing him? She was too beautiful, his own golden angel. That was the problem.

"Well, Celwyn isn't a traitor."

He flicked at the shell of her ear with his tongue and sighed deeply. "Nay, neither is Father MacDuff. I take it back. Can we—"

"MacDuff?" Catie squirmed until she could see Jamie's face. "What's Father MacDuff got to do with this?"

"Would you please forget about Forbes just long enough to kiss me, Catie? I'm a starving man here."

"First, tell me about Father MacDuff."

"Witch."

"Your ally," she corrected him, a singsong lilt in her voice.

"Father MacDuff is Celwyn and Bronwyn's uncle." Jamie closed his eyes and waited. Surely now, she'd be satisfied and give him the kiss she'd promised.

"Why is his name MacDuff, then?"

Accepting that he'd never get himself kissed unless he answered *all* of her questions, Jamie opened his eyes and explained. "MacDuff was the first Cameron priest. Every priest since then has taken the name to honor him. MacDuff's real name—this MacDuff," he clarified before that raised yet another question in her busy mind, "was born Gregor Forbes." Jamie let out a telling sigh and his breath fanned her face. She gave him that slow blink he thought might just be the sexiest thing he'd ever seen.

"Oh." She tugged his beard. "Jamie?"

Her voice had grown husky, sweet and deep, and she licked her lips. He nearly groaned. "Aye, love?"

"Aren't you ever going to kiss me again?"

She sounded forlorn, and he started to remind her he'd been trying to do that very thing for what seemed forever, but the sweet longing in her eyes had him forgetting to be annoyed with her and wanting to make her smile. He liked Catie's smile. He hated that it made him soft in the head, but he did like her smile. It was . . . warming.

He claimed her soft lips, and captured her sweet sigh.

"Jamie," she murmured against his mouth. "The things you make me feel . . ."

Her sexy whimper reached out and grabbed hold of his heart. He couldn't answer. Something warm and good blocked his throat. So he told his sweet Catie that she made him feel too, the only way he could: with his kiss. Tender little kisses and longer, loving ones.

And then, to the soothing sounds of the fire, he rocked her long into the night.

Catie checked the shelf and the floor in front of it, and then behind it. The glaring gap between the book spines disturbed her, though she had no idea why, and again she cursed the archives' poor lighting. It was midday but, even with the candles lit, the blasted place was so shadowy she wouldn't see an elephant tromping around unless it wore a headlamp.

She checked the catalogue cards at her desk. An eerie feeling came over her, lifted the little hairs at her nape. She moved closer to the candle, then read the card. "Explosives?"

Cricket growled, low and throaty.

Half-expecting to see Jamie, Catie turned. "What's wrong, Cricket hon—"

Something slammed against the back of her skull.

Her head jerked. Her glasses flew to the floor. Blinding

pain knocked her to her knees, and she sprawled on the floor.

Cricket was going crazy; snarling, growling, and barking as if his mouth were full.

The attacker!

Catie couldn't move. Why couldn't she move? "Cricket! Guard!"

The dog brushed against her side and barked furiously. A little click sounded. The door? She strained but heard only Cricket's pants, her own heart jack-hammering, threatening to beat right out of her chest. The attacker had gone.

Catie couldn't focus. She blinked, then blinked again, but the hazy blur still didn't clear. Terrified, she wrapped her arms around Cricket's neck and buried her face in his scruff. "I can't see, Cricket. I can't see!"

The dog's wagging tail thumped against her side, and he licked at the tears on her cheeks she hadn't realized were falling.

The door opened.

Oh God, he's back! She pointed toward the noise. "Cricket, attack!"

"Nay!" Jamie yelled out.

Jamie. *Jamie!* Catie tried to make her voice work, but fear paralyzed her throat. She couldn't utter a sound.

Then Jamie was at her side, squatting down and sounding worried. "Why are you ordering Cricket to attack? Catie? Catie, darling, what's happened?"

"Someone hit me," she finally managed.

"In here?"

"Aye." She swallowed hard, trying not to panic. "Jamie, my head hurts and I—I can't see straight. Everything is fuzzy."

Jamie scooped her up in his arms. He too was shaking.

Within minutes, he had her tucked into her bed, and Dr. Patrick on his way. In his Grim-Reaper tone, he ordered her to stay put, then stepped into the hall with Iain. Why Jamie bothered to close the door between them was beyond her. Annie could surely hear his shouts in New Orleans.

"I'm wanting her guarded." Jamie dropped his voice. "And I'm wanting to know how the hell someone got past Thomas to her this time."

Catie felt sorry for poor Thomas. Jamie was likely to injure the man—if he wasn't injured already. Thomas had been right outside the door. How could the attacker get past the man without harming him? Fearing he couldn't had her worrying.

"Damn it," Jamie raged on. "That's twice she's nearly been killed in me own home."

Iain said something she couldn't make out, but Jamie's acid response sounded crystal clear. "I told her not to worry. She's my ally. She trusted me to protect her."

Catie did trust him, and she'd proven it. When she'd asked what he'd learned about the first attack, Jamie had told her he and his men had not yet found anything concrete. He'd asked her not to worry, to trust him. And she'd put the matter out of her mind. She'd even quit complaining about having Cricket or one of Jamie's men underfoot all of the time. She bit her lip. And now . . . this.

Dr. Patrick arrived, examined her eyes, removed the stitches from her arm, and then assured her that her vision would clear come morn. For now, she should just rest.

"I'm going to give you an injection, Catie," he said. "A sedative so you'll sleep well through the night."

"No."

"Ordinarily with a bump on the head, I wouldn't," the doctor said. "But you never lost consciousness, and there are other considerations to take into account. In my judgment, you need this."

"I don't want it."

"Catie," Jamie said. "Please, love. You need a good rest."

She didn't want to admit she was afraid to go to sleep, but she was. What if the attacker came back while she was doped to the gills? She could die in her sleep without even a chance to defend herself.

"I'll be with you, lass," Jamie whispered close to her ear. "So will Cricket."

He knew. God love his heart, he knew. She nodded. "Okay, Jamie."

"Okay." Jamie repeated her to Patrick as if only he had heard her.

Patrick filled a hypodermic. "Turn onto your side, Catie."

Her heart pounded hard. "There are men in the room."

"Be gone, Father," the doctor said. "You too, James."

"I'm no leaving."

There was no doubt in her mind Jamie would be staying. Comforted by that, Catie informed the doctor. "Jamie doesn't count. We're allies."

"Ah, I see."

Those famous Scots words: *I see.* Catie sighed.

Jamie held her hand, but spoke to Patrick. "She's meaning there's no need for me to leave because we're allies. I count most, of course."

"Of course." Patrick jabbed the needle into Catie's hip.

The sting seemed to last forever "That must be one healthy shot."

"Aye, it is. I intend for you to sleep tonight."

He pulled out the needle then gathered his things. At least, that's what it sounded like he was doing. She closed her eyes. Not being able to focus had made her stomach queasy.

She heard Patrick talking at the door. "She'll sleep tonight and probably most of tomorrow. I'll be back for a look-see tomorrow afternoon. Let your ally rest tonight."

The men's voices grew more distant, and Catie's cheeks burned hot.

Letty squeezed her hand. "James is worried, dear heart, not angry."

"I know."

"Has your vision cleared?"

"Not yet." She swallowed back the fear that it wouldn't clear.

"It will. You're not to worry."

"I know."

Letty pressed a warm cup of tea into Catie's hands. "Did you see anyone?"

"No." Catie sipped from the cup. "It was too dark. He hit me from behind."

Celwyn added another quilt to the bed, then tucked it up around Catie's middle. "I'm no understanding any of this. We've never had such goings-on at Cameron."

"I angered the men yesterday. They know I'm a Yank, Letty."

"What, I'm asking, has that to do with this?" Letty paced by the fireplace.

All Catie could make out was a blur of neon green, swishing back and forth. "Bronwyn took offense to me just hearing about clan matters. The men surely took offense to me questioning their loyalty. Don't forget, I ordered one to take off Jamie's colors."

"Jamie?" Celwyn asked, sounding baffled.

"James," Letty explained, clearly pleased.

"Ah, *Jamie*." Now Celwyn too seemed pleased.

Letty came closer to the bed. "When James arrived at the hall yesterday, what exactly did he say?"

"Thomas was asking who I was—because I had on Cameron colors." Feeling her face heat, Catie sipped at her tea. "Jamie only said I was a Cameron ally."

"What?" Celwyn gasped.

"What were his *exact* words?" Letty asked.

"Mmm." Catie thought back. "I'm not sure exactly. I think—yes. Jamie said, 'She's a Cameron ally.' Then one of the men asked whose ally, and Jamie said, 'Mine.' "

"Ah, I see." Letty patted Catie's hand. "Rest easy, then. No Cameron would harm a hair on your head, dear."

"Mine," Celwyn repeated breathlessly. "But that means—"

"Shh. Catie's eyelids are drooping. We've pestered her long enough. She should rest now."

"My thoughts exactly." Jamie's voice carried to them from the door.

"Come along, Celwyn." Letty's green blur blended with Celwyn's brown one and they moved toward the door. "Remember what the doctor said, James. Catie needs rest."

He didn't answer, but Catie would bet her medallion he was frowning. She heard Celwyn whisper, "He said she was his."

"Aye," Letty answered not bothering to lower her voice. "They're finally allies."

Jamie grunted, closed the door, then sat beside Catie on the bed. "Are you wanting some more tea?"

"No, but would you take this?" She passed the cup.

He put it down on the table beside the bed. "How are you feeling?"

"Foggy."

"Ah, the shot is working, then."

"You will be here." She hated the plea she heard in her voice.

"I've given you my word, lass. That is a trying habit you Yanks have, Catie, making a man promise everything twice." He smoothed her hair back from her face. "Are you hurting?"

Such a pitiful voice. She nearly smiled. "I'm fine."

"Have your eyes cleared?"

"Not yet."

"Then you're no fine, darling. I would have the truth."

"Okay, the truth. I'm scared," she confessed. His arm came around her shoulder, his weight against her side. "I've wanted to be in Scotland for as long as I can remember, and now that I'm here, some jerk wants me dead." She shuddered and he held her tighter. "You know, Jamie, when I get over being scared, I think I just might be mad."

His tone turned tender. "Are you wanting Sir Andrew, lass?"

"No, I'm—" She stopped herself. She'd been about to tell Jamie that what she was wanting was a good cuddling. But he'd taken off his boots, leaned back against the heavy headboard, and was now in the process of pulling her into his arms. Maybe she'd finally stop shaking. In Jamie's arms, she felt safe.

The medication was working its magic. Her eyelids felt heavy. "I'm cold, Jamie."

He pulled the quilt up over them then settled back on the pillows. She snuggled to his side, hooked a leg over his thighs, then pressed a grateful kiss to his shirt front. "Have you found Thomas yet?"

"Not yet, lass. The men are still searching."

She had to force herself to ask. "He's really missing?"

"Aye, I'm fearing he is."

"You should be with your men, looking for him."

"My place tonight is with you. It'd be the same for any Cameron." He pecked a kiss to her hair. "Go to sleep now, lass."

"I can't. Not until I know Thomas is all right." She rubbed at her nose. "Your shirt's scratchy."

He took the flannel off, and she slid back into his arms, her hand coming to rest on his bare chest. Could anything in the world feel better? "Jamie?"

"I'm no taking my pants off, darling, and that's that. I've got orders to let you be."

Catie smiled. "I wasn't going to ask you to take your pants off."

"Oh." He sounded disappointed.

That had her giving his chest another little peck. "Thomas is single, isn't he?"

"Aye." Jamie gave her a little squeeze, then returned to

rubbing her back. "Your voice is thick, love. I'm knowing you'll no sleep, but close your eyes just to rest them, mmm? And let me soothe you."

"If you do, I'll cry again. I'm really not a crier, Jamie. I want you to know that. Before I came here, I hadn't cried in years and years."

She'd cried her heart out on the phone to him the night Sir Andrew had broken their engagement. But of a mind to go along with her, Jamie didn't remind her of that truth. Instead, he kissed the top of her head. "I think a good cry might be just the thing—to clear your eyes." He pressed a light kiss to each eyelid. "A little sniffle might not hurt, either."

"You want me to cry?"

He didn't, which is exactly why he'd suggested she do it. The woman was contrary and, though she might be forgetting that fact, he wasn't. "I'm wanting you to release some stress, is what I'm wanting. Though truth is truth, and you don't much look stressed at the moment." Jamie brushed her hair back from her face. She looked like an angel and smelled as sweet as heather in spring. The muscles in his stomach clenched. "And I'm wanting for you to say you won't be leaving Cameron, Catie. That you won't be leaving me."

She gave him a sleepy smile, and slurred, "Compromise?"

"Terms?"

She looked at him, slumber-eyed. "Dance with me at the Christmas Eve party."

"Agreed." The woman was daft about him. Of course, she wasn't going to leave him. But he'd be lying if he didn't admit her reassuring him had settled the quiver in his stomach.

She pressed a fingertip to his lips. "Shh, I'm not finished."

He waited, stilling his hand on her back.

"Sing to me."

The tension ebbed from his body, and he kissed her fingertips. "Anything."

"When you sing to me, I know everything is going to be all right. I love you for that, Jamie."

His eyes grew moist. His sweet Catie hadn't led an enchanted highbrow life, after all. "I'll sing to you always then," he promised. "Whenever you're worried or afraid."

"Soothing." Smacking her lips, she burrowed against his side. "Whenever I'm needing soothing."

"Aye, darling. Whenever you need soothing."

She gave him *that* look.

"Oh God."

"What?"

"I'm thinking you've got that look."

"What look?"

"The one that says you're about to do something Yank."

"I am."

She slid up his side until she brushed his lips. "You're needing kissing."

"You're supposed to be sleeping now, Catie." He gave her lips a firm peck then pressed her head down against his chest. "Mind your wing. The stitches are out, but it's tender."

"It's my arm, dear. When it hurts, I'll know. Right now, you're the only thing hurting me."

He loosened his hold.

"Nay, love," she whispered. "Hold me tighter."

Love. His heart nearly stopped. She didn't realize she'd said it, of course. The woman was drugged to the rafters. But she had said it. To keep his emotions under control, he forced his voice brisk. "You're instructing me, darling."

"Aye, and getting damned impatient at your slow response, too."

Scots, through and through. He smiled. "You're delicate—petite, lass. You've been injured and shocked, if you'll recall. You need to sleep now."

"Thank you for reminding me and getting me worried again. Repay, Jamie." She puckered her lips.

"I'm not going to get you to sleep otherwise, am I?"

"Nay." She slid him a goofy grin.

"Well, when a man has no choice . . ."

She met him halfway, and kissed him lovingly, longingly, pressing her sweet body close to his, sweeping his calf with her toes. Before he totally forgot why he was in her bed, he pulled back and held her firmly against his chest. "There, are you satisfied?"

"No, actually, I'm not."

"Stop that and go to sleep, Catie Morgan." He jerked her hand away from his thigh, planted it firmly on his chest, and then held it there.

"More," she whispered against his mouth.

"Witch," he mumbled against her lips. The woman was bent on provoking him. He groaned, definitely liking being provoked by Catie, and kissed her until her lips went slack.

Ah, his angel sleeps. He rolled until Catie lay on her back. Her hair had fallen over her face. He smoothed it back, marveling at the way her lashes swept her cheeks. A flood of tenderness welled inside him from somewhere down deep. He loved her. The thought hit him like a sharp blow. God help him, he loved her with all his heart.

And someone wanted her dead.

He stared at the ceiling. That someone, he feared, had done serious injury to Thomas. The only Cameron who would break his laird's guard duty was a dead Cameron.

It wasn't a matter of *if*, but of *where* they'd find Thomas's body. The questions were, Who had killed him? And how in hell was Jamie going to convince Catie that Thomas's death wasn't her fault?

* * *

My my, how touching. Singing to her yet again, Cameron?

They say she can't see straight. That's as effective as blinding her, eh? I know exactly how you feel about her being attacked twice in your own castle, right under your mighty nose. As guilty as hell.

A pity she must die, really. She handled your men well, and women with grit are rare. But, of course, she must die. You've marked her.

Oh, it was wise of you to have Thomas and Cricket guard her, and I'm sure you're eager to search for Thomas yourself, but there's no need to rush. He'll wait. Cricket did surpise me, grabbing at my sleeve. Shocked me, really. My mistake. I let myself forget that he's your dog. And you do love your dogs, don't you, Cameron?

I'm saving them for last. For now, I'm concentrating on your ally. I've decided the exact moment she must die: After the Christmas Eve party, I'll be waiting. . . .

I'm going to make her confess she loves you on her knees, then punish for it. I would have her know you're the reason she's suffering. And, aye, it will take a lot of suffering to satisfy me now.

Then I must learn who attempted to usurp my right to kill her.

Aye, there are two of us. Another surprise, eh, Cameron? One for me, as well. But one that heated my blood. You see, I'd planned to return the explosives book and then to kidnap your Yank. I could kill her at my leisure. But when I arrived, someone else was already attempting her murder.

Isn't it exciting? I have a competitor!

Unfortunately, I don't know the identify of that person yet. And, for a change, that leaves us both wondering the same thing:

Who else could possibly want your sweet Catie dead?

Ten

"Ah." Celwyn smiled across the kitchen table at Catie. "You'll love the party."

Catie rolled out the flour dough with the pin, then paused to rub the tip of her nose. "The castle looks great, doesn't it? I love holly sprigs and seeing the tree lit up." A tender knot formed in her chest. "It's magnificent."

"My, my." Celwyn tilted her head. "I think you're a wee bit awed by it all."

"Christmas here is . . . different."

After moving the steaming teapot to the counter, Celwyn filled two cups. "Different?"

"Aye." Catie brushed the raw dough with a concoction of melted butter, cinnamon, and brown sugar. "For the past few years, I've spent Christmas with Annie and Andrew's family."

"What did you do?" Celwyn set a cup near Catie. "Sing carols and such?"

"No." Catie avoided Celwyn's eyes. "The parties were huge affairs with hundreds of people. Very stiff and very formal."

"You don't sound as if you enjoyed them very much."

"I didn't," Catie confessed. "I usually spent the entire time trying to keep Andrew and Annie from killing each other."

"Ah, your godmother didn't like Andrew overly."

"She didn't like him at all." Catie set the bowl and brush

aside, then dusted her hand against her thigh. Speckles flurried in the sunlight coming in through the window.

"That can keep a party lively." Celwyn placed the angel cookies on baking sheets, then pressed lines into their wings with the tines of a fork. "What about before then? With your own family?"

Catie shifted the raisin box, shook some out, then sprinkled them over the dough. "There were parties then, too."

"More enjoyable ones I hope."

" 'Fraid not," Catie said. "My father was as difficult to please as Andrew."

"Lud, Catie. Haven't you ever had a happy Christmas?"

"Well, sure," Catie lied, putting the box down on the counter. "Just not ones like I wanted." She wiped her hands on the dishtowel. "What would your perfect Christmas be like?"

"Oh, I don't know," Celwyn hedged.

"Yes, you do. Tell me."

At the table, Celwyn dropped down onto a chair, then propped her chin on her hand. "I'm thinking I'd be strolling through the hedge maze with Colin."

"The Ferguson?" Catie folded the dough into a roll. The strong scent of cinnamon tickled her nose.

"Aye." Celwyn's voice grew dreamy. She sighed, stood up, then put the cookie sheets into the oven.

Catie had serious doubts about that appliance. It looked like a torture chamber from hell. She was still a little miffed with Jamie for not telling her sooner about the generators, or about the gas stove. This morning, Letty had told her that sections of the castle even had central heating! She bit a smile from her lip. Yet, there was something to be said for Jamie's deceit. He had helped her dry her hair with the heat from a candle. Not very efficient, but darned sensual.

"Colin's a good laird." Celwyn checked the oven temperature, then adjusted the knob. "I know James is upset about the loch, but Colin's only trying to be fair and to do what's right."

"I'm sure he is. Celwyn, does Bronwyn know how you feel about Colin?"

"Aye, she does."

"Oh." Figured. Nothing was sacred to that woman.

"I know. You saw her go riding with him the other day."

"I could've been mistaken."

"Nay, it was him." Celwyn sighed. "Bronwyn will be through with him before long. She flits from man to man like a bee does to flowers."

"I see." Catie rolled her gaze heavenward. Now these Scots had her saying it.

"Colin is so handsome."

"Is he a good man inside?" Once Catie had thought Andrew gorgeous, but his heart was as cold as stone. To be truly happy, Celwyn needed a warm, mild-tempered man.

"Aye, he's wonderful." Her dreamy expression faded to one of hopeless misery.

"Well, what's wrong with him then?" Was the man dying from some dreaded disease?

Her chin quivering, Celwyn twisted the dishtowel. "I'm loving the man and he isn't even knowing I'm existing."

Cricket whined and slinked under the table. Typical male. A woman gets a little emotional and he hides. Catie spared him a frown, then looked back at Celwyn, glad this was a universal problem easily fixed. "What you've got to do then is to show the man you are existing."

"How?"

"You could start by asking him to dance at the party tomorrow night." Lifting a sharp knife, Catie began slicing the cinnamon log.

"I couldna do that!" Celwyn paled, looked ready to faint.

Catie stopped mid-slice to roll her gaze heavenward. "Are you sure you're Bronwyn's sister?"

"Don't be comparing us, Catie. I know I'm lacking."

"You are not. And don't be saying you are."

"You can afford to ignore the truth. You've got your man."

"What?"

"James is daft about you."

Was he? Or was he just plain daft, and she just happened to be the woman in his castle? "We're allies." All that Letty had told her about an ally being more important than a wife couldn't possibly be true. She'd just been in one of her more eccentric moods and, regardless of what he said, Jamie was just shoring up her ego because she'd told him Andrew considering her not stimulating had snipped her wings too close.

Celwyn pulled the oven door open to peek at her cookies. "Me getting Colin to be my ally, well, I just can't do it."

Having finished the last of the slicing, Catie put the knife down on the counter. "Celwyn Forbes, are you in love with the man, or not?"

"Aye, I'm loving him, Catie."

Boy, did Catie recognize that forlorn look. It too was universal, and she'd seen it in the mirror on her own face more than once when she and Andrew had been at odds.

"You're not understanding. Colin's a laird. He—"

"He hasn't realized how lucky he is . . . yet." Catie put the first of the cinnamon rolls into a pan then set them aside to rise. "Tomorrow night at the party, you just ask him to stroll through the hedge maze with you."

"Just ask him?" Celwyn gasped and wrung the front of her dress so hard she nearly choked herself to death. "But he's a laird, for God's sake. I canna just ask him, Catie. Oh, no. I canna be doing that."

Catie didn't know whether to hug Celwyn or to shake her until her teeth rattled. "Even a laird has feelings, Celwyn. He's still a man. Now you ask him and, when he agrees and you're out under the stars, you kiss him, too."

"He'll laugh in my face," Celwyn looked mortified.

Catie propped her hands on the table. "I'm saying he won't."

Celwyn gave her a doubtful look. "Then he'll swear I'm daft." She paced a short path between the table and the oven, her hands pressed against her stomach. "Oh, Lud, I'll faint."

"You won't faint. He'll kiss you back, and you'll both like it." She considered warning Celwyn she would get weak-kneed—if Jamie's kisses were any gauge—but she'd surely keel over and never risk kissing Colin, Catie decided against it. Instead, she shrugged. "What's the worst possible thing that could happen?"

"I have to think about that. He could get sick. Or tell me he hates me. Or—"

Before Celwyn could consider every God-awful scenario in the book, Catie set another filled pan aside, grabbed an empty third, and interrupted. "If you don't lay a kiss on the man that has him overcome with gratitude, you're no Scot, Celwyn Forbes."

"He'll be overcome, all right—with shock."

"Shocking a man on occasion is good." Catie wasn't sure about that with all men but, when she surprised Jamie, he seemed to like it. Andrew, on the other hand, hadn't. But then Andrew was English, and unless the happening was work-related and promised to be lucrative for the firm, he wasn't much interested in surprises . . . or in the expected.

That bit of clear thought had her frowning. Andrew wasn't a man who enjoyed much. Deciding that deserved some thought, she promised herself to consider it later.

"We've been friends for the longest time," Celwyn said. "Colin and I have always done things together—just not man and woman things. We've fished the loch and ridden the moors, but, nay, never any man and woman things." She filled the sink with hot soapy water and then tested it with her fingertips. "If I go kissing him, he'll think I've lost my mind."

"He'll be wondering how he could have been friends with such a special woman for so long and not realized she felt more."

"All right, stop your harping. I'll do it." Celwyn slung suds on the floor, wagging her finger. "But if he hauls me before my laird saying I've gone daft, it'll be on your head."

"I'll risk it." Catie repeated the words Jamie once had said about marrying her. A tiny corner of her heart wished he'd ask her again. Not that she would accept. She couldn't. She didn't really want to marry him, but she sure liked the idea of him wanting to marry her.

"What are you wanting for your perfect Christmas, Catie?"

She cocked her head and bit down on her lip. "I want to dance, to hear the bagpipes, and to feel Jamie holding me." She lifted a brow and slid Celwyn a knowing look. "Really holding me, and showing me he wants me."

"He does." Celwyn turned away from the sink and saw James standing at the kitchen door, his finger over his lips, shushing her.

Drying the rolling pin, Catie paused and looked out the window. "Oh, he wants my body—and that's nothing to sneeze at. I'll tell you, Celwyn, feeling as if you can't stimulate a man can sure do a number on a woman's ego." Would Catie ever forget Andrew's, *No, Catherine. I'm sorry to say it, but I don't find you particularly stimulating?* She swallowed against the hurt the memory brought with it, then recalled Jamie soothing her, and felt better. "But that's not all I'm meaning about Jamie."

"What are you meaning, then?"

Catie stared out the window at the rose bushes, and let herself dream. "I'm meaning I could die happy, if just once Jamie would hold my face in those big hands of his," she paused and cupped her hands, "give me that you're-lovely-darling look of his, and say, 'Catie, I'm of a mind to love you, lass. Before, during, and after . . .'"

She turned away from the window and toward Celwyn. "That's all. Then I'd have a perfect Christmas."

Celwyn hiked a shoulder, dripping water and suds onto the floor. "Before, during, and after, what?"

Catie gave her a wistful smile. "He'd know."

When Celwyn looked back toward the door, James Cameron was gone.

From across the hall, Jamie watched Catie talking with Bronwyn the Terrible. His ally looked bewitching, more like a temptress than an angel in her black gown, with its low-cut back, and her high heels. But, from her expression, thinking the woman wasn't pleased would be akin to thinking Attila the Hun had a wee bit of a temper. What had Bronwyn said to rile Catie now? If she ruined his ally's perfect Christmas, he'd forget sparing MacDuff's feelings and ban the woman, and that was that.

Skin to bone, the two women were as different as night and day, and he couldn't help wondering how he'd ever found Bronwyn attractive. She was a beautiful woman, aye, but hard. And though most, he supposed, would consider her body perfect, it offered none of Catie's sweet softness.

His ally visually scanned the hall and, when she saw him, she smiled. His heart lurched, and he promised himself she'd smile later, too. This would be her first of many perfect Christmases with him.

Her medallion caught the light and glinted. Jamie stiffened. She'd damn well take Andrew's medallion off first, though. Jamie wasn't of a mind to be loving his ally while she was wearing another man's jewelry. Aye, the more he weighed the matter, the more certain he was she shouldn't be wearing that medallion at all.

He strode across the hall, excused them from Bronwyn, and then guided Catie through the maze of people toward the fireplace, where they'd cleared the floor for dancing. The trying woman complained the whole way, and he let her. But on taking her into his arms, he gave her fair warning.

"If you're of a mind to foul my mood by bending my ear, Catie lass, don't. Be contrary later, after tonight."

"I know I've been fussy and I'll hush, since it's Christmas Eve, but I'll say this first." She paused to be heard over a woman's laughter. "You're not cooperating very well with my diplomacy lessons. I was in the middle of a conversation with Bronwyn about the first Cameron laird. She seems very knowledgeable about him. You didn't even let me—"

Jamie kissed her quiet. Catching the beat of the music, he pulled her close, snuggled her to him, promising himself that if she kept her complaining about him interrupting when he raised his head, so help him, he'd kiss her until her lips gave out. When she forgot her surprise and settled into the kiss, he parted their mouths, then whispered close to her ear. "I'm sorry, darling. But it is your own fault."

"My fault?" She gave him a little look denying responsibility.

"Aye. You decorated my hall, and this is the only place in it you saw fit to put mistletoe." He tilted her chin up so she could see the little bunch tied with a red satin ribbon. "I was of a mind to hold you, love."

She drew in a sharp breath that had her breasts brushing against his chest, then expelled it slowly. "Oh."

His angel looked bemused, and a wee bit dazed. Lesson learned. To get Catie Morgan out of a complaining mood, kiss her 'til she's starry-eyed. Though he was a man fond of a good impassioned argument, he liked kissing her better. "Oh?"

"Just oh," she said, giving him a docile look and a half-smile that set his heart to banging against his ribs.

"You're looking bonny tonight, Catie."

"I'm glad you're hexed," she murmured against his chest.

He smiled above her head, his cheek against her crown. "Aye, I am that."

"Jamie, did you mean it?"

"What, lass?"

"About wanting to hold and kiss me?"

His love needed reassuring from the toenails up. And tonight he'd be giving her all she needed. "Aye, darling. Both are pleasing things." He rubbed their noses, then teased her, putting that deep growl in his voice that gave her those wee shivers. "It's your dress, I'm thinking. It's sexy, Catie."

"Really?"

"Aye, love. Seeing your back bare puts a man in the frame of mind for touching and holding, and more."

That earned him a dazed little smile. "So are you—looking sexy, I mean." She let her hand drift down his side to his hip. "There's nothing quite like the sight of a strong man in a . . . kilt."

He caught that mischievous glint in her eye and issued a second warning. "Don't be calling my kilt a woman's skirt. I'm saying I'll suffer none of your neutering this night."

Swaying to the music, she laughed throatily and rubbed her fingertips down the front of his jacket. "I wasn't thinking that."

"Oh."

"Well, aren't you wondering what I was thinking?"

"I fear, I'm knowing." He grunted at her soft laugh. "But, aye, I'm wondering." The woman had the most intriguing mind. Warped logic, to be sure, but damned intriguing.

She tugged at her lower lip with her teeth. "I was thinking that knowing what's under your kilt is . . . warming."

He groaned. He knew she'd baited him, and had asked anyway. "Don't start, love." Some warning. He sounded as weak as a beggar.

The Yank witch clearly wasn't worried; she laughed in his face. He would have been miffed, but the laugh had come straight from her heart. And that warmed him right out of his snit. It warmed far more than his body, too. It sweetened his soul.

"Do so many people always come to your castle on Christmas Eve, Jamie?"

We have 4 FREE BOOKS for you
as your introduction to
KENSINGTON CHOICE!
To get your FREE BOOKS, worth
up to $23.96, mail the card below.

FREE BOOK CERTIFICATE

Yes! Please send me 4 Kensington Choice (the best of Zebra and Pinnacle Books) Historical Romances without cost or obligation (worth up to $23.96). As a Kensington Choice subscriber, I will then receive 4 brand-new romances to preview each month for 10 days FREE. I can return any books I decide not to keep and owe nothing. The publisher's prices for Kensington Choice romances range from $4.99-$5.99, but as a preferred subscriber I will get these books for only $4.20 per book or $16.80 for all four titles. There is no minimum number of books to buy and I may cancel my subscription at any time, plus there is no additional charge for postage and handling. No matter what I decide to do, my first 4 books are mine to keep, absolutely FREE!

Name _____

Address _____ Apt. _____

City _____ State _____ Zip _____

Telephone ( ) _____

Signature _____
(If under 18, parent or guardian must sign)

Subscription subject to acceptance. Terms and prices subject to change.   KF0897

KENSINGTON CHOICE
Zebra Home Subscription Service, Inc.
120 Brighton Road
P.O. Box 5214
Clifton, NJ 07015-5214

His hall was crowded to overflowing with laughing, dancing people. "Aye, but there's even more at the Festival of the Brides." Seeing a raised elbow encroaching, Jamie pulled Catie closer and then turned to take the jab in his shoulder. When his hand settled low on her back and touched bare skin, he shuddered.

"It's a lovely party, isn't it?"

"Aye," he whispered. "The hall looks—" He started to say cluttered, but considering the amount of work Catie had invested in decorating this past week, he thought better of it. He was of a mind to romance his woman, not to suffer a fit of her temper.

"Festive?" she suggested.

"Aye, festive," he quickly agreed.

Appeased, she nestled against his shoulder. "I like this song. Do you?"

He listened. A soft and mellow ballad, perfect for making love. He liked it a lot.

"Will you sing it for me sometime?"

He looked down at her upturned face. Love. Trust. Both were there in her eyes. Was the lass recognizing either? He gave her a sweet kiss, just a gentle brushing of lips to tell her she aroused his passion, aye, but also a need to be tender in his heart.

Lairds were supposed to feel ruthless, not tender. Tradition forced them to lie. But to his way of thinking, since lairds were mere mortal men, they had a God-given right and obligation to feel both, and they should be honest with themselves about their emotions. And with their allies, for no woman on Earth touched a laird's tender side more. "I'll sing for you later," he promised, his voice gruff. "When we're alone."

A tap on his shoulder claimed his attention. Iain. Jamie ignored him, hoping his second would go away, but the irritating man persisted, tapping again. Jamie frowned at him. "What?"

Iain smiled back. "I would ask to dance with your ally, Laird. 'Tis the season for sharing and goodwill."

"Thank you for that reminder," Jamie said, giving the man a scowl that warned a dance best be all he shared, then looked to his lady, resisting a grimace. "Catie?"

Not of a mind to exercise restraint, Catie gave Iain a fair grimace of her own. "If I dance with you, will you challenge Jamie for me?"

Iain's eyes stretched wide. He looked stunned, and Jamie well imagined his second was stunned, since, except for during the festival, that particular custom had ceased to be tradition somewhere around the twelfth century. Not that Jamie felt the least bit guilty for his small deception. Catie's ego had needed the shove, so he had given it to her. Now he could only hope his second didn't get him tossed on his foolish elbow for his trouble.

"A challenge, eh?" Understanding winked in Iain's eyes, and he answered cryptically. "Well, I'm thinking that depends."

"On what?" Catie asked, looking far from pleased.

"Would ye be planning on stomping me toes?"

"If you're planning on challenging Jamie, I might."

Iain rubbed at his neck and pretended due consideration of the matter. Jamie nearly laughed. The man had started feuds with less thought.

"Aye, you're surely worth stomped toes, lass," Iain said. "But I'm thinking that to spare me aching feet, nay, I'll no challenge the laird for ye. 'Twill be a simple dance, no less, and no more."

Catie dazzled him with her smile. "In that case, I'd be delighted."

Jamie watched them, not much caring for the way Iain was looking at Catie, but before he could make a fool of himself by hauling the woman off the dance floor and back into his arms where she belonged, he reminded himself it was a simple dance, no less and not a damn bit more, then forced himself to look away. Several other Camerons had Iain's same hexed look, and they too were looking at Catie. A sorry streak of jealousy knotted Jamie's stomach muscles, but he refused to move. Truth was truth, and looking at her still dazzled him. He'd give them time to get used to her hexing. Aye, he'd be patient, too. He'd give them another five minutes. Then he'd start knocking heads together.

Colin Ferguson stepped to Jamie's side. "Your historian is very graceful."

Jamie nodded.

"I've heard she held her own with your clan."

"Of course." Jamie had to bite the pride from his voice. To express pride to another laird would prove he had expected less from her: a grave insult to Catie.

"I'm no meaning to interfere in Cameron affairs, especially in those of its laird, but gossip is spreading through the village and the clans, James. I thought you should be knowing."

Jamie folded his arms akimbo, then raised a questioning brow. He'd listen, but he damn well wouldn't tolerate any unkind tongue-wagging about Catie.

"They're saying she's a Yank."

Jamie resisted an urge to roll his gaze to the rafters. "You heard her talk, Colin. You know she's American."

The younger laird smiled. "Aye, I was jesting. Though she has confused some."

"Oh?"

Colin nodded. "I'm told she mimics you well."

Jamie caught the admiration in Colin's tone and allowed his pride to swell his chest. Iain spun Catie on the dance floor, and her laughter carried on the air to Jamie. Inwardly, he smiled. She was happy here. With him, and with his people. "She's loyal to me, aye, Colin, and to America. But Catie is her own woman."

Clearly pleased by that disclosure, the young laird cleared

his throat. "Then you'll no mind me inviting her to join me—"

Jamie shot the man a blistering glare. "You'd be inviting my ally, Ferguson."

Colin backed up a step, as shocked by Jamie taking an ally as his own clan had been. "I see."

For all the gossip the man had heard, that clearly had escaped his ears. "Aye, I think you're beginning to."

Celwyn joined them, and Jamie again recalled the kitchen conversation he'd overheard between her and Catie. Tonight, he wanted everyone happy. "Your pink gown suits," he said, then nudged Colin to notice with an elbow to his ribs.

The man let out a telling grunt. "Aye." He rubbed at his side. "You look lovely, lass."

Celwyn gazed up at Colin in adoration. "Thank you."

Jamie waited a full ten seconds for Colin to be seeing what was in front of his eyes, but the dull-wit just stared at Celwyn as if she'd sprouted a spare head. He gave the man's ribs another jab to get his fill attention.

"What?" The young laird shot Jamie a fierce frown.

The dance had ended, and Iain and Catie were returning. If Jamie didn't interfere, she would. Wanting to please her, he gave Colin a knowing look. "The hedge maze is looking particularly festive, Ferguson. Catie and Celwyn have strung it with twinkling lights."

Jamie thought it a foolish waste of generated electricity. From his expression, so did Colin. But Catie had asked so sweetly, so Jamie had agreed, not that he intended to make a habit of letting her hex him right out of his opinions. The woman had a stubborn streak as wide as his, a fine Scots trait in a woman, but she'd never in her life had a happy Christmas. He'd bet his tassels on that. And since he meant to be giving her a perfect Christmas, the first of many perfect Christmases for them, he'd let her get riled so he could soothe her and then, in the end, he'd gone along with her. Pleasant, that soothing. He gave Colin a nod, and swore to himself if the dimwit didn't get his meaning this time, he'd quit being subtle and just pound it into his thick skull.

Finally, light dawned in the man's eyes. "Um, I've a fondness for twinkling lights. Would you like to show me the maze, Lady Forbes?"

Lady Forbes? Colin hadn't called Celwyn *Lady Forbes* once in his life. No one had, for that matter. It wasn't a proper title. But, Jamie swallowed a chuckle, Colin likely never had seen Celwyn as a woman before now, and the dawning had him a wee bit rattled.

Her eyes lit up from the bottom, fairly twinkling. "I'd like that very much, Laird Ferguson." She circled his arm, and then they walked toward the hall entry.

Jamie nearly snorted. At least they were both acting dippy. Or was it dopey? He'd have to ask Catie.

Colin asked Celwyn, "When did you become a woman on me, lass?"

"I've been a woman for years, Colin Ferguson. You never noticed I was a girl."

Jamie chuckled, thinking Colin would be shaking his head over that a lot in the future.

"Where are they going?" Catie asked. Her cheeks flushed and her eyes sparkling, she looped her arm with his.

"To see the hedge maze." Jamie pretended that statement held no significance. He didn't dare to look at Catie for fear she'd realize he'd overheard them talking in the kitchen. He didn't want to ruin his surprise. And he wondered for the thousandth time that day if she'd come to him at the fire. And for the thousandth time, he assured himself that she would. The question was whether she'd come willingly, or be dragged.

"The hedge maze?" She gave him a suspicious look.

"Aye," Jamie said. "Colin's had a fondness for twinkling lights for years."

Catie let out a little squeal of delight and hugged him. Jamie hugged her back and laughed.

"I'm thinking you—" she began.

He pressed a finger to her lips. "If you go kissing me now, lass, I'll be hauling you up the stairs to your chamber, and that's a promise."

"Ah, your weakened condition." She rubbed their noses, not looking at all upset but damned pleased with herself. "And what would we do once we were up there?"

The hope that he'd cure her flaw was clear in her voice. Warming, and it had him growling from deep in his throat. "Everything I've wanted to do since I first heard your sexy voice on the phone."

"God, Jamie, whisper." She clamped a hand over his mouth. "Someone will hear."

He nipped at her palm. When she jerked her hand back, he laughed in her face. "I've told you before, lass. I'll no have you embarrassed about loving me."

"It's not that." She blushed to the roots of her hair. "It's private."

Ridiculous. Nothing to do with a laird's love life remained private. "Are you thinking anyone in my hall isn't already knowing, lass?"

That question earned him an outraged frown he'd not soon forget. "Knowing and *knowing* are two different things, you barbaric beast."

"Nay, not yet. It's still my timid self you're seeing." He gave her a wicked grin and a devilish promise. "But soon, love."

Letty waved a cherry red scarf at him. "James!"

When he glanced her way, she pointed to her watch. He nodded acknowledgment, then told Catie, "It's time."

"Time for what?"

Jamie tweaked her nose. "Wait for me here, darling."

He wasn't going to answer her. Again. Catie crossed her arms and then drummed her fingers against her forearm. Only God knew what the man was up to now. She liked that, and blamed her idiocy on the thin Highland air.

He walked toward the entry. Was he forgetting her, then? Nay, the hall tree. He snagged the cloak she'd worn riding, then returned to her with it. When he draped it over her shoulders, she swore she caught a whiff of spring grass along with Jamie's heated cedar scent.

He adjusted the hood, tied its dainty ribbons with his big fingers, then touched their lips together for the merest twinkling. Catie nearly purred. There was something intimate and potent in Jamie clothing her in his colors. She gave him a soft smile.

"Don't be hexing me now, love. They'll be waiting for me," he said, wrapping a possessive arm around her shoulder.

They joined the group emptying out of the hall, then walked down the landing steps to the upper bailey. The air was cold and clear and the torch-lit path to the hedge maze looked beautiful with flames dancing in the wind.

"Stay here with Father MacDuff and Letty." Jamie brushed her cheek with a kiss, then whispered, "And don't be watching any one man overly long, Catie. I'm wanting to stay timid tonight."

The man didn't have a timid bone in his body. But he thought he did. Darling, that. He walked away, toward a huge heap of wood limbs and brush. Near the path to the hedge maze, he pulled up a torch staked in the ground, then lit the fire. Soon the bonfire blazed, warming her cheeks even from this distance. Then everyone fell silent, and the faint strains of bagpipes grew louder and louder.

In an enchanting display of Scottish tradition and virility, seven formidable giants, including Jamie, formed a precise row before the fire. Iain stood to Jamie's left, a distinct gap stretching between the two of them—a missing man formation? Thomas?

The fire glowing at their backs, the men were all dressed in their kilts, their shoes freshly shined and glossy, their jackets' silver buttons twinkling in the firelight. The men playing the bagpipes stopped on the torch-lit path and the sweet strains from their instruments filled the crisp, night air.

The music tugged at some forgotten cord in her, lulling, arousing, then reached in, squeezing a tender hold on her heart. She looked at Jamie. Firelight danced on his hair, on his beard, in his eyes, and he began to dance with the others, his steps controlled and measured and in perfect unison, but physical, abandoned, and extremely impassioned. The ripple of his muscles, the raw energy he poured into his dramatic movements, the intense emotions that flickered over his face, mesmerized her. Her heart began pounding a slow, hard beat, and she suffered a powerful, primitive urge to touch him. To just . . . touch him.

" 'Tis a wondrous sight, eh, lass?"

She heard Father MacDuff, felt him touching her elbow, but she couldn't make herself glance away from Jamie. His lure was too potent, his gaze too compelling. She finally managed a nod, and was grateful for it.

"Aye, I see her, Gregor," Letty said. "Why are you surprised? I told you they're allies. . . ."

Allies. Freely chosen. Beloved. Catie blinked, then blinked again, surprised to find it true. Jamie indeed had somehow captured her heart. Every nook and cranny of it. He was watching her too, and even the blazing fire couldn't compete with the heat in his eyes. Her blood thickened in her veins, a slow burning started somewhere deep inside her, and the urge to just touch him strengthened to a blinding need to hold him.

The music stopped. Catie barely noticed. The other dancers rejoined their parties and accepted their profuse praise. People all around her were laughing, chatting, and milling away.

Father MacDuff bade her good night.

Letty wished her a happy Christmas.

Catie mumbled something unintelligible about it being early yet, and stared at Jamie, awed and humbled and oddly pleased that looking at a man had never before affected her this way. He just stood there, watching her, as if he were waiting. . . .

Waiting, aye. For her.

She forced her feet to move, to take her closer to the fire. Forced herself to walk the walk to James Cameron that she sensed would forever link their lives. Why crossing that short, ten feet between them bore such significance, she didn't know. But it did. She felt it just as surely as she felt the fire's heat growing hotter with her every step.

A foot in front of him, she stopped. He looked magnificent. His chest still heaved from his dancing and sweat sheened his skin. He didn't smile; in no way welcomed or shunned her. This decision was hers alone to make. Holding his somber gaze, she said the only thought that took hold in her mind: "I came, Jamie."

"Aye." So serious, so worried, he lifted his hands to cup her face. His fingertips trembled against her skin. "I've a need to say this, sweet Catie. I'm knowing you believe you're loving Sir Andrew, but—"

"I'm not." She covered Jamie's hands with hers. She tried to nod to add weight to her words, but his fingers had tightened on her face and she couldn't move, so she let him see the truth in her eyes. "I thought I was, but I'm . . . not."

Jamie swallowed and rubbed a tiny circle on her chin. "Are ye sure?"

Her darling Scot, so intense, so emotional. "Aye, Jamie."

He kissed her then, achingly sweet and tender and, when he had, he again looked into her eyes. "I've a story to tell ye, lass. About a laird who was feeling empty and alone." His thumb strayed, brushed over her lips, then he circled her shoulder with his arm and began walking between the burning torches to the hedge maze.

"Which laird? You?"

"Nay, no me, darling," Jamie said, not surprised at all that she'd taken him for the empty and alone man. Until she'd come to Cameron, he had been. He led her into the maze, down its winding path. The twinkling lights reminded him of stars. Pleasant, that. A reasonable use of generated electricity, after all. " 'Tis James."

"Ah, James." She curled her arm around Jamie's waist and snuggled close.

Their sides brushed with each of their steps. When they rounded a corner, Jamie stopped and pulled Catie into the shadows. "James was a very lonely laird."

"If he was as ruthless as you say, that's probably why he was lonely, Jamie."

He frowned at her, hoping she could see it in the dim light. "I'm wanting to get on with my story, lass."

She laughed at his reprimand.

The woman had no respect. "Catie."

"Sorry."

She didn't sound at all sorry; traces of laughter lingered in her voice. "The laird was ruthless—he had to be—but he was hurting, too, darling. And that can be making a man seem heartless when he truly isn't. But James changed, Catie."

"He didn't."

Clear as his stream, she wasn't believing him. "I'm saying he did. Now, hush and listen."

"You're getting testy, Jamie," she warned. "James Cameron was ruthless and heartless. The man didn't change."

Jamie wasn't getting testy, he *was* testy. If the witch would stop hexing him and act like a proper ally should, he could be getting done with this romancing business and on with the loving. "By damn, James changed, and don't you be disputing me further on the matter."

"Charming."

"Catie, yer pricking my good nature."

"Sorry, go on."

He tamped his temper and continued the tale. "On the

night of the feast at the Festival of the Brides, King Edgar made James a laird, and Forbes's clan became Clan Cameron."

"Edgar gave James a woman, too." Catie looked up at Jamie and explained. "It's in one of the old diaries."

"Is it now?" Well, she was ruining his romancing strategy good and proper, wasn't she? "Then I suppose you've read about James's angel."

"His angel?" Catie looked puzzled. "No, I haven't heard about any angel."

"Ah," Jamie said, feeling a twinge of excitement. All hadn't been lost. That was the best part of the story—for a time like this. "An angel came from the mist."

"Oh, her. She wasn't an angel, Jamie, she was a woman. And she named Forbes as a traitor to Edgar."

"An angelic woman she was, Catherine Morgan." Jamie let her see his impatience, then softened his tone to instruct the trying woman. "You're making me telling you a romantic tale damned difficult, lass."

"Romantic?" Her tone went husky and she smiled, looking more than a wee bit angelic herself. "Oh." She flattened her palms against his chest and looked up at him. "Tell me more."

Aye, this was more like it. He eased his hands beneath her cloak and clasped the curve of her sides at her waist. "She was the most beautiful woman James ever had seen. She came to him by the fire, and she kissed him as he'd never before been kissed. James felt her passion and her desire, aye, but even more he felt her love for him. It seeped into his every pore and spread like honey down to the very marrow of his bones, and it changed him forever."

"Oh, my," Catie whispered, bemused and sagging in the most warming way against Jamie's chest. "I expect he did change, then."

"Aye, he did." Jamie squeezed her sides, then let his

hands wind around to her back to hold her up, and a wee bit closer. "He was challenged for her."

"No! Someone challenged him for her after seeing how much she loved him?"

Outraged. Pure and simple. Darling, that. "Aye, two men."

"Damn barbarians."

"The battles were fierce."

"I knew there'd be blood in this story." Catie frowned and heaved a sigh that had her breasts flattening against his chest. "I just knew it."

Jamie smiled at her disgust. "James won."

That had Catie smiling again and giving him an adorable off-handed shrug. "Of course. He was a Cameron, if you'll recall."

Jamie laughed out loud. "Aye, he was that." The woman became more Scots with each passing day, and even more a Cameron.

"Jamie," she said, sounding troubled. "Did he kill the men, or just wound them?"

He considered telling her the truth, but she looked as worried as she sounded, and knowing she took exception to James's letting blood, and that blood and romance wasn't an appealing mix for softening his woman, he compromised with a half-truth. "Nay, just wee injuries."

"Good." Her relief was immediate. "I'd hate to think your ancestor killed for his angel."

Jamie frowned at that comment but held his tongue, more or less. "You do make it difficult for a man to hold on to diplomacy, love. Here I am, trying to soften you up, and you're bent on talking about killing."

"Why?"

How should he know why she was talking about killing? He lifted his brows. Sometimes the woman's thoughts scattered like leaves tossed by the wind. "I canna be knowing, since—"

"Why are you trying to soften me up?"

"For . . . later." He let her see his intentions in his eyes, hoping he could get her to call him her love again without her being drugged to the rafters.

"Oh." A mere whisper, that.

Now exactly what was she about? "Oh?"

"Finish your story, Jamie."

He didn't bother to complain about her insulting him. Sure as she drew breath, the woman would be insulting and bossing him 'til his clan planted him on the ridge near Harry. Still, her eyes enchanted him, and Jamie prided himself for being so patient with this romancing business. He was hard and hot and eager to be loving his woman. "James married his angel, and that's that."

Catie snuggled closer still and rested her head against his chest. "It's a very romantic story, Jamie."

"Aye, I was hoping you'd think so."

After a long moment, she backed away, and they walked on in silence through the shadows and flickers of the twinkling lights.

When they neared the center of the maze, Catie stopped on the path. The wind tugged at her cloak. "Jamie?"

Hearing something bothersome in her tone, he stopped at her side. "Aye, darling?"

She gave him her witch's smile. "I'm soft."

He laughed, a wee bit surprised by her blunt admission. "Come on then, Catie." He grabbed her hand, then took the path at a good clip. "Now's no time to be dragging your feet, I'm thinking."

"For crying out loud, my feet are barely touching the ground. Some of us don't have tree trunks for legs, you know."

He scooped her up and growled into her neck. "Aye, some of us are delicate—I'm meaning petite." Recalling the woman's opposition to feeling fragile or delicate, he rushed down the path.

"What in God's name is the hurry?" She thunked against his chest with each of his jarring steps. "Is the devil after us?"

"Nay, lass." At a break in the hedge, he opened a creaky old door, then grabbed a torch from the walkway.

"Where are you taking me?" She sounded worried.

"Does it matter?"

Did it? Catie paused. Once, he'd stated his objection to her always asking him where and why. He'd taken those innocuous questions as a lack of trust, not curiosity. But she did trust Jamie with all her heart, and it was past time to let him know it. "No, it doesn't matter at all."

He rewarded her with a kiss that made her glad she wasn't trying to walk. Soft and weak, she'd have fallen flat on her face.

The tunnel walls were damp and brown, and the air smelled musty from disuse. Though still curious about their destination, she refrained from asking. She was alone with Jamie, and as he was fond of saying, that was that. For her, it was more than enough.

When he passed the first door and took the second, she realized they'd gone down, through the winding tunnel, and then up again. Thanking God she wasn't in the dark hole alone, and that the torch hadn't gone out, she tightened the circle of her arms at his neck and snuggled to him even tighter.

Soon they emerged in a huge fire-lit chamber that smelled of cedar. He put her down on the stone floor, then lit candles on the fireplace's mantel and on the chests beside a massive oak bed that dominated the room, as well as her thoughts. He was finally—thank God, finally—going to cure her flaw.

Jamie extinguished the torch. As moisture came seeping from the logs, the fire in the hearth sizzled and hissed. The flames teased the screen, leaping streams of blue and gold that played on the floor and the high ceiling, and had the room toasty warm and smelling like Jamie. She liked it.

He turned from the fireplace, his expression as masked and as hard as it had been on the moor when she'd stepped out of the helicopter and onto Cameron land for the first time. She could almost be frightened of him, so solemn, so stern, but on the moor back then he'd held heather, and another memory of something he'd once told her crossed her mind. *I've never had an ally before, nor a woman in my chamber, for that matter.*

The light at his back made shadows of his eyes, and his voice turned serious, gruff. "This is my chamber, Catie."

The brazen, arrogant, and experienced man literally had run to bring her here, yet he now seemed uncertain and nervous. How very darling. "I thought it was."

He stiffened as if he expected she would bolt and he'd have to catch her. "I'm wanting you in it."

She stepped closer to him, her heart nearly beating right out of her chest. "I thought you did."

Jamie didn't touch her. "You came to me at the fire. Be ye knowing what that means, lass?"

So much emotion on his face! Her throat went thick. "When James's angel went to him and kissed him, he knew then that he loved her."

"Aye" Jamie tensed even more, and creases of worry lined his face. "But he knew more, too, Catie. He knew she accepted him. Him, and his heart."

Jamie's meaning wasn't lost on her. She'd kissed him at the fire unknowing. But if she kissed him again now, she'd be accepting him and his heart. Forever. A thousand tiny sparks of conflicting emotions ignited inside her, yet one emotion grew stronger until it smothered the others: He was her ally, and she wanted him.

Closing the space between them, she stretched on tiptoes to touch his beard, and whispered against his lips. "I came, Jamie."

He swallowed hard, drew in a sharp breath against her lips, and she kissed her rustic giant, sharing with him all she was feeling, her certainties and her fears. Their lips melded, their tongues thrust deep, and Catie felt the same magic James had shared with his angel, for her Jamie's love seeped into her pores and spread down to the very marrow of her bones.

On parting their lips, he stepped back and lowered the cape's hood from her hair, then untied its ribbon at her neck with gentle hands that were far from steady. The cloak slid down her body to the floor.

"I'm wanting you to take off Andrew's jewelry, lass." Jamie's whisper rasped thick with emotion.

Andrew. Not Sir Andrew. Aye, her giant was intensely emotional, and the quiet pleading in his eyes touched her so deeply she was afraid she might weep. He was jealous, and his ally wearing another man's jewelry beat at his pride. How hard it must have been for him to bring her here, not knowing if she'd agree or refuse him, not knowing if she'd willingly remove the medallion he believed had been given to her by another man. Not knowing if she'd kiss him again by his chamber fire, or walk away from him. She rubbed the disc between her forefinger and thumb. "My father gave it to me, Jamie."

He drew his brows together in a frown that crinkled his tender skin.

"As a child. For my birthday. I always wear it." She smoothed away his frown with a fingertip, wanting to reassure him about Andrew without mentioning the man's name. He had no place here, and she didn't want him intruding. "Jamie—"

"Shh. . . ." Jamie's expression softened, then softened some more. "I'm needing to tell you what's in my heart." He again cupped her face in his hands, his thumbs gentle. "Catie, I'm of a mind to love you, lass," he whispered, his burr growing thicker with every word. "Before, during, and after."

She drew in a sharp breath and paled as white as winter clover. "Oh God, you heard!" Darting him an accusing glance, she pulled away. "I could die. I could just die."

"Aye, I heard, Catie." He drew her back into his arms. "But it's the truth, I'm saying." He lifted her chin and waited until she looked up into his eyes. "I *am* of a mind to love you, lass. Before, during, and after." He sighed, resigned. "Simply put, I'm not just needing you until after the festival. I'm needing you all my days. Forever. Darling, you're in my heart."

She stared at him a long moment, too emotional to speak, then a tear slid down to her cheek and Catie touched his face, his wonderful beard, and whispered past the lump in her throat. "I need you too, Jamie."

"Only me?"

Andrew. Why couldn't the man forget— That day astride Thunder, he'd found it degrading. He needed to know it was not just any man's loving, but his loving, she needed. "Only you," she promised.

Jamie groaned his relief, tightened the circle of his arms, and kissed her as he'd never before kissed her, wet and hot and filled with longing. Reeling from the intensity of their emotions, knowing he was recanting his vow and opening his heart to her, exposing his hopes and dreams and fears and innermost secrets, she met his needs joyously. Their tongues danced, as Jamie had before the fire, passionately swirling and seeking, stirring sensations that burned deeper and hotter and seared more quickly than any blaze could hope to burn.

In a fumble of arms and fingers and unsteady hands, he slid down the zipper of her dress and bunched the fabric in his big hand, smiling at her rushing with the buttons of his jacket that seemed to have grown too large for the button-holes, yet too small for her eager fingers. He stilled suddenly. Had he changed his mind then? She frowned up at him. "James Cameron, don't you even think about stopping. You're going to cure my flaw right now, and that's that."

"Aye, darling, I am. Just as soon as you get my sleeve out of this damn zipper." He shook his arm, nearly pulling her off her feet. "I'm thinking an inferior Englishman de-

signed the damn thing. A Scot would have the good sense
to stay with buttons, I'm thinking."

"Just leave it, until after," she said, hoping he wasn't going to get sidetracked and start on one of his international
tangents with Scots ranking superior. She tried wiggling out
of the dress, but it just wouldn't slip past the flare of her
hips. Jamie, too, tried, and they twisted and bumped, begged
and cursed, but her zipper and his sleeve proved more stubborn and failed to cooperate.

Jamie let out a bellow that had her ears ringing and, with
a mighty tug, tore the sleeve from his jacket and shirt, the
dress from her back.

Stunned, Catie went stiff as a board, but he let loose a
victory whoop that had her laughing again. Her man was
stimulated and that, too, was that.

"I'll buy you another," he promised, tossing the items
onto the floor, then glanced at her. He stilled long enough
to give her a frown. "Well, hell. Now you're tight-jawed,
aren't you?"

"You scared the bejesus out of me." She might just keep
that torn dress as a souvenir forever. "Truth is truth, Jamie,
and I've never before had a man rip off my clothes."

"I'm wanting to love you, woman. And don't you be lying
to me. You're more Scots than Yank now, and you've never
feared me. Nay, not even when you were inferior."

She'd been plenty terrified of him, and more than once.
But it wouldn't do to let him know it. He'd lord his Scots
superiority over her for the rest of her life. "Nay, I never
have feared you," she lied, wrapping her arms around him
and tugging down on the wool at his hips. "Now, lose this
kilt or—"

"I'm saying, darling, you're not much acting like a timid
virgin."

Was that good or bad? She looked into his eyes, saw the
beat in them, and decided it was a pleasing thing to the man.
"When you touch me I don't feel shy or timid. I feel starved,
Jamie."

With a wonderful impatient grunt, he smothered her lips with a filling kiss. Feeling fabric grate against her hands on his hips, she started to pull back to finish her threat, but suddenly her thighs were pressing not against scratchy wool but against warm, bare skin, and, liking the feeling very much, instead of complaining, she nestled closer.

"You're a trying woman," he said, nipping at her neck. "Always bossing."

She nibbled at the underside of his chin until he begged her to stop, then nibbled some more, down his neck to the soft hollow of his throat, and added wicked flicks of her tongue to the torture.

The awful man laughed. When she opened her mouth to complain about that rudeness, he thrust his tongue into her mouth and pulled her into an emotional spiral that seemed to whirl on forever. Oh, but he could say anything he wanted, do anything he wanted, if only he'd keep on kissing her.

He let his hand skim down the length of her leg, awakening nerve-endings, tantalizing skin and, before she could react, she stood barefoot and her dainty heels hit the floor with healthy thunks. Her Jamie wasn't just an impatient man, he was eager. She loved him for that. In his arms, she couldn't feel more stimulating, or more wanted and needed.

When they were naked, he lifted her to him, and they hugged, skin to skin, breasts to chest, heart to heart. Jamie let out a sigh that ruffled the hair at her temple and arrowed straight to her soul, so full of contentment she felt sure she would faint or cry. Had she ever before felt so poignant? So alive? So beloved?

She couldn't resist touching him, letting her fingertips drift over his shoulders, blade to clavicle, sweep down his biceps and across his hair-roughened chest. When her palm grazed his male nipple, he shuddered and she gasped, amazed that such a simple touch from her could arouse such a potent response in him. A surge of feminine prowess rippled through her, and flooded her with joy as pure as sunshine, as tender as a lover's smile. "You like me touching you."

"Aye." He breathed at her neck, lifting her higher, pulling her flush against his length. "I like it, lass."

She more than liked it. She loved the feel of his warm body pressing against her warm body, the feel of his big hands, so tender and gentle, caressing her, the feel of the hard and rigid part of him pressing deep into her belly, telling her more clearly than any words could of the pleasure he found in holding her. She loved the sweet murmurs he breathed against her skin on shallow rasps of breath, the telltale quiver of his muscles responding to her touch that had her aching for all of him, the burning sensations that flowed through her like hot honey and pooled deep in her thighs. She loved the cedar and salt smell of his skin, the sounds he made, the tender look in his eyes that made her feel beautiful and beloved.

They fell together onto the bed, her on her back, Jamie hovering over her. He studied her inch by inch and she stilled, not embarrassed or uncomfortable, but wanting desperately to touch him: a desire burning so strong she had to bunch the twisted sheets in her hands to survive the wait. She would let him look his fill, explore as he desired, even if it killed her, for her heart knew that she and Jamie had come together in love and, because they had, there was no room between them for discomfort, or shame, or anything that didn't honor and celebrate the treasures true love brings to those lucky enough to find it.

"You're beautiful, lass," he said, then kissed her lovingly, longingly, achingly sweet and hauntingly beautiful, warming her body as he'd warmed her heart.

She rolled onto her side, let her hands drift down him, rib to hip, stomach to thigh. "You're beautiful, too, Jamie," she whispered against his mouth, rubbing their noses. "Are there Scottish traditions about making love?"

"A few," he hedged. "What are ye wanting to know, lass?"

"Can I kiss you whenever I want?"

"Aye, whenever you want." He nibbled at the soft fleshy part of her earlobe.

This prospect, too, he found pleasing. She gave his sides a little squeeze to thank him, then crawled on top of him, and stretched out, full-length.

Jamie let out a swoosh of breath. "Mind your knee, love," he said, then cupped her buttocks in his hands and cradled their hips. He had all the experience but his ally had needs of her own and no hesitation at seeing them filled.

"Jamie?"

"Aye, darling?"

"I'm of a mind to love you." Her eyelids dropped to half-mast, and her love for him shone in their brilliant depths. "Before, during, and after."

Jamie's heart nearly burst in his chest. She loved him, aye, and in her own way, she'd admitted it. Knowing she'd been hurt and yet had risked her heart again had him awed by her spirit. And to be hearing and believing true what he feared never hearing nor believing again. . . . He choked on the flood of feelings hammering at his heart, inflamed him, and his need crept into his voice. "Say it, lass. I would have the words."

She took his lips instead. Her hands taunting, squeezing, caressing. His body rocking from the sweet torture, he pulled her hard against his thrusting hips. She let out a sexy whimper, and he rolled her onto her back then hovered over her, kissing the soft skin at her eyes, the hollow of her cheek, the shadowy lobe and shell of her ear, and the bonny little dip in her stubborn chin. She arched her neck, her hips, and he whispered the loving words his sweet Catie needed to hear, the loving words he needed to say.

Ablaze and kissing her tempting skin wherever his lips happened to touch, he finally reached her breast and lingered, flicking at its peaked center, suckling lavishly, cupping his hand and warming its mate, paying homage. Her hands in his hair, fingertips pressing against his scalp, he kneaded, drawing on her nipple, stretching and elongating it until, sweet and responsive, she arched up off the bed to meet him. He could easily spend a lifetime adoring Catie, of that he felt sure as certain.

She let out a little whimper and again arched from the bed. "Too tender!"

He released her breast and adored her ribs, one by one, then moved down her body. Before she left his bed, she would feel his touch head to heel: the traditional sealing of an alliance, signifying the giving and acceptance of the vow that from this moment on they belonged to each other and were bound forever by heart, soul, body, and spirit.

"Jamie," she whispered at his shoulder, sounding uncertain and a wee bit frightened. "I hurt."

"Aye, you're supposed to ache for me, lass," he reassured her, hurting plenty himself. But tonight he would have just this once to love her. His darling ally would be too tender for more, and his need to give her reason not to mind the soreness to come was great. He'd no have his sweet Catie recalling the pain of losing her virginity more than the pleasure of him loving her. "Just a little longer, love," he rasped against her soft stomach.

Sliding down on the bed, she reached between them and stroked his belly. He jerked, then shuddered, and she curled her fingers around him. Nearly coming undone, he fused their mouths in a furied mating of lips and tongues. Nothing in his life had prepared him for loving his ally. No sexual encounter ever had touched him, not all of him, not like this.

Protection. Good God, he'd almost forgotten. He pulled back, smiling at Catie's grumbled protest, reached to the chest beside the bed for a condom, then quickly fitted himself. "I'm no stopping, love. I promise."

"Then hurry, Jamie." She growled that instruction. "I'm suffering here, if you aren't knowing."

Even now, the woman gave him hell. "I'm knowing," he assured her. How could he not be knowing? Did she think he was made of steel? His heart thrumming in the wild rhythm of a primitive ritual, Jamie settled himself between her thighs, and asked for the reassurance his soul still desperately needed. "Who's loving you, woman?"

"Only you." Damp tendrils of hair framed her face. She wrapped his hips with her thighs and held him to her. "Don't leave me, Jamie."

"I'm no leaving you, love." He slid forward, flexing his elbows, rounding his spine, and brushed their chests. "I'm coming deep inside you now. It'll hurt a wee bit at first, darling. I'm wishing it wouldn't, but—"

"I'm hurting now," she interrupted, groaning her protest. "Hurry, Jamie."

He thought he might have smiled. Truth is truth, and he wanted to be inside her so badly he couldn't really recall if he did or not. "Kiss me, Catie. Kiss me with all you feel for me."

She met his open mouth eagerly, fanning her fingers flat on his shoulders, and arching her sweet hips. And deeply moved by her trust, he arched his body, letting the last of his resolve to never again be vulnerable to a woman fall, then drove forward with a powerful thrust, burying himself inside his sweet ally.

The pain hit her hard. He stilled, worked diligently to soothe her and, when she lifted her hips, unable not to move her sweet body for wanting him, he began the melding of body and spirit that would merge their flesh for a time, their hearts and souls forever.

Catie unleashed her passion, gave as much as she took, and he lost himself in her yearning, tumbling deeper and deeper into love's bliss. Soon, she whispered against his shoulder, "Jamie, what's happening to me?"

He heard her fear, her near panic, and soothed her with gentling words. "I'm taking you to heaven, Catie. My heaven," he ground out, feeling her muscles clench, her body stiffen. Her expression shifted, enraptured, and, there at the edge, she dangled for the longest time. He gave a final thrust that drove her up on the bed, and she shook with warming spasms that carried him with her.

When the explosion inside him eased to slow pulses, then finally to satisfying tremors, he collapsed and rolled to his side, bringing her with him. Sweat-slick, chests heaving and breathing hard, they lay cooling, calming, but not yet ready to part. And she began that sexy rubbing with her toes against his calf. Smiling, he opened his eyes and cupped her face in his hands.

"And after, Jamie?" she asked, her eyes wide and seeking.

"And after, love," he promised, then claimed her sweet mouth to seal his vow.

Good God, Cameron, I'm going to explode!

There's only one thing that arouses me more than hearing you and the Yank having sex. The sounds of death.

When I saw you by the fire, I knew tonight would be the night. Getting Thomas's body out of the tunnel in time was a challenge, but I did it. Now it's back in the secret passage, though I doubt it'll remain there long. The stench of rotting flesh isn't conducive to keeping secrets.

And then I listened to you make love. Ah, the mighty Cameron laird caught in the throes of passion, as weak and as vulnerable as any other man. You cried out her name when you came. I felt the force of it. Rapture. Sheer . . . rapture.

Aye, I was wise to wait to kill her. Your regret will be much greater now, your guilt much deeper. And both will be with you soon, for when she returns to her chamber tonight, I will be waiting.

I've watched you for the longest time, and you always dismiss your women soon after sex. Satiated, you've no further need of them. Knowing that, has the swirling in my loins growing stronger by the minute. She'll come to me still bearing your scent. Suffer me punishing her with your seed still inside her body.

I'm going to touch her while she dies.

Eleven

Catie stood at the window, looking out into the night.

Jamie had awakened the instant she had left his bed. But her clothes were strewn with his near the fireplace and she hadn't gathered them, so she wasn't of a mind to be leaving. He held his silence, content to watch her, knowing giving herself to him had touched her deeply, likely confused her a wee bit too, and she needed to give all her new feelings time to settle.

The moonlight silhouetted her slender body, nude and perfect to him. Looking at her, remembering, he warmed. Making love with her had been the most awesome experience of his life. His sweet Catie loved with her body, aye, but her loving came straight from her heart.

He'd meant to teach her the art of physical love. Instead, she'd taught him that physical love is but a wee part of a much deeper spiritual love. He'd told her he was taking her to his heaven. Arrogant and shortsighted, that. His sweet Catie had knocked him on his foolish elbow and then had taken him beyond heaven. She'd taken him to a new realm where all is acknowledged, accepted, and made pure. The revered realm rarely glimpsed by man but, traversed, is recognized immediately: personified love.

The fire crackled in the grate. He heard her breathing. A sniffle? Was she crying? He listened closer and this time her sniffle was distinct. Tossing back the quilt, he went to her, the stones cold against his feet. Standing at her back, he put his hands on her shoulders. "Catie?"

She stiffened and whispered in a shaky voice. "I should go back to my room now."

Her tone bothered him. She sounded uncertain; as if she didn't know what she should be doing, and was worrying about it. "Why, love?" Didn't she want to be with him now? Nay, nay, it couldn't be that. She'd told him, *and after*.

Holding her gaze on the bailey beyond the window, she shrugged. "Isn't that what you do after making love with someone you aren't married to? You don't cling, you get up and go home."

Ah, now he knew what she was about. The woman was unsure of her place. Jamie turned her to face him with pressure to her shoulder. The moonlight set the tears on her cheeks to glistening. He pretended not to notice them to spare her pride. "You are home, lass."

She dropped her gaze to his chest. "I should go."

"Nay, Catie." He waited until she looked up at him. "At the fire, you came. Your place is with me now."

"Is this one of those Scottish lovemaking traditions you mentioned?"

It wasn't, of course, but she was upset and he didn't want her upset. He wanted her happy. "Aye."

Clearly seeing through his deceit, she frowned up at him. "It's after, Jamie. Are you still loving me?"

Yet another insult. He'd told her once already, but she seemed so rattled he couldn't not reassure her again. He brushed her wet cheek with his lips. "You're my ally, I would remind you. I'll always be loving you, lass."

She gripped his bare sides, her fingers cold, her grip firm. "You told me once you'd been in love with Bronwyn, that loving was different than being in love."

"Aye, I did."

Her eyes were wide, serious. "I didn't know what you meant then, Jamie."

Hearing fear and uncertainty in her voice tore at his heart. "But you know now."

She nodded.

Pleased, he held his smile. She wouldn't understand. Not yet. It was too soon for her to have reconciled the matter. "Are you loving me, Catie? After?"

He'd asked the question though, if she said she wasn't, he didn't know how the hell he'd make her change her mind. She would change it of course, even if he had to hold her under lock and key until she cleared the clutter and saw the truth. He knew she loved him but, he stroked her cheek, from the troubled look of her, his sweet Catie was still mired in the muddle.

"I don't want to hurt you, Jamie, but it would help me to talk this through. I'm confused."

"I've told you before darling. I'll be your friend, your husband, your lover. Whatever you need."

She covered his hand on her shoulder and laced their fingers. "I feel so much for you, but I'm not sure it's love. I thought I loved Andrew, but tonight at the fire, I knew I never did." She arced her neck and leaned back against his chest. "Now I'm feeling all these wondrous things for you. But are they love? Are they, Jamie?"

Sure she wouldn't see it, he smiled and kissed the top of her head. "Are your feelings for me the same as they were for him?"

She shook her head. "No. Well, they're similar in some ways, but even more different."

Catie Morgan loved him, and that was that. Jamie kissed her head again to let her know she'd pleased him. He had the strongest urge to take her back to bed and prove it to her, but she first had to come to terms with loving him on her own. Only then would her fears settle and her head accept the message from her heart.

She turned in his arms and pressed her cheek to his chest. "I just want to be with you. To see you smile, to hear you laugh and sing." She looked up at him and touched his beard with a trembling hand. "And I want to hold you, Jamie. To keep on holding you forever."

Even forever wouldn't be long enough, he thought, looking deeply into her eyes. Seeing no regret, no guilt, he realized her tears had been poignant ones, not sad ones.

"Give your feelings time to sort, love. Everything will be fine."

"Promise?"

She knew he kept his promises, and her asking pleased him greatly. "Aye, I said it didn't I?"

Her wee smile satisfied him she was soothed again. He kissed the tips of her fingers, then lifted her into his arms.

She grunted and curled her arms around his neck. "Are you taking me back to my room, then?"

He nipped at her neck. She had the sweetest skin. "Nay, I'm taking you where you belong." Crossing the stones, he put her down in his bed, got in with her and then drew the quilts up over them.

She snuggled into the crook of his arm. "I belong with you now."

"Aye." He wrapped his free arm around her as well. "Holding me forever."

She kissed his chest over his heart. "Thank you, Jamie."

"For what, love?"

"For giving me a perfect Christmas."

Something warm and good burst inside him. Jamie cuddled her close and they began talking, whispering stories of past Christmases tender to their hearts. Stories of childhood hopes and disappointments, and triumphs. They dreamed, and teased, and touched. And just before dawn, Jamie again made love with his sweet Catie; slow and gentle love, for their urgent needs had been satisfied, yet their need to come together burned strong.

Now she slept in his arms, her lips parted, her silver-tipped lashes sweeping her cheeks. He smiled against her hair, for the first time in his life, a content man. He didn't feel driven by any need to prove himself, or his heart. His mind, body, spirit, and soul were at one with the woman in his arms, and he couldn't help but wonder. Would life ever again feel this good? This perfect, and this good?

On the heels of that thought came another. One that promised a future full of contentment. He and Catie had tomorrow. And the day after. And weeks and months of years after that. He had a future with Catie in his arms, sharing his life.

He traced the delicate slope of her nose with his fingertip. Oh, they'd fight. His Catie had a fierce temper and she was a mite stubborn. In truth, the woman likely would give him more than his fair share of hell. She'd probably drive him to drink a time or two, especially if she kept nagging him to fly her damn Yank flag from his tower. But that, he vowed, he'd never do. King Edgar would rise from his grave to take back Clan Cameron, and Harry would be standing at Edgar's side urging him to be quick about doing it.

Aye, the woman would make Jamie miserable at times. But at other times, he'd be happier than a man had a right to be feeling this side of heaven. She'd probably start her screeching in the morning too, when he gave her his Christmas gift. It'd definitely prick her temper.

He could hardly wait.

The first rays of Christmas dawn sneaked into the windows and streamed across the room. Nuzzling Catie's neck, he closed his eyes. Tonight he'd ask her to become his wife. And when she agreed—of course, she would agree. By God, she would—then he too would have a perfect Christmas.

Catie and Jamie faced each other, sitting Indian-style on the bed. He'd stoked the fire and the logs crackled in the grate taking the chill out of his chamber.

"Two?" he asked, accepting the wrapped gifts for which

he'd just paid her the ransom of one kiss each. "But I gave you three kisses."

"One was free." She shrugged. "You needed kissing."

"Ah, you're a wicked woman, I'm thinking. And it was you who needed that third kiss. I was quite content with two."

"You Scots sure lie easily, James Cameron."

"Scots never lie, Catherine."

Ignoring his clipped tone, she shook the long box in her lap. Her breasts jiggled too, taunting him, and he wanted her again, but her ginger steps to her chamber to get his gifts proved her too sore. Aye, he'd have to be timid and considerate, and hope it didn't kill him.

"Is it a hundred pairs of glasses?" She reached up and wiggled the frames of the pair resting on her nose, a naughty gleam in her eye.

He squelched a groan. "Witch."

"You love it."

" 'Tis painful, love."

"It isn't. It's fun."

"That's true." He moved the gifts from his lap and feigned a groan. "But, aye, it is painful, darling. Look what seeing you in glasses is doing to me." He thought it best not to mention that seeing her nude body aided in the effect.

"Jamie!" She flushed a pretty pink, and jerked the sheet up over his thighs.

"Nay, woman." He tossed the covers back. "You did it. Now you'll be seeing the suffering you're causing."

The devil danced in her eyes. "Well, we can't have you suffering." She slinked forward like a loving cat and thumped against his chest, flattening her soft breasts against him.

"You're supposed to fall backward, dear. I'm knocking you off your feet—in case you aren't knowing."

"Oh." He could have mentioned he hadn't been on them, but he didn't. Like a dutiful ally, he fell backward on the bed, and pulled her with him. When she rested full-length on him, he smiled up into her shining eyes. "Aren't you wanting to open your present?"

"I am," she said, staring at his mouth. "The very best present of all."

"Catie darling, I'm willing, but I doubt you're able."

She mimicked his burr. "I'm of a mind to love you, Jamie. Would you be denying your ally your loving on a perfect Christmas morning?"

He raked her hair with his fingers and dragged her down to receive his kiss. Against her mouth, he warned, "Nay, but if you canna walk for a week, woman, it'll be your own fault."

"I accept full responsibility," she whispered, nipping at his lips. "You're hexed."

"Aye, you wanton witch." He sighed and drew a lazy circle around her lips with the tip of his tongue. "I'm hexed." And unless God was napping, he'd be hexed all the rest of his days.

He lost himself in her kiss and reached down between them to caress her soft curves, skimming her full breasts, her tiny ribs, the flare of her sweet hips. Stretched flat, his hand spanned her abdomen, hipbone to hipbone. When he finally touched those soft curls, that tender part of her, her sweet flesh beckoned, and he suffered a series of quaking tremors. His Catie was hot and wanting him. "You're starving, love."

She made sexy little noises and arched against him. "Aye, you awful man."

He raised her hips and rubbed her flesh with his. "It'll hurt a wee bit, Catie. You're tender."

"I'm needing feeding, love, not instructing." Before finishing her statement, she guided him to her, impaling herself. Letting her head loll back, she groaned. "Jamie, this is . . ."

"Painful," he said. "Aye, I tried to tell—"

She looked down at him, her hair falling forward over her breasts and sweeping his chest, her expression not of pain but of bliss. "Wonderful," she stammered and began moving on him. "Truth is truth, and wonderful is what I was thinking."

He shuddered. "Aye." Cupping her full breasts in his hands, he reveled in the sweet joining of their flesh, the communing of their spirits.

"Jamie," she rasped, her eyes desire-glazed, unfocused.

She was getting close. He held her at her ribs, his big hands nearly spanning her, and brushed tiny circles on her skin with his thumbs. When she began making those sweet noises he loved, he pushed her back, astride him, stroking her soft center. She jerked, letting out a telling groan that had him near climax.

"Jamie." She looked down, rapture in her eyes. "Oh, Jamie!"

She let her neck arc back. Her hair hung in gleaming golden strands to his thighs, creating an arousing friction so filling. She thrust, then thrust again. He rolled her peaked nipples between his forefingers and thumbs then gently tugged; bowing his spine, lifting his hips from the bed until his buttocks hollowed, giving her all of him. She hissed in a breath, then cried out and, feeling her sweet throbbing, he held her hips and thrust harder and harder, until her spasms slowed, certain the pressure in his loins would kill him. Caressing his orbs, she flexed her muscles, and he closed his eyes, let her take him. The pressure in his loins shattered, and he shuddered with each pulsing throb.

When a long while later he opened his eyes, she was watching him, smiling her angel's smile. She bent low, kissed him languidly, luxuriously, telling him how much their loving pleased her. "And after, Jamie?" she asked.

His heart full, he cupped her face in his hands. "And after, love."

She nuzzled his palm, then his neck. "I suppose I should mention that we neglected something."

"What?" He certainly didn't feel neglected.

Catie pointed to the condoms on the bedside chest.

He'd forgotten. How could he have done that to her? "Oh God, Catie. I'm sorry."

Her lower lip was swollen from their kisses. She worried it with her teeth and avoided his eyes. "I'm not."

Stunned, he just stared at her for a long moment. She wasn't irresponsible. She knew the risks. How could she not be furious with him? She had been a virgin, he reminded himself. "Catie, I could have just made you pregnant. You are knowing that, aren't you, lass?"

Her voice went husky and she gave him the slow blink that drove him wild. "Aye, you awful man. We could have done that very thing."

She wasn't opposed. Jamie swallowed hard and let that truth wash through him. Even without marriage, she wasn't opposed to bearing his bairn. Opposed? He looked at the curl at the arch of her lips. Nay, she wasn't opposed, she actually seemed damned pleased with the prospect.

"Merry Christmas, Jamie." She kissed him between his brows.

Her smile took his breath. He smiled back at her, feeling its warmth and her love down to his bones. Catie wanted him and their bairn. Tender inside, he whispered softly. "Merry Christmas, love."

"Gift or no, I'll no be flying your damn Yank flag from my tower, Catie Morgan." Jamie glared back up the steps at her and wagged a finger. "And I'll be hearing no more on the matter."

She didn't look at all worried, or convinced. Three steps behind him and heading down, the trying woman laughed so hard that at any moment he expected she would fall and break her lovely neck. She caught her skirt and swished it, giving him a bonny view of her shapely thighs and a warming glimpse of lacy panty. The woman was a temptress, sure as certain. He hadn't been this enamored since puberty.

"I love my dress, Jamie. Pink is one of my best colors, don't you think?" She twirled around on the step.

"What I'm thinking, woman, is you're going to fall and crack your skull."

She fell.

He caught her in his arms before her feet touched the steps, and her laughter echoed in the stairwell. She pecked kisses to his cheek, his beard, and any skin her errant lips happened upon. "You wonderful, wonderful man."

"Catie."

"Shh, I'm repaying you." She rubbed their noses. "I knew you'd catch me."

He laughed. "Aye, you wee darling witch. I know you did."

"Do you want me to stop repaying?"

He pretended to consider it. "Not yet."

Then I'll repay you for this morning."

"You should be cursing me for neglecting my duty to you." That he hadn't protected her still had him shaking his head. How could he have let that happen? The wee witch had turned his mind to mush. Aye, to mush. Pure and simple.

"Nay, I'm blessing you for doing your duty so well."

"Catie, darling—"

"Shh," she said, pressing her fingertip to his lips. "Let me enjoy my dream a bit longer, Jamie."

He meant to talk to her about this. Them having a child together was too important to not thoroughly discuss. But the look on her face had him opting to postpone that discussion. Catie Morgan's eyes twinkled. She was happy . . . and so was he. Aye, he'd wait until after he proposed to her tonight. He sent her an arrogant look. "You may keep kissing me, then. Repayment for my possible contribution."

"Nay, I don't think I will."

"Catie." His tone was threatening.

She laughed in his face, then kissed him again and again, nuzzling huskily. "Grrr, Jamie. I think instead I'll eat you up."

"If you don't stop hexing me with your sexy growls, Catie Morgan, I'm going right back up those stairs with ye. 'Tis warming to a man to be knowing his woman is wanting his bairn, in case you aren't knowing."

"Bairn?"

"Babe," he translated. The trying woman now had him talking Yank—on Christmas, no less.

"The idea has merit." She curled her arms around his neck. "But it's past noon. Everyone will think we've—"

"Everyone will *know* we've been doing exactly what we have been doing."

Far from embarrassed, Catie purred. "I liked it, Jamie."

His heart thundered. His ally was pleased, and not minding her soreness in the least. He stopped on the steps and looked into her bewitching eyes. "Of course, you did."

"Arrogant barbarian."

An endearment if ever he'd heard one. "Scots."

"Same difference." She kissed him again.

"Ah, sweet Catie, I love your kisses. But, hexed or no, I'll fly no Yank flag from me tower, love."

She rubbed their noses. "Jamie, honey, please."

"Nay, lass." Now why was he half-tempted? Damn his spinning head.

Catie smiled and curled her fingers in his beard. Against the corner of his mouth, she murmured. "But even when I hex you, I don't let you suffer. It's just one little flag—"

"Nay, love." He kissed her to soften his refusal.

"One day you will fly my flag, Jamie."

"Nay, I'll not. Not if it's a Yank flag, Catie Morgan, and that's a promise."

She laughed. "Aye, James Cameron. You will. I'll catch

you at your weakest moment. I just have to figure out when that is, and then you won't be able to refuse me." She nuzzled his neck. "Maybe it's when you're inside me. Is that when you're weakest?"

"Nay, that's when I'm strongest," he lied. "Adrenaline."

"Do you like the way I strengthen your adrenaline?"

He looked at her and laughed. Any stronger and he could be a self-propelled rocket exploring Pluto. "You're improving. You're a fast learner, love. Why in no time—"

She gasped. "You're lying, you beast. You loved sleeping with me, and that's that."

"Nay, you snitch all the covers." That earned him a healthy whack to the chest. "If you're through inflicting bodily injury on me, I'm thinking I'll finish. I was of a mind to say I liked making love with you." He smiled at her disgruntled expression. "Aye, at that, you're not bad." He couldn't resist. "For a Yank."

"I'm getting angry, Jamie."

Aye, she was. Her gaze was shooting daggers at him. He softened his voice, deepened his burr. Catie liked his burr. "I'm wanting to repay, lass."

The look in her eyes softened, though she pretended she was still miffed. "Well?"

"Kiss me, Catie."

She smiled and complied, then tickled his ribs. "Grrr."

"You're a witch, woman."

"Aye, I am. And you'd best be remembering it. I'm getting better at hexing all the time."

"Catherine, what in God's name is that man doing to you?"

Catie stiffened. Her laughter stopped, her smile faded.

Jamie looked down at the man who'd asked that question and frowned. Letty and Father MacDuff stood at the foot of the stairs with a woman about Letty's age Jamie never had seen before. She stood beside the man who had spoken to Catie. He reeked of Yank. Smooth Yank.

Jamie stared at him until the man backed up a step, then walked down the stairs, a silent Catie still in his arms. "Letty, who are these people in my hall?"

Thin and dressed like Letty in red and bright green, the aged woman stepped forward and kissed Catie's pale cheek, then stretched up and kissed Jamie's. Ah, she had to be Annie. And where her loyalties rested was perfectly clear.

"Merry Christmas, children," Annie said, her eyes sparkling. "I'm—"

"Annie," Jamie said. "Merry Christmas and welcome to Cameron."

"You've given me a pleasant welcome indeed, James, dear. Catherine, you positively glow!"

"She probably can't breathe. That giant has her in a death grip." This from the puny Yank.

Jamie growled and deliberately insulted the man. "Who are you, lad?"

"He's Andrew, Jamie." Catie sounded faint.

She looked pale, tense and wary, which riled Jamie's temper. "Do you want me to beat the bastard?"

"Nay, it's Christmas."

"Oh." Now what did he do with the man? He shouldn't have asked. Sir Andrew deserved a beating . . . aye, and a blessing. He'd deserted Catie, after all, leaving her for Jamie. But, by damn, he'd hurt her, too. "Not even a wee bit of a beating?"

"Nay, not on Christmas."

Jamie swallowed his disappointment. What was the man doing here? "Oh."

"Oh?" She blinked.

Jamie's stomach muscles clenched. Andrew had come for Catie. But he'd take her only over Jamie's dead body. "Just, oh."

Andrew stepped forward. "Catherine, I hate to intrude on this enlightening conversation, but you could at least remain civil long enough to speak."

"Hello, Andrew." She ruffled Jamie's beard, a strange look on her face, as if she feared it'd be the last time she touched him.

"If you aren't of a mind for me to beat him or to toss the man out on his foolish elbow, we could just go back upstairs until it isn't Christmas anymore," Jamie whispered.

She looked as if she were considering it, then shook her head. "He'd just wait, and it'd ruin Christmas all the same."

A thread of panic threatened, and fear seeped into Jamie's stomach. "And after, Catie?"

She smiled at him, bittersweet, and her eyes filled with tears, but she did not answer.

"Well," Letty's voice rang out. "Andrew has asked to speak to Catie for a moment. I've told him he may use your hall, James."

Andrew nodded. "Preferably with her standing on her feet. Alone."

Jamie stood statue still.

Annie touched his arm. "Put her down, James."

Did the woman know how much she asked of him? He'd waited so long for Catie, and now . . . He looked into Catie's godmother's eyes. Aye, she knew.

He kissed Catie's chin, then set her to the floor.

She walked toward Andrew, paused near the door, then looked back at Jamie. None of the joy she'd shown just minutes ago remained in her now, and that worried him. "You came, Catie," he said, reminding her that she'd given herself to him.

Her chin quivered. She stared at him for the longest time, and finally her lips flattened in grim determination. She walked past him, then disappeared around the corner of the entry.

"Where is she going?" Andrew asked.

No one answered.

Andrew let out a brittle laugh that grated at Jamie's ears. "Is Christmas always so solemn here?"

Again no one answered.

Jamie glanced at Letty, at Annie, then at MacDuff. Celwyn joined them and she looked no different than the rest. All serious. All waiting with held breaths. It seemed only Sir Andrew remained in the dark, unaware that his, Catie's, and Jamie's futures were being decided by the woman at that very moment.

Jamie would let her make her decision, but she'd no be leaving him, and that was that. Unless . . . What if she truly wanted to go?

She rounded the corner. Jamie's heart swelled and damn near burst. He blinked, then blinked again, not at all convinced his eyes weren't tricking him.

Catie walked across the hall toward him, smiling the most beautifully serene smile he'd ever seen. And around her shoulders hung a cloak. His cloak. His Cameron colors.

The decision had been made.

"I came." She paused and touched his beard. "And after, Jamie."

He blinked hard, his eyes blurring, his voice thick. "And after, love."

Everyone except Andrew laughed. Jamie kissed Catie until he feared he'd split her lips. "Go on, woman. Give the man the news that's gonna have him kicking his own arse for the next fifty years."

She smiled. "I can't."

Jamie frowned. "You'll tell him he's not wanted here, Catie. I'll no be sharing you with another man."

"I should stuff your tassel in your mouth for that, James Cameron. I can't go tell Andrew 'he's not wanted here' because you, you darling, barbaric beast, have me dangling."

Jamie laughed, kissed the meanness right out of her, then set her to her feet.

She sniffed. "If you think that's repayment, you're wrong, dear."

He smiled, not at all opposed to her demand for repayment. "Anytime, sweet Catie."

"Aye, exactly."

Letty and MacDuff linked arms with Annie. "We're going to the kitchen for coffee. Join us, James."

"In a moment. I've something to do that can't wait."

Letty smiled. "Aye, I imagine you do."

Jamie kissed her soft cheek. " 'Tis a merry Christmas indeed, aye, Letty?"

"Aye. Aye, it is that."

He walked into the chapel, remembering the night after Harry had died, then three days later when he'd had to damage the door to pull Letty out. Today, Jamie closed the repaired door softly, reverently.

At the tiny altar, he bent to his knees and closed his eyes, feeling grateful and humble as only a man who knows he's been given life's most precious treasure can feel.

His hands folded, he looked up at the rough-hewn cross bathed in flickering candlelight and let quiet peace settle over him. "I'm thinking You sent Catie to me because she needed proper loving. I dinna know it then, but so did I. I'm no alone or empty anymore. She fills my heart with her laughter and my soul with her love. You've blessed me as You blessed my kin, giving me an angel." A hot tear rolled down Jamie's cheek. "I would thank You, Lord."

He closed his eyes, bowed his head.

The chapel door opened.

Jamie turned and saw Father MacDuff walking up the aisle between the wooden benches.

He sat down on the bench in the first row, his expression grave. "Catie was with you last night?"

"Aye," Jamie said still on bended knee.

"So Letty was right, then." MacDuff sighed. "She told me you'd made Catie your ally last night."

Jamie frowned. Why did MacDuff look so worried? "Nay, we were allies before she came to Cameron."

"Sweet Mary." MacDuff crossed himself. "Before you had even seen her?"

"My heart recognized her from the start." The moment he'd heard her voice, he'd known. Jamie walked over, then sat down beside the priest. "You're worrying because we've been intimate, I'm thinking, but there's no need. She's in my heart and I mean to marry her, Father. You've my word on that."

The priest's face bleached a ghostly white and several intense emotions flitted across his face. The man was battling in an internal war, to be sure. But why? "Surely you see that marrying Catie is what I must do."

"Because it's your duty?"

The hope in his voice had Jamie deepening his frown. "Because I'm loving the woman."

MacDuff rose, paced a short path between the altar and the bench, then strode through the break in the split rail around the prayer bench. He stopped behind the altar then ran his fingers over the stone wall.

"Father, what are you doing?" Jamie stood. Priest or no the man had best have a good reason for . . . for taking a stone from the chapel wall?

"There's a priest's hole back here, James," MacDuff said over his shoulder.

He reached in and pulled something out. It was a book. A dark brown, worn-looking book. "What is that?"

MacDuff replaced the stone, then turned to face Jamie, his hand trembling. " 'Tis a diary, James."

A shiver crawled up Jamie's spine. "The diary Letty found after Harry died?"

"Aye." MacDuff took off his glasses, his eyes sad. "I'm breaking Letty's confidence in giving this to you—that's something I've never done in our forty years together. But I've wrestled and wrestled with this issue, and my loyalty must go to my laird."

The wrinkles in MacDuff's face pitted deeper and, for the first time, Jamie realized the man had grown old. "Father?"

"I've loved your grandmother for as long as I can remember. I know, it's a shameful sin for a priest to be loving a woman in that fashion, but that's the truth of it."

"I know." When MacDuff's jaw gaped, Jamie added, "You're a priest, Father, and a fine one, but you're human, too. Don't be judging yourself so severely for your human feelings. Your Maker is merciful of human feelings, as well He must be, having gifted them to you."

MacDuff smiled. "Thank you. I guess my reason for being at Cameron is to receive spiritual counseling as much as to give it." He waved toward the bench. "Please, sit down."

MacDuff's concern worried Jamie, but he did as the priest asked.

"I'd give anything not to have to tell you this. Catie's a fine woman, and I'm sure as certain she's loving you as much as you're loving her." The priest's eyes grew suspiciously moist, and sadder still. "But you canna marry her, James."

Fear scattered in Jamie's chest. There was a desperate edge in MacDuff's tone that warned he had strong reasons for his opinion. "Why not?"

"Read this, then you'll understand." MacDuff passed the diary. "Know I've had it authenticated. The parchment and ink are both genuine twelfth-century—eleven hundred, actually."

Jamie took the diary, lifting a curious brow. "What, I'm asking, has some diary written over nine hundred years ago to do with me marrying Catie?"

MacDuff looked Jamie straight in the eye. "I'm sorry to say, James, that this isn't just some diary. It's your Catie's diary."

* * *

"Sit down, Andrew." Catie motioned toward the little rosewood settee. Instead Andrew moved toward Jamie's rocker. Catie blocked his path. Silly, but she didn't want Andrew sitting in Jamie's chair.

Andrew gave her a questioning look, but moved to the settee. Catie studied him, and waited. Even with all his traveling, he wasn't the least bit rumpled. The only creases in the man's slacks were the ones down the leg fronts that should be there. His shoes weren't scuffed or even dusty, and his white shirt cuffs weren't tinged with so much as a smear or a smudge. His tie was crisp and neatly clasped, not loosened for comfort, and not one short, black hair on his head dared to be out of place. He looked . . . perfect. Perfect, and totally awful.

She cocked her head. Had she really once thought him the most handsome man ever created?

Surely not. He looked prim and proper and dull. She tried to imagine running her fingers through the hair at his nape. But there was no hair at his nape. He had a nice face, but it lacked character and depth, and it was as bare as a baby's behind. There were no tiny lines near his eyes from squinting against the sun, no curl to his lips from smiling. And, when he looked at her, there was no warmth lighting his eyes from the bottoms that made her feel like he saw her with his eyes, but also with his heart.

He wasn't . . . Jamie.

"I've missed you, Catherine." Andrew crossed his legs and rotated his foot.

She didn't answer. She couldn't. It had occurred to her that once she'd settled in at Cameron, the only time she'd thought of Andrew had been when Jamie had mentioned him. That sort of stunned her.

Andrew draped his arm across the back of the settee. "Now that you've satisfied your Scottish whim, I want you to come home. It's time we married."

Married? Her married to *Andrew?* Catie watched him

stand up and shook her head. "You never wanted me. You wanted the law firm."

He put his hand in his pocket, drawing his suit coat back behind his arm. "You've changed, Catherine." Andrew studied her from head to toe, and his expression grew quizzical. "You look . . . softer."

"I stopped trying to please you and started pleasing me again."

He frowned. "You were in James Cameron's arms."

"Aye, I was. And I liked it."

"You're sleeping with him?" Clearly shocked, Andrew held up a hand. "No, don't answer that. I don't want to know."

"I wasn't going to answer you," she said. "Where or with whom I choose to sleep is none of your business."

"Technically, that's true." He clasped her hand. "But I came here to take you home. You belong with me." He flushed red from the neck up. "Forget what I said about . . . you know, sexually. We'll have a good life together, Catherine. I promise. And you know that's what your father wanted."

More promises. More empty, wasted words. More emotional blackmail. It was all so clear to her now, and it sickened her. Her father had trapped her into doing what he'd wanted her to do. He'd used his approval and his love as rewards to entice her to fall in line with his plans. And when she'd denied him, he'd withheld his approval and love, and had showered her with guilt. Andrew was merely an extension of her father. He used the same tricks. The same manipulations. The same shallow, empty blackmail.

She lifted her chin and kept her voice soft. "No."

"No?" He looked stunned.

"No," she repeated quietly, finding it easier than she'd expected to refuse him. "I don't love you, Andrew. I thought I did, but I don't. And you don't love me, either." She patted his hand, then let go of it. "We both deserve love."

"You *are* sleeping with him." Andrew walked to the fireplace, then turned his back to her. "Cameron is an uncouth savage in a woman's skirt, Catherine. How dare you let him paw you?"

"I dare what I choose." Catie smiled. "And his skirt is called a kilt, Andrew. Trust me, it's not at all feminine. To you, I suppose Jamie might seem a bit barbaric, but to me, he's perfect."

Andrew glared over his shoulder back at her. "Christ, his hair is almost as long as yours."

"Aye, it is." She laughed. Andrew's objections being what her own once had been struck her as funny. But now what Andrew claimed as Jamie's liabilities were in her eyes a few of his assets. "James Cameron is a good man, Andrew. He's warm and loving, and when he looks at me, there's something in his eyes that makes me—"

"Lust." Andrew grabbed her shoulders. "What you're feeling is lust. Women do it, Catherine. They wait so long to have sex that, when a man finally copulates with them, they fall head first into lust, thinking it's love."

Copulates? How tame and clinical, and how like Andrew to explain the most magical event in her life in polite, bland, and totally inadequate terms. She too once had thought lust was what she was feeling for Jamie. But *copulate?* She smiled to herself. Andrew would never understand. "Maybe some women do mistake lust for love, but I'm not one of them—not anymore."

"Lust," Andrew insisted. "It can't compare with what we had."

"It can't. You're right. But not in the way you think." She wasn't succeeding; the muscle was twitching under Andrew's left eye. Did his courtroom adversaries recognize that telling sign as easily as she did? Andrew's ego would suffer, but not like hers had. She couldn't wound him as deeply because he hadn't deluded himself about being in love with her. Still she gently squeezed his hands to soften the blow.

"The simple truth is that James Cameron stimulates me, Andrew. My mind, my body, my spirit and heart—all of me."

"And I don't."

She shook her head. "I'm sorry. I don't want to hurt you, but it's Jamie I want. I need him, Andrew."

"I guess that's it, then. You'll be staying with him."

She nodded. "For as long as he wants me."

"I see."

"Aye, I believe you do." She released his hands and took a step back. Knowing Jamie would approve, if not insist, she added, "I'll return your ring."

"Keep it. I bought it for you," he said, walking toward the door. Just inside, he stopped and looked back. "I'll leave tomorrow."

She nodded.

"Catherine?"

"Aye?"

"If you should change your mind, well, I'll be here."

"I won't," she said, admitting to herself what her heart had been telling her for weeks. She loved Jamie.

Catie left the hall and went to the kitchen. Annie, Letty, Father MacDuff, and Celwyn were seated around the table, drinking coffee.

Annie slid Catie an expectant look. On hearing the conversation pause, Catie smiled. "Aye, I told him I'd be staying."

"Aye?" Annie lifted her brows.

Catie nodded. "When in Scotland . . ." She walked to the counter and got herself a cup, then poured it full of steaming hot coffee. It smelled good. "Where's Jamie?"

Father MacDuff nearly choked to death. Letty and Annie both tapped on his back, driving the poor man's belly into the table's edge.

Annie avoided Catie's eyes. "I believe he and Bronwyn stepped into the rose garden. She, um, had something to tell him about Mr. MacPherson." Annie sent Letty a pleading look. "Or was it about Mr. Kirkland?"

"She's going to learn the truth, Annie Morgan. There's no sense in lying to the woman." Letty frowned, then looked at Catie. "It was about Thomas, dear."

A flash of fear streaked into her stomach. "Has he been found?"

"Aye, Iain found him just a few minutes ago."

Letty was reluctant to disclose much, and that worried Catie. "Is he . . . all right?" Her voice cracked.

Father MacDuff stood up, then covered her hand with his. "I'm sorry to say, Catie, our Thomas has gone home."

Puzzled, she frowned. "Home?"

The look in his eyes grew tender. "He's dead, lass."

"Oh God." Catie gasped and held her stomach. She couldn't move. Couldn't talk. Thomas had died. Guarding her, he'd died!

Father MacDuff put his arm around her shoulder. "I know this is shocking news, but you mustn't be sad—"

"*Sad?*" She cried, "*I killed the man!*"

The priest shook his head. "Nay, lass? You can't be taking the blame for something that isn't your fault."

"He was protecting *me.*"

"But—"

Catie turned and fled from the kitchen. She had to see Jamie. To tell him how sorry she was that she'd caused the death of one of his men. In her mind, she again saw Thomas, facing her in the hall. His leathery skin, his softening eyes. And again she heard him ask, *Who are ye, lass?*

Oh God. He was dead. Dead.

She left the hall afraid that, before she could get outside, she'd be sick. She jerked open the door. Cold air slapped her in the face with the force of a good left hook. Dragging in deep lungsful of frigid air, she headed from the castle landing down to the upper bailey wall. Her face stinging from the bitter cold and her fingers and feet going numb, she reached up and touched her cheeks. They were wet with tears.

Cricket bounded up to her, and Catie dropped to her knees on the snow-covered ground then hugged the dog, burying her face in his scruff.

When she opened her eyes, she saw Jamie in the rose garden with Bronwyn. He stood rigid, his arms hanging at his sides. Bronwyn stepped close to him, wound her arms around his waist, then kissed him, and Catie's heart again shattered. She watched, unable to look away, and suffered anger, hurt, and a sense of betrayal ten times worse than any she'd felt with Andrew.

Jamie lifted his hand to Bronwyn's shoulder. Catie waited, sure he would set the woman back on her heels. He'd been stunned. That was all. But now he had recovered and he would push Bronwyn away.

He didn't. He held her shoulder. Held her!

Catie couldn't bear to see anymore. She turned her back, ran down the slope to the lower bailey stables. Iain was coming out of the first stall. Catie swiped at her cheeks and called out. "Iain, saddle Thunder."

Jamie's second frowned. "Thunder is too much beast for a tiny wisp of a woman."

"I've ridden him every day for the past month, Iain. Now, saddle that horse."

"I'd rather not." His frown changed, his look grew tender. "James was with you then, and 'tis clear as day at present you're a wee bit upset, lass. Maybe Firefly, hmm? The mare's much gentler—"

Catie clenched her hands into fists. "Damn it, Iain, saddle Thunder or I'll ride him bareback."

"All right." He turned to the stall where Jamie kept his stallion. "It'll take me a few minutes, lass."

"Fine. I'll wait outside."

Catie went out into the fresh air and breathed deeply. God, but she hurt all over.

When Iain finally led the great black beast out of the stable, she let Thunder sniff her hand. He nuzzled her, and she stroked his velvety hide, leaning forward to rest her forehead against his nose.

"Be careful," Iain warned. "Thunder hates having his nose touched."

She turned until her cheek rested on the horse's muzzle. "Nay, he likes it." She stilled her hand and rose. Thunder proved her right; tossing his head until she rubbed him again.

Iain's eyes stretched wide. "Even the laird canna do that to the beast."

"Help me up, Iain." She should be embarrassed, crying like this in front of him. And she would be, later. Right now she hurt so badly she just couldn't give a flying fig.

"Nay, Catie, I'll not." He shook his head. "Cricket would rip out me throat."

She frowned. "Cricket, stay put, please. Now will you help me, Iain?"

He stepped toward her, wary-eyed. "Are you sure that dog won't come at me? He's done it before, I would remind you."

"He won't," Catie promised.

When she was fully seated, Iain wasted no time in backing away. "Where're ye going, lass?" He kept a watchful eye on Cricket.

The dog hadn't moved. Men, she thought. "I'm going to the stream to have myself a Class-A cry for killing Thomas. Then I'm coming back to box Bronwyn's ears for kissing my man. After that, I'm going to scorch your laird's ears with some allied instructions he'll not soon be forgetting, and then I think I might just tell him to haul his huge self into the chapel where I'm going to—"

Iain's jaw hung loose.

"Oh God, Iain," she cried. "Thomas is dead. He's dead, and it's my fault."

"Nay, it's not, Catie." He looked up at her, the wind plastering his collar to his neck, the frigid air making frost of his breaths.

She nodded her disagreement. Her heart was in her throat.

"It's not. Truly, Catie." He shuffled his feet in the cold dirt. "You dinna kill Thomas."

"Thank you for trying to make me feel better. But I know the truth." She sniffed. "They say you found him."

"Aye, I did."

Afraid of seeing censure for her in his eyes despite his reassuring words, she focused on his boots. "Did he suffer?"

"Nay, lass. You've me word on that."

She squeezed her eyes shut. "Did he have a family?"

"The clan."

Catie did look at Iain then, and wished she hadn't. He looked uncomfortable. But then he had known Thomas all of his life. Iain had to be hurting, too. "Thomas didn't have any immediate family at all?"

"Nay, no wife. No ally, either."

She took up the reins. "I'm so sorry," she said, then dug her heels into Thunder's flanks and headed out to the open moor.

Jamie looked down into Bronwyn's eyes and lowered his hand from her shoulder. "Merry Christmas."

"Merry Christmas, James." She sighed. "I hate to be critical, love, but there was a time when your kisses were infinitely more . . . exciting. I've seen you kiss Letty's cheek with more enthusiasm than you just kissed me."

"Aye." The diary in his hand burned his palm. Catie. Going back in time to James? Feeling his blood pound in his temples, Jamie shuddered.

The sound of a horse's hooves grew loud, then louder. He

looked through a watchman's hole in the bailey wall and saw Catie astride Thunder, riding hell-bent-for-leather toward the moor with Cricket dogging her heels. His heart ached. She looked magnificent.

"James! James!"

Iain came running toward Jamie. "What is it?"

"Catie," Iain said, winded. "She's taken Thunder—"

"I saw her," Jamie said. "She can handle him. The beast is gentle with her, and Cricket will keep her safe."

"Aye, but—"

Jamie frowned. "Let her ride, Iain."

His second cocked his head, clearly puzzled. "But she's feeling Thomas's death is her fault."

"As well she should." Bronwyn thrust out her chin.

Jamie glared at his former lover. "Are you blaming Catie?"

"If Thomas hadn't been guarding her, he'd still be among the living."

How had Jamie once thought himself in love with the woman? "Say no more against my ally, I warn you," he told Bronwyn. "Catie didn't stab Thomas in the back."

"True." Bronwyn bent to the hard edge in James's voice. "You're right, of course, James."

He turned to Iain. "Let Catie ride for a while, but bring her back before dusk."

Iain looked at Jamie as if he'd lost his mind. "You're no going to get her?"

Jamie didn't answer. Every emotion in him was at war. He wanted nothing more than to go get Catie, but the book in his hand forbade him that honor.

He walked back to the castle, the contents of the diary weighing heavy on his heart. He had to talk to Andrew, and what Jamie had to say to that man weighed heavy on his soul. But he had no choice. If Catie stayed away from Cameron she would be safe. Not being here, she couldn't go back to James.

Aye, to protect her, Jamie had no choice. God give him strength.

He had to ban Catie from Cameron.

Cricket lay before the hearth in Catie's chamber.

Catie glanced over and saw the dog, watching her pace. His head resting on his front paws, he moved nothing but his eyes. "Is he ever going to come home, Cricket?"

Jamie had been gone to the village for most of the day, and he'd avoided her the rest of it. "He knows Thomas's death is my fault," she told the dog. "That's what it is."

She again knocked on the door between their chambers, though she knew Jamie wasn't there, then again tried the knob. It wouldn't budge. He'd locked it. Her chin quivered and she clamped her jaw shut. "Pretty clear signal, Cricket. He doesn't want me."

She couldn't blame him, but it hurt. Oh God, how it hurt.

She staggered back to her bed then crawled in atop of the red quilt. In fifteen minutes she had to go downstairs for dinner. Jamie would definitely be there. So would Andrew and Bronwyn and the rest of them. How in the name of God could she face them? Any of them, much less all of them? How could she stand for all them to look at her knowing what every one of them was thinking?

It's your fault Thomas is dead.

You killed him.

Murderess!

When Catie stepped into the dining hall, everyone already was seated. She had to endure this, she told herself. They deserved the opportunity at least to blame her face to face. Letty sat on Jamie's right—Catie's usual chair—and Annie on his left. The only empty chair was one beside Andrew. Her heart in her throat, her stomach pressing against her backbone and burning like fire, she walked to the empty seat.

Andrew stood up, then pulled out her chair. She sat down, watching Jamie. He followed her with his gaze, but she had no idea what he was thinking. His expression masked, he didn't move or speak a word. No one did.

Celwyn began serving the meal. Andrew, Catie noted, seemed to be in fine spirits, but everyone else at the table seemed extremely sedate, whispering softly, if at all. Catie pushed her food around on her plate, hoping to God the meal would be over soon so she could go back to her room. She wanted them to have their chance, and she'd given it to them, but she couldn't stand much more of this. The tension was suffocating.

Midway through dessert, Andrew tapped his wineglass with his spoon. "Friends and family," he said.

When the quiet buzz ceased, Andrew smiled. Catie looked at Jamie. Grim and determined came to mind, and refused to go away. Spasms and a bitter certainty that something awful was about to happen snaked through her stomach. She looked away, stared down at her bowl of strawberries in chocolate sauce.

"I have an announcement to make," Andrew said. "But first, I'm sorry about Thomas." When Jamie nodded acceptance of the condolence, Andrew went on. "That said, this day also bears good news I'm delighted to share with all of you. Catherine and I have reunited."

She gasped, darted her gaze to Jamie.

He didn't move.

He said nothing.

He looked at her as if she were a stranger. No warmth. No love. Nothing.

Nothing.

When she realized that he wasn't going to say anything, she stood up. "Jamie, this—"

He came to her and took her hands. His eyes solemn, he

pressed her wrist to his lips. "I hope you'll be very happy, Catherine."

Catherine. Not Catie, but *Catherine*. She blinked, then blinked again. He blamed her. He didn't want her. God help her, she would love him forever and he didn't want her. "And after," she whispered, choking on tears.

He stared at her, and said nothing.

Her heart broke. "You lied to me, Jamie. You said Scots didn't lie, that you always kept your promises, but you lied to me. I'll never forgive you for that."

She turned and left the dining room. Near the door, she looked back and saw Bronwyn's satisfied smile.

Hot tears flooding her eyes, Catie fled to the stairs, hurting as she'd never before, hurting some place so deep inside she didn't know exactly where it was, only that she couldn't hold all the pain coming from it. And this time, God help her, Jamie wouldn't be there to soothe her.

In her chamber at three the next morning, Catie faced the truth. Jamie would not come. He'd never come again.

Crossing her chest with her arms, she combated the constant aching inside and sat down on the edge of the bed. She understood him blaming her about Thomas. She understood about Bronwyn kissing him. That kiss meant less than nothing. What Catie didn't understand, would never understand, was him breaking his promise to her. He'd kept his word.

Until now.

He'd said he loved her and she'd believed him. When he'd held her at the fire, and when they'd made love, she'd been so certain. Lust, Andrew had said. But he'd been wrong. She and Jamie had made love. Before her talk with Andrew, when Jamie had seen her in his colors, he'd had tears in his eyes. He couldn't have pretended those, or the feelings he'd shown her. *He couldn't have!*

But, she forced herself to face the facts, all of that had

happened before she'd shamed him and his clan. Before she'd killed Thomas.

Nay, Jamie would shed no tears for her. And she couldn't stay in Cameron and have their relationship be different. She couldn't bear seeing him hate her, seeing regret in his eyes whenever he looked at her. Not after seeing them look upon her shining with love.

She had to leave Cameron.

Somehow, she had to find the courage to tell Jamie she was leaving, the courage to not break down when she saw his relief that she was going. And she had to find the courage not to tell him that she loved him. Once, he'd asked for the words and she hadn't been ready to give them to him. She'd never given him the words.

And now, she never could.

My, my, what a day!

Such strange twists fate delivers at the most opportune times, eh, Cameron?

The Yank looked devastated at dinner. So did you, though she was too blinded by her own pain to notice.

All that to celebrate, and then to come face to face with my competitor in the archives. It's almost too much joy.

I wasn't at all surprised by my competitor's identity, of course, for those attacks on your sweet Catie too were motivated by destiny's call.

We compromised quickly and formed an alliance of sorts. Our mission?

To destroy you.

Twelve

Father MacDuff sat alone in the first row on the chapel bench. Bent forward, he had his head buried in his hands.

Jamie sat down beside him. "Help me, Father. I don't know if I can let her go." His voice cracked. "She's all I've ever wanted. I . . . need her."

"I'm so sorry, James." The priest looked up at Jamie's grief-stricken face. His brows knit, and MacDuff slumped back against the seat. "You believe what you've read in the diary, then?"

"How can I not believe it? I've seen Catie's writing often in the archives. It's the same. The diary's been authenticated. It tells of Letty bringing her to Cameron." Jamie drew in a breath that heaved his shoulders. "How can I not believe it?"

"I canna answer that, Laird. I've come to terms with this oddity myself, and you'll have to do the same."

Jamie raked his fingers through his hair. "I've searched and searched for a way to keep her with me, but she's not safe in Cameron. She's suffered two attacks already and, if what this diary says happens, really does happen, then she'll be gone forever." His insides twisted into knots. "Only God knows what could happen to her. I can't let her risk this." He passed the diary to MacDuff.

"If you don't risk it, you could die." MacDuff's voice shook, and he gripped the book hard. "Letty's life would be changed forever. Her Harry will not exist."

Jamie smelled MacDuff's fear, tasted it on his tongue, yet

there was nothing he could do to stop it. Never in his life had he felt so helpless, so vulnerable and so damn helpless. "Letty and I have talked over the matter."

"And Letty agreed Catie should leave Cameron?"

"What else could we do, I'm asking?"

"But the clan—"

"Iain will see to their needs."

Father MacDuff stared down at the diary. His fingers gripping its spine turned white. "The lass thinks you blame her for Thomas's death."

"It's even worse." Jamie looked over at the priest, knowing his eyes mirrored his inner torment. "She blames herself." He rubbed at his forehead. "I've no choice but to let her believe it."

"Otherwise, she'd not leave you."

Perceptive, as always. Jamie nodded and sat silent for a long moment. Where was the light at the end of the tunnel? Why couldn't he see himself in the years ahead without her? Why could he so easily see her without him? "I've talked with Andrew. He'll be taking her back to New Orleans tomorrow."

"You threatened him, you're meaning."

"Only if he hurts her again." The man had wounded her tender spirit something fierce already, and Jamie couldn't forget that, or let it happen again.

"Aye, he told me." MacDuff scratched at the book cover with his nail. "He's bent on marrying her. You're knowing that, of course."

A knot as big as his fist lodged squarely in Jamie's chest. His heart felt like a dead lump. "Aye, I'm knowing." He curled his fingers until his nails bit into his palms. "But I love her, Father. I'd rather she be his wife than to be knowing I'm living in a world she's no longer in."

"James, he's English." MacDuff swiped at his glasses. "Catie will never be happy with the man."

Catie, married to Andrew, loving him, having his children, laughing with him, and going to him to soothe her. Jamie without her. Empty and alone. Aching, and never free from the torment of knowing all he'd lost.

Hollow inside, he looked up at the cross above the altar. "I pray she will be happy. I pray he fills her heart with laughter, and her soul with love."

"The gifts she gave to you," MacDuff whispered.

"Aye." His eyes burned and stung. "Aye." Too emotional, he could say nothing more.

"You're asking too much of her, James," MacDuff said softly. "When a woman like Catie loves a man until his heart and soul are content, she can love no other man the same. She's got no choice in the matter. If it helps you to face the years that come, if they come, know you'll always hold her heart."

"But with him, she'll be alive."

"Aye, alive." MacDuff nodded then replaced his glasses on his nose. "But every bit as empty and alone as you, James."

Catie, unhappy? Empty and alone? Jamie hated the thought of it. But what could he do? He again looked to the cross. A single tear slid down his cheek and trickled into his beard. "Nay, Father. Catie will no be alone. Never alone. She'll leave Cameron, aye. She must. But she'll no be alone." His heart would always be with her.

Just after dawn, Catie stepped into the kitchen. Father MacDuff was sitting by himself at the table, drinking a glass of milk. Was he troubled, or ill? "Father?"

He looked up. Dark circles pitted the skin beneath his eyes. "Morning, Catie."

Pulling her robe more tightly closed against a chill, she frowned. "You're not ill again?"

"Nay. Nay, I'm fine."

"Can't you sleep?" He didn't look peaked, not really, but something was bothering him.

"Nay, I'm having one of those reflective nights we all

have at times, lass." He gave her a sad smile. "I've been thinking about my life here." He looked down and twirled his glass, his mind clearly far away. "Did you know Harry drank a glass of warm milk before bed? He studied Cameron history then. Every night, last thing before bed. How Harry loved Scotland. I miss him."

A funny feeling locked around Catie's stomach. She tried to shake it, but couldn't. "Father, was it a habit of Harry's to drink the milk every night?"

"Aye." He smiled, bittersweet, then sipped from his glass. "Regular as sunset."

The feeling grew stronger. "The night Harry died, was his milk tested for cyanide poisoning?"

"I'm no sure." Father MacDuff frowned and shifted uneasily on his chair. It creaked under his weight. "Catie, lass, why would you be wondering a thing like that?"

"I don't know." She answered honestly. "I guess it's something Jamie told me once. He said Harry simply drank his warm milk and went to sleep."

"Aye, that's true."

"He hadn't been sick or anything before then?"

"Harry?" MacDuff chuckled, but it sounded forced. "Nay, lass. Harry was as healthy as a horse."

"Healthy horses don't die in their sleep," she said. "That's what is bothering me—I think." She ran a fingertip over the back of the chair. The polished oak felt slick and smooth. "What officially killed Harry?"

The priest sobered, the seed of doubt in his mind clear in his eyes. "The coroner said, 'natural causes.' "

"What does that mean?"

"I'm no sure." He stared into his own glass of milk. "But Harry didn't suffer, Catie. His expression was at peace. Yet—" MacDuff paused, his wrinkles settling into a distinct frown.

"What is it, Father?"

"Nothing really." He shook his head.

"Tell me what you were going to say."

"Well, I've heard about the pallor of death all my life. In my duties, I've seen it many times. The departed look pale and ghostly. Their skin has a waxy look—from the lack of blood circulating, you see. But Harry was . . . pink."

"That isn't common, I take it."

"Nay. Nay, it isn't." He scratched his head. "Funny, until now, that never occurred to me."

Seeing she'd lost the priest's attention, Catie shifted the subject. "Have you seen Jamie?"

"Aye, he left at dawn for the stream. I think, on Thunder, unless it's raining."

Catie swallowed a fresh surge of tears. She was sick to death of crying. "I'm leaving with Andrew in a few hours, and I wanted to tell Jamie. . . ."

"He knows, lass."

She looked into his kind eyes. "Father, what am I going to do? I love Jamie and he hates me."

"Nay, he doesn't. But he's under a lot of pressure right now, lass. If you love him, you'll do what's best for him."

"Leave?"

Father MacDuff didn't answer. His silence screamed inside her mind. She looked down at the floor. "Jamie won't be back before I go, will he?"

"He's busy with clan matters, lass. 'Tis often the case for a laird."

She pressed her lips together to keep them from quivering. "Thank you for your kindnesses, and for that lie. It's the truth that right now I need it." She drew herself up. "I'd best finish packing."

He nodded. "I'll miss you, Catie."

"Will you do something for me?"

"Anything."

Tears trickled down her cheeks. "Will you tell Jamie good-bye for me?"

Again he nodded.

"Thank you." She sniffed. "And will you also tell the clan that I'm sorry about Thomas?"

"No, Catie," he began, his own eyes misty.

"Please." She balled her hands together and pressed them to her chest. "Please, just tell them. I'll pray for Thomas, Father. And for forgiveness."

"I know, lass."

She turned and left the kitchen.

The helicopter's whirring props stirred up a raw wind that chilled Catie to the bone. Standing on the cold ground, her emotions churning, she shivered and looked at Letty. "I'll miss you."

The old woman inhaled deeply. "You'll be back, Catie Morgan. Scotland is in your blood."

Catie hugged her and, feeling Letty tremble, stiffened. "Oh God, this is so hard."

"Aye, it is." Letty sniffed. "I would offer you this advice, dear. Never, in all your life, give up on love. When you can't carry yourself, love will carry you."

"I'll remember."

Catie turned to Father MacDuff and hugged him. His sad eyes shone suspiciously bright. The wind must be bothering him a great deal. "Remember your promises to me, Father."

He cleared his throat. "I'll no forget them, lass."

She nodded, then moved to Celwyn. "Your walk with Colin went well?"

"Aye." Celwyn wrung her hands and started weeping. "Lud, Catie. What arc we gonna do without you?"

"You'll be fine." Catie nearly cried herself. "I wanted you to know," she said, then paused to grip control of her emotions. "I had my perfect Christmas, Celwyn. It was . . . wonderful."

Andrew touched her shoulder. "It's time, Catherine."

She nodded then offered Bronwyn her hand. "Good-bye."

"Good-bye."

Annie sighed. "I'll see you in a few weeks. I'd still rather go home with you now."

"No, I need some time alone."

Her godmother nodded. "Call me."

"I will."

A distant rumbling grew loud. Thunder? Her heart beating hard against her chest wall, she spun around and saw Jamie, astride the huge black stallion, bearing down on her.

Andrew backed up against the helicopter. "Move, Catherine! Move!"

Catie stood fast.

Jamie brought the huge beast to an abrupt halt, so close to her she could feel the air expelled from Thunder's flaring nostrils, feel his heaving sides brush against her arm. She looked up at Jamie and the pain etched in his face shattered her heart.

"I'll wait inside," Andrew said.

"James!" Letty cried, tears streaking down her face. "Don't let this happen. You can't let this happen!"

Father MacDuff wrapped his arm around her shoulder and patted. "There, there, lass. What will be, will be."

Jamie switched to Gaelic. "You forget the diary, Letty. It's my life or Catie's. I love her. By damn, I love her *aw frae the bein*. I canna stop her from going. I canna!"

"Aye, but not like this. She'll hate you!" Letty warned him.

He drew in a sharp breath that swelled his chest. "Aye, she will hate me. But she'll live, Letty. She'll live!"

God, how Catie wished she knew what he'd felt so deeply. Except for his 'all from the bone' phrase, she'd understood nothing. As soon as she got home she vowed she'd learn Gaelic, to speak and to translate it.

"Catherine," Andrew called from inside the helicopter. "We'll miss our flight."

Her heart thundering, she touched Jamie's bare thigh and

looked up at him, looking down at her. And she cried. She didn't care that he saw her tears, that her pride lay tattered. She loved him and she was losing him. And she couldn't *not lose him.* "Jamie, tell me you came. Tell me, after. *Please!"*

"Oh God, love, I canna." He lifted her into his arms and crushed her to him. "I canna, but, if I could, I'd give all I own to give you the words." He kissed her temple. "I'll miss you, love, *aw frae the bein."*

His clan. He was banning her out of duty to his people. Because he both loved and hated her. The man and the laird couldn't separate, couldn't overcome, and couldn't reconcile. She sobbed into his chest and touched his beard. "I'll miss you more, Jamie."

He kissed her tenderly, pressed a white clover into her hand, then curled her fingers closed around it. "Be happy, Catie Morgan. I'll be having your word."

"Not without you. How can I be happy without you?"

"I'm begging you, Catie. For me, please."

Jamie begging? The pain in his voice ripped her heart to shreds. And because she knew how much that cost him, knew how badly he needed the lie, she gave it to him. Biting her lip, she touched his wonderful beard one last time. "Aye, Jamie." She glimpsed her sachet, peeking out of his jacket pocket. "You have my word."

"Catherine," Andrew called again.

"Jamie, why?" Her voice grew urgent, despondent. "Why are you sending me away?" He had to feel something for her or he wouldn't be here, not like this, not hurting every bit as much as she was hurting. "Why are you doing this to us?"

"I have no choice." Jamie clenched his jaw and put her down on the ground. His expression grew hard, determined. "I have no choice."

Thomas. The clan. Love and hate. Hopeless, she turned then stumbled to the helicopter, but hearing Thunder's hooves pound the earth, she gave in, willing to suffer any amount of pain for just one more look at him.

Thunder reared, and man and beast struck the magnificent pose portrayed in the hall's painting of James. Catie drank in the sight, greedily snatched it into her heart, and held it captive there. God help her, this would be her last glimpse of him forever. And she took comfort in knowing that her heart would recall vividly every detail. Every detail. "I love you, Jamie," she whispered the words he'd wanted and now never would hear her say, then stepped into the helicopter.

The bitch isn't dead, but her leaving is just as good. You're devastated, eh, Cameron?

You gave her white clover. The Yank didn't understand the meaning, but I do. "Think of me." You were telling her goodbye forever, and she didn't even know it.

Her heart remains here with you. Your heart has gone with her. How tender. How touching. How perfect . . . for me.

I can now proceed with my plans. First I'll see to your flock, I think. Nay, nay, first the Ferguson. You see, I've been instructing him in his opinions, through my emissary, of course. And she's done an admirable job with him. However, he's failed me. And for that, the fool will soon learn the penalty.

A good dose of death should do the trick, eh?

The question is, Whose death?

His?

His woman's?

Or both?

It doesn't matter really. Regardless of who dies, the blame will be yours.

Thirteen

Annie crossed her chest with her arms. "All right, Letty Cameron, I've had it."

Letty rubbed at her forehead and gave the cross above the altar a last pleading look, then hauled herself up from her knees to her feet. "When a body's praying, Annie, you could be a wee bit more patient, I'm thinking."

Annie dipped her chin and stared at Letty over the top of her glasses. "This castle has been like a tomb since Catie left. James is miserable. You're worried sick. Every time I've talked with Catie, I can tell that, even though six months have passed, she's not stopped missing James. And Celwyn and the good Father MacDuff are moping around looking less chipper than the Grim Reaper."

Letty groaned. "Go home, Annie."

"You've been telling me that since December. It's now June. And, unless you tell me what the devil is going on around here, you'll still be telling me to go home come next June."

"It's nothing you can do anything about. I vow it. Please, just let the matter rest." Letty walked to the bench then plopped down. Lord, what would Harry do? She'd prayed and prayed for answers, but none came. Holding on to her faith was proving harder by the day. Especially when she looked into James's eyes and saw the pain and emptiness he felt. His desolation broke heir heart.

"Letty!"

She looked up at Annie. "We have to keep praying, keep believing that everything will settle right. That's all any of us can do."

Annie grimaced. "My goddaughter's suffering, Letty Cameron. She loves your grandson. You called him to stop her from ruining her life with Andrew. Now she's back with Andrew, her heart is with your grandson, and she's suffering more. We can't just pray. We've got to *do* something."

"James loves her, too," Letty said sharply, responding to Annie's censure. "Can't you see that?"

"Well, why are we just standing around, letting them hurt for each other? If they lack the sense to set matters straight, then we should do it for them. We can't go on doing nothing."

"Nothing is *exactly* what we're going to do. We've no choice."

Annie frowned. Letty had spoken to her hands, and her shoulders had slumped. Letty Cameron hadn't slumped her shoulders in her life. Annie plopped down beside her friend and stared open-mouthed. "I don't believe you're saying this. They're hurting, Letty."

"Didn't you hear me? We've got no choice."

"Why don't we?"

"James had to let Catie go."

"Because of Thomas and how the clan would feel?"

"Nay, Thomas had nothing to do with it."

"Then why?"

Sighing her resignation, Letty went to the priest's hole. She scraped her knuckles removing the stone, but finally retrieved Catherine Morgan's diary, then passed it to Annie. "Read this, and then you'll understand."

In the hall, a trembling Annie found James rocking in his chair and staring into the fire. She wrapped herself with her arms. "It's cold tonight, isn't it?" After reading the diary, would she ever feel warm again?

He didn't look at her, or answer.

Annie swallowed and persisted, needing to speak her mind whether or not James wanted to hear what she had to say. "I know you're hurting, James. And now I understand why."

Silence.

She licked her lips. "Please talk to me."

"I canna." His Adam's apple bobbed and his knuckles on the chair arms went white. "I'm knowing you're meaning well, Annie, but this pain runs too deep. It's best left inside me."

"I know about the diary." Her voice came out as a mere whisper.

He didn't so much as blink. Just stared into the fire, looking as lonely and lost and as hollow as Catie sounded on the phone.

"Then you're knowing why she can never return to Cameron, or to me."

"You could go to her."

"I canna. I'm laird here. My first duty is to my people."

"I don't know that Catie shouldn't come back to you." Still he didn't look from the fire, but determined, Annie went on. "What I do know is that you and Letty, Father MacDuff, and everyone else around here, including me, knows about the diary. Everyone except the one person who ought to know about it."

James looked at her then, his torment riddling his eyes with deep and distorting shadows.

"Oh, James." She cupped his jaw in her hand. "Everyone is making decisions about a life except the one person best able to make those decisions because the life being decided is hers. Catie is in pain, dear heart. She believes you love and hate her. She believes it's her fault Thomas is dead. I've shamed her for that, but I shame you for it, too. Her guilt is understandable, if unjust. But your shame is greater.

You've let her suffer that guilt without lifting a finger to stop it."

"I love her, Annie. I *love* her. Can't you see? I had to let her believe those things or she'd no leave me and go where she would be safe."

"Don't you dare tell me you love Catherine. Don't you dare." Annie narrowed her gaze. "You can lie to yourself, James Cameron, but you will not lie to me. You don't love my goddaughter. If you did, you'd tell her the truth. You'd trust her to do what *she* thought best. You'd work this out *with* her, not decide *for* her. And if you loved her, you would never, never, let her suffer like this, James."

"By damn, woman, don't you understand? I've no choice. Catie loves me. She'd damn the risks and come home. She'd come home, Annie, and I'd lose her forever." Pain contorted his face, agony riddled his eyes. "I canna wake up of a morn and know I'm living in a world without her. I canna do it, Annie!" He leaned forward, buried his face in his hands, and his broad shoulders shook. "I canna do it. . . ."

Annie touched her hand to his back, softened her voice. "It should be her decision too, dear heart. It's her life, and she has a right to know."

He glared up at her, his expression raw, his voice lethal. "Are you wanting her dead? If I bring her home, I'll be killing her, Annie. Just as surely as if I'd run her through with a sword, I'd be killing her. That's what you're asking me to do here, damn it, and I willna kill her. I willna kill her."

Annie shook her head. "Do you want her married to Andrew?"

"Aye. If marrying him will keep her alive, by God, I do."

Annie sat down on the hearth's stone ledge. The fire warmed her back. "There's something you don't understand. To Catie, marriage to Andrew and death are one and the same. Before you go through with this without telling her, think about that. Think with your heart. And you think while knowing that, regardless of the risks and dangers to you both, one thing will never change. You love each other, my dear, and even death doesn't kill love. You have proof of that right here in your castle. Look at Letty and Harry." She paused and squeezed James's shoulder. "Love burns on until the spirit dies." A tear rolled down Annie's wrinkled cheek. "Regardless of where Catie is, without you, her spirit will die."

"Nay. She promised me she'd be happy." Panic etched his voice. "She promised."

"She lied."

James stilled.

"Tell her the truth, my dear. Let Catie decide the course of her own life. You've no right to decide for her. Andrew learned that by losing her. Don't you lose her, too."

Jamie crushed Catie's heather sachet in his fist. The scent roused strong memories of her that had his heart numb. He lay abed, staring blindly at his chamber ceiling. Zeus and Cricket lay near the crackling fire, their shadows elongated on the beamed wood. The homey sounds, so comforting all his life, seemed hollow now. As empty as his heart.

June. Only June? It seemed Catie had been gone forever. He dreaded the days, but God, how he hated the nights. The hours stretched ahead of him, crept by slowly, forcing him to remember, to relive over and over every moment he'd spent with Catie.

But more than the nights, he hated his bed. She'd been here with him. Shared herself, accepted him, loved him. God, how she'd loved him. And, every night, he awakened reaching for her and, on opening his eyes, he'd see her standing by the window, looking out onto the bailey courtyard. He'd hear her sniffle, and know once again that her tears were poignant ones, tears she cried because he'd touched her heart. And when he awakened in the mornings, the first words he heard were hers, nagging him to fly her damn Yank flag. He regretted he hadn't given her that. And then the memories of her in his arms, loving him, would flood his mind and he'd drown in them until they disappeared, leaving only the cold emptiness that chilled his soul to ice.

Cricket came to his side of the bed, whined, then went to the door leading to Catie's chamber. Jamie's heart wrenched and he squeezed her sachet until little specks of crushed potpourri sprinkled onto his chest. "She's gone, lad."

The dog groaned a pitiful growl and scratched at the door. Zeus lay by the fireplace, looking as forlorn as Jamie felt.

Catie was gone. She wasn't coming back. She was with Andrew now.

And again, Jamie felt empty and alone.

When Jamie became aware of his surroundings, Catie was making love to him.

Though more asleep than awake, he knew he lay flat on his back, fully aroused. His chamber as black as pitch, he strained to make out her silhouette but couldn't and, afraid that this was a dream, that if he moved she'd disappear, Jamie lay still, closed his eyes, and savored.

Her mouth seared him. He dug his fingers into the sheets and twisted them in his fists. She placed something in the center of his chest. Heather. Her sachet? Nay. Nay, it lay on the nightstand. When she shifted and impaled herself on him, he broke out in a sweat that soon ran in rivulets down his chest, and he nearly cried out. This wasn't happening. It was a dream. Aye, a dream. He doubled his efforts to remain still, to not do anything to jar himself awake.

Catie said nothing, just moved on his body, her hands at his shoulders, the heather crushed between them. Harder and harder she thrust, lifting him higher and higher, closer and closer to climax. Unable to stand the stillness, he reached for her. His hands cupped the curve of her shoulders, then slid over her skin up to her neck. Something felt odd, but she'd taken him too high; he couldn't concentrate intently enough to figure out what. The pressure in his loins grew furied and intense. So intense. "I'm going to come to you, Catie," he rasped on ragged breaths. "Are you ready, love?"

"Yes. Yes, James," she whispered huskily. "Come now."

He let go, crying out her name. Her spasms blended with his own, and he reveled in fulfillment.

Too soon, she lifted herself off of him. "Catie," he reached out, but she eluded him. "Don't go. I'm of a mind to hold you, lass."

"Sleep, James," she whispered. "You've no been sleeping well. That's why I came. I'll always come to you."

Depleted and exhausted, Jamie closed his eyes. "And after, Catie."

"Aye, after." She stroked his damp forehead, her hand steady and as cold as ice. "Rest now. Rest. . . ."

Before the words died in the night, Jamie lay fast asleep.

Just after dawn, Iain yelled and banged on the chamber door, awakening Jamie. "Laird? Laird?"

"Aye, come in, Iain." Groggy, Jamie rubbed at his jaw and sat up in bed. The sheets tangled around his legs. He shook himself loose, looked up at Iain, and frowned. "What's wrong?"

"I've just come from the village. One of the Ferguson's men is dead."

"What happened to him?" Naked, Jamie stood up and reached for his kilt. Why the hell did he smell heather? He glanced at the nightstand. Ah, Catie's sachet.

"He drank from the Ferguson's flask."

Jamie stilled. "Cyanide?"

"Aye." Iain confirmed Jamie's suspicion. "That's what Dr. Patrick is saying."

Jamie grabbed his boots, sat down on the side of the bed, then jerked them onto his feet. "Are they knowing who's responsible?"

"Nay." Iain shifted, looking uncomfortable.

"But MacPherson is saying that, since his and Ferguson's tests agreed with Kirkland's and not yours, you tried poisoning Ferguson to prove the loch water was unsafe. MacPherson's saying he has proof."

How could he have proof of something that never happened? "What proof?"

"That, he wouldna say."

Jamie grimaced. "Leave it to MacPherson."

"Aye," Iain muttered. "The cut-throat bastard."

"Have Thunder saddled and meet me out front."

Iain nodded, then left the chamber.

Jamie reached for his shirt and saw a sprig of crushed heather in his bed. He stopped and stared at it, his stomach furling. It hadn't been a dream. Catie had come to him.

He ran to her chamber door, then jerked it open. "Catie?"

Cold. Dark. Empty. He looked back at the flower. She had been here. They'd made love. Yes. She'd said her Yank yes. And she'd called him James.

He frowned. The only time Catie Morgan called him James was when he'd pricked her temper. Then that something strange he'd felt when they'd made love hit him. The woman who had come to him had come bare-throated.

Again Jamie saw Catie holding her medallion between her fingers. Again he heard her telling him that it had been a gift from her father, that she wore it always.

He'd had sex, aye, but he'd not made love with Catie.

Feeling violated, Jamie quit his chamber and headed down the stairs. Before he reached the bottom step, he decided he had to know for certain. He sat down in his rocker, then dialed the phone.

She answered on the second ring. "Hello?"

His throat went dry. It hadn't been her in his bed. Along with a strong surge of disappointment, he wondered, Who, then had come to him?

"Hello," she repeated.

Jamie squeezed his eyes shut and savored the sound of her voice. God, what he would give to see her just one more time. To feel her hands on his beard, just . . . one more time.

"Just a minute, Andrew. No, I don't know who it is."

Andrew. Jamie's hand shook. He swallowed hard and forced himself to replace the receiver.

Long after she heard the disconnecting click, Catie held the phone to her ear. She had to hang up. Her hand was shaking. Why couldn't she make herself hang up? Had it been Jamie?

Andrew walked over. Hearing the dial tone's droning buzz, he pried her fingers from the receiver, then put it down. "He isn't going to call, Catherine. It's been nearly six months."

She stiffened her shoulders, bracing for the pain, then let her hope die. Again. "I know."

Andrew turned her to face him with a hand to her shoulder. "He doesn't want you. Accept that and let's get on with our lives. Marry me." His voice changed to an urgent whisper. "Your Scottish barbarian is no Lochinvar. He isn't coming after you. But I'm here. Marry me, Catherine."

Catie clenched her jaw. "I don't want anyone else, Andrew. I've said it again and again. Why don't you hear me?"

He let out an exasperated sigh. "I hear you. I've always heard you. I just can't believe that rather than marry me, you'd choose to spend your life alone, lusting after a savage who screwed you then threw you out!"

Catie slapped him hard. Her fingers stung. His cheek bleached white then stained red with the imprint of her hand. "How I spend my life is none of your business. Nothing I do is any of your business. Shut up and butt out of my private life, Andrew Huntley. Do you understand me?"

"I'm sorry, Catherine." He rubbed at his jaw. "That was crude."

"Don't, okay? You were wrong, but at least you were honest. Maybe for the first time ever, you were truly honest with me about how you feel. For God's sake don't apologize and ruin it." She jerked away. "Look, just let me sign the damn papers so you can go."

He walked over to the desk, then held out a pen. "The firm's assets have doubled since I took over."

"So I see." She scribbled her signature at the check marks, then looked up. "Do you want to buy me out?"

"Yes, I do. I can't stand seeing what he's doing to you. What you're letting him to do you."

"Fine." She dropped the pen. "Have an outside attorney draft the documents."

Andrew gathered up the papers, then slid them into a manila envelope. "You don't want to see me again, do you?"

"I'd rather not, no."

He nodded. "Catherine, I know you love James, but you can't let him destroy your life."

"Destroy it? Andrew, Jamie *is* my life. He's all that matters to me." She gave Andrew a wistful smile, tears slipping to her cheeks. "That's what you don't understand. Without him, nothing much matters. He didn't screw me and throw me out. He—"

"The hell he didn't."

Clenching her jaw, she insisted. "He had no choice."

"God, you're so naïve." Andrew shook his head. "How can you believe that nonsense?"

"It isn't nonsense, and I believe it with all my heart. Jamie keeps his promises, and he promised he'd love me forever."

"Jamie *used* you," Andrew argued. "And, contrary to what you're saying, you are letting him destroy you."

She gave him a negative nod. "No. No, Jamie showed me what love between a man and woman should be. Precious and beautiful." She gave Andrew a little shrug. "I miss it. I miss him. But I won't settle for less. Not now that I know what love can be like."

Realization that it was over between them lit in Andrew's eyes. "I hope some day you find love again, Catie."

Catie. Not *Catherine*. She gave him a genuine smile. "Thank you." The words sounded normal, but she knew they were empty. She loved Jamie. That kind of love came to a woman—a very lucky woman—only once. "I hope you do, too."

Looking as guilty as sin, he rested his forehead against the door. "I promised not to tell you this, but since things between us are over, I can't see why I shouldn't."

"What?"

"James asked me to bring you home to protect you. It wasn't that he didn't want you. He didn't think you were safe."

Her heart lurched. "He did *what?*"

"That's all I'm saying. If you want to know anything more, you'll have to talk to James."

Andrew walked out, then pulled the door shut.

It had been the longest six months of her life. With Annie still in Scotland, Catie had rambled around the huge house alone. In her suite, she gave the phone a forlorn look, lifted Jamie's photo from the piano, then touched the flat glass and remembered the feel of his beard. And in her mind, she recalled his voice. *Would you mind if of an eve I called you about her? When a man's worrying about his kin . . .*

Why not? Why shouldn't she check on her godmother? Annie was the only family she had left, and Scots didn't hold exclusive rights on worrying about their kin.

Catie paced the floor. Jamie's asking Andrew to bring her home didn't strike her as odd. But him asking Andrew to protect her, did. Especially when she coupled that with Jamie telling her he had no choice but to send her away. He had called her "love" and he had wished he could give her the words to make her stay. This wasn't about the clan or forgiving her for what had happened to Thomas. It wasn't

about Jamie, the man, and Jamie, the laird, being at war
with himself, loving and hating her. At least not solely.

At 3:00 A.M. she placed the call. Old habits die hard.

When Jamie answered, she nearly lost her nerve. Oh, God.
Just to hear his voice. Just to—

"Hello?" he repeated. "Catie?"

He knew. She couldn't talk. An ache so sweet blocked
her throat. She squeezed the receiver so hard she ached,
hand to elbow.

"Catie, love. Is that you?"

Love. He didn't mean it, not as he once had, but she had
heard hope in his voice.

"Are you kay-oh, darling?"

She bit her lip and put her hand at her thumping chest.
God, this hurt. "Okay," she corrected him.

"Whatever! Are you well is what I'm wanting to know."

"I needed to hear your voice." She bunched up a portion
of the quilt in her fist. She needed so much more.

"Is Sir Andrew there?"

"Nay." Annie clearly hadn't told Jamie that there had been
no reconciliation. "How's Annie, Jamie?" Catie finally managed.

"Fine."

Brisk. Curt. Well hell, what had she expected? That the
man would welcome her with open arms? She dipped her
chin and ploughed on, repeating the words he'd once said
to her. "Um, I was wondering. Would you mind me calling
you of an evening to see about her? Annie's not understanding about my worrying, Jamie. But I am worried."

He didn't answer.

Her hand on the phone grew clammy and she squeezed
her eyes shut. *Please, God,* she silently prayed. *Give me
this. Just let him talk to me. Let me hear his voice.*

"I'm knowing Annie phones you twice a week, Catie."
Jamie blew out a sigh that crackled through the phone and,

she swore, ruffled the tiny hairs on her neck. "What's Sir Andrew done to you, lass?"

Catie. He'd called her *Catie.* A tiny flicker of hope sprang to life. "Nothing."

"Nothing?" Jamie sounded shocked.

She gave the receiver a quizzical look. "Nay, Jamie. Nothing."

"Well, what the hell is wrong with the man, then? Bah! Never mind. He's English, and that's that. Give me his number, love. I'll have a chat with him and explain his duties to the man."

She didn't know whether to laugh or cry. Jamie sounded angry, but he wanted Andrew to do his duties? Could that be? "No, Jamie. I—I mean Andrew hasn't done anything wrong."

"Oh."

How could one word express so many emotions? Relief. Disappointment. Regret. The implication that Andrew had been doing something right hung between them.

"Catie, why are you calling me, darling?"

She sobbed. She tried not to, but she just couldn't help it. "I miss you, Jamie. I know you hate me because . . . of Thomas, and I know . . . you don't . . . want me, but . . . I . . . miss . . . you."

"Catie, don't cry, love. You know I hate your tears."

"I'm trying to . . . stop, Jamie. Really, I am. I think . . . something happened to me . . . in Scotland. I've turned into a woman who . . . goes on crying jags . . . at a blink. I . . . hate . . . it."

"Catie, please."

Rally! She demanded herself to stop sobbing. Rally! "Oh, Jamie. I know I'm not handling this very well. But can we please just talk? Just until I get used to losing you? I know women aren't supposed to be saying these things but, damn it, I feel them. When I lost you, I lost my love and my best friend. I hurt." She sniffed again. "I hurt . . . so bad, and . . . I . . . need . . . you."

"I'm knowing, love." He went quiet, then talked on. "Have you discussed this with Sir Andrew, darling? If you're needing soothing, he's the man you should be turning to, I'm thinking."

He didn't want even this between them. Not even this. Oh God, how could she stand it? She forced a strength into her voice she didn't feel. "I'm, um, sorry I bothered you. Don't worry. I-I won't call again."

She hung up the phone.

It rang minutes later. Half an hour after that. It rang at five, again at six, and at seven.

Then it stopped ringing.

Jamie sat in his rocker and stared at the fire. Just before 3: 00 A.M. New Orleans time, he lost the battle. Catie might be with Sir Andrew. He might be doing nothing wrong. God, how it hurt to know he could be doing something right. Jamie might be doing what he had to do to protect her. But there were two things he couldn't do.

He couldn't stop missing her.

And he couldn't stop loving her.

His darling ally was hurting. And he'd promised to always soothe her, whenever she was hurt or afraid and, if she was feeling a grain of all he did, she was suffering a lion's share of both.

Before he remembered all of the reasons he shouldn't, he called her.

"Jamie?" She sounded breathless.

He forced his voice light. "Ah, Catie, lass. And how are you this fine eve, I'm asking?"

"Better."

He heard the smile in her voice. "Better is good, I'm thinking." So much inside him lay simmering, waiting to be shared. Because he couldn't, he settled for what he could share with her.

"And you?" she asked.

"Better." God, but she sounded wonderful.

"How are—"

"How are—"

"You first," he said, smiling. That, too, felt good. It had been a long time since he'd been of a mind to smile.

"Nay, you."

The woman was Scots to the bone. Converted, pure and simple. "Catie, darling, it's time for being honest. This call has naught to do with Annie, nor Letty, nor MacDuff, nor Celwyn, nor Cricket, nor anyone else—not even Bronwyn the Terrible. This has to do with you and me. Truth is truth, and I'm missing you something fierce, lass."

"God, Jamie. I've missed you, too."

She was crying; he could hear it in her voice, feel it deep inside. Looking into the fire, he remembered the nights he'd rocked her in his arms, the night he'd held her here and explained what being an ally meant to him. God, how he ached to hold her. "I'd like to call you of an eve . . . to talk. Would you be of a mind to agree, love?"

"Aye, I would." She paused. "Jamie, what does the clover mean?"

He smiled. So she had gotten the white clover. He'd sent it to her every Monday since she'd gone. No card, no words. Only the clover. "It's a mystery, lass. We Scots love mysteries."

"I looked it up." Her voice grew deep. "Is it the same in Scotland as it is here?"

He closed his eyes. "Think of me."

"Oh God."

His eyes snapped open. "Catie?"

No answer.

"Catie, talk to me."

Silence.

"Are you crying, love?" He straightened in the rocker. "Catie?" A searing ache ripped through his chest. His eyes burned and a hot tear rolled down his face to his beard. "Please, Catie, don't be crying, lass. It—"

"I've thought about you, Jamie." She sniffled, then yelled lustily. "I should reach through this damn phone and beat you bloody."

Jamie smiled. The fire's flames blurred. He blinked to set them to rights. She was fine. "Ah, now you're getting violent. And you were the one always saying Scots were the bloodthirsty barbarians. You hated stories with blood in them, too. Remember James?"

"This isn't a story, damn it. This is our lives!"

"True."

"Well, what the hell are you doing, then? You can't wait to get rid of me. Then you send me these clovers to keep my heart broken, and now you say you miss me. I should do something God-awful to you, James Cameron."

"Of course, your heart has suffered. You're engaged to an Englishman, I would remind you. If that flaw isn't enough to break a woman's heart, I'm confounded as to what is." He grunted lustily. "The English make lousy lovers, Catie. 'Tis a well-known fact that they lack the passion for loving. Now, the Scots—"

"I agree," she interrupted. "Yours is a lusty, hot-blooded breed."

"Aye. 'Tis good of you to finally notice, I'm thinking."

Catie seriously considered scorching his ears. She lay down on her bed and growled. "Oh, I noticed."

"Of course, lass. You're a lusty wisp of a woman yourself . . . for a Yank."

"For a Yank, Jamie?"

"Now, don't go getting floppy, darling. I was meaning, for any woman."

"You said Yank. Specifically."

"Aye, but I was meaning any, so help me."

"You're lying," she said. "But I forgive you. You are an inferior Scot, after all."

"I think we have to redefine our alliance, Catie."

Redefine? Her heart nearly stopped. Catie clutched her pillow. "Jamie, please don't tell me you hate me. I can take almost anything, but I can't take that."

"You're forgetting that you're a strong woman, I'm thinking."

"You've said that before, but it wasn't true then, and it's not true now. I hurt, Jamie. I hurt like I never knew a body could hurt."

"I guess it's good then that your ally is strong enough for both of us, eh?"

"My . . . ally?" She put her hand to her throat. "Are you still my ally, Jamie?"

"I'm wanting you to listen to me—with your heart—and never forget what I'm about to say to you, Catie. Promise me."

"I promise." She stiffened on the bed, terrified that she was about to lose him again.

"Catie, I'm of a mind to love you, lass." His voice shook with emotion. "Before, during, and after. Since the first time we talked on the phone, in my heart, you've been my ally. And you will go on being my ally until the day I die. But I canna—"

"You don't hate me," she said breathlessly. "You don't blame me for Thomas, either."

"Hate my ally?" He blew out a sigh he obviously meant for her to hear. "I'm sure I explained our alliance clearly. Aye, by damn, I know I did. Dinna I tell you, woman, that an ally is always there for his ally? Good times and bad. Skinned or on the hoof?"

A communication foul-up? Slang? Surely it couldn't be that simple. She sat up in bed. "But then why did you—"

"I told you, I had no choice, darling. You had to leave Cameron."

"Because of the attacks. The threats on my life." She

groaned. It was all so clear now. "Damn it, Jamie, I think I will beat you bloody."

"Nay, that was but part of it, though no wee part you should sniffle at, I'm saying. But were it that alone, I'd have kept you guarded or at my side until I'd killed the threat."

He'd given her back to Andrew so she'd be safe. Jamie had been there for her, acted as a proper ally, sacrificed her to protect her. She stared daggers at his photo. "I'm coming home."

Silence.

"Did you hear me, Jamie?"

No answer.

"At the fire, I came. You said I belong with you. You said you wanted me with you, holding you forever. You don't lie and you didn't break your promise. Scots don't lie, and why the hell it took me six months to figure this out, I don't know. But I understand now. Scots don't lie, and I'm coming home, Jamie."

"Not now, darling. Please."

The fear in his voice shook her to her roots. Jamie feared little. Until this moment, she would have sworn he feared nothing. "Are you telling me you did lie? That you don't want me with you anymore?"

"I'll no lie to you ever, love. I'm wanting you—God, how I'm wanting you—but the matter is complicated, lass. I canna—" He sighed his frustration. "I canna explain, Catie. I would ask you to trust me."

Trust him? For her own good or not, he'd broken her heart, let her suffer through six months of sheer hell, and now he wanted her to trust him?

"I'm wanting your word. Tell me you won't come home." The fear in his voice grew stronger, more urgent. "Swear it, love."

She frowned at the receiver, confused and shaken. "Then you come to me. I need you, Jamie."

"I canna. Odd things are happening, lass, and my duties are here."

"What odd things?" A shiver crept up her spine, and the roof of her mouth tingled.

"Someone attempted to murder the Ferguson."

"Colin?" Her heart raced. "Poor Celwyn must be terrified."

"Aye. The woman's required a fair amount of soothing, according to Ferguson. His water flask was poisoned. One of his clansmen drank from it, Catie. He died."

"Cyanide." Just like the loch. She knew it as well as she knew Jamie's test results on the loch water were the only accurate ones.

"Aye." The hairs on Jamie's neck stood on end. How had Catie known that?

"Was Harry's milk checked for cyanide?"

"Harry?" Jamie set his coffee cup back on the little table at his elbow. "Elwin—"

"Who is he?"

"The coroner. He said—"

"I know what he said, Jamie. But ask Iain about it for me, okay?"

"Harry was eighty years old, love. He went to sleep."

"He drank warm milk, every night. He read Cameron history, every night. He hadn't been sick. Think about that, Jamie." She let out an exasperated sigh. "Do you know even one stubborn Scot who would die in his sleep without a whimper?"

Jamie stilled the cup midway to his mouth and frowned through the steam. "I'll ask Iain."

"Promise me."

"I've said I will. That *is* a promise." The lass had a valid point about Harry. The man never had done anything quietly. Would he die without a ruckus? Nay, he wouldn't. Why hadn't that occurred to Jamie? "Aside from you questioning my honor again, I'm having the feeling you're knowing something you're not telling me, Catie. I dinna care for the feeling."

"I don't know anything for fact," she said. "But I have this horrible feeling Harry's death was no accident."

"Why?" An eerie belief that she was right settled deep in Jamie's belly.

"Harry was healthy. He was still crazy about Letty. He was a content man, Jamie. A lusty, content Scot doesn't just die quietly in his sleep."

"You're lying to me. Aye, omission is lying, darling." Cricket brushed against his leg and propped his head on Jamie's knee. The pup was missing Catie. Jamie patted him and scratched Cricket's ears. "What else?"

"Harry drank warm milk every night before bed, right?"

"Aye."

"He read Cameron history every night before bed, right?"

"Aye, 'tis common knowledge, darling."

"Exactly."

He frowned. The woman's mind was warped. "Exactly what are you meaning, I'm asking?"

"Habits, Jamie. Commonly known habits. He was healthy—just like your parents."

"My parents?" A shiver raced up his spine and slammed into the roof of his mouth.

"Aye. Don't you think it all odd, Jamie? Even a little extraordinary? Your parents were perfectly healthy people with better sense than to swim in the loch in the dead of winter. Yet they drowned swimming. And Harry went to bed perfectly healthy, yet he died in his sleep."

Every muscle in Jamie's body clenched. "Are you suggesting they were murdered?"

"I'm not suggesting anything. I'm saying it's odd. When you add me coming to Cameron and having two attempts made on my life, Thomas being killed while guarding me, and now the Ferguson's man—well, it's odd, Jamie. Pure and simple."

"People die, lass."

"I know that. But it seems to me there's a lot of *healthy* people dying. And all of them have one thing in common."

"What?"

"You."

"How does the Ferguson tie to me, I'm asking?"

"Through Celwyn. All right, in a fashion, they're all connected to you." Catie sighed, seeing the stretch from Jamie's maid to the Ferguson laird something Jamie hadn't considered significant to this problem. "Something else, too."

Jamie was almost afraid to ask. "Mmm?"

"Have you noticed that many of the deaths have to do with liquids? With cyanide?"

Jamie thought about that. "I'll ask Iain about Harry's milk first thing in the morning. But I must tell you, love, that the coroner's reports term Harry's death—"

"Natural causes."

"Aye, my parents, too."

"I know. Father MacDuff told me. That has me wondering, too, Jamie. Pink skin and the smell of almonds are indicative of cyanide poisoning. I looked it up."

"What the hell does that have to do with Harry?" This set of circumstances grew more bizarre by the minute.

"Father MacDuff said Harry didn't have the ghostly pallor of death. His skin was pink."

"Aye, 'twas. I recall."

"Were your parents pink-skinned, too?"

Jamie sat straight up. "Oh God."

"I'm coming home."

"Nay. Nay, darling, you canna. What about Sir Andrew?"

"We're talking about murder here, Jamie. Your family. My allies. What the hell does Andrew—"

Cricket perked up his ears and slid under Jamie's feet, diving for cover. Aye, the pup had heard Catie yelling through the phone. "You're to marry the man, I would remind you."

"I'm coming home."

"Nay."

"We're allies. Good times and bad. Skinned or on the hoof."

"Catie, I'll no be—"

You would ask your ally to break Scots tradition?"

Clearly the woman was of a mind to be stubborn, and she had him dead to rights. "Tell me you're still engaged to Sir Andrew."

"Why?"

"Because then that changes things. I *am* connected to all these things, Catie—including the attack on the Kirkland. Sure as certain, you were in danger here because of your relationship with me."

"I'm coming home, damn it, and that's that."

"Things canna be as they were before between us," he warned. "I'll no let you risk your life. You canna ask that of me, love."

"I know it'll have to be different. I won't ask, but I am coming."

"Will you be bringing Sir Andrew with you?"

"No."

"You're talking Yank."

"I *am* a Yank."

Maybe on paper, but not in her heart. He frowned into the fire, his mind whirling. "You have to leave before the festival. I'll no have you here then, and that too is that, Catie."

"Why? Before you wanted me there specifically for the festival."

"Trust me."

She didn't hesitate. "All right."

He smiled. As long as she left before then, she'd be fine. He'd watch every moment and see to it she left Cameron before the diary events started. "When will you come home, love?"

"Tomorrow."

Tomorrow. His sweet Catie. He would see her one more time after all. He should refuse, but the need in him was too great. He'd managed not to call only because he'd hoped she would reconcile with Andrew and Jamie hadn't wanted to interfere. But now he knew the truth. And he could die a content man, seeing her one more time. "Until then, think of me."

Her words rushed out. "Jamie, don't hang up. Not yet."

"Nay, love. You're needing soothing."

"Aye, I am. And I'm thinking you could use a wee bit of soothing yourself."

"That, too." While he had much to do with all these suspicions coming to light, nothing rated more important than seeing to the needs of his ally. He dropped his voice. "Are you in bed, Catie?"

He heard her sharp indrawn breath. "Aye. Are you in your rocker?"

"Aye, darling, I am."

She let out a little whimper. "Are you wearing your kilt?"

"Aye."

"I can't wait to touch your beard, Jamie."

What was he doing here? Had he lost his mind? Harry, his parents, maybe murdered, and Jamie was going to allow his ally to return to Cameron? Nay, he'd been selfish. Blinded by his need to see her. But he couldn't do it. He couldn't see her again and put her in harm's way. He forced his voice hard. "You're hexing me again, Catie. I canna let you come home. It's too dangerous. Even more so, if you're right about my kin."

"I'm coming home, Jamie."

"Nay. I canna have you here and not hold you, love. I canna do it."

"I'm coming home."

"By damn, nay!"

"It's an ally's duty—"

"To respect and trust her ally's judgment. Aye, it is. You will not come home."

"Why?"

"Because I love you, Catie."

"But that's exactly why I should come. You need me."

"Aye, I do. I need you alive and well and safe."

"Jamie. . . ."

"Quit trying to sway me with your soft sexy voice, Catie. Truth is truth, and I know you're to wed Andrew. That's that. But you're in my heart, lass, and you won't let go. I canna put you in danger."

Her own heart soared. He loved her. She was in his heart. He was afraid for her. She'd give in gracefully . . . for now. There was little sense in worrying him a minute longer than necessary. "Will I ever be able to return to Cameron?"

"One day."

"Why not now?"

"Things aren't settled."

"When will they be settled?"

"I'm no sure."

"When will you know?"

"I'm no sure of that, either."

"Jamie?"

"Trust me, love. Please."

"You weren't honest with me." He still wasn't telling her everything. But he would. "You let me leave Cameron thinking you hated me. And you've let me cry my heart out over losing you for six months."

"I was being diplomatic."

"You?"

"Aye, me. Chivalrous, too, by damn. I was protecting you."

His groan roared in her ear. He clearly hadn't meant to disclose that. "Why? What were you protecting me from?" The attacker, but was there more?

"You took seven stitches in your arm, suffered a second attempt on your life, and you must ask me that?"

Catie stared at the receiver. "What aren't you telling me?"

"I've flopped over every loaf in Cameron and have found no evidence that leads to anyone. I'm floundering in dead ends without knowing who tried to harm you."

There was more. Definitely more. "And what else, Jamie?"

"I canna say."

"Can't or won't?"

"Canna."

"All right I'll trust you, then . . . for now. But I—"

"I know." He heaved a sigh that she was sure had hiked his shoulders. "You want me to call."

"Aye."

"I will, lass."

"Promise."

"I said it. Lord, but that's a trying habit of yours, woman, making a man promise everything twice. 'Tis degrading, I'm thinking."

He didn't sound degraded, the darling, arrogant Scot. "Sorry. I'll repay . . . as soon as it's safe."

"Aye, you will that. And you'll no hex me anymore, Catie Morgan. I'm putting my foot down on that—and you'll no hex my animals or my clan, either."

Catie smiled and mimicked his soft, sexy burr. "Sing to me, Jamie."

He groaned. "I just tell the woman not to hex me, and she goes and gets all sleep-soft and sexy-sounding. What's a man to do, Cricket?"

When the dog barked, Catie smiled.

"Kay-oh. Kay-oh. Don't rile yourself into a snit. I'll soothe her."

Catie didn't correct him. "Aye, Cricket's right. I need a lot of soothing, Jamie."

Rather than answer, he began to sing. She listened, welcoming his sweet song into her heart. It had been so long. . . .

Knowing he could be in danger, knowing he could be slated as the next victim, did the man honestly expect her to stay away?

She'd leave first thing in the morning, of course. And she'd bring him heather. *Lonesomeness*. That, too, she'd looked up. She had been lonesome. And, God love his heart, so had her ally.

Tomorrow she'd see him again. And tomorrow night, with luck, she'd be in his arms. He wanted her there. Whether or not he would take the risk of admitting it was another matter, but he did want her there. And heaven knew she didn't want to be anywhere else. Aye, she'd go to his castle, but Jamie would have to come to her bed. He'd sent her away. And while she knew now he still loved her, she also knew he intended to love her from a distance. She could push him, but truth is truth, and she just couldn't take any more rejection from him. He would have to come to her.

Her decision made, she curled up in bed and concentrated on his sweet love song, concentrated on tomorrow, on who could be threatening their lives.

Iain and Bronwyn stood near the coffeepot. Reaching for the sugar, his hand brushed hers, and she smiled up at him. Jamie saw it all, and frowned. The last thing he needed was his second getting hooked up with Bronwyn the Terrible and her muddling his mind. They had too many issues that might well all be connected to consider and resolve.

"Pass the bacon, Celwyn," Father MacDuff said.

"Don't." Letty gave the priest a frown. "Your cholesterol level is already up to two-eighteen. Are you trying to kill yourself, dear?"

Jamie looked across the table and saw the priest frowning back at Letty. MacDuff liked her fussing over him, that was clear. With his mouth, he grimaced, aye, but behind his glasses, his eyes adored. Kirkland and Ferguson noticed, too. Both were eager to be done with breakfast and to move on to discussing these odd matters.

Annie sent Jamie a knowing look. He winked at her. "I talked with Catie last night."

Everyone fell silent. Jamie pretended not to notice.

"Well?" Letty twisted the orange scarf knotted at her throat. "What did she say?"

"About what?" Jamie took a bite of toast.

Letty shot him a look of sheer disgust. "About anything."

"She's wanting to come home."

Celwyn squealed, leaving no doubt about her delight. Jamie silenced her with a sharp look. No one else seemed to react. "She's engaged to Andrew again."

Bronwyn looked totally uninterested. Iain scratched his neck and downed another full glass of orange juice, then scratched his neck. Ferguson and Kirkland masked their feelings on the matter, though Jamie sensed their surprise at Jamie's ally marrying an inferior Englishman. Letty, Mac-Duff, and Annie muttered. Celwyn wrung her hands until her knuckles were raw, and Jamie sighed. One of these people had attacked Catie twice, had meant to kill her, but from their reactions, Jamie couldn't be knowing which one.

Bronwyn poured herself a second cup of coffee. "If she's engaged to Andrew again, then why is Catherine coming back here?"

"To finish her work in the archives," Letty said. "She left in the middle of her duties. I wrote her a scathing letter she'll not soon be forgetting for doing it, too."

Jamie sat back and continued monitoring their reactions. "I've told her to come," he lied. He'd made her promise not to come. Still, his instincts noted nothing uncommon from anyone.

Iain returned to the table, then buttered a slice of toast.

"She's been attacked here twice, James. Surely you've no forgotten that."

"And been marked with the thistle," Kirkland added.

"I've no forgotten any of it. But she was my ally then."

"You broke the alliance?" That from Ferguson.

"She's marrying an Englishman, Colin."

Understanding nodded all around, save Letty, MacDuff, and, of course, Annie.

"Well," Iain said. "At least she'll be in no danger here now."

"Aye," MacDuff agreed.

Jamie prayed it proved true.

That comment started a flurry of conversation. Jamie listened to snatches of it, satisfied now that Catie would be safe here. They had two weeks until the festival. And, though she'd promised him not to come, if he knew his darling ally—he checked his watch—in about six hours, she'd arrive.

I'm sitting at your table, eating your food, and shaking my head at your arrogance, Cameron.

I can't believe you're letting the Yank return. If she's foolish enough to do it, by God, I'll kill her.

I wanted to give you the lion's share of my gifts the week of the festival but, if the bitch is returning, I don't dare to wait. If not for the repeated sloppiness of my competitor, you never would have realized a battle was being fought. I'm sure you've cast blame, if only in your mind and, for that reason, the one most suspect will be eliminated.

I'll use cyanide, of course. On him and on your flock. I want you to know you're being punished. That I can punish you. And I want you to wonder.

Who will die next?

Fourteen

Jamie rode out to the sheep-washing shed, his rifle slung over his knees. Outside the wooden fence, he halted Thunder, and watched Iain, preparing the blackface sheep.

The wind was brisk, and Jamie squinted against it. The sheep looked a dusty gray and, downwind from the flock, he caught the distinct scent of almonds.

"Iain, wait!" Catie had said cyanide smells like almonds. "Dinna wet the sheep!"

Iain shouted the halt order to the other men, dropped the long hose, then walked over to the fence. Dirt smeared across his left cheek. "James?"

"Separate one from the herd and wash only it." Jamie grimaced. "An ewe. And have a care to keep the water off yourself."

"Only one?"

"Aye."

Jamie sat stiff in his saddle, his hand resting on the rifle's stock. Iain lifted the hose and put the water to the ewe's back. The gray washed right off, puddling at the animal's hooves.

"Should we go on with it, James?" Iain called out.

"Nay." Thunder whinnied and sidestepped. Jamie flexed his knees to still the horse, his gaze riveted on the ewe. First, it let out a little bawl, then within seconds it began convulsing.

Jamie warned the gaping men. "Dinna touch her! Dinna touch the water to them, or to yourselves!"

Thunder grew anxious, uneasy. He too smelled death. Jamie patted the horse's neck.

Iain ran back to the fence. "What is it, James?"

"Cyanide." Jamie lifted his rifle and put the ewe down.

"Who?" Iain asked.

Jamie returned his rifle to its place near his knee. "I dinna know."

"MacPherson." Iain expelled an angry oath and slung a cloth to the ground. "Nine hundred years, and that bastard laird still holds to the feud."

Jamie gave Iain a reprimanding look. "We've no proof MacPherson had anything to do with this."

"Aye, we do." Iain looked up at Jamie. "I saw two men in MacPherson colors herding the flock this morn."

"Where?"

"Near the loch. Away from it, actually, which is why I thought nothing of the incident. Your opinion on the loch water ain't exactly a secret among the clans."

Jamie narrowed his eyes. "See to the flock, Iain. Dry wash them."

"Aye," Iain said, giving Jamie a knowing look. "Are you wanting men to go along with you?"

"Nay." Jamie settled in the saddle, preparing to ride. "I'll be seeing to the matter myself."

Jamie spurred Thunder, turned the horse toward the moor leading to MacPherson's. The sounds of a helicopter's props split the chill air. Thunder reared. Jamie shifted his weight easily, in no danger of losing his seat. Still, his heart began a slow, hard beat. *Catie*.

He searched the sky, spotted the helicopter, and watched it set down. The brush and grass bent to the pressure of the wind, and soon Catie stepped out.

The first thing he noticed was her flat stomach. She wasn't

pregnant. He should be happy about that, but disappointment
hit him hard. He'd failed to fulfill her heart's desire.

God, but she looked beautiful.

On the ride to her, he saw her waving her hand, rushing
the pilot to leave. Jamie had to turn his head to hide his
smile. Catie was seeing to it that he couldn't send her back,
at least not right away.

He forced his expression hard. She stood beside her pink
suitcase, her back as straight as a staff, her hands folded
before her, her expression deceptively serene. The blustery
wind caught her pastel pink dress and had it furled in soft
folds at her knees, clinging seductively to her thighs. And
she was wearing her glasses.

Aye, his darling ally was scared stiff, pure and simple.
He'd have to be timid, he supposed. But . . . Now what was
that the trying woman was holding?

He drew closer, flexed his knees, and stopped Thunder
directly at Catie's side. Heather. Lord help him, she'd
brought him heather. He pretended not to notice and cursed
his soft head for telling him he smelled spring grass.

She lifted her face to the sun to look up at him. "Now
before you get angry—stop snarling at me, Jamie. I don't
like it—I want you to listen to what I have to say. I had to
come. You can bellow, rage, glare at me until your eyes
bulge, and you can even call me a Yank, but—"

"You *are* a Yank."

"You know what I mean." She glanced down to his thigh.
"My point is, I am not leaving." She looked back up at his
eyes, but she didn't smile. "I'm never leaving you again."

He could have kissed her—or blistered her backside.
Since he couldn't do one at all, and the other would forfeit
the pretense that she was no longer his ally, he stared at her
instead.

She rolled her gaze, letting him know in her not so subtle
way that his stares didn't bother her even a wee bit, and
stroked Thunder's nose. The damn horse nuzzled her. Evi-

dently, Thunder's reaction to seeing Catie was smarter than his master's. He was getting petted. "Get up here."

She stepped closer, then reached up to him. He lifted her and, seeing her smile, planted her on his thighs, then spurred the horse. "Crazy, damn Yank. I should drop you on your foolish elbow. I knew you'd put yourself in danger to be with me. Didn't I tell you I was being chivalrous in sending you away?"

"Aye, you did."

"Then why did you break your promise? That's a damn sorry thing for an ally to do to her ally, Catie Morgan."

"Technically, I didn't promise not to come home, Jamie." She gave him her witch's smile. "But since you assumed I had, I'll gladly repay."

"I should put you over my knee."

"You wouldn't dare."

"I damn well should."

"Maybe," she agreed. "But you won't."

That, in her singsong voice. The one with the lilt that made him daft. "By damn, Catie. Don't you know that just the thought of you coming to harm ties me in curls?"

"Knots," she corrected.

"Whatever!"

"There's no need to shout, Jamie. I do know, and that's exactly why I'm here." Catie smiled to herself, leaned back against Jamie's chest, and let him rave. He was miffed, pure and simple. But after he let off enough steam to power a paddleboat a thousand miles or so, he'd come around. She should remind him about her luggage, but, nay, she wouldn't. If someone chose to steal her clothes, then she'd just do without. Jamie was annoyed enough without provoking him further. Soothing him wasn't going to be easy but, she sighed contentedly, it was going to be wonderful.

His fingers felt like steel bands on her ribs. She relaxed against his chest and covered his hand with hers. She wouldn't interrupt his fussing to ask where they were going.

He would expect her to, but even when he wasn't roaring at her the man did find her questioning his actions offensive. Since he hadn't once in his rantings mentioned sending her away again, she'd indulge him. They were headed toward the stream, anyway. True, that wasn't her choice of final destinations, but it'd do for now. When they arrived at the babbling, rock-strewn body of water, she'd be in Jamie's arms again, feeling his kiss. And in his arms was her destination of choice—and her destiny.

He stopped beside the stream. His arms tightened around her and she reached back over her shoulder to stroke his beard. Hot honey surged through her veins.

He pressed his face against her hand. "You're wearing Sir Andrew's ring."

"Aye." She swallowed hard. Jamie had given her no choice but to pretend that she and Andrew had reunited.

"Why?"

She glanced back at him.

"Don't lie to me, Catie. You're no marrying the man, or you'd already have tied the bow."

"Tied the knot."

"Whatever!"

She didn't answer his question, and she had no intention of answering it, either. Sooner or later that would occur to the man. If she admitted she wasn't marrying Andrew, Jamie likely would have the helicopter carting her away from Cameron before she could sneeze. But if she said she was marrying Andrew, she'd be lying to Jamie. Either way, he'd be even more furious with her for coming home. He was plenty peeved already, thank you very much. She opted for silence, and just looked at him.

"I've told everyone you're marrying Sir Andrew, lass, and we're no longer allies."

"I thought allies were forever."

"Except when one of them marries an inferior Englishman of her own free will."

"Another tradition." She grunted her thoughts on that. And on him not bothering to entertain the thought that a Scot might marry an Englishwoman of his own free will.

"I'll be having none of your sassing on the matter," Jamie warned her. "I'm protecting you, Catie. Sure as certain you were attacked because of our alliance."

"Why?"

"I'm not sure. But why else would anyone here hurt you, I'm asking?"

"I'm flawed."

"You *were* flawed." His gaze warmed. "You're not anymore."

She loved him for that. "I mean, I'm a Yank."

"Aye, but Scots don't kill Yanks. We just don't like them."

"Charming," she muttered. "And so very diplomatic."

"Aye, but save your compliments for later. We canna be as we were before, love. Not now. There are eyes everywhere—and you're wearing another man's ring, I would remind you."

"So I'm just your historian, back here to finish my work in the archives?" She swatted at a horsefly on Thunder's neck. "Is that what you're saying?"

"Aye. My historian." He stared at her hand, at Andrew's ring.

He resented it being there, and she recalled his opposition to her medallion when he'd believed Andrew had given it to her. Is the ring what had put the strain in Jamie's voice? "Has something else happened?"

He nodded. "The MacPhersons were seen herding me flock away from the loch this morn."

"Why in heaven's name are you letting your sheep go near that pit?" She drew in a sharp breath. "You're not letting them drink—"

"Nay, Catie. Do I look crazed? I'm not knowing how they got there, but Iain saw MacPherson men leading the flock back onto Cameron land."

"Then you should go and thank MacPherson for saving your flock and end the feud."

"Oh, I'm going to thank him, all right."

"Jamie. You've got that look."

"What look?"

"Are you going to give MacPherson hell for saving your flock?"

"That depends."

"The man did you a kindness."

"Dusting my sheep with cyanide is a kindness?"

"Oh God." She swayed and near fell out of the saddle.

Jamie closed the circle of his arms, held her tighter. "I'm sorry, lass. I wasn't of a mind to snap it on you like that."

"Spring," she corrected. "You didn't mean to spring it on me."

"Whatever!"

She turned her head, pressed her cheek flat against his chest. "How many died?"

"Only one. I smelled the almonds."

"Oh, Jamie."

"The poison didn't activate until the ewe was wet down, Catie."

"Wet?" His parents had been wet. They'd drowned in the loch, yet their skin had remained pink.

"Aye. Until it was hosed with water, the ewe wasn't suffering any ill effects."

She frowned. "Jamie, did you ask Iain about Harry's milk?"

"Not yet."

"Damn it, I'll do it myself."

"You've no need to get miffed, lass, and you'll do no such thing. I'll ask him. I've been a wee bit busy with the sheep this morn. That's all."

"I find this all so odd. Your parents and the Ferguson's man, dead because of water. Someone selling the loch water in Edinburgh. Kirkland's attack near the dam, and him vowing the water's safe. He has to know that only an idiot would believe him. Even with multiple tests backing up his absurd claim. And now your sheep." She stared at a dark spot on the toe of Jamie's boot. "That's a lot of incidents involving water, don't you think?"

"Aye, I do. Which is why you must stay engaged to Andrew."

"I haven't said I wasn't engaged to Andrew," she reminded Jamie with an affronted sniff.

"Well, if you are engaged to the man, then you shouldn't be sneaking your hand up under me kilt, I'm saying."

She jerked her hand back from his thigh.

The awful man laughed. "Forgive me, love. Touch me all you want. I forgot your fiancé is English."

"Jamie," she warned him.

He caught her hand and put it firmly on his bare thigh. "Nay, love. Don't be blushing, now. I'm sure you're starving for the feel of a lusty Scot."

"Jamie, I'm in no mood to listen to your—"

"Aye, darling, I'm knowing," he whispered and pulled her hand further up on his thigh, under his kilt. "You're wanting soothing."

"Will you stop?"

He smiled into her hair. "That depends."

"On what?" she asked, clearly annoyed with him.

"On whether or not you're of a mind to compromise." The trying woman attempted to pull back her hand. He refused to let her.

She gave him a resigned sigh. "Terms?"

"Tell me," he demanded.

"Exactly what are you wanting to know, Jamie?" She glanced back at him.

"Are you engaged to Sir Andrew?"

She shrugged. "That depends."

He let her see that she'd displeased him—again. "I'm

saying, either you are or you aren't going to marry the inferior Englishman who has you starved, Catie Morgan."

"I'm weighing the matter," she said, just to annoy him.

It did. And while he stated his particular objections, in minute detail, she ignored him and set her mind to puzzling out this water mess. Someone was out to hurt Jamie. All of the attacks affected him. But who? And why?

Bronwyn, maybe? No, she was too busy flexing her feline claws on any man who looked halfway decent in a kilt to bother. And she'd definitely not attacked Catie. She wasn't as thick, and she lacked the physical strength. Besides, Celwyn had vouched for Bronwyn's whereabouts during the knife attack. Iain? If Jamie died before fathering an heir, Iain would gain most. He'd become laird. But he'd taken the Cameron water sample to Edinburgh and had gotten accurate results, and him killing the flock reeked of him cutting off his nose to spite his face. Iain wouldn't kill what would become his own flock. There'd be little left to inherit. Celwyn? She seemed a highly unlikely candidate. Absurd, even. Letty? Father MacDuff? Ridiculous, Catie decided. Ferguson? Possible, but only barely. Celwyn said he was a good man and Jamie had spoken often of him being a good man, only inexperienced. Kirkland? Maybe. Jamie strongly opposed the dam and the laird was greedy. But Kirkland had been attacked. Though he could have set that up to remove suspicion from himself as a suspect. MacPherson?

Catie blinked, pegging her candidate.

"I'm feeling slighted here, woman. By damn, insulted, too," Jamie said. "You're ignoring me, I'm thinking."

"We should get home, love," Catie said, not concentrating on what she was saying but on how she could arrange a meeting with the MacPherson.

Jamie didn't move. She glanced back at him. He seemed stunned. What had she said? Done? Her hands were on the saddle, it couldn't have been that "Jamie?"

"I'm wanting to kiss you, Catie."

"You can't."

"Why the hell not?" He sent her a grumpy frown she adored. "I'm knowing I'm needing to be timid here, but have you forgotten we've been apart for six months?"

Forgotten the most hellish time of her life? Not bloody likely. She countered. "Have you forgotten Andrew?"

"Now you must admit, love, Sir Andrew is a forgettable sort."

She lifted a brow. Jamie looked torn between kissing her and flinging her off his horse. How very darling. She patted his thigh. "You're starving, mmm?"

"Aye, I am. And after calling me your love, if you've a compassionate bone in your body, you'll feed me."

Had she said that? No. No, she couldn't have. He was teasing her again. She turned around to face him, certain he'd not let her fall. "If I had a compassionate bone, or a lick of sense, I'd scorch your ears. You let me spend six months—*six months*—alone."

He smiled and softened his voice. "You missed me."

He looked a little too pleased with himself for her liking. "Nay, you awful man. Only an angel could miss a barbaric beast with hair almost as long as mine and a scratchy beard on his Scots face."

"You want me to shave?" He rubbed at his jaw, rustling his whiskers. "I thought you liked my beard, lass, but if you're of a mind for me to shave, I'll shave."

She jerked his hand down from his beard and narrowed her eyes. "Don't you touch one whisker, James Cameron. Not one."

"Ah, you are loving my beard. Aye, 'tis most manly, I agree. And you missed me, too. Nay, don't lie. You missed me, pure and simple. Go on, lass, confess. 'Twill only hurt—"

"I did *not* miss you. Not at all," she lied. "Not a smidgen, not a wisp. Not even for a second."

"You're lying, sweet Catie."

The lilt in his voice pricked her temper. "Yanks do that."

"Aye."

"But Scots are better at it," she countered. "Scots promise you forever. They steal your heart and tease you with a taste of their love. Then they snatch it back. After you're half-dead from heartache, then they say they were protecting you and ask you to trust them and, fool that you are, you do it, knowing sure as hell they're going to knock you on your foolish elbow."

"Catie."

"Nay, Jamie. Scots are superior—aren't you always saying so?"

"I've missed you, lass."

"Of course, you've missed me." She shrugged, bumping his chin, resting on her shoulder.

"You're a wee bit sassy, I'm thinking."

"No man wants a rug."

"True, but he doesn't want his hexing witch raging, either."

"You're shouting again." She stiffened her spine.

"Aye, I am. And I'm thinking, I'm going to be shouting more."

"Why?" His eyes weren't angry. Not angry at all.

"If my shouts set your ears to ringing, I'm thinking you might just be of a mind to shush me like you used to—"

She clamped her hand over his mouth. His breath warmed her skin. "Like this?"

He kissed her palm. "Nay, love." Lifting her chin with his fingertip, he breathed against her mouth. "Like this."

His kiss was gentle, warm and wonderful and filling. His tongue sought and met hers, then swirled in a rapturous dance, joyful at being reunited. Catie sighed her contentment and leaned into him. His arms tightened around her, and he deepened their kiss. Aye, he was glad she was home.

And so was she.

* * *

"Iain?" From the stable door, Catie saw him soaping a saddle in the first stall. "Hello."

"Ah, Catie. 'Tis grand you're home."

"Thank you." She walked over to him and draped her arms over the wooden slats. "May I ask you a question?"

"Aye." He stopped rubbing his brisk circles on the saddle's seat and gave her his complete attention.

"When Harry died, did you take the glass he drank milk from that night in for testing?"

"Aye, I did. Nay, wait." He paused and scratched his neck. "Aye and nay, Catie."

"Well, which is it?"

"Aye, I left to bring the glass to the coroner's office, but, nay, I dinna actually take it."

"Why not?" The smell of the soap blended with that of hay and leather and horses. "What I'm meaning is, Did the milk get there?"

"Aye. Well, I suppose so. I met Bronwyn on me way to the village. She was seeing Elwin that night and said she'd bring it on in."

"Elwin, the coroner?"

"Aye."

"Bronwyn?"

"Aye." Iain returned to his rubbing. "I appreciated her help. As I'm sure you can imagine, things were in an uproar here what with Letty locking herself into the chapel and Celwyn carrying tales to the village. Half the clans thought Letty had lost her mind, though she hadn't, of course."

"Sounds as if there was a lot of confusion."

"Aye, there was that." He sent her a puzzled look. "Why are you asking about this, Catie?"

She smiled. "I need to record it in the records."

"Ah. How's the work going?"

"Fine, but slow. There are so many gaps that need filling in." She rubbed at her nose. The stable was warm, heating the blend of scents. Strong, but not unpleasant. "Iain, I need a favor."

"What?"

He wouldn't like this any more than Jamie so she gave him her best smile and most pleading look. "I want to get the records as complete as possible, but to do that, I need help."

"I'm sorry, but I'm lacking on the matter. I'd help if I could but—"

"You can."

"How?"

"You can arrange a meeting between me and the MacPherson."

"The MacPherson?" Iain's jaw went slack.

"I need to talk with him—to fill in the gaps. Bronwyn told me at the Christmas Eve party that MacPherson knows all about clan history."

Iain shook his head. "Nay, the laird would be having none of it."

"MacPherson?" She frowned.

"Nay, James. Truth is truth, lass. James would throw a bloody fit."

Catie lifted her chin. "I don't need James's approval, Iain. I work for Letty." When he didn't seem to be softening, she clicked her tongue to the roof of her mouth. "Never mind. I'll just drop by for a visit."

He looked mortified. "You can't be doing that!"

"Of course I can."

"But—"

"I mean to talk with the man. I have to, to do my job right."

Iain lost his fluster and looked resigned. "I'll ask, but don't expect much of a response. The Camerons and the MacPhersons have been feuding—"

"I know, over nine hundred years."

"Aye. The MacPherson surely won't be much pleased by

the Cameron's ally wanting to meet with him." Iain frowned.
"And, begging yer pardon, Catie, but the Cameron won't
like it worth a tinker's damn, either."

"I'm not his ally anymore. I'm engaged to Andrew, Iain."
She didn't like lying to Iain, but Jamie had made her see
the logic in the charade. She'd have more freedom to find
out what exactly was going on here, and have more safety
in doing it, being Andrew's fiancée rather than Jamie's ally.

Maybe tonight she'd tell Jamie that she wasn't engaged.
If he hadn't riled her temper, she would have told him the
truth already. But he had, so she'd just let him go on thinking
what he would. Still, it worried him, and more worry right
now, her darling barbaric beast just didn't need. Not telling
him had been heartless, but she'd no intention of letting him
suffer six months. Nay, the very next time she caught him
being tender, she'd tell him the truth.

Catie rode Thunder to MacPherson's castle, doing her best
to stay upright in the saddle. Thunder was behaving beautifully, but since they'd taken the moor to the glen and then
crossed onto MacPherson lands, she'd been ogled by angry-
looking clansmen who made no bones about not wanting
her there. Squelching the urge to hide her feet, she firmly
reminded herself she wasn't trespassing. MacPherson expected her.

Stopping near the keep, she saw a man standing on the
landing with a white bandage strapped across the bridge of
his nose. He was near Jamie's age, she suspected, but
shorter, thicker, and his skin looked like leather. Next to
Jamie when he was livid, MacPherson was the meanest looking man she'd ever seen.

It took every drop of courage she could muster to not
turn and run. His scowling at her wasn't helping her fight
her fear, either. She dismounted, dropped Thunder's reins,
and instructed the horse to stay put. Then she offered the

laird her hand, deliberately reminding him she was a Yank. "Thank you for meeting with me, Mr. MacPherson."

He didn't take her hand. Instead, he folded his arms across his chest. "Laird."

"Sorry."

"You're Cameron's ally."

The man could be civil. She didn't answer his question, just held his glare and prayed to God she hadn't already broken any odd, Scottish traditions. If the Scots were steadfast in anything it was in their fondness for a multitude of odd, little traditions. For every occasion.

When he realized she wasn't going to answer him, he grunted. "We're feuding with the Camerons. I'll keep his horse as repayment."

"For what?" She gave him a good glare. "I've not insulted you."

MacPherson shrugged. "I like him."

"Well, you can't have him." She put a protective hand on Thunder's nose. He nuzzled, as he always did, for more petting.

"Bah! You've ruined the beastie. He's soft." He shot her a disgusted look. "Nay, I'll not take him."

Was the man serious or not? Did she thank him for not stealing Jamie's horse? No, no gratitude. He was Scots, wasn't he? He wouldn't respect anything but strength. Catie looked him straight in the eye. "Did MacPhersons dust Cameron sheep with cyanide?"

His eyes closed to slits. Her life flashing before her eyes, she held her glare. A full minute passed.

"Nay."

"I didn't think so."

"Why?" He sounded surprised.

She smiled to confuse him. "Would MacPhersons wear their colors to herd Cameron sheep away from the loch?"

"You tell me."

"Nay, they wouldn't."

He grunted. "What would MacPhersons do?"

She shrugged. "Drive them *into* the water, of course."

He laughed. "Welcome to my castle, lass." He held out an arm to lead her inside.

She stayed put on the grass. "I thank you for your welcome, but I can't go inside, Laird. I'm loyal to the Cameron."

"Ah."

He seemed a little surprised by that, but not at all upset. In fact, his eyes got a nice little twinkle in them. He was much kindlier looking when he wasn't scowling, snarling, or grimacing. Almost attractive.

"Well, I'll say this for ye, lass. Ye've a more patient soul than yer laird."

"Your nose?" she asked, trying not to flinch.

"Aye." He fingered the bandage. "Your man has a hell of a right."

"Mmm." She nodded her agreement. "A decent left, too, I expect."

Again he laughed. This time, she joined him.

"So what is it you're wanting, Catie Morgan?"

"The truth."

He guffawed and whacked his thigh. "You expect a MacPherson to tell a Cameron ally the truth?"

"Aye, I do. You're a MacPherson, I know, but you're also Scots. I'm relying on your honor, Laird. Will you give me the truth?"

A flicker of admiration lit in his eyes. "Aye, lass. I will."

"You didn't send anyone to Cameron to kill me, did you?"

"Nay, we don't settle our grudges murdering wee women, nor attacking them either. Not even bonny Cameron women."

"You don't strike me as a murderer, I must admit." She sat down on the grass below the bottom step and crossed her legs, Indian-style. "And no MacPhersons have been selling the loch water in Edinburgh, either, have they?"

"Nay." He sat down on the bottom step and braced his elbows on his knees. "No MacPherson would touch that water."

"Why then did you say your test results came back safe?"

"Because they did come back safe."

"Yet you don't touch the water."

"It stinks."

He had her there. She looked up at him. "Why didn't you tell Jamie you haven't been doing these things?"

Her question surprised him. His eyes widened and he drew back. "If you'll recall, we're feuding, lass."

"I haven't forgotten."

"Call me Duncan."

"I haven't forgotten, Duncan, but an old feud is no reason to lie."

"I dinna lie!"

Now she'd done it. The man looked furious. "I do apologize, Duncan."

He gave her a lofty sniff. "I dinna lie. That bullheaded laird of yours dinna ask me."

"I see." And she did. In a strange way, MacPhersons and Camerons were mirror images; two sides of the same coin. "But you have been blaming Jamie for everything wrong going on in the village and throughout the clans."

"Everything?"

"Aye. The Ferguson man's death, for example."

"Well, of course."

"Of course?"

He laughed. "Don't get your hackles up, lass. 'Tis my duty to blame Camerons for any ill. We're enemies. And James made it awfully easy to blame him for the Ferguson man's death—and for Kirkland's attack, I might be adding. Leaving the heather on his chest was a sure sign."

"A sure sign? What sign?"

"Everyone knows James Cameron is partial to heather, lass. After seeing that, it was my duty to blame Cameron."

"Your duty?"

He cocked his head, sent her a puzzled frown. " 'Tis clear you're not understanding the traditions of the feud."

More traditions. Now why didn't that surprise her? "What started this feud, anyway?"

"What else?" MacPherson slid her a wicked grin. "A woman."

She gasped again. "Your clans have been enemies for nine hundred years because of a woman?"

"Nay. The feud goes back to 1100."

"James." She frowned. "I knew it."

"Aye, James Cameron," MacPherson said, respect in his tone.

"At the Festival of the Brides, right?"

"Aye. Are you knowing the story, lass?"

"Nay, I think not. At least not all of it. But with James Cameron, *everything* happened at that festival."

"Cameron fought for the woman. MacPherson challenged. And Cameron killed MacPherson with a hard blow to the chest."

"Killed him?"

"Aye." He grabbed her shoulder to halt her swaying. Are ye all right, lass? Ye look as if ye've seen a ghost."

Wee injuries, Jamie had said. But he had been softening her up just then. "I'm fine. Only a little confused." She frowned. "Men fighting and killing each other happened a lot back then. So why the feud?"

"Oh, it wasna the Cameron killing the MacPherson what caused the feud, lass. It was Cameron offering Clan MacPherson repayment for the killing what done that. 'Tis truth the MacPherson was not well liked by his own people. A nasty bit of a temper, he had."

She remembered what Jamie had told her about trespassers, about them implying the holder was too weak to hold onto what was his. "So the MacPhersons declared war on the Camerons because the Cameron's offer of repayment implied the MacPhersons were weaker. Is that it?"

"Aye." Duncan MacPherson narrowed his gaze. "They say yer a Yank. But ye dinna sound Yank, nor think Yank, either."

"I've learned Gaelic and my heart is Scots," she explained, then nodded to let him know she meant what she'd said.

He frowned his confusion.

"I'm hexed," she confessed.

"Ah, I see."

That, he understood.

"Ye know, lass. Back then, the MacPhersons might not have been so miffed at the Cameron, but he'd already fought one battle that night. The man was winded starting out."

The hairs on the back of Catie's neck stood up. "Who else did he fight?"

"The Kirkland. He—"

Shock pumped through her. "The Kirkland?"

"Aye, his clansmen found the woman. That gave him first rights to her." MacPherson sighed. "Cameron wanted her badly, though."

"How badly?" Why did Catie have the intense desire to cover her ears to keep from hearing Duncan's answer?

"Badly enough to give the Kirkland the loch for her."

"Kirkland Loch used to be Cameron Loch?" She remembered Catherine Forbes's diary, and that James had renamed the clan and the loch. It was the same loch!

"Aye. Until that night."

She crossed her arms and frowned. "Why doesn't anyone tell me anything around here?"

"I am telling ye."

Catie huffed. "The woman they fought over. She was the woman from the mist, wasn't she?"

"Aye." Duncan tucked at a fly buzzing around the toe of his boot. "Well, actually, she was an angel."

Catie's heart thundered in her chest. "What was the angel's name, Duncan? Do you know?"

"Aye." He nodded. "Her name was Catherine."

Catie sat down at her desk. The archives were not her favorite place at night, and that was that. She accepted the fact, then began looking through the marriage records. In the column beside James Cameron's entry, she found "Catherine" listed.

The diary! Catherine Forbes's diary.

No, Catherine Forbes had been sure James Cameron had been about to kill her.

"Well, hell, Catie," she muttered to herself and crawled from her chair. The man was Scots. Passionate. Lusty. Contrary. Of course, Catherine Forbes thought he'd kill her. But James Cameron just as likely married her.

Catie shuffled through the box, pulled out the diary, then looked for the entry.

Catherine had written nothing more the night of the feast in 1100 where Edgar had given her to James. Skimming through the pages, and converting the dates to the Gregorian calendar, she paused on an entry dated June 24, 1102: the night of that year's Festival of the Brides feast. She read the entry.

Finally, tonight at the feast my James married me. He teased me about disappearing on our wedding night, as his first wife had, but I believe he truly worried for he kept me close to his side throughout the eve. I accused him of having faerie dust in his eyes. He laughed and kissed me dizzy. It wasn't faerie dust, of course. My James loves me. But for another kiss like that one, I'll surely be accusing him again. . . .

Catherine flipped back to the beginning of the book. James had married twice. And his first wife had disappeared on the night he'd married her.

She read through the years of Catherine Forbes's life, through the births of her three children. When she'd read the last entry, Catie closed the book and then her eyes, wanting to savor for a moment the glow the diary had left her feeling. Catherine Forbes Cameron had been happy with her James. Content and fulfilled.

But not another word had been mentioned of James's first Catherine. Catie set the diary aside and pulled out the records book again. "1100. Wedding. James Cameron to Catherine." She then turned to 1102. "Wedding. James Cameron to Catherine Forbes."

He'd married two Catherines!

Catie snapped the records book closed. Two Catherines, and all these centuries later, his namesake too, would marry a Catherine.

Catie stood up, called Cricket, and then left the archives.

In her chamber, she smiled into the shadowy cheval glass. Jamie would marry her. He just didn't know it yet.

My, my, Cameron. It appears your love for your sweet Catie has turned bitter. Tonight you looked at her as if she meant no more to you than one of Letty's dinner guests. I wonder if it's so, or if you're deliberately trying to trick me, to protect her.

Ah, you canna be trusted, and I well know it. How did you know the sheep had been treated, eh? Would it surprise you to know I never intended for them to die? True. I merely wanted you to see that I could kill them. And I did.

The hatred between Camerons and MacPhersons runs even deeper now. Strange, on seeing your bandaged knuckles, the Yank didn't so much as blink. Did she already know what you'd done?

Bah, keep your secrets, Cameron. Tonight I'll be watching from the tunnel myself, and if you go to the Yank, or she comes to you, then I'll know the truth. I have to say, I'm not caring for the changes in her, since her return. She's more spirited. Almost pretty, for a scrawny Yank.

It will be such a pleasure to watch her die.

Fifteen

Jamie lay waiting.

The fire in his chamber sizzled. So did the fire inside him. Just knowing his sweet Catie was in her chamber, a mere wall away, had him hard and hot. She *would* come to him. Whether or not she was engaged to Sir Andrew, Jamie wasn't sure. At least, in his mind he wasn't sure. In his heart, he knew she belonged to him, just as he belonged to her. But engaged or no, she *would* come. She had to; her heart couldn't let her leave him again without coming to him, no more so than his heart could let her go.

He squeezed his eyes shut. The festival would begin in two days. Tomorrow she'd return to New Orleans and, thus far, she had not come. She'd worked in the archives. She'd gone to see the MacPherson, which Jamie didn't like one wee bit: a fact he fully intended imparting to the trying woman, just as soon as she saw fit to tell him she'd done it. And she'd ridden the moor, hexing his horse and his dog, good and proper. Even Zeus rolled her eyes at Cricket's frisky behavior these days.

Aye, the woman was a menace. A trying bit of baggage that tested his endurance to the limits, and if she didn't get her darling nose back into joint and her cute little arse back into his bed soon, he might just lose what wee bit of sense he had left.

That, too, was her fault. Not knowing if Andrew's god-forsaken ring being on her finger was the ruse Annie claimed, or if Catie really had engaged herself to the inferior Englishman again, was driving Jamie insane. And not knowing the truth of the matter, he couldn't go to her. Not if she sincerely had given herself to another man.

His heart swore she would only ever belong to him, but the lass should be telling him the truth. He sighed and laced his fingers behind his head. MacDuff and Annie were right. Catie would no be happy with Sir Andrew, and he'd never know a moment of peace, married to her. Jamie could lock her in the dungeon, he supposed. Aye, to keep her from ruining her life and to spare Sir Andrew the hell of loving her, Jamie could be doing that. He'd be doing the man a kindness. Aye, saving his sanity and his life. Catie's lust would surely kill an inferior Englishman. The woman needed a Scot for loving, and that was that.

Aye, she should be locked up. He shifted on the sheets then pulled the quilts up to his chest. She'd worked her way into his heart and into the hearts of his people. Hell, she had his clan eating out of her hand, bossing them in the festival preparations as if she'd been born bossing them. She planned on staying, pure and simple.

The muscles in Jamie's gut clenched. He couldn't lock her up. Or allow her to stay. Engaging in a bit of fancy was pleasant enough but, truth is truth, and he had to make her go . . . again. He'd do it, of course; he had no choice. And he'd pray for a miracle. Pray that after the festival, Letty's life with Harry would remain unchanged, and Jamie himself would still be here.

Maybe he should tell Catie about the diary? Annie was right; this was Catie's life. But, nay, he couldn't tell her. She would stay. To save him, she would stay, even if it meant forfeiting her life. Instead, he would risk forfeiting his life and keep Catie safe. That was honorable. Chivalrous. Loving. But Annie had been right about one thing. Love burns on. Even dead, Jamie would miss her.

Aye, and even with him dead, she would miss him.

Pain arced through his chest. He closed his eyes and suffered it, grateful to be alive to feel it. When the wave calmed to a dull ache, he whispered into the darkness, "Come to me, Catie. Please, come to me."

Deep in the night, Zeus's low growl broke the quiet of the fire. Jamie heard it, and heard Zeus stop. It was too dark to see, but nails clicked on the planked floor. Cricket's. And he wasn't alone. The heavier steps were Catie's.

Jamie held his silence and waited, his heart thudding a hard beat. She stood beside his bed; he felt her there, felt her looking down on him, though he knew she could see him no better than he could see her. Sensing her uncertainty, his heartbeat sped up to an erratic thumping against his ribs. She was torn, deciding whether to stay with him, or to go back to her chamber. He didn't move. It was one of the hardest things he'd done in his life, but the woman must make the decision on her own.

She reached over to his nightstand, and he smelled heather. She'd found her sachet.

"Jamie?" she whispered.

Oh God. "Aye?"

"It's awfully cold tonight."

It was June. Mild, with barely a chill to the air. Yet Catie was a proud woman. He'd no wish to be making her forfeit her pride, but he'd no desire to be making an ass of himself, either. He needed to be sure as certain of her intentions. "Is the fire in your chamber low?"

"Nay, but it's not warm enough. I'm cold."

He'd gladly give her the lie. He lifted the edge of the quilt. "Come to bed, Catie."

She slid in beside him and, when she settled, he pulled the quilt up over her. She hugged the edge of the bed, careful not to touch him. He balled his hands into fists in the dark and vowed he'd not touch her first, not even if he had to sleep on his damn hands. "Better?"

"I'm still cold," she whispered. *"Aw frae the bein."*

She was timid. The woman had half his clan outraged, the other half laughing, all of them loving her and, with him, she was timid. But why now? She'd never before been timid with him.

Confusing, that. Catie always had stood her ground. But, this seemed different and— Oh God, fool that he was, he should have realized that, aye, this was different. And he should have damn well reasoned it long before now. Sir Andrew had made the lass feel unstimulating. After one night in his bed, Jamie himself had let her leave him thinking he hated her. The woman's wings had been clipped short again.

Determined that this be the fastest wing-sprouting in history, Jamie turned onto his side, dragging the quilt with him. "Come to me, Catie. I'm of a mind to hold you, lass." His heart nearly stopped. What if she refused? What if—

He didn't have time to finish the thought. With a wee whimper, Catie scooted across the sheets and nestled to him. His throat thick, he closed his arms around her and absorbed her shivers. She was cold and, God help him, wearing a silky camisole and lacy panties. He almost groaned.

"You're so warm," she whispered close to his ear, then touched her nose to his neck.

"Don't you have any nightgowns, lass?" He swallowed, then swallowed again, determined to keep his hands firmly at the center of her back.

"I usually sleep nude, but—"

"You got dressed to come to me?" Now what exactly was a man to make of that?

"Aye." She sighed, her flesh warming. "There just wasn't enough heat."

There was more than enough heat now. She needed him. Engaged or no to Sir Andrew, she'd come to Jamie because she needed him. And right or wrong, he needed her. Tomorrow she would leave him again. His heart rebelled, his soul mourned. Aye, he needed her.

She grazed his chest with the tips of her fingers, nipple to nipple, rib to rib, navel to throat.

Smelling sunshine, heather, and spring grass, he hissed in a breath. "Catie?"

"Mmm?"

"You came," he reminded her, giving her one last chance to object.

"Aye, I came." She grazed his beard with her cheek and whispered into his neck with a sweet tremor that rocked him to the core. "You're nude too, Jamie."

He swallowed hard. "Aye."

She touched the tip of her nose to his chin and sighed, her breath fanning his beard. "I want to touch you."

"Are you wearing Andrew's ring, lass?" Sounding harsher than he'd meant to, Jamie kissed her temple to apologize.

"Nay, I took it off."

It was clear they both had recalled his objection to her medallion, when he'd thought Sir Andrew had given it to her. Jamie smoothed her hair, her wonderful silky hair. His voice deepened. "If you stay in my arms, I'm going to make love to you, woman."

"God, I hope so."

He lifted her chin with his fingertips and claimed her lips in a searing kiss. She met him halfway, those sexy whimpers coming deep from her throat. Did she know how those wee, desperate noises warmed him? He groaned and thrust his tongue deep into her mouth.

No gentle lovemaking, this. Lips crushed to lips. Greedy hands clutched and groped, demanded the flesh it sought, yield. Desire proved too powerful, too frantic for tenderness, for gentle loving. This mating was primal, primitive, as urgent and base as a smothering man's need for air. Needing to be inside her, Jamie reached toward the chest for a condom. Halfway there, he halted. He waited a full minute for her to object, but she didn't. *She still wanted his bairn.*

The knowing inflamed him, and when he drove into her wet heat, he found her hungry for him, as eager as a withered plant starved for sunshine and water. Their hips clashed, pounded their fury; their hands roamed, caressing, seeking and claiming the wants and needs of their flesh, their spirits, their hearts too long denied the soothing and solace of each other's arms. They'd withstood the forced separation and endured, but fearing the coming separation would keep them apart forever, their emotions raged.

Yet this was Catie. His sweet Catie. And she needed loving, aye, a tender and gentle loving that, *please, God,* would give her their bairn. Jamie gritted his teeth and forced himself still. When he could talk, his face at her temple, he asked, "Catie, love, are you all right?"

"Not now, Jamie," she gasped, writhing beneath him.

He'd hurt her. She wanted to get away from him. Remorse tearing at his stomach, flooding him with guilt and regret, he bowed his spine to leave her.

She locked her thighs around his hips. "No!"

"I dinna mean to hurt—"

"Jamie," she shouted. "I'm suffering here, damn it. Forget diplomacy and being chivalrous, and tend to your duties."

Stunned, he laughed, and kissed her hard. His darling Yank was every bit as needy as he. Losing himself in her passion, he gave desire free rein to take them where it would.

Her hands in his beard, she cried out his name. Wanting to see her face, he cursed the darkness, feeling her arch her back, tense, and then her spasms. Knowing conception was possible had the spiral in his loins weaving in on itself with his thrusts, weaving tighter and tighter, the pressure more and more intense. Painfully intense. And then he was there with her, dangling. He sank himself, the pressure shattered, and he spilled himself into his sweet Catie.

Long moments later, still too moved to speak, he held her in his arms, and felt a tremble. Whether it was him or her, he couldn't tell, but it didn't matter. Since they'd first spoken on the phone, they'd been one. And, when he could, he kissed her; gave her the tenderness, the gentleness, and the whispered love words he'd been unable to give her before finding relief. He started to roll to her side, but she held him to her, curling her fingers into his sides, and whispered, "Don't leave me, Jamie."

"I'm too heavy, lass." He rolled then, and brought her with him.

When she settled on top of him, tangling their legs, as she often did, he let his hands drift up and then down her spine. "I've missed your loving, Catie."

"Of course."

He laughed and smoothed her hair back behind her shoulder. "Of course."

"You've missed me out of bed, too." A wee shiver had her vibrating against him. "My back's cold, Jamie."

He lifted the quilt over her, then nuzzled her salty-skinned neck and followed her dainty medallion chain to the soft spot at her throat. "Aye, love. I've missed you out of bed, too." She curled her fingers in his beard. So gentle, so tender. Would he ever tire of feeling Catie's hands on his face?

"You want me."

How could a woman who turns his mind to mush with her loving sound needy of reassurance? He could just say he wanted her, but Catie was too wise to his ways. She'd feel slighted, pure and simple, and he'd no leave the love of his life feeling anything but sure of his love. Sure enough to last her a lifetime, just in case. "You're getting sassy, I'm thinking."

"I've always been sassy." She rubbed her nose against his beard, rustling his whiskers. "I'm being diplomatic and honest, unless—are you saying you don't want me?"

"Nay, I want you, woman." He squeezed her tight. "More than I've a right to want you."

She rewarded him with a loving kiss. "I knew you did."

"I meant for you to know it."

"Is that why you forgot, um, you know." She'd dropped her voice, sounding timid again.

"Protection?" He smiled into the darkness. The woman was a hellcat in his arms, yet she couldn't bring herself to say the simplest things. "Nay, love. I dinna forget."

"I didn't, either," she confessed, sounding as guilty as sin itself.

Wanting to ease her fears, he kissed the tip of her nose. "I know."

"I meant for you to know."

With another smile, he settled back on his pillow.

She snuggled to his side and twirled a fingertip in the hair on his chest. "Jamie?"

"Aye, love."

"I want you to know that I meant what I said. I'm never leaving you again."

The woman sounded as serious as a heart attack. He sighed, rolled away, then lit a candle beside the bed.

"Why do you do that?" she asked. "We've got generators. Why do you use candles in our chambers?"

Our chambers. Aye, God help him, she truly did plan on staying. "I'm partial to candles. They're more romantic." That earned him a smile he'd be remembering fifty years from now—if indeed he were alive in fifty years. "Catie, darling."

She interrupted. "Are you needing a blade of spring grass, Jamie?"

He was worried, sure as certain. "I'm wanting you here with me, love. But you have to leave Cameron tomorrow, as we planned and you agreed."

She looked a word away from tears but, when she spoke,

it was defiance he heard in her tone. "Tell me why. Tell me you don't love me, Jamie. You tell me that, and I'll go."

He pulled her into his arms and let her see his anguish. "You would leave me no choice but to lie to my ally to keep her safe? Catie, dinna ask that of me, please."

"Oh God. You *do* still love me."

The surprise in her voice hurt. "You're my ally, lass. I explained the ways of allies to you. Aye, I know I did, and more than once."

"But that was before Thomas—"

"Shh." He pressed a fingertip to her lips. "I'll explain again. You're a Yank, I'm recalling. Aye, and at times you Yanks are notoriously slow to know the heart's truth."

She frowned at his rebuke.

He cupped her face in his hands, softened his tone. "Catie, I'm of a mind to love you, lass. Before, during, and after."

"Oh, Jamie." Tears spilled down her face.

He kissed her damp eyelids, the salty tears on her cheeks, the dip in her quivering chin, the sweet slope of her red nose. "No more tears now, mmm? I'm loving you, darling, but you've chosen Sir Andrew as your mate, and that's that. You have to go back to him."

"You love me, yet you're sending me away again. To Andrew?"

"Because I love you with all my heart, aye, I am. You're in danger here." Jamie stroked her chin with the pad of his thumb until it ceased its quivering. "I can bear anything in this world except knowing I let something hurt you, Catie. I canna live with knowing I failed to protect you. With Sir Andrew, you'll be safe."

"Will I see you again?" Her eyes shone her resignation.

"Aye," he promised, sure that even if he died, she would see him in her mind's eye. She looked resigned, but something lingering in her tone troubled him. "Again and again."

"But not here." She let her fingertip slide down his ribs.

"Nay, no here."

"When?"

"I'm not knowing the answer to that."

"And you want me to marry Andrew?"

Jamie couldn't say it. He should, but God forgive him, he couldn't make himself do it. "I would have you safe and well and happy."

"Without you?"

His heart splintered. "Aye, without me."

"I can't be happy without you, Jamie. I tried because I promised, but it didn't work. I can't do it, and you asking me to, is asking too much."

"I'm knowing, lass. But I ask it of you to soothe my soul." He hated the raw pain in his voice. He hated it, but letting her see how he felt down deep inside was the only prayer he had of her realizing the importance of her happiness to him. "I could never be at peace knowing you're not happy."

She looked at him, her hand trembling on his beard. "Promise me I'll see you again."

"You'll see me again, darling."

Catie gave him a slow blink, brushing her cheeks with her lashes. "When we were separated, I thought about you every night, Jamie. And every night I listened for the phone. I waited and I remembered."

"What did you remember, love?" Her face to his chest, he lifted a strand of her hair and let it run through his fingertips.

"You talking to me in Gaelic. I've learned it now. And I remembered riding Thunder with you, and how much you love me in glasses."

"Aye, I do that."

"I'd pretend."

"About what, darling?"

"About us." She rubbed his chest with her cheek. "I want to dream with you, Jamie. Like I dreamed of you."

"What would you dream?" He closed his eyes.

"That we had children, and grandchildren. That we had a whole lifetime together. We loved well, Jamie. We fought too, sometimes, but we mostly loved."

"Our grandchildren would find my fondness for you in glasses amusing, I'm thinking."

Their grandchildren. Catie's heart nearly burst from her chest. He was dreaming with her, aye, but a man who would dream couldn't mean for her to marry Andrew. The awful, darling barbarian. "Our grandchildren," she said in her most haughty tone, "will be furious with their hard-headed grandfather because for thirty-odd years he's insulted their sweet and lovable grandmother—namely, me."

"Nay." He cuddled her in his arms. "My grandchildren would never side against me, love."

"They will. Especially when they learn that not only have you insulted me, but you've refused to repay."

He dipped his chin and looked down at her. "How, I'm asking, have I done that?"

"Your tower is lacking, James Cameron. I couldn't help but notice that Old Glory is still absent."

"Your Yank flag." He blew out a sigh that had her near giggling. "By damn, Catie. Are we back to that again?"

"Aye, we are." She nibbled at the underside of his chin. "And if you think I'm bad about it, wait until our grandchildren get a hold of you."

He harrumphed and pulled her on top of him. "No worry, I'm thinking. Our son will set you to center on the issue."

She pressed her cheek to his chest. "Will he be laird of Cameron, do you think?"

"Of course. And our daughter—"

Catie kissed him, not wanting to wait another moment. When she released his lips and nuzzled his neck, he sighed his content.

"And our daughter will no doubt be as stubborn and as beautiful as her mother."

"Aye, in your eyes, you darling man." Catie showered his eyes, his forehead, his temple with sweet warming pecks.

" 'Tis good of you to notice how lovable I am, I'm thinking. I was feeling a wee bit slighted that it was taking you overly long." He pretended a totally unconvincing sigh, and let his hand drift down her side to her hip. "Aye, our daughter will be stubborn, sure as certain. Just to spite us, she'll probably even befriend . . . a MacPherson."

"You know." Catie gasped and whacked at his chest with the heel of her hand.

He nodded, giving her a look that told her he knew, and he was not pleased.

"I intended to tell you, Jamie."

"When?"

"I don't know." She shrugged. "Maybe right after our son is born. Aye, that would have been my best chance to catch you in a good mood."

"Catie." He grabbed her shoulders and squeezed. "Are you saying—"

"Nay, Jamie. I'm not pregnant." She gave him a disgruntled look. "You sent me away and, before, you were too careful with *those*." She pointed an annoyed fingertip at a condom on the chest beside his bed. One she'd evidently put there, since he hadn't, and it hadn't been there when he'd gone to bed.

He frowned to let her know what he thought of that remark. "We've made love more often without protection than with it, lass, and you well know it."

"True. But I'm still of a mind to become pregnant, dear." She cocked her head. "Would you consider working a wee bit harder at curing that little flaw?"

The woman could hex the devil himself. Still he did his duty and uttered a reprimand. "Catie."

"Okay. Okay. I really wasn't directing you, Jamie." The man did take serious exception to being directed. She worried her lip, and gave him her sweetest smile. "Would you *please* work a wee bit harder at curing that little flaw?"

She heard him swallow. "You're wanting my son . . . now?"

"Your daughter, too." She tilted her head to give him one of those slow blinks he said turned his mind to mush. It wasn't honorable by his standards, she supposed, to deliberately attempt to manipulate him, but this was a very important matter, and those sometimes needed a little shove. "Twins do run in your family, Jamie. There were three sets in the sixteenth century. And in 1579—"

"Catherine," he interrupted, giving her a scowl that had her fighting a cringe. "Are you forgetting you're to marry another man?"

"But you're my ally. I'm trying to be diplomatic here, Jamie, but if you're going to force an inferior Englishman's children on me instead of curing my flaw yourself—as any proper Scots ally would—well, I'm not sure exactly what to think about that."

"Flaw?" He guffawed. "Truth is truth, woman, and what you're wanting is my loving."

"That, too." She rubbed their noses, then taunted the shell of his ear with the tip of her tongue. "But I am wanting our baby, dear."

"God, Catie. I'm going to have a serious talk with Annie about your attitude. And 'tis no a baby—that's Yank. 'Tis our bairn you're wanting."

He might be yelling, but he was arching his neck so she had better access to kiss him. That was a good sign. "Bairn. That's what I meant, Jamie. Aye, our bairn is exactly what I was meaning. Bairn." She nodded emphatically, brushing his neck with the tip of her nose, then stilled and gave him a curious look. "What's wrong with my attitude?"

He rolled his gaze heavenward, clearly seeking patience. "You're supposed to want a husband first, then a bairn."

"Thank you for that instruction, dear. But I don't need a

husband. I might want one, but I don't need one." She laughed huskily, nipped at his earlobe, and then raked it with her teeth. "I have an ally."

The woman was a witch. Pure and simple. And a wicked witch, at that. He lowered his hands down her back to her hips, over the swells of her buttocks, then gently squeezed. "You should be wanting your husband's bairn, love."

He was giving in; his voice lacked any strength or substance. A little more distraction, and he'd come around. "But my ally is my freely chosen partner." She mimicked his brogue. "When you're wishing, do you wish for things that should be?" She looked deeply into his eyes. His gaze heated to the smoky emerald that set her stomach to fluttering. "Or do you wish for the miracles you desire in your heart?"

"I see."

"Aye." She licked the tip of his ear. "I think you're beginning to."

"God, Catie, the things you make me feel."

"You understand, then?"

"I'm seeing your point." He kissed her temple. "But that's no saying, I'm agreeing."

"If you don't want to do your duty and make me pregnant, James, just say so."

"I dinna say I'm opposed to having a bairn with ye, Catie. We just made love without protection, if you'll recall. 'Tis just that things aren't settled." They'd been sparring true, but had she truly forgotten her vow to leave Cameron? The thought alone had him aching. "Your timing is God-awful, lass."

"With a barbaric Scot for an ally, there is no good time," she argued. "I could die of old age waiting for things to settle."

That truth hit his heart like a sledge. If not now, if not tonight, he and Catie might never have another chance.

She brushed his face with her cheek until her lips hovered

FESTIVAL 353

his. "Please, Jamie. It doesn't even have to be twins. Just one wee bairn."

His heart decided, damning his logic and all of his reasons why they shouldn't, and his body reacted, trembling its pleasure at knowing Catie still wanted to share the miracle of life with him. A slow fire ignited deep in his loins and grew to a raging blaze.

He rolled her onto her back and loved her with a fierce protectiveness, a gentle yearning that welled from his heart. And in his mind, he saw his sweet Catie standing naked at the window, her body swollen with his bairn.

His nostrils filled with the distinct scent of spring grass and he eased himself into her warmth, beginning the loving he prayed would give her heart its desire. He prayed for her safety and content, and that this wouldn't be their last time together, forever. And when he came to her, knowing she could conceive, the mighty Cameron laird wept.

Jamie wouldn't come to see her off. Catie had his word, and she could only hope he kept it. If he didn't, he'd scorch her ears for a century or two and then skin her alive.

"Psst." Why wouldn't Celwyn turn away from the sink? Catie peeked further around the kitchen door. *"Psst!"*

Celwyn spun around and her eyes stretched wide. "Catie!"

"Shh!" She pressed her finger to her lips. "Come here."

Water dripping from her wet hands down the front of her dress, Celwyn rushed over to the door. "James said you'd gone."

"I lied. I can't leave him again. I just can't." Catie rushed to add, "But he can't know I'm still here."

"Why not?" Not looking at all happy about being drafted into a conspiracy to deceive her laird, Celwyn dried her hands on the front of her green skirt.

Before she rubbed them raw, Catie grabbed them and held

them still. "I'll explain later," she promised. "Right now, I need help."

"What kind of help?"

"A costume for the festival."

"Come on, then," Celwyn said, brushing past her and heading for the stairs.

In the attic, she went straight for an old trunk. In it, Catie found a floor-length cream-colored chemise, a deep, wine red bliaut, and a scarf-looking thing about twelve feet long, woven in Jamie's colors. "What is this, Celwyn?"

Her friend smiled. "That's a bridal girdle."

"A bridal girdle." Catie stared at the object. "Mmm, and what does one do with it?"

"One wears it around one's middle . . . like this." Celwyn wrapped the thing around Catie's waist.

"I see." What in heaven's name was the purpose—ah, the colors. The Cameron colors.

"Nay, you clearly don't." Celwyn laughed. "But you will."

Catie sat down atop the trunk. "Okay, shoot."

"Nay, you don't shoot it." Celwyn rolled her gaze as if she were speaking to an unruly child. "You wear it to the festival. All of the brides wear one."

Maybe it wasn't to identity your clan alliance. "What for?"

"To let her man know she's willing."

"Willing?" Catie frowned again, not sure she liked the sounds of that at all. "Willing to what?"

"To be claimed."

"I don't understand."

"That's clear." Celwyn dusted the trunk lid with a swipe of her hand, sending dust sparkles flying, then sat down beside Catie. "Take me, for example. I'm loving Colin, so tomorrow, I'll wear a bridal girdle woven in his colors. He'll see it and, if he wants me for his festival bride, he'll claim me."

"And if he claims you, what exactly does that mean?" Catie gasped. "You're not married to him, are you?"

"Only for the festival."

Catie felt relieved. That, she supposed, was a tradition too odd even for Scots.

"Unless we're both willing and wanting to wed," Celwyn added, fingering a crevice in the lid of the old trunk. "Then, Father MacDuff will wed us proper at the feast."

"Really?"

"Aye, really." Her cheeks flushed a pretty rose. "There's no lovemaking, of course. Well, except for Bronwyn. Truth be told, she does as she pleases, with or without a festival."

"Are you going to wear Colin's colors tomorrow, or was that just an example?"

"Nay, I'm wearing them."

"Has he—"

Celwyn's sigh heaved her slender shoulders. "Until recently, we were getting along well. But he's only kissed me so far."

"In all this time?" Catie grimaced, sounding as disgruntled as Celwyn herself about that. What was wrong with the man? "He is genuine Scots, isn't he?"

"Aye, full-blooded." Seeing Catie's confusion, Celwyn turned from rosy pink to deep crimson. "I'm a virgin."

"That's not a bad thing, so don't be sounding as if it is. But it does explain his neglect." Catie remembered Jamie's reticence on learning she was a virgin. She'd thought for ages he'd never cure her flaw. "Who's Colin sleeping with, then?"

Celwyn's expression crumpled and she started wringing her hands. "I don't know. But she's special to him."

"He tells you about her?" Catie couldn't help but shout. Celwyn had shocked her.

"Nay, but I'm knowing. After he's been with her, he's angrier." A good frown clearly showed her feelings on that matter. "Truth is truth, I don't much care for him angry."

"Box his ears," Catie advised her.

"I'm loving the man. I don't want to have to box his ears to get him to love me back." Celwyn frowned. "Besides, he's having a few problems with his other woman that he has to satisfy."

"Satisfy." An odd choice of words. "Is that exactly what he's told you?"

"Aye, that's what he said, in those very words. He can't come to me until he satisfies the problem." Celwyn shrugged and fingered the bridal girdle. "Bronwyn says he's sexually frustrated."

"Bronwyn?" Catie resisted an urge to shake her head. "What's she got to do with this?"

"Nothing." Celwyn lowered her voice to a conspiratorial whisper. "But who better would be able to give knowledgeable advice about sexual things?"

Catie saw Celwyn's point. Bronwyn did have a reputation for being well versed. "You're willing to share Colin with this other woman, then?"

"If I have to." She scrunched her mouth, telling Catie that the idea held less than a little appeal. "I don't think it's wise to make a laird angry."

"Good grief, Celwyn. You're forgetting he's a man. He might be a laird, and he might be sexually frustrated, but no man wants a woman who's a rug. The reason he's frustrated, I'm saying, is because he's a man being loving with the wrong woman. His heart wasn't in it. He's wanting you."

Celwyn's jaw gaped. "Do you think that's possible?"

"I do." She related what Jamie once had told her. "When a man's loving a woman, making love with her is different. Aye, that's why Colin isn't satisfied. He isn't loving her."

Celwyn's cheeks flamed, and she looked down at the floor. "Truth be told, I'm thinking she's the one not satisfied, Catie. She always instructs him on clan matters. Bronwyn says instructing a man right then dampens his mood, and then he can't satisfy spit much less a lusty woman."

"Well, it doesn't make a flying fig's difference who's not satisfied, the result is the same," Catie said, waving off those comments and hoping she was right. "Any woman can warm his body. But if he's being loving with the wrong woman, she can't warm his heart and soul. He might as well dunk himself in the loch."

"Nay." Celwyn frowned.

"Aye."

"Stop teasing, Catie. This is a serious challenge."

"I am serious." Catie looked out the window, then turned to Celwyn. "The way I see it, you have two choices. You can either dunk him in the loch, or seduce him."

"Seduce him!"

"Close your jaw. Your man needs you, pure and simple."

"Lud, Catie, I canna be seducing the man. I dinna know how."

Before Celwyn could wring her hands clear off her arms, Catie laughed and pretended knowing a spitting lot more on the topic than she did know. "That's easy."

"It is?"

"Aye, all you have to do is kiss him." Seeing Celwyn's doubt, Catie nodded to reassure her. "Not just a peck of a kiss, though. Seducing takes a good, thorough kissing, and then it just happens."

Celwyn bit down on her lower lip. "I can kiss him." She warbled her brows. "I like Colin's kisses."

Catie gave her a smile and an encouraging nod. "Of course, you do."

"I'll do it." Celwyn expelled a relieved breath, and her eyes shined. "I'll seduce him—*if* he claims me."

"Well, if he doesn't claim you, just remember that a Scotsman loves nothing more than a good brawl. If you love him, you give the man hell, Celwyn. That'll make him love you back."

"Catie?" Celwyn rubbed the girdle through her fingers. "Will you wear James's colors?"

"Aye." Catie looked out the window. "Though I doubt he'll claim me. He thinks I'm still engaged to Andrew."

"Aren't you?"

"Andrew's a pompous ass."

Celwyn frowned. "Don't you think you should be telling James you're not going to marry Andrew, then?"

Oh brother. Jamie would cut out her tongue if he found out she'd messed up his charade. "I didn't say I wasn't going to marry him."

"But you're loving James. That's as clear as the nose on your face. You canna give your heart to Andrew, nor your body either, I'm thinking, not when you're loving James. Nay, I canna see the likes of you marrying a man without giving him both."

"You know me well." Catie's face heated. "But you mustn't tell Jamie this. He, um, isn't knowing, and we've got to keep it that way until he comes around to the idea of me staying." Well, now she'd done it, and she had to explain. "He's worried about my safety."

"Ah." Celwyn flushed guiltily. "Bronwyn did mention to me that you were abed with James last night."

"How did she know that?"

"Iain knew, too. So did Colin."

"But he doesn't even live in the castle."

Celwyn shrugged.

Wonderful. Everyone in Cameron would know. Hell, in the entire Highlands. Jamie would throw a Class-A fit. "Is there anyone who *doesn't* know?"

"Annie and Letty, though I imagine they suspect. And Father MacDuff, of course. Everyone protects his sensibilities."

"Everyone protects themselves from his stern lectures."

"That, too."

"How did Bronwyn find out, anyway?" Catie asked, thoroughly vexed. Jamie wouldn't take this news well at all. Not at all.

Celwyn laughed. "Bronwyn knows everything going on in Cameron. In the entire Highlands. Pillow talk, she says."

Frowning at that disclosure, for there was nothing she could do about it, Catie collected the slippers that matched her costume. "I'll stay up here tonight so Jamie won't see me. Could you smuggle me an iron up here?"

"There're no outlets." Celwyn held out her arms. "Let me do it for you."

"Are you sure?"

"Aye. I'll leave them in your chamber downstairs."

"But—"

"James will go out at dawn. You'll be safe, dressing there."

"Thank you."

Celwyn smiled at her. "Lud, Catie. I'm glad you're staying at home."

So was Catie. In her heart, Cameron had become her home. That left only one heart to convince she belonged here. But it resided in an arrogant and stubborn man.

Jamie.

Ah, Cameron, you love her and she loves you. We must celebrate, eh? Tomorrow. Aye, tomorrow, for that's when all my plans will come together.

I've dusted her chemise and bridal girdle with cyanide. Because the Yank has a knack for evading me, I've also soaked her chemise in DMSO. Why? To open her pores. A touch of any liquid and she'll fairly drink in the poison, and then she'll slowly die. And you'll watch her.

There. The thistle is secure at the end of her girdle, as are the three black ribbons. You'll be challenged for her, Cameron. But regardless of your prowess on the battlefield, you'll lose. The Scotch thistle is at the end of her girdle with her three black ribbons. You see, I've also treated the ribbons, and when you're sweaty from battling for your bride

*and she ties the ribbon to your bare arm, aye, you will grow
weaker and weaker and you, too, will die.*

It's an effective method. As your parents proved.

*I think I'll have you and the Yank buried naked. A visual
symbol that I've stripped you of everything. What think you
of that, eh?*

*Tomorrow will be a fine day. You expect your Yank to die
from cyanide, too, eh? Well, she won't.*

*Nay, tomorrow your angelic Catie will be blown to bits
in an explosion that will rock the Grampians. You'll see it
happen, of course. But you'll be too weak to stop it.*

*Amazing, eh? Exciting, too. I will have won and no one
else will truly realize a battle has been fought.*

*Well, almost no one. My competitor ally will know. And
he canna be trusted. If he betrayed you, he'd certainly betray
me. Still, his assistance has been appreciated so, with him,
I'll be merciful and kill him swiftly.*

Sixteen

Jamie took his place with the other three lairds at the head of the competition battlefield, wishing the festival were over, and not just about to begin. Colorful flags stretched waist-high in two long lines, forming a lane for the bridal procession, but it was of little interest to Jamie. His Catie wouldn't be among them. She'd kept her promise and returned to the States yesterday. He was relieved and worried. His heart was heavy and he just wasn't up to all the laughter and fine moods filling the air.

On the other side of the flag-decked lane, the clans had gathered. From the number of colorful tents and banners he counted, about seven hundred had come for the festival. Some of the men wore kilts; more wore the pre-tartan version of the kilt, the blanket-like plaid. A good number wore hats, too. Their cockade feathers tucked securely in the bands to depict their clan alliance.

Jamie didn't wear a hat, or his kilt. He wore what he wore every year: a replica of the first Cameron laird's plaid, knotted at the shoulder, pleated and wrapped around his waist, and belted with a strip of leather.

Smiling faces and the buzz of excited voices drifted on the warm, summer wind. Aye, it would be a successful festival. If it proved to be his last, so be it. The truth of the tragedies would come out. Patrick and the coroner had been granted permission to exhume Harry's body and those of Jamie's parents. The good doctor would prove they all had been murdered with cyanide. The killer or killers would be caught, tried, and punished. Iain would care for Jamie's people, MacDuff for Letty, and . . . and Andrew for Catie.

An ache swelled in Jamie's chest. Catie. His sweet Catie. If he should cease to exist today he'd forfeit his life with but one regret: just once he would have heard Catie tell him she loved him. She did, of course. But just once he would have the words.

Duncan MacPherson tapped his club in the dirt, then propped himself on its end. He squinted against the sun's glare. "Are ye competing today, Cameron?"

"Nay, no today." Jamie locked his gaze on a mother holding a bairn to her breast. Had Catie conceived? Aye, maybe he had two regrets. He wished he could know. If he had to leave her, he wished he could know that she had their bairn to comfort her, to care for her, to remind her of him in the years ahead. She'd no be forgetting him. There was solace in that.

Colin Ferguson and Robert Kirkland joined them. Kirkland rested his hand on the hilt of his sword. "Why aren't you competing, James?"

"I've no interest in any of the brides."

Colin Ferguson's brown eyes flickered regret. "I guess what they're saying is true, then."

Jamie looked at Colin, noticing the quiver of green and white feathered arrows strapped to the young laird's back.

"What's true?" Kirkland lifted an appreciative brow at a young woman walking past dressed in MacFie colors.

She took one look at Kirkland's colors and snubbed the man. MacFie women stuck to their own men for the most part, so none of the lairds paid much attention to her arrogance.

"James sent Catie back to America," Colin said.

"Aye, I did." Jamie nodded, knowing Celwyn had told Colin. He'd likely soothed her way into the night. She'd been weeping since Catie had left, though she'd appeared quite calm this morn. "For now."

"Damn." MacPherson muttered.

Jamie glared at the man, and MacPherson gave him a wicked grin. "The lassie's got grit," he said. "For a Cameron."

The buzz of the crowd grew louder. Jamie turned to watch the procession of the brides. They rode on white mares saddled with silver girths around the bases of their necks, red feathers in their bridles, and colorful ribbons plaited in their manes and tails. Nearly forty of them, all dressed the same in cream-colored chemises and wine-red bliauts. Only their bridal girdles differed. They'd chosen their prospective festival husbands and donned their men's clan colors.

Were it not for the diary, Catie would have been among them. Disappointment shafted through Jamie's chest, and he looked away.

"My, my, would you look at her?" Kirkland chuckled. "And first in line, too."

Bronwyn. Jamie frowned. Wearing a green girdle with red and white threads. The customary three black ribbons dangled from its end.

"Colin, 'tis your colors she's wearing." The MacPherson's eyes warmed appreciatively. "Bonny, she is."

Jamie had to agree. Her hair gleamed blue-black in the sunlight, floating down her back, and her eyes looked like huge sapphires. But her heart was as cold as the ridge in deep winter. How could she do this to her kin? Celwyn would be devastated. And, if she knew, Catie would be furious.

Jamie looked at Colin and silently groaned. The man looked dazed.

He stepped up to Bronwyn's horse and grabbed its reins. "You wear my colors, Lady Forbes."

She gave him a smile that set nearly every man who saw it to sighing. "Aye, I do."

Colin nodded. "Then I claim thee for my festival bride."

"I'll bet he does," Kirkland whispered to MacPherson. "Aye, every laird should have Bronwyn as his bride—once."

"Aye." MacPherson chuckled. "Come Monday, the Ferguson will look on honeymooning differently, that's sure as certain. Hell, I couldn't walk for a week."

Kirkland gaped. *"You* claimed a Cameron?"

"Nay, she's a Forbes," MacPherson countered, then lowered his voice. "I know they're one and the same in the matter of the feud, but I was hoping to plant a bairn in her belly. Enemy or no, could you resist ploughing her?"

"I didn't." Kirkland glanced over at Bronwyn. Her eyes were beckoning Colin to bed already. "I claimed her three years ago, remember?"

"Aye, seems I do. And seems I recall you stepping a bit gingerly for a time thereafter, too."

"Three days." Kirkland confessed on a wistful sigh, then caught himself and adjusted the sword at his hip. "Kirklands are stronger than MacPhersons."

Duncan MacPherson let out a healthy snort. " 'Twas a full week, Robert. Don't be trying to lie to me about the woman. I well remember ploughing her."

Jamie pretended not to hear them. Bronwyn was a Cameron and, if he heard their conversation, he would be duty-bound to defend her honor. But to do that, he'd have to forfeit his own. The woman had earned her reputation, pure and simple. Since he couldn't take exception to the truth, he feigned being deaf as a stone, and held his silence.

Colin looked starstruck. Jamie sent the laird a disgusted look he didn't see, then a measuring one. Lust, pure and simple. Colin would not be following the festival tradition and marrying Bronwyn after the feast. But he would be following the lairds' tradition of marrying her for the festival. Jamie doubted the man would have any regrets, or that he'd be walking normal in less than a week. Truth is truth, and there was something about being a bride that stimulated Bronwyn Forbes.

Celwyn broke the line of the brides, turned her mare, then rode like the wind over the field to the open moor. Jamie grimaced, watching her go. Colin would have something he should regret, after all, though he likely wouldn't know it. His gaze on Bronwyn, the young laird hadn't seen Celwyn go.

MacPherson cleared his throat. When Jamie looked at him, a wide grin split his leathery skin. "Since you'll no be competing, Cameron, I guess yer ally is looking for her a new man."

"What?"

"She's a bride." He lifted his chin to point.

"I'll kill her." Jamie spun to follow MacPherson's direction. Midway down the line of brides sat Catie, dressed as a bride, and looking more beautiful than he had ever seen her. *God help him, she'd stayed.*

Kirkland raised up, looking damned pleased. "I thought you sent her away."

"I did," Jamie said from between his teeth. "When it comes to leaving me, my woman's a mite stubborn."

"She's a Yank with a Scots heart." MacPherson scoffed. "Of course, she's stubborn. Damn pity she's flawed."

"Flawed?"

"Aye, Cameron. She's loyal to ye, ain't she?" MacPherson drew himself up from his perch and grabbed the club. "But since ye want the lassie dead, I'll be taking her off yer hands."

"You'll not," Jamie said in a lethal tone that had the other two lairds laughing.

"Well, ye'd best haul yer arse over there, then. She's just kicked a Brodie in the ribs for trying to claim her. Now a MacFie is trying his luck." MacPherson scratched his neck. "Them MacFies have a plucky reputation for their breeding. Stamina of stallions, I hear." MacPherson chuckled. "Hell,

Cameron, if ye ain't quick, ye'll be fighting half the clans
in the Highlands afore nightfall."

Jamie grimaced and strode over to her, knowing the others
had followed. He stopped behind MacFie, crossed his chest
with his arms, then waited.

"No," Catie said, looking down at the man. "Though I
thank you kindly for your offer, I've chosen my festival husband. See?" She held out her hand. "I already wear his ring."

Sir Andrew's ring. The sight infuriated Jamie. Maybe he
wouldn't kill her. Maybe just to annoy her, he'd make the
woman live.

The young man shook his head. "But I'm a MacFie, lass.
Ye canna marry better than a MacFie. 'Tis a well-known
fact that we make fine husbands. We plough our women
regular, and plant more than our share of fertile seed."

*Ploughing. Planting. A husband. Not a festival husband.
A husband.* Those were the ones. The last remarks Jamie
was willing to hear. He hardened his voice to match his
expression. "MacFie. Take your hand off my woman's knee
now, or you'll be drawing back a stump."

Catie jerked up. "Oh God."

He didn't look at her.

MacFie swallowed hard and looked back. "Uh, Laird
Cameron?"

Letty and Father MacDuff hurried over. "Catie!" Letty
screeched. "What are you doing here?"

"Calm down, lass." MacDuff patted Letty's hand. "She's
here, and done is done."

"MacFie," Jamie shouted. He was out of patience and
that, too, was done. "This is your last warning, lad. Unhand
my woman."

The man scooted back, looking at his hand as if it were
a foreign object. "I-I dinna know she belonged to you."

"Now you do."

MacFie apologized, his words tripping over themselves in
their rush to get out of his mouth.

Jamie listened until he considered hitting the man just to shut him up, then simply turned his back and glared up at Catie. She was as white as her mare, clutching the saddle horn in a death grip. The wind had little tendrils of her hair clinging to her cheeks and her teeth were buried in her lower lip. She was beautiful, and scared stiff. She was here. And as MacDuff had said, done was done.

"Letty," he said, holding Catie pinned with his gaze. "The aquamarine."

Letty pulled the ring off of her finger, then passed it to him.

Jamie took it, then stepped toward Catie. Her chest was heaving and the look in her eyes held so much hope. She was his, aye, and he hers. Whatever tonight or tomorrow brought, they would face it together. She, by damn, had seen to it that they'd no other choice.

Feeling tender and shaky, he cupped the ring in his palm. Then, just as James was said to have done to his Catherine, Jamie bellowed at her. "You wear my colors, Catie Morgan."

"I'm not deaf, James Cameron, and I don't care much for your tone." She sent him a look so stiff with reprimand it couldn't be misunderstood.

The crowd gasped, and fell silent.

He crossed his chest with his arms, planted his feet apart, and narrowed his gaze. It wouldn't take long for her to realize her error. She'd publicly insulted him, but she would make amends—one way or another.

She glanced around at the solemn faces. Letty's worried look had Catie nibbling at her lower lip, streaking the pink tint coloring it. "I'm sorry, Laird, for shouting at you. But I would remind you that I only reacted to your shout." She gave him an angelic smile. "Still, I will gladly repay for the offense."

A collective "Ah . . ." rippled through the crowd. She'd hexed them. Now why didn't that surprise him? His wee, darling witch could hex the devil himself. "I said, you wear my colors, Catie Morgan," he repeated, refusing to soften his stance. The woman had the power to hex, but she damn well had to accept her duties, too. When she gave her word, she was honorbound to keep it. She had agreed to leave even before she'd returned, and he meant for her to know he'd not forgotten that minor detail.

Catie cringed. "Aye, I do, Jamie."

"Then I claim thee for my festival bride."

Standing at Jamie's back, Kirkland whispered to MacPherson. "If his voice gets any harder, he'll have the lass falling off her horse."

"Don't accept him, Catie," MacPherson called out. "A laird can kill his bride legal, and Cameron sure as certain looks ready to murder."

She laughed; deep and lusty, rich and warming. "Duncan, don't be ridiculous. Jamie would never harm me."

"Not harm, lass," Kirkland corrected her. "*Kill* is what the MacPherson said. Though it'll be costing me a fine fight, I'm of a mind to be agreeing with him."

"That, either," she replied, traces of laughter still lingering in her voice. "Tell them, Jamie."

He held his stance, and said not a word.

Her smile faded. "Jamie?"

Well, finally, he'd gotten her attention. The woman was worrying, and it was damn-well time. "I might."

"Jamie!" She gasped then frowned. "I don't think they realize you're teasing, dear."

Again, he just looked at her.

She studied him, long and hard, then gave him that slow blink that drove him wild. "But I know you are."

His ally knew his ways too well. With a grunt she couldn't miss, he grabbed her hand and tugged off Andrew's ring, scraping her knuckle, then tossed the diamond down into the dirt, which earned him a healthy glare. He glared back at her and shoved the aquamarine onto her finger. "There, are you satisfied? You're my bride, Catie Cameron. Now you wear *my* ring, and don't you be taking it off."

"Catie *Cameron?*"

"Aye, 'tis custom for a bride to take her husband's name for the festival."

She cupped his jaw in her hand. "Aye, Jamie, I'm satisfied."

She smiled down at him. Beautiful. So soft and loving that he almost forgot why he was furious with her. The diary. . . .

Catie leaned down and whispered. "I told you I never would leave you again, Jamie. On the moor, when I first returned and," she whispered, "I reminded you when we were loving. You wouldn't have me lie to my ally, would you, dear?"

"You did lie. When you were still in New Orleans, you promised you would leave Cameron before the festival."

"That particular promise came from the Yank in me." She nodded, stretching her eyes wide. "With Scots being superior, I'm thinking you'll forgive me that little flaw."

Kirkland and MacPherson nodded, fully understanding that the Yank was just acting true to a Yank's nature, and James should be forgiving her.

He wasn't so accommodating. "Scots or Yank, you lied to me, woman."

"Nay, not to you. *For us.* I know you don't want to need me, or anyone else, for that matter. But you do need me, Jamie. And, God knows, I need you."

"The woman *is* yer ally, Cameron." That reminder from MacPherson.

And Kirkland nodded his agreement. Letty and Father MacDuff, and now Annie, too. That fine woman added an I-told-you-so look that set his teeth on edge, mostly because he now saw the rightness of it, when before he hadn't. *Us.* Jamie sighed. Aye, it should have been that way from the start. Not him protecting her, or her protecting him. They should have faced everything together, as us. He softened his voice. "Aye, I need you, love."

"Of course." She shrugged, straightened in the saddle, then smoothed down her skirt.

He nearly laughed.

"I challenge."

The humorous urge died. Jamie turned to stare at MacPherson. "What?"

"I challenge." MacPherson grinned at Catie. "Ye've got grit, woman. Aye, I'll take ye."

"I'm not a horse, Duncan. You can't take me."

"I can challenge, though," he countered, looking far too pleased with himself for her liking. "And I do. Aye, I challenge ye for her, Cameron."

With a clean conscience, a good heart, and proper conviction Catie could have thrown a Class-A fit. The man didn't want her. He wanted to rile Jamie, who was plenty riled already, thank you very much. "Duncan, no! I—" Jamie's glare had her shushing and tightening her knees against her mare's sides. A little time and distance, and he'd calm down. Not long. Four or five days ought to do it. Six days, max—provided Duncan butted out now.

"Name your weapon," Jamie said. "Catherine, don't you dare move that horse."

She jerked straight in the saddle and relaxed her knees. "I wasn't," she lied, doing her best to muster up a serene smile. Cricket's snarl would just have to do. There was a time for truth, and one for sense. At the moment, sense definitely carried the most rank.

Grinning, Duncan lifted his lethal-looking club.

"Naturally." Jamie frowned. "Iain, would you get my club from the hall?"

"Aye, Laird."

Kirkland smiled. "I challenge, too."

Catie groaned. "What for? I don't even know you."

"I want a good fight." The laird shrugged. "A festival ain't a decent festival without a good fight, lass. And unless

I miss me guess, no man here is in a finer rage than the Cameron."

She couldn't dispute that. Jamie looked fit to be tied.

"Weapon?" Jamie all but gnashed his teeth.

Kirkland touched the hilt of the sword at his hip. "This'll do."

"Naturally," Catie muttered. Seeing Jamie's reprimanding look, she crossed her mouth with her fingertips.

MacFie opened his mouth. Jamie wagged a finger at him. "Don't even think it, lad. The woman would make you crazed within a week."

Catie stared daggers into Jamie's back. The man needed a good dose of diplomacy, and she was just irritated enough to give him one that'd knock him to his knees. She reached into her chemise pocket, pulled out her glasses, then slipped them onto her nose. "Jamie."

He turned and drew in a breath that swelled his chest. The sunlight caught the hair there and streaked it a shimmery gold. Gorgeous, that. She dropped her voice. "May I speak with you for a moment, dear—privately?"

She heard Father MacDuff's "Sweet Mary" and Letty and Annie's soft laughter. That was sure to get Jamie's temper up again. Yet he didn't appear to have heard them. He wasn't smiling, but he finally had lost that murderous gleam from his eyes. "Jamie?"

"I have challenges to eliminate, Catherine."

Catherine. He'd heard, all right. Good grief. She bolstered her courage, then tried again. "Please, dear. Just for a moment."

"I'll wait," Kirkland said.

"Me, too. She's asked ye so sweetly," MacPherson chimed in, his grin as crooked as his sense of humor. "Don't worry, lassie. When yer mine, I'll no make ye plead for my attention."

Jamie stepped toward MacPherson, his eyes glowing as dark as sin. "Touch her and die."

" 'Twill be a worthy death, I'm thinking." MacPherson laughed. "But I'll wait, 'til after I win her."

Good God, the men looked ready to really fight. Maybe she should faint. Nay, with all their little traditions, they were bound to have one for feuding where they'd just walk over her supine body and tangle, trying to rip out each other's throats. "Jamie, *please.*"

Jamie whistled for Thunder then swept Catie off the mare's back, planted her on Thunder's, then mounted behind her. Before she realized she'd moved, they were headed out onto the open moor.

Far from the view of the crowd, near a patch of wild heather, Jamie jerked the horse to an abrupt halt. Maybe Thunder's stirring the pungent odor would keep Catie's spring grass scent from softening Jamie's head. By damn, he needed clear thoughts. "I should murder ye, lass."

"I'm not worth the bother." She turned around to face him, then straddled his hips.

He tightened his hold at her waist to keep her from falling. "Damn it, Catie. You've got to quit doing things like turning astride without me knowing your intentions ahead of time. You'll fall and crack your head."

She curled her arms around his neck and scooted higher on his thighs until their bodies pressed intimately close. "You'll catch me."

Complete trust. Total faith. A knot lodged in his throat and the diary weighed heavily on his mind. "There might come a time when I canna catch you, love."

"You will, Jamie. I believe it."

He didn't dispute her. But he couldn't tell her about the diary, after all. In his heart he knew he should, but not knowing was kindlier. Owing her that and so much more, he kissed the tip of her nose. "You gave me your word, darling. Why didn't you go back to the States like you promised?"

"I couldn't leave you again." Her cheeks turned rosy. "I explained this once, Jamie. Weren't you listening?"

"Aye. But I was . . . thinking," he improvised, not of a mind to tell her he'd been distracted with wanting her just then. "I'm thinking I might have missed a wee bit of your explanation."

"You were worrying," she said, looking displeased by that. "The whole truth is that I came. At the fire, I came. I belong to you, and you belong to me. You're my ally."

"I'm your festival husband."

"That, too." She rubbed their noses.

He whispered against her mouth. "Then do your wifely duty, woman. Soothe your husband's anger."

"You're wanting kissing, James Cameron, so don't pretend you're demanding repayment."

"I'm no pretending, darling. Pay me now, for my anger is great."

"I rather like you angry, I think." She let out a sexy whimper against his mouth. "Actually just after you're angry. When we're," she ground their hips, "repaying."

"Hexing witch," he growled and claimed her mouth in a hard, hot kiss that left them both trembling.

She pressed her face to his chest and purred. "Jamie, what does the stone mean?"

He pecked a kiss to her crown. The wild leek didn't mask the sun-warm scent of her hair. Spring grass. God, help him. "It's a Scottish mystery."

"I'll look it up," she warned. "I know it's a symbol. Everything you've ever given me is a symbol."

"Aye." He rubbed lazy circles on her back with his thumb.

"The heather means *lonesomeness*. We were both lonely, weren't we?"

"Aye, darling we were." He closed his eyes. How could he tell her that they might soon be faced with that loneliness again?

"The clover means *think of me*. I do, Jamie. I think of you a lot."

"I know. Me, too, love." He buried his head at the curve

in her shoulder and kissed her neck. He had to tell her the truth. He'd been guarded about her safety, but she had been brave. Knowing she was in danger at Cameron, she'd still come to him. Come, and stayed.

"And the stone? What does it mean?"

Feeling her nails lightly scratching his bare arm, he confessed. "The aquamarine stands for courage, love, and success in a dangerous mission."

She stiffened in his arms. "What dangerous mission?"

Panic churned in his stomach. "Any you might face."

Her expression changed from serious to somber. "I have some things to tell you. Important ones."

He ordered his muscles to relax. They ignored him. "All right."

"I talked to Iain," she said. "Bronwyn took Harry's milk in for the tests."

Jamie stiffened. "Are you accusing Bronwyn?"

"Nay, though I'd be lying if I didn't say that I have my suspicions. When I talked with MacPherson, he said the men found heather on the Kirkland's chest, when he was attacked with the shovel."

"Ah, then that's MacPherson's proof."

Catie nodded. "Jamie, did you ever give Bronwyn heather?"

A shiver crawled up his backbone. "Aye, I did."

"So she knew its significance to you."

That set him to thinking. "Aye, but my fondness for the heather 'tis no secret, darling. Many know of it."

"She knows a lot about Cameron history." Catie fingered his plaid, just over his clavicle. "From Harry, do you think?"

The shiver grew stronger and lingered. Thunder sensed it, sidestepped and neighed. Jamie gave the horse a reassuring pat, though he was feeling far from reassured himself. "Aye. Through the years, they discussed it often."

"I see." Catie reared back and gave him a slow blink. "Thank you for claiming me, Jamie."

"You knew I would."

She shrugged. "Of course."

He smiled; he couldn't help himself. Passports be damned. The woman was Scots, and that was that.

"Celwyn says that when a festival husband claims his bride, she must repay him with a kiss—for honoring her. Is that true, Jamie?"

He had no idea, but Catie wanted kissing. "Aye."

She leaned into his chest. "Repayment, Laird Cameron, for claiming me," she whispered huskily, then kissed him thoroughly.

When she pulled back, he let out a low whistle. "You curl my tassels, love."

She laughed and flicked at the black tassels at his boot tops. "They don't look curled to me."

"You're not through repaying me yet."

"I'm not?"

"Nay."

He could almost see her thinking. Her mind was a maze. How could he not look forward to hearing what she'd come up with next? He should prick her temper. She'd said she liked their kisses just after he was angry best. But it was the soothing the woman liked. "You're failing me in your wifely duties, Catie."

"Failing you?" She gave him a suspicious look. "How?"

"You're not even knowing?" He frowned. "What should I expect from a Yank?"

"Don't start, James."

He gave her an affronted look. "When a festival husband accepts challenges for his bride, it's her duty to repay him for defending her honor. You've been remiss and not repaid, yet you tell me not to start?" Before she could answer, he deepened his frown and added, "Aye, there's the rub. And I'm still angry with you for not returning to America, Catie. Yank or Scots, a lie's a lie, pure and simple."

"If you'll stop bellowing, I'll repay you, James Cameron. Lord, you're charming."

"Aye, I am."

"Barbaric beast." She crushed his lips with her kiss.

It was longer, deeper, than the first, and when she drew away from him, he shuddered in protest. Her eyes looked as soft as young heather and her lids drooped the way they did when she was wanting him inside her. His muscles clamped. "Catie?"

"Aye, Jamie."

"I'm still angry with you." Thunder agreed, snorting and stomping a hoof, ready to get moving.

"Aye, but you're not yelling anymore."

"Nay, but you're not out of debt, either."

She gave him a puzzled look.

He closed his arms around her and pulled her tight. "I accepted two challenges."

"Aye, you awful man. You surely did." She stroked his beard, smiled, then again claimed his lips.

By the time the kiss ended, he was dizzy.

She rubbed her chin against his bare shoulder, letting her lips taunt his skin. "Jamie, a lie is a bigger debt than a challenge, wouldn't you say?"

"Aye, I would." She looked pleased by his answer. What was the maze-minded woman thinking of now?

"Well, I think we should go to our chamber. So I can repay—for the lie."

The woman was wanting loving, pure and simple. He broke out in a cold sweat. "We have a festival going on, lass."

She raked the lobe of his ear with her teeth. "I'm soft, Jamie."

His heart slammed against his ribs. An excuse hadn't worked. Maybe being obtuse would slow her down. "Aye, darling, soft and sweet."

"Nay, Jamie," she said, clearly losing her patience. "I mean, I want you."

"Of course, you do. You're my ally and my festival bride." He gave her a look laced with reprimand. "If you didn't want me, I'd be feeling more than a wee bit slighted, I don't mind saying."

"I mean," she said from between her teeth, "I want you now."

Annoyed from head to heel. Darling, that. He cast her a quizzical look.

"When a bride is starving is no time for a dutiful husband to be pretending ignorance, or to be dragging his feet, Jamie." She folded her arms across her chest. "In case you aren't knowing."

He laughed at her outrage. "What I'm knowing is that I canna wait that long to be loving you, Catie."

"Then love me here."

"Astride Thunder? The scent will make him crazed."

"You're making me crazed," she said in a singsong voice, then mimicked his burr. "I'm of a mind to be loving my husband, Jamie. Would you be denying your bride?"

"Hold on." He snapped Thunder's reins and dug in his heels.

"Where are we going?"

"Do you know, woman, you ask me that on damn near every ride we take? It puts a man in the frame of mind that you're not trusting him, I'm saying. I dinna like it."

Catie thought about it. She had always asked—except when she'd returned and left her luggage on the moor.

They rode to the little wood leading to Jamie's stream, then cut through the thick pines. Sun-dappled, their shadowed trunks looked nearly black. He stopped the horse in a cluster of them, dismounted, then looked up at her. "Now I'm angry again," he said. "I'll tell you, lass, when you're of a mind to, you can sure dampen a man's mood."

She lifted her chin and slid off Thunder's back.

Jamie caught her before she hit the ground and gave her a disgruntled look. "I just told you not to be doing that kind of thing without warning me."

"You caught me, didn't you?"

"Aye, but I—"

"Shut up, Jamie."

"By damn, Catie, that's no way to be talking to a laird."

She backed out of his arms, stripped down to her skin, then leaned back against the trunk of a huge pine. For a long moment, she just looked at him and listened to the sounds of crickets and the rushing stream, and she thought what she'd thought every time she'd truly studied him. "You're beautiful, Jamie."

While he undressed, he drank in the sight of her, his gaze warm and loving. When he was as naked as she, he joined her at the tree and then propped his hands on the rough bark at either side of her head. "Men are not beautiful, lass."

"You are to me." She stroked his beard. "Sometimes when I look at you, I'm awed."

"Because I'm Scots?"

She smiled. "Aye, because you're Scots."

He rubbed their noses. "Nay, my sweet Catie. You're awed for the same reason I am. Because we feel so much for each other."

"Jamie?"

"Mmm?" He kissed a path down the curve of her jaw to her chin.

"It'll always be this way between us. I want you to know you're in my heart."

He drew back, looked deep into her eyes and saw that was true. She still loved him, yet even now she was unwilling to give him the words. "I'm knowing, darling."

Her eyes were solemn, her expression serious. "I'm wanting you inside me now, Jamie."

Holding her gaze, he lifted her then turned his back to rough bark. She couldn't be ready for him, not yet. But rather than trying to tell her and pricking her temper, he'd just show her. He eased her down until flesh met flesh, and his knees went weak. She was ready. Warm, wet, and welcoming. He groaned and entered her in one long stroke.

Catie wasn't just ready, she was on fire, and eagerly meeting his sweet thrusts, gently grazing his hard chest with her breasts. His silky hair taunted her nipples, so sensitive and aching. He held her hips and arched to her, pleasuring them both, and his eyes glazed, desire burning in their depths. She caressed his shoulders, pressed a hand against the bark of the tree, then thrust hard, wanting all of him inside her to hold. "Jamie, I like making love outside." The sun felt sinfully good on her bare skin.

He shuddered, took her breast in his mouth, then suckled and mimicked his strokes until she swore her insides had turned to flame. And then he tugged hard, arousing a hungering ache in her core. She let her head loll back, heard whimper upon whimper escape from her throat. Their strokes grew shorter, faster, more furied, the honeyed heat hotter and hotter. She heaved a shudder and held his face in her hands and, looking into his eyes, she felt the rush, the pooling of desire so deep inside, and then the dangling; the sweet, wonderful dangling. Shivering, she looked down to where their bodies joined, gasped for breath and held it, making her flat belly concave. Jamie thrust, then thrust again, and fulfillment washed through her in pounding waves. Jamie shuddered, thrust hard, then buried himself, the expression on his face naked and raw and earthy, and deep inside, she felt him pulse.

She held him close, chest to chest, heart to heart, and wondered. After today, could she ever again be satisfied with making love indoors?

On the ride back to the battlefield, Catie palmed Jamie's hand at her waist. "I'm glad you're not mad at me for staying."

"I'm miffed, love. But I knew you'd be staying."

She tapped the backs of his fingers. "You didn't."

"Aye, darling, I did." He pecked a kiss to her nape. "I'd hoped you'd keep your word so you'd be safe but, truth is truth, and I suspected you wouldn't."

For an angry man, he sounded pleased. "Why?"

"You're Yank."

She let out a very indelicate snort. "You said I'd converted."

"Aye, I did, sweet lass."

"You're not making sense." She fingered the three black ribbons dangling from her bridal girdle.

"Residual effects."

"Ah, my conversion isn't complete, then."

"It is, except for a few rough edges." He growled and nipped her neck. "But I'm willing to smooth them out."

"Because it's your husbandly duty?"

"Because I love smoothing you, lass. You do have the softest skin."

"You're hard." Thunder's neck gleamed blue-black in the fading sunlight. She gave his neck a gentle pat.

"Aye, truth is truth. Whenever I'm around you, I am—Ouch! Careful, woman, you'll have my ribs black and blue."

"For a month, I hope."

He rubbed the spot where she'd jabbed him. "You want me soft?"

She nearly laughed. "Softened. There's a major difference, you know."

"Aye, I'm knowing."

Plucking a bit of bark from her bliaut, she worried her lip. "I wouldn't mind you telling me you like making love with me. You've never told me that."

"There are things you've never told me, too, Catie. But I don't mark you for a month."

"You're doing your damnedest to mark me forever, James Cameron." They had made love without protection . . .

again. And he'd surely marked her heart forever. "Why don't you just say you like making love with me and be done with it?"

"I'm fighting for you, I would remind you. That should tell you something."

"It does." She shifted on his thighs and lifted her chin. "It tells me you love a good fight which doesn't surprise me, considering you're Scots."

"Are you thinking I won't win?"

She guffawed. "Of course you'll win. You're a Cameron." Her faith pleased him; he was rubbing her stomach, wasn't he? "And, after you win, I'll reward your bravery with two kisses."

"At least two kisses," he amended.

She smiled at his arrogance. How very darling. "Hurry, Jamie." She reached back and stroked his beard. "I'm needing to be close to you."

"Nay, I've something to say. The danger has not passed, love, it's grown worse. I've claimed you in the presence of all the clans, I would remind you. I want you to stay close to me. No meandering, kay-oh?"

She didn't bother to correct him. In truth she couldn't. Catherine Forbes's diary entry flashed through Catie's mind. Her James had kept her close to him throughout the festival, too. And then at the feast, he'd married her. Would history be repeating itself on that, too? "Okay."

"If you're agreeing, then why, I'm asking, are you frowning?"

"There's something very basic in all these happenings that's hiding on the fringes of my mind."

"It'll come, love. But until I say otherwise, I want your body and your mind close to me and paying attention to what's going on around you. And stay away from the Kirkland's dam, kay-oh?"

"Okay," she corrected and lifted his fingertips for a peck

of a kiss. What was she missing? Something basic. Something simple. But what?

On the battlefield, Jamie dismounted and then helped her down, holding her a bit longer than necessary.

MacPherson yelled out. "Cameron, are ye ready to battle? The Kirkland's panting to take ye down."

Catie's heartbeat sped. "I don't like this, Jamie. The Camerons and the MacPhersons have hated each other so long. Did you know James battled a Kirkland, too? He lost the loch, Jamie." She nodded to prove she was telling the truth. "Nay, I don't like this fighting one bit."

Jamie kissed her quiet. When she opened her eyes, Celwyn, Letty, Annie, and Father MacDuff had joined them.

"Put the woman down, Cameron," the Kirkland snickered. "The sword's the chosen weapon. She's the prize."

To MacPherson's laughter, Catie stepped to Letty's side. "They won't really hurt each other, will they?"

"Of course not, dear. Stop your worrying." Letty patted Catie's hand. "It's a friendly battle. They only fight to first blood."

"First blood!" Catie's bones chilled to ice. "You mean, Jamie could be *stabbed?"*

"Now, Catie, calm down, lass." Father MacDuff said, offering her a consoling look. "James is a good fence."

That made her feel better. "Is the Kirkland?"

"Excellent," Letty said. "Gregor, I could use a glass of ale, I'm thinking. Would you be a dear?"

"Aye." He left, then worked his way through the crowd.

"Excellent versus good. That doesn't sound like an even match to me, Letty. But Jamie will win. He said he would and, God knows, the man's too contrary not to keep his word."

"Aye, he is contrary. Stubborn, too. But the Kirkland is very good with the sword."

"Jamie's better." Catie thrust out her chin, her gaze darting between the men. If Kirkland spilled so much as one drop of Jamie's blood, she'd breach his dam, and that was that. Her feet would just have to fend for themselves.

Jamie took his sword from Iain. It was a God-awful looking thing. The blade, a full two inches wide, caught the slanting sunlight and gleamed menacingly. Her stomach sank to her knees, and she looked away, scared to death she'd humiliate him by fainting.

Until she saw Celwyn, and her tear-streaked face.

Jerking Celwyn by the arm Catie led her a few paces away to where a bonfire had been readied for that night. "Where have you been? Why are you crying? And why weren't you in the bride's procession?"

"I was." Celwyn choked on a sob. "But Colin claimed a bride before he saw me."

"No!" Blast and damn.

"Aye, he did." She wrung her hands in her bliaut.

"Stop that." Catie swiped at them. "Who did he claim?"

"Bronwyn."

"Bronwyn?" Catie shouted. "But she knows you're in love with the man!"

"Aye, she's knowing." Celwyn sniffled. "But she hates the Fergusons more than she loves her kin."

Catie shook her head. Another odd tradition, she supposed, but for the life of her she couldn't make this one out. "If she hates the clan, then why did she wear his colors?"

"She's a laird's bride every year." Celwyn lowered her voice. "She hates all of them, Catie. Because their clans supported the Cameron against the Forbes."

Catie frowned. "When were *they* enemies?"

"When James—the first James—became laird of Forbes clan."

"I should have known James Cameron would be mixed up in this. Even dead the man is a menace. There was blood spilt over the matter, too, wasn't there?" Again Catherine Forbes's diary came to mind.

"Not if it's going to get you riled up again."

"Never mind, Celwyn. I know there was. James Cameron and bloodletting were synonymous."

"I think you're being a wee bit unfair to the man. A Forbes did almost cost James his life, in case you aren't knowing."

"Nay, I didn't know that." Catie saw a little boy sucking the tip off his ice cream cone. His own corner of paradise. Cute expression, that. "But I'm sure James asked for the trouble. He was a ruthless laird."

"Aye, and loved by his people for it, too."

"Ruthless," Catie mumbled, an idea flashing into her mind. She turned and ran back to where Jamie and Kirkland had squared off. "Kirkland, wait!"

"Catie, now's not the time—"

She looked at Jamie and disputed him, knowing fully well she'd pay later for the insult. "It is, dear." Turning her gaze on Kirkland, she smiled. "If you win, you get me—for the festival. What does the Cameron gain?"

"A ribbon, a kiss, and a hell of a fight." Kirkland laughed.

The gathered crowd watching laughed, too. Catie affected Jamie's arms akimbo stance. "Say you I hold so little value, Robert Kirkland?"

Kirkland frowned, saw Jamie's shrug, then looked back at her. But he didn't answer.

"I've been thinking," she said.

"Oh God."

She glared at Jamie. "I heard that."

"I meant for you to hear it."

She rolled her gaze heavenward, then looked again at the Kirkland. "I've been thinking. If you win, then the Cameron loses what he values most—me." God would forgive her that white lie. She only hoped Jamie would. He was a tad less understanding. "But when the Cameron wins—"

"If he wins," Kirkland smoothly corrected.

"Whatever," she snapped. "My point is, what do *you* lose?"

"Nothing." He shrugged. "I'm the attacker."

Catie frowned as if perplexed. "Are you inferior?"

"What?" he roared.

Jamie groaned like the dying. Catie ignored him. He'd catch on . . . eventually. "It's a reasonable question, Robert," she insisted. "Are Kirklands inferior to Camerons?"

"Nay, and dinna—"

"If the Kirklands are equal to Camerons in ability and skill, then why are they not equal in risk? I would think fighting with unequal terms would tarnish the Kirkland honor."

Behind her there were mumbles of agreement. The Kirkland and Jamie looked a scant step away from inflicting mortal injury—to her. "I believe the Kirklands are honorable," she said quickly. "As are the Camerons." She tilted her head. "To prove that, I think it only fair that the Kirkland should risk that which is most important to him, just as the Cameron is doing."

Kirkland drew up his arm and tipped his sword back over his shoulder, effecting a lazy stance. "Which is?"

She pretended consideration. "Your ally?"

"I have none."

"Your wife, then?"

"Nay, I've no wife, either."

She sighed. "I guess we'll have to settle for the dam, then. Though I don't mind telling you, I'm not overly pleased at being considered of equal value to a clump of mud in a polluted pit of water." She paced, refusing to look at either of the men. Kirkland, for fear he'd see the truth, and Jamie, for fear the anger in his eyes would knock her to her knees. "No, I'm not sure the dam will do at all."

Kirkland's men were goading their laird to put the woman in her place. She bit her lips to keep from smiling. If Kirkland refused, he'd look weak and dishonorable to all the clans. If he accepted and lost, Jamie would win—and breach the dam.

She should salvage Kirkland's pride, she supposed, for the sake of future diplomacy. The clans wouldn't forget this battle any more than James Cameron's had been forgotten. She'd not be responsible for the Camerons fighting the Kirklands when they were still feuding with the MacPhersons over a woman.

She paused her pacing and looked at Robert. "Are you sure as certain the dam is the most important thing to you?"

"Aye, it is." His bellow had her nearly jumping out of her skin.

"All right, then. I accept." She smiled. "You're an honorable laird, Robert. Your clan's trust in you is just."

"Damn right." He stabbed the earth with the tip of his sword.

"Get on with it, then," she said, forcing an impatience she didn't feel into her tone. "If the Kirkland wins, he gets me. If the Cameron wins, he gets me and the Kirkland breaches the dam. Agreed?"

"Aye," Robert snapped.

"Aye," Jamie said, giving her a wink.

Catie returned to Letty's side. Leaning close, she patted Catie's hand. "Harry would have loved you as much as I do, Catie. I expect that what he's done will hit Robert right about . . . now."

Robert's startled expression quickly changed to one of fury, and he leveled it on Catie. Jamie let out a war cry and began the battle.

Kirkland was smoother-moving, but Jamie was stronger and no slouch. Again and again, their blades arced through the air and clashed. Each dull clank sent Catie's heart lurching.

Jamie thrust with the first in a series of flashing moves that taxed Kirkland. Sweat beaded on his forehead, on Jamie's broad back, on Catie from head to toe. She thanked heaven she hadn't been born at a time when battles raged. She would have made a lousy warrior's wife.

Kirkland was vulnerable. He cursed Jamie and sidestepped a powerful downthrust. Jamie deflected the return and Kirkland kicked up a cloud of dust that covered him and Jamie with a fine brown layer, dulling their sweaty sheens. Again and again their swords clashed and glinted in the sunlight. One moved forward, the other back, the advantage shifting again and again. Nearly crazy from the suspense, Catie couldn't breathe. She couldn't stand watching, but she couldn't stand not watching, either.

Kirkland feinted left then dipped right. The tip of Jamie's sword nicked the Kirkland's arm. Kirkland let out a string of curses that had mamas covering their babies' ears.

Jamie stepped back, found her in the crowd with his gaze, and waited.

She ran to him, hugged him around the waist and pressed kiss upon kiss to his dusty chest.

Laughing, Jamie dropped his sword, lifted her high in the air, then spun around. "You are a treasure, lass."

"Of course." Dizzy as a duck from his spinning, she planted a quick kiss to his mouth. "You're not hurt?"

"Nay." The twinkle in his eyes warmed.

She swallowed hard. Every inch of his bare skin was streaked. Dust over sweat. He smelled wonderful. Earthy. Man and cedar and earth. Her voice grew thick. "You won."

"Of course."

She smiled. "I knew you would."

"I know."

"Clever, wasn't I? To get Kirkland to breach the dam?"

"Aye, if he holds to his word."

The Kirkland joined them. "I hate to have to be saying this, James, but, aye, I'm glad you bested me."

"I'm expecting you are."

"Keep the woman. She'll make you crazed."

"Robert." Catie stiffened her spine. "I think I'm taking offense to that remark."

"Aye, but you've earned it. You're a Cameron to the

bone." He glanced back to James. "I'll be breaching the dam, if you'll be keeping the woman."

Jamie's hold tightened, warning her to stay quiet. "I'll be keeping her."

"When will you breach the dam, Robert?" Catie asked.

"Later." He slid her a wicked grin. "I said I would, and I will."

"But when?"

"Now that," he gave his hat a jaunty tip, "we haven't yet negotiated."

"You're reneging?"

"Nay, you'd have me lynched," he predicted. "But I'll breach the dam when I see fit."

Scots pride, she decided. "I'm sure you'll do the right thing. You are the Kirkland, after all, and a Kirkland wouldn't go back on his word."

"He'll keep his word." Jamie squeezed the dickens out of her ribs. "The Kirkland's earned his respect."

Kirkland nodded and walked off.

MacPherson laughed. "Rest up, Cameron. I'm going to fight hard, I warn ye. Nay, I never could resist a woman with grit."

Catie sent him a frown to let him know what she thought about that comment. Duncan laughed until he shook. These Scots did find humor in the most God-awful things.

Minutes later, Catie saw Bronwyn near the big yellow refreshments tent and strode over. "Why did you do this to Celwyn? You know she loves Colin."

Bronwyn frowned. "I would think you'd have enough to deal with in your own love life to be bothered with anyone else's."

"Jamie and I have no problems."

Bronwyn lifted a haughty brow. "Very generous of you, Catherine, to forgive him for sleeping with me while you were gone."

Catie nearly fainted. She did her best to hide her shock.

Jamie hadn't. He wouldn't have. But Bronwyn looked too smug to be lying. By God, Catie'd kill the man with her bare hands. "Lust means nothing," Catie said. "Your sister, not Jamie, is what I'm meaning to discuss here. Celwyn loves Colin. You don't. So why did you do this to her?"

"She would have married him." Bronwyn sipped from her glass of lemonade. "Celwyn is too weak to be a laird's wife. Even you should be able to see that."

"She isn't weak. She's strong. Quiet-strength, it's called."

"Celwyn?" Bronwyn laughed. "Aye, she's strong. As strong as an impotent drink—or a damp fuse. She'd never help his people prosper." Bronwyn's expression grew hard, silk over steel. "Only one Forbes handled a Cameron and, in the end, she bent to his will. She let him destroy her clan and rape her people of their birthright, all in the name of love."

Raped birthrights? Destroyed her clan? Celwyn's words came back to Catie. Bronwyn hated all the lairds. Supporting James against the Forbes. The explosives book, the cyanide drinks, Jamie's sheep, the heather—all flashed through Catie's mind. She stiffened, her blood drained to her feet, and the taste of fear grew bitter on her tongue.

Colin came, looped arms with Bronwyn, then led her away. Catie watched them go, too stunned to move. Bronwyn had taken Harry's milk for testing. She'd been there. During the tragedies, she'd always been there. And Jamie's parents? Water-activated cyanide? If Bronwyn had managed to dust the sheep, had she also managed to dust Jamie's parents?

Catie lacked proof but, in her heart, she knew her questions about Harry's death, about Jamie's parents, the Ferguson man, and Thomas's murders had been answered. *An impotent drink.*

Bronwyn had murdered them all.

Why?

Forbes. Cameron.

Scots.

Vengeance.
Oh God. "Jamie!"

"Colin, love." Bronwyn ran a lingering fingertip down
his forearm. "Would you do me a favor?"

"Aye."

"I forgot to tell Catie that James is wanting her down at
the dam. Would you mind?"

"Nay, I'll tell her."

Colin turned, glad to be away from Bronwyn for even a
few minutes. She might be wonderful in bed—her reputation
made bedding her hard to resist—but she was awful company. Where the hell was Celwyn, anyway? He shook his
head. He'd thought for certain she'd wear his colors, but
Bronwyn had told him yesterday Celwyn had decided
against becoming a bride. Disappointing, that.

He saw Catie talking to Celwyn, and hurried over.
"Where have you been all day?"

"Here and there," Celwyn said.

"Ah."

Celwyn frowned at him. "What are you wanting, Colin?"

"I'm playing messenger. Catie, James is wanting you at
the dam. He says you're to come right away."

"The dam?" Catie looked surprised, and maybe a little
stunned. "Are you sure he said I'm to go to the dam?"

"Aye, I'm sure."

"Thank you," Catie said, then left them, looking more
than a wee bit baffled.

Celwyn looked at Colin and sighed. The man still hadn't
noticed she'd worn his colors. But James had. Hadn't her
laird offered her a few comforting words and a bit of advice
on bringing Colin to heel? Seduce him, James had said.
Funny, he and Catie even thought alike. Catie. . . . James?
Panic welled and burst in her chest. *James!* "Oh, Lud,
Colin—*Catie!*"

"What is it?"

"Who sent Catie that message?"

"Bronwyn."

"But James is on the battlefield. He's *no* at the dam!"

"He probably got tired of waiting—"

"Nay!" Celwyn started running. "Catie's in danger!"

From the edge of the field, Celwyn saw him, battling MacPherson with the club. "James!" she screamed. *"James!"*

He stopped, spun around.

"Bronwyn sent Catie to the dam—to meet you!"

The dam! Jamie dropped the club, his heart in his throat. He ran full-out, the diary burning in his mind. "Oh God. Oh God," he chanted, his words keeping time with his feet. *"Catie!"*

"Jamie?" Catie stepped onto the dam and into the damp shade, a heavy, swirling mist blanketing her feet. Could Jamie really have slept with Bronwyn? He hadn't thought Catie would be coming back, but . . . Well, hell, what did it matter? They were apart for a long time. Jamie was a virile, lusty man and, when she got ahold of him, she was going to scorch his ears, anyway—if Bronwyn had told Catie the truth—after she told Jamie how neatly all her suspicions led to Bronwyn's guilt. "Jamie?"

An eerie feeling seized her and the fine hairs on her neck stood on end. Someone was watching her.

Turning in a slow circle, she scanned through the mist, but she saw nothing unusual, heard nothing that should cause her worry. Not so much as a single cricket, nor a rustling leaf. Still, something had aroused her instincts and that eerie feeling wasn't going away.

Jamie wasn't here. The eerie feeling grew stronger, and she shivered. No way was she going to stay here alone. Jamie's warning echoed through her mind: *Stay close to me. Stay away from the dam. Stay close. . . . Stay away. . . .*

His war cry split the silence.

She darted her gaze and saw him running toward her, stark fear on his face. "Catie!" he shouted. "Run to me, Catie! *Run!*"

Something flashed in her peripheral vision. Bronwyn. *Oh God!* What was happening?

"Sweet Christ, Catie, run!"

She bunched up her chemise and started toward him.

The dam exploded.

Seventeen

Long after the others deemed looking an exercise in futility, Bronwyn searched. At the edge of the wood, she stepped over a fallen branch. The dry leaves littering the ground crunched under her feet and pricked at her ankles. It would be pitch dark in minutes, and still there was no sign of—

A telltale crackle split the quiet. Someone was coming.

She hid behind the trunk of an old pine and, seconds later, came face to face with her competitor. "You scared the hell out of me."

"Nay," the man said. "You lack the sense to fear even the devil."

She frowned. "Where are the damn bodies?"

"I dinna know." He shrugged a bony shoulder. "But James was too far away. He couldna have been . . ."

"Blown to bits?" she suggested, lifting a haughty brow.

The man turned green. Bronwyn laughed. "I can say it, even if you can't."

"There's no trace of either of them."

Bronwyn squeezed her eyes shut. If during the battle Kirkland hadn't stirred up the dust to dry their sweat, Cameron would have been too weak to run to the dam. He wore the Yank's black ribbon on his arm, but there had been no moisture to activate the poison. "Damn him. Can't the man even die as he should? Why was he there?"

"Celwyn summoned him. She heard Colin tell Catie—"

"Aye, aye." Bronwyn waved impatiently to silence him. "I should have killed Celwyn last night."

"Never mind the woman is your sister, she's a Cameron. You've no need to be killing Camerons. The laird wasn't supposed to die."

"So Celwyn's a Cameron. So what?" Men were such fools. Follow the rules, even when murdering. She stepped around a tree, mindful of its gnarled roots protruding from the ground. "Don't waste your glares on me, my dear. Our opinions on Cameron differ. The laird had to die and Celwyn, by God, should have died."

"Bent on killing your own flesh and blood." The man shook his head, his face mottled red, his voice full of disgust. "Feel you no remorse, woman? No ties to your own kin?"

"Of course not. I'm a Forbes, darling. We learned the art of betrayal long ago."

"Aye, and that's exactly why Forbeses are Camerons today. I would think that would have taught you the cost of betrayal, as well as the art."

Bronwyn sneered at him. "Just find the bodies, hmm? The explosives were potent, aye, but not so much that they would remove all traces of the bodies." She gave him a feline smile. "Bodies don't just disappear," she snapped her fingers, "like that."

Catie opened her eyes.

Thick mist made fog of the air. She blinked, trying to focus her eyes and her thoughts. Where were her glasses? She patted the earth beneath her. Where was she? And why had she fallen asleep on the ground?

Facedown, sprawled on an uneven slope, she touched her medallion for comfort and turned her head. Through the damp mist, she saw the loch. Even now the water sparkled clear in the thin haze of twilight. How . . . odd.

Oh, God. The dam. . . . The explosion! Jamie!

Hearing voices, she looked toward the sound. Two men, the younger wearing Kirkland colors, the older dressed in an unfamiliar purple and green plaid, stood together, whispering in hushed voices. Why were they talking in Gaelic?

Catie strained to hear and to translate.

"Nay," the Kirkland warrior said to the other. "You're no in danger. Who would suspect the Forbeses of treason?"

The older Forbes started walking again. Catie closed her eyes, feigned sleep, and prayed the men didn't crush her under their steps. No Scot—especially one discussing treason—would appreciate a Yank overhearing the discussion.

"What the hell is that?" Forbes asked.

"What?"

"There, in the mist."

The footsteps came closer. She swallowed a gasp. Could they hear her heart thundering?

Kirkland squatted down beside her, his knee brushing against her side. "An angel."

"She's lovely as one, I'm agreeing, but her chest is heaving. I dinna think angels breathe."

Her mind whirled and her pulse pounded in her temples. Where was Jamie? Surely he'd come any minute now. Why hadn't he come already? He was her ally—her festival husband, too, damn it—and when he did come, she was going to have a serious talk with him about changing his opinions without telling her. Ordering her to stay away from the dam, then instructing her to meet him there, then not waiting until she could get there. Maybe Colin had misunderstood—Bronwyn.

Damn it, Catie should have known. Jamie hadn't sent her there. Bronwyn had!

The Kirkland stood up. "You'd best get on with your mission before Edgar notes your absence. I'll take the lass to the battlefield. Looking at her should keep everyone busy 'til you get back."

Chuckling, the Forbes left, his footfalls growing more and more faint.

Edgar? *Edgar?* Wave upon wave of shock rippled through Catie. She forced herself to get a grip on her wild thoughts. Nay, they couldn't mean *the* Edgar. Not the first James's king. That'd be impossible. Catie peeked out from behind slitted eyelids.

When the Forbes stepped out of sight, the Kirkland warrior bent down and touched her shoulder. "Lass? Lass? Be you ill?"

She opened her eyes and answered in Gaelic. "Nay. I—" She paused, some sixth sense warning her not to tell the warrior about the explosion. "James?"

"Nay." The warrior helped her to her feet, then brushed bits of dirt and grass off of her girdle. "I'm no James, lass. Come on, I'll take ye to the field. Ye wear the same colors James Cameron is ken to wearing, so I'm thing he's the James you're wanting."

"Aye, James Cameron." She wanted to weep. What was wrong here? For one thing, the loch was clean, the water clear, not the least bit black or polluted. And for another, the Kirkland warrior still spoke every word in Gaelic. So had the Forbes.

The Kirkland man led her to the competition battlefield. The clans formed a wide circle, the field in the center, and at least a dozen more banners than she recalled flew from tall wooden staffs.

When had they moved everything around? The yellow refreshment tent was gone. A green and white tent stood where it had been. She blinked and looked at the people. They wore no kilts. Not one. All of the men wore plaids like Jamie's, knotted at their shoulders, their knees bare. The women wore hats, chemises, and plaids pleated and bound at their waists—except for the brides. They were dressed like Catie. Odd. She'd definitely seen lights before the explosion. And where were all of the Camerons? She scanned the crowd, but saw not one Cameron plaid. Not one Cameron banner. She glanced up at the castle's tower. Surprise bolted down her backbone. The Cameron flag was absent from the tower!

Edgar. Her footsteps grew hesitant. Nay, it couldn't have been *that* Edgar the men had been discussing.

A huge bonfire burned in the center of the battlefield. Remembering it from earlier in the day, and remembering Camerons had become Camerons *during* the festival at the feast, Catie breathed easier. That's why there were no Cameron plaids or kilts and the flag was missing. It was another festival tradition. Of course it was. But what about the explosion? Maybe she'd just fallen asleep and dreamed that horrible nightmare about the explosion. Everything was clearly fine here, and the man was taking her to Jamie. Aye, it must have been just a bad, bad dream.

Now she felt foolish for letting it upset her so much. Good Lord, she'd given herself a hell of a fright, and over nothing. Thank God Jamie didn't know about it. He'd flaunt his Scots superiority over her until she was old and gray.

The matter settled in her mind, Catie looked around at the festival husbands competing against challenging attackers with the club, the sword, and the bow. Many brides looked on with anxious faces, though a few seemed totally uninterested.

Near the corner of the fire, she saw Jamie. He had his back to her, but he was upright. He was alive! Though it had proven just a dream, it'd been a wicked one that had felt real. She was so glad to see him. And, truth is truth, she could use a little soothing. She hiked up her gown and fairly ran to him. "Jamie!" Tears sprang to her eyes and flowed down her cheeks. "Jamie!"

He turned toward her. So did the man at his side. He'd shaved off his beautiful beard. He didn't smile; looked worried. Good thing, too. She'd told him not to touch a single whisker. Oh, hell, what did it matter? His beard would grow back. She'd be angry with him for shaving later. Much later.

She ran from the mist to the clear air near the fire and threw herself at him, planting kiss upon kiss to his clean-shaven jaw, his cheeks, his eyes, his neck. "Oh, Jamie. Jamie."

He lifted her to him and she found his lips. "Jamie," she whispered her relief then kissed him thoroughly, pushing her tongue deep into his mouth and swirling it with his.

Laughing, she rubbed their noses. "Oh, Jamie, I—"

"Ye wear my colors," he said.

She laughed deeper. "Aye, you awful man!" Because he was emotional and his burr so thick she could barely understand him, she kissed him again and squeezed his broad shoulders. Lord, but he seemed tense. She sniffed and definitely smelled spring grass. Her poor darling likely had chewed on a thousand tender blades after telling her to stay close to him and her dozing off for a nap. "I'm all right. Really, I am. You can stop your worrying."

But truthfully, he didn't look worried. He looked dazed. "Ah, Jamie, love, you're needing soothing," she whispered. And because she needed soothing herself, she kissed him again. Longer. Deeper.

He returned her embrace, kissed her deeply and, when she felt his hardness pressing into her belly, she let out the whimpers she knew he loved. Yet, for all the kiss's familiarity, his response felt unusual, less loving and more lusty.

Of course, it was lusty, she chided herself. He was Scots. She'd just been missing and the man was worrying, for God's sake. Her Jamie was a physical, virile man. Of course, being highly emotional, he felt lusty.

Yet something continued to niggle at her. Something that didn't settle quite right. Puzzled as to what it could be, Catie ended their kiss. "Jamie?"

He gave her a strange look. "Ye wear my colors."

"Aye, Jamie," she agreed, impatient to tell him Bronwyn had committed the murders. "I have something to tell—"

"Then I claim ye for my festival bride."

"Aye, darling, I know you do." She patted his chin, gave him a quick smile, then hurried on before he could interrupt her again. "That's all settled. I'm your bride and you're my husband. Now, what I have to tell you is—"

"What is yer name, lass?"

She hushed midsentence, and stared at him. He looked so serious. "Jamie? Honey, this is no time for humor. I'm trying to tell you that I think Bronwyn—"

"I canna understand ye, lass."

She'd reverted to English. Why was he choosing now of all times to be cute about this stuff? Another little tradition? "Don't start, okay? This is important."

"Okay? What is this—okay? And what's more important for me to be knowing than my bride's name, I would ask?"

"Jamie!" Had he been injured? He didn't look injured, but . . . She felt his skull for any lumps. "It's me—Catherine. Don't you know me?"

"Aye, I'm knowing ye, love." His look vowed he did recognize her, heart to heart.

Still, something didn't feel right.

"Cameron, I challenge."

Good God, why now? Catie swung her gaze to see who'd uttered that untimely comment. Without her glasses, and from this distance, the man looked fuzzy, but his voice rang clear and the blurred image fit. "MacPherson, you stop that. I've got no time for any more nonsense from you on this challenging business. I've got to tell Jamie something vitally important."

She looked back to Jamie. "I'm serious, dear. I know who—"

"I accept," Jamie told MacPherson as if she'd not said a word.

"Ah, finally a sparring match worth watching," a third man said.

Catie glared at him. Walking toward them with a priest, the man had a satisfied look about him that infuriated her. "Could you kindly not encourage them, sir? I have to talk to Jamie."

"Who are ye, lass?" the old man asked.

"Catherine," she said. Why was everyone talking in Gaelic? Why couldn't Jamie understand English? Why did he choose *now* not to be in tune with her feelings and thoughts? Most likely more damn festival traditions. With Scots, it had to be that.

Jamie set her down to the ground. "Catherine, ye willna be rude to yer king. Apologize."

She frowned her confusion. A ribbon of fear wound up her spine, through her stomach and chest. "My-My king?"

"Aye." James nodded toward the old man with scars sprinkled on his arms and shoulders.

He had bushy gray hair and kind eyes. Was this another tradition? She'd do anything at this point to get to talk to Jamie alone. She had to tell him about the conversation she'd had with Bronwyn. Catie gave the old man a smile. "I do apologize, Majesty."

"Come, Catherine." He nodded. "During the battle, I would have you stand with me and MacDuff."

She didn't move. Jamie gave her a gentle shove. Her eyes still weren't clear. Why hadn't she asked that Kirkland warrior to help her find her glasses?

Jamie and MacPherson each took a club, and the battle began. When MacPherson slipped on a patch of wild leek, a pungent odor filled the air—and Jamie hit the MacPherson a hard blow to the chest.

MacPherson fell flat on his back like a toppled tower, hitting the ground with a dense thud.

"Ye kilt him!" A warrior in a MacPherson plaid yelled out. "Cameron kilt the MacPherson!"

Oh God. Oh God. Catie wrapped her arms over her chest. It was really happening. Just exactly as Duncan MacPherson had said that it had. *A hard blow to the chest—in 1100!*

Edgar.

"Majesty?" Catie said urgently, having the devil's own time trying to catch her breath.

"Aye?"

"What is your name?"

MacDuff nearly choked to death. "You dinna know yer own sovereign's name?"

"Please!"

"Edgar, Catherine."

It wasn't a dream. He wasn't Jamie. He was James!

"Oh God." Shock pumped furiously through her. She looked to where MacPherson lay stretched out on the ground. *A hard blow to the chest. 1100. This isn't possible!*

But the proof lay there in the dirt before her eyes.

Later, she'd admit her insanity. She rushed to MacPherson, dropped to her knees, swept his mouth with her finger, jerked his head back, and began CPR.

"Catherine," James bellowed. "You'll no kiss a corpse!"

She cast him a pleading look. "I can save his life, Jam— James."

He crossed his arms. They all did, and formed a wide circle around her.

"He's dead, lass."

"He's . . . stunned. Please, James. *Please!*"

He gave her a curt nod.

Catie Morgan dipped her head and began CPR. She also did her damnedest to convince herself that she had not somehow wound up in 1100 with the first Cameron laird. She placed her hands in the proper position on MacPherson's chest and counted her pumps. Then she again bent to his mouth.

It was a dream. It had to be a dream. She'd been knocked out by the explosion. Of course, that was it. Any moment now, Jamie would wake her up and she'd be in their chamber, snuggled up to his side. Again she returned to the pumps and counted. Her thoughts rushed on. Jamie would laugh at her for entertaining such foolish ideas as traveling through time. He'd—

A pulse! Thank God, a pulse. She straightened and checked again. It grew stronger. His lashes fluttered, then MacPherson opened his eyes.

"Hi," she whispered, then smiled up at James.

"He was dead."

"The blow to his chest stunned his heart," she explained. "But he'll be all right now."

James narrowed his eyes and took up that God-awful stance Jamie effected when annoyed. "He was dead."

"Aye, but he's all right now." Really, the man could be a little nicer. Maybe even a little grateful. Gratitude wouldn't kill him.

"You're admitting you raised him from the dead?" James looked shocked.

Brushing a pebble out from under her knee, she darted a glimpse at the others. They all looked shocked. "Oh God, this isn't a dream."

"A nightmare, aye, it is that." A MacPherson warrior said.

"She admits raising the MacPherson from the dead?" MacDuff worked his way to James's side.

"I didn't raise him from the dead. I did CPR. It's a . . . a medical . . . a healing I learned at . . . home."

"She's a witch!"

Some woman yelled that damning accusation. Soon the others were chanting it. Catie couldn't decide whether to faint or to have a heart attack herself.

James held up his hand. The crowd quieted and he asked, "Where is yer home?"

Oh God. Now what did she say? She licked her lips. "James, I—"

"You will answer, woman," he roared.

"Through the mist," she said without thinking. "Far—far away."

James turned to Edgar. "She's likely a witch. I would ask that MacDuff put her under guard in the chapel. Mayhap to cleanse her soul?"

Edgar appeared disturbed. He didn't look at her. "Aye."

James stepped closer and glared down at her. "Ye'll do no more hexing here, woman. Do ye ken my meaning?"

No, she didn't understand. Not at all. "Hexing?"

"CPR."

"You would rather I'd let the MacPherson die?"

"I'm saying the dead should stay dead. If he's different, I'll kill you myself."

Kill her? Her knees gave away. Good God, James meant to *kill* her!

Edgar and Father MacDuff each grabbed an arm and held her upright. She looked from one of them to the other, wild-eyed. "Father. Majesty. I'm not a witch. I swear it!"

"Take her," Edgar told two warriors in Forbes plaids.

"MacDuff, keep yer cross in your hand."

"Aye, James. I will."

Catie gasped then did what any woman with sense would do in her situation. She passed out cold.

The chapel looked fresher, but much the same. Benches, a few stools, a rickety desk in a shadowy alcove, a railed-off altar hewn from wood, and a prayer bench for kneeling. The cross above the altar was bathed in candlelight, just as it had been every time she'd ever seen it.

Fingering his palmed cross, Father MacDuff sat down and suggested she pray for her soul.

Catie nearly fainted again. "Do you think he's going to kill me?"

"Ordinarily, nay. But James has been under a lot of pressure of late."

Catie gave the cross a forlorn look. She just plain didn't need more trouble right now. She closed her eyes for a scant second. The man was a Cameron. Jamie was her ally and festival husband. She had to do what she could to help his kin—before that kin killed her, thinking her a witch. Resigned to do her duty, she asked the question taunting her conscience. "What kind of trouble?"

MacDuff shifted uneasily on the bench. "He'll have to tell ye that himself, Catherine."

"He's a Cameron, Father. Where I come from, I'm considered a Cameron." That was true. Jamie's clan had accepted her. Jamie himself had called her Catie Cameron.

James entered the chapel. His expression grave, he walked past the two guards posted at the door then stopped beside the priest. "Explain yourself, woman."

He wasn't holding a cross, she noticed, but truth being truth, he looked too mean to need one. Catie swallowed hard and moved a little closer to MacDuff. Surely a priest wouldn't let James kill her in cold blood. "I'm not a witch."

"The MacPherson is well?" MacDuff stood up, then moved to her side.

"Aye," James said. "He's fine."

"Of course, he's fine," Catie said, forcing impatience into her tone. If she seemed at all surprised, she'd convince James that the recovery was unexpected. "Where I come from, CPR is common. Many, er, healers restart a stunned heart that way."

He doubted her. That was clear in his eyes.

"Father," he said. "Mayhap you should hear the MacPherson's confession, just in case."

The priest gave Catie an apologetic look, then left the chapel.

With each of his retreating steps, she felt her heart sink a little deeper into despair. He passed the two guards at the door without pausing. Their wary expressions made their thoughts clear. She was on her own against James.

"Now, woman, I would have the truth."

"I've told you the truth." Catie's knees shook so hard she could barely stand. Every awful comment she'd ever heard about James Cameron's ruthlessness echoed in her mind.

"I'm no witch, James." She stiffened her spine. "I'm from the future. I know it sounds, er, daft, but, when I awakened and attended the Festival of the Brides this morning, the year was nineteen ninety—"

He laughed in her face. "Yer imaginative, I'll give ye that, Catherine."

"I'm telling you the truth." The guards were smirking, and avoiding her eyes. They didn't believe her, either. Well, hell.

"Nay, lass. You're hexing."

She glared at him. "Your namesake, James Cameron, is my festival husband in my time. He would believe a woman from your time."

"He'd not. No Cameron would be such a fool." James lifted his chin. "He'd believe you were hexing, just as I do." He paced a short path between the altar and the front bench, staring at her. "What is that at your neck?"

She touched her medallion. Her father'd had it engraved! "Look at it, James."

Though clearly hesitant, he walked over and lifted the medallion. His fingers brushed against the skin between her clavicles. She inhaled sharply. "Look at the back of it," she said, barely whispering.

"Nineteen eighty-nine!"

She nodded. "It was a gift from my father." A man who in 1100 hadn't yet been born. Her mind whirled, and fear knotted in her throat.

"Ye say yer James Cameron's woman. Have you proof of this claim?"

"My word. And . . . And this." She held out her hand so he could see the aquamarine, but no recognition lit in his eyes. "My Jamie—"

"Yer belonging to me now, lass, and I'll no have ye calling this Jamie yours. Ye came to me at the fire wearing the colors I ken. I claimed ye, and ye acknowledged my claim."

"But I thought you were my Jamie!"

He shrugged his indifference to that protest, then narrowed his eyes at her. "We favor?"

His eyes grew familiarly somber, but James's clean-shaven face reminded her poignantly that he was not Jamie. "Aye, you favor." An aching longing for her own Jamie wrapped around her heart and squeezed.

"But he is no here, and I am." James rubbed at his jaw. "Aye, ye belong to me now."

She looked at him through pleading eyes. "My Jamie is in trouble, James. A murderess intends to kill him. She's killed his grandfather—his parents, too, I think. She's poisoned the loch, and—" Feeling tears well, Catie paused and took in a deep breath. "She's hurt a lot of innocent Camerons."

"Camerons are a clan?"

"Aye, a fine one, too."

He looked like he wasn't sure what to believe. She touched his bare arm and looked up, willing him to see the truth in her eyes. "She blew up a dam in the loch, James. I was there at the time. So was Jamie. He could have been hurt. Maybe even—" She shook her head, unable to say that God-awful word. "I don't know . . . But if he's alive, she *will* kill him. When the dam exploded, I think Jamie saw her running away. I'm not sure. But even if he didn't, Jamie will soon have Dr. Patrick's test results. He's exhuming the bodies. But she could attack Jamie before then. Oh, James, don't you see? I have to get back to my Jamie."

"Aye, I'm seeing. Yer saying ye ain't a witch."

Thank God. "Nay, I ain't a witch."

A light lit in his eyes. "Yer an angel, then."

She didn't know what to say. Witches burned, didn't they? Angels were revered—or at least she thought they should be revered. Revered beat the socks off burned, and that was that. Though, she didn't think she was dead, and to be an angel she would have to be dead, wouldn't she? Either way, he looked awfully pleased with the prospect of her being an angel, and surely even these barbarians would treat an angel with more mercy than a witch. But what if she claimed she was an angel and they proved she wasn't? They'd take serious offense to that.

At a loss as to what to say, she opted for the truth. "Hell, I could be anything. This morning I was mortal, but then Bronwyn Forbes wore the Ferguson's colors—poor Celwyn was so upset—and then Jamie claimed me and gave me the aquamarine. Lord, but he was angry that I'd stayed. I was so happy—until MacPherson challenged and Jamie accepted, and the Kirk—"

"Wait!" Scowling, Jamie grabbed her upper arms. "Yer making me daft, woman." He led her to a bench and then shoved down on her shoulders until she sat. "Start at the beginning—and go slowly, eh? I'm a mere mortal, I would remind ye."

He sounded just like Jamie. Bittersweet, Catie told her tale. She began with Harry dying and Letty coming to New Orleans and told James everything she could remember that had happened between then and now, even voicing her doubt that Bronwyn could have dusted Jamie's sheep. A woman would have been noticed in the field. She had to have had a man do that. An accomplice. But who?

James's frown wasn't very encouraging. It kept growing deeper and deeper. The guards at the door pretended not to hear a word and kept their expressions firmly fixed. At least they weren't glowering at her anymore. That was a good sign, wasn't it?

When Catie couldn't think of anything else to say, she just stopped, folded her hands in her lap, and then waited.

James remained quiet for a long moment. Then he rubbed his jaw and stood up. "For understanding an angel, we're needing a priest, I'm thinking." He turned to the guard on the left. "Summon MacDuff."

Both guards gave James a healthy nod that went a long way toward restoring Catie's confidence. He might not believe her, but he wouldn't kill her.

James talked with the remaining guard until the priest returned and sat down on the bench beside Catie. The poor man was huffing. When he caught his breath, she whispered, "He doesn't believe me, Father. I swear I've told him nothing but the truth, yet he doesn't believe me."

The tears she'd fought since accepting what had happened to her refused to go unshed any longer. In silent streams, they slid down her cheeks. She lifted the loose edge of the bridal girdle and dabbed at her eyes, swearing if she sobbed or sniffed even once, she'd find the nearest cliff and just jump off.

Father MacDuff studied James. "He's under pressure, lass. I'm afraid this oddity won't help him with his troubles."

"What troubles?"

The priest seemed reluctant to say. Catie patted his hand. "I would remind you I'm a Cameron, Father. James is my kin."

The priest gave her a measuring look, then dropped his voice to a confidential whisper. "An English sympathizer who's a Kirkland warrior, is being watched. He's carrying secret information to the English—information Edgar suspects James is giving the warrior."

"It's a lie. You cannot mean—"

"Aye, Edgar suspects James of treason."

"Treason!" Catie gasped, jumped to her feet, effected Jamie's outraged stance: feet planted apart, arms akimbo, expression and tone lethal. "James Cameron is no traitor to Scotland or to his king. Take me to Edgar."

"Catherine," the priest said gently, obviously intent on placating her.

She was having none of it. "By damn, MacDuff, take me to Edgar!"

"Quit your curses, lass. I know James is innocent." The priest's expression softened, yet he still looked fearful of her. "But how are *you* knowing he's innocent?"

"The man's a Cameron, and you dare to ask me that?" She held her hard stance, miffed to the rafters. "No Cameron would betray his country or his sovereign. He'd have to forfeit his honor. Even dead Camerons do *not* forfeit their honor."

"Catherine, why are ye glaring at MacDuff?" James asked from her side. "Are ye hexing him?"

She looked at James, opened her mouth to answer him, then changed her mind.

"Nay, she's no hexing me, James," MacDuff said quickly.

James sat down beside the priest. "The guards tell me the Forbes's daughter is a faerie doctor. Mayhap she can cure this Catherine."

"A faerie doctor?" Heaven help her. "James, I am *not* sick."

James glared at her. "Now slowly, tell us what you're about. We're mere mortals, I'm reminding ye, so be easy."

Catie frowned to let James know what she thought of that remark, then again told her tale.

By the time she finished, their expressions, and those of the two guards, had changed a hundred times.

"Is that all, then?" James asked.

God, he looked as if she'd given him a bloody weather report! "Yes, I believe I've told you everything."

"Yes? What is yes?"

"Aye." Catie slumped. "It means, aye." *God, Jamie. Where are you? I need you!*

James stared at her for a long minute, stood up, then walked out of the chapel without a word or a glance back in her direction. Catie nearly cried again.

Father MacDuff patted her arm, his tone compassionate. "Give him time, lass. He's weighing the matter."

Did she have any choice? She nodded her resignation. "Do you believe me?"

Father MacDuff walked to the back of the altar, loosened a stone, then removed a leather-bound book. He passed the book to Catie, then pointed to a small desk in the alcove at the side of the chapel. "Ye'll find what ye need there, lass, to write out yer thoughts. 'Twill pass the time 'til James returns."

"Father, has James given Cameron Loch to the Kirkland yet?"

"James Cameron owns no loch, lass." He gave her a puzzled look that pitted a wrinkle between his brows and caused a ton of acid to dump into her stomach.

"He will, Father." She swallowed hard. "And when he does, you must *not* let him give it to the Kirkland. In my time, that has the innocent suffering."

"Why?"

"The Kirkland is greedy. He dams the loch and that taints the wildlife. When the people eat the fish, they get sick," she improvised and stopped there, afraid to try to explain electricity or ecobalances to a man from the twelfth century, who at different times considered her crazy, an angel, or a witch. At present, she had no idea in which direction he was leaning, but she wasn't risking one thing more.

"When yer done, ye may put the diary back into my priest's hole for safekeeping."

"Where are you going?" She hated the panic in her voice.

"To have a wee talk with James." MacDuff stopped at the chapel door. "I'm believing ye, lass."

He turned to the guards. "When she's ready, take her to James's chamber above stairs."

"His chamber?" Catie sputtered.

"Aye, he's claimed ye. But ye need not fear him."

"He's said to be ruthless."

"Aye, he is that."

MacDuff's smile left no doubt but that he considered ruthlessness an asset. Catie swallowed a sigh and then sat down at the desk.

Her mind whirled. How could she be trapped here? Through her studies and her work in the archives, this time wasn't alien to her, but she was certainly alien to it. And what in God's name was happening in her own time?

What was happening to Jamie?

Eighteen

Something shuffled.

Catie opened her eyes and saw James, standing beside the bed and looking down at her as if he couldn't quite figure her out. She scrunched the pillow, afraid to move.

"Ye defended me to MacDuff."

Was he pleased or angry? Unable to tell, and unwilling to risk being wrong, she didn't answer him.

"I would know why, Catherine."

Now his tone matched his expression, but neither offered an atom's worth of comfort. He was still in a black mood.

"I defended you because you're a Cameron." She smoothed her hair back from her face. "And because you look so much like my Jamie."

James sat down beside her on the bed. "Do people in your time sleep fully clothed?"

He believed her. Wide awake now, her heart hammered. "At times."

He rubbed at his jaw just as she'd seen Jamie rub at his a thousand times. "You're loving my namesake, I'm thinking."

"Aye, I'm loving him," she confessed. Was Jamie alive? Well? Worried? Unbidden tears threatened. To fight them she plucked at the nubby blanket. "But I never told him. I wish just once . . ."

"What, lass?"

"I wish I'd given him the words." He'd asked for them, and she'd refused. God, how she hated it that she'd refused him.

"Come." Leaning back against the headboard, James held out his arms. When she fairly flew into them, he closed them around her, holding her close. "I'm knowing yer worrying about your Jamie, lass, and I'm thinking yer missing him, too."

She sniffled against his shoulder where his plaid joined his bare skin. "Aye, James, I confess I need a little soothing. My Jamie sings to me to soothe me. He has such a warming voice." That memory brought a fresh bout of tears. She buried her face in his chest and let them flow. She deserved a fair portion of self-pity. "He probably thinks I'm dead."

"Nay, lass." James swept her back with a gentle hand. "Jamie knows ye live."

She looked up at him, forlorn and hoping for reassurance. "Do you really think so?"

"Aye, I'm sure of it." His eyes warmed. "He would feel it."

Catie pinched up a bit of his plaid to dry her eyes. Looking at James had her stomach fluttering. "I hope you're right. My poor darling is probably searching high and low for a sprig of spring grass."

"Spring grass?"

She nodded, bumping his chest with her chin. "Chewing on a tender blade helps a man with his worrying."

"Ah." He pressed her head to his chest then stroked her hair. "Close yer eyes now, and I'll sing to soothe ye . . . for my kin."

Catie settled in. It was cowardly, giving into her emotions like this, but she'd be stronger tomorrow. Surely no later than the day after.

The steady rise and fall of his breathing lulled her. And when he began singing a soft ballad, she closed her eyes and ordered herself to relax.

The song sounded familiar. Had she heard it before? She must have . . . somewhere.

She tried to recall, but couldn't. Hearing it did make her feel better, though. She craned back her neck and looked up at the underside of his chin. "James?"

He looked down, his eyes lighting from the bottom like Jamie's. "Thank you for believing me. And for being understanding about me feeling sorry for myself."

" 'Tis good of ye to notice I'm being chivalrous, Catherine." He gave her a little smile.

"I noticed."

"Yer welcome, darling. Close yer eyes now and rest a while."

Catie smiled at him. If he had a beard, she would swear he was her Jamie. Drawing comfort from that, she closed her eyes and let his singing soothe her.

"Catherine. Catherine, please."

"Wake up, lass." Someone jarred her shoulder.

She snapped her eyes open. "Father MacDuff?"

"Aye." He looked worried. "Wake up now."

She sat up. "What is it?"

"Hurry." He urged her out of bed. "The Kirkland has challenged James for you—just as you predicted."

"Oh God. He didn't accept. You told him not to accept, didn't you?" MacPherson had told her that James had first fought the Kirkland, but obviously he hadn't.

"Aye, I told him. James hasn't accepted yet, but if we don't hurry, he soon will."

At the chamber door, the two guards from the chapel stopped them. Father MacDuff spit out the reason for their rush, and the guards came with them.

Outside, the feast was about to begin. Catie pushed through the throng of people, many of whom were more drunk than sober. The smell of ale nearly knocked her to her knees.

Near the fire, someone grabbed her arm. She looked back and saw the MacPherson. "Please, not now, Laird. I'm in a God-awful hurry."

"I'll delay James," Father MacDuff said, scooting past her.

Just in case she'd insulted the man—Scots were awfully touchy about their little traditions—she bobbed what she hoped would pass for a decent curtsy and smiled at him. "Yes, Laird MacPherson?"

The older man smiled. Like Duncan, this MacPherson looked much kindlier when he smiled. A large group of men all clad in MacPherson colors stood behind him.

"You're no wearing a wimple," he said.

Hoping to heaven a wimple was the headdress she thought it, she touched her hair. "I'm a bride." In her time, none of the brides had covered their hair.

"They say I was dead."

The crowd circling them grew larger and more quiet. Catie's knees were knocking together so hard she was sure he could hear the racket. The heat from the fire warmed her face. If she wasn't careful here, she could wind up killed whether or not James Cameron believed her. "You weren't dead, Laird. Your heart was only stunned. I kept it working until it was normal again."

He stared at her. "I must repay."

Repay. Thank God. He wasn't going to kill her. This time, her smile was genuine. "Aye."

An appreciative flicker lit in his eye. "Your demand?"

"You're a very important laird. My demand will be steep."

His chest puffed and his lip curled. "Aye."

He was pleased. Breathing easier, Catie licked at her lips and scanned the crowd for James or MacDuff, but saw neither of them. "MacPhersons must always be allies with the Cameron."

"The Cameron?" MacPherson frowned. "Mean you James, angel?"

"Aye." The crowd hissed with whispers. Whether they were pleased or outraged, she couldn't tell.

"James is a fine man, but he's no a laird, lass."

"You've requested my demand and I've stated it. To repay, you must promise me that MacPhersons and Camerons will always be allies. Right or wrong. Skinned or on the hoof. I would have your word on this, Laird."

"Catherine?"

Hearing King Edgar's voice, she turned and curtsied. "Aye, Majesty?"

"You could demand the MacPherson's fealty for yourself, yet you ask only for his clan's alliance with James Cameron. I would know why."

"The MacPherson's loyalty is to Scotland and to you, Majesty, as is James's," she said, recalling Edgar's doubts about James. "That's as it should be. As a Cameron, I should follow Cameron beliefs and traditions, don't you agree?"

"Aye, I would say I do—so far."

"Well, no Cameron would demand more of another man than of himself. It'd stain his honor."

"I dinna ken yer meaning, lass, though I confess to liking the sound of it." The king stepped closer to her.

She looked up at him. Edgar was a giant of a man. A shame really that he'd never married. "A Cameron respects his allies and his alliances, but he'll give his loyalty only to his country and his king."

Edgar's gaze grew piercing. "And who are ye loyal to, Catherine?"

She held his gaze. "The Cameron."

A frown knit his bushy grey brows. "There is no Clan Cameron, lass. Are ye loyal to James, is that yer meaning?"

"Aye," she said truthfully. "I'm loyal to James Cameron."

King Edgar laced his hands at his back and paced a short path, clearly thinking. A long moment later, he stopped. "I would have yer pledge, Catherine."

James stepped up to her side. The air seemed suspended, the gazes of the spectators expectant. Catie gazed up at Edgar. "Are you a fair ruler, Majesty?"

The crowd collectively gasped. James groaned. MacPherson cleared his throat, trying to drown out her words. All of their reactions irritated her. "I have to know, James. I doubt you'd be loyal to an unfair king, but I need to hear it from him myself. I can't pledge loyalty to a king I'm not sure as certain is a fair man, and I can't believe you'd want me to."

James gritted his teeth. "If you don't hush and give your pledge, I'll have to kill to keep you alive, Catherine."

Catie gasped. "King Edgar would never permit that." She frowned then asked him. "Would you?"

"Nay, I wouldna." He smiled. "Dinna worry, James. I'll no harm the lass. She's pleased me."

"Pleased you?" James sounded positively shocked.

"Aye." Edgar clasped Catie's hand. "Her vow is one she takes to her heart. Loyalty from the heart does indeed please me." He nodded at her. "You have me vow that I'm a fair ruler, Catherine."

She smiled up at him. "Should I kneel, then, Majesty?"

" 'Tis tradition to kneel before one's king, Catherine."

That from James, sounding clearly exasperated, too. She held off a frown, though she had to work at it, knowing now exactly where Jamie had inherited his arrogance. Holding onto James's arm, she dropped to her knees. "You'll have to tell me the words," she told James, then explained to Edgar, "this tradition is new to me."

She bowed her head and crossed her heart with her hand. No one told her to, but it felt right somehow, and no one took exception, so she supposed it hadn't broken one of their million odd traditions. James knelt beside her and then began speaking softly. She repeated him word for word and, when she was done, a rough hand cupped the crown of her head. She opened her eyes and looked up. Edgar was touching her . . . and smiling at James.

Catie swallowed the knot of emotion in her throat. Edgar once might have doubted James's loyalty, but she didn't think he doubted James anymore. Her Jamie would be proud, and acting as if he'd expected no less from her.

Edgar helped her to her feet. "I am pleased with ye, Catherine."

"Of course, Majesty." She'd just given him her vow. How could he be displeased about that?

His eyes widened, then Edgar laughed. "Of course."

"Cameron, I challenge," a man cried out.

The crowd parted and the Kirkland strode forward. Even without her glasses, the resemblance between him and Robert was uncanny.

" 'Twas a Kirkland warrior what found this angel from the mist," he said. "I would claim her."

Catie stepped closer to James then clung to his side. "Can he do that? Two men found me, James, but first thing, I asked for you."

"Two men?" He glanced down at her.

"Aye."

"I saw only the Kirkland warrior."

"The Forbes was with him," she explained. "But he went south to complete his mission . . . before Edgar got wind of it!" She gasped. "Forbes is the traitor."

"Bring them to me." Edgar shouted at a guard, then leveled his hard gaze on Catie. His voice turned as cold as sleet. "Ye've accused one of my lairds of treason, Catherine. You will accuse him to his face."

"Aye, I surely will." She held tightly to James's arm. "Truth is truth, and I heard what I heard, Majesty."

He nodded. "Until the guards return with the Forbes, stay where you are."

"Yes, Majesty."

James put a protective arm around her shoulder. "Edgar, the woman is mine."

The king looked from James to her, then back again. "Aye. If I can, I will support your claim, James."

A long hour later, the guards returned with the Forbes. The heat from the fire didn't touch the chill in her bones. Catie felt frozen with fear.

King Edgar returned to the fire. "Are these two the men you overheard, Catherine?"

"Aye." Catie nodded. She forced herself to look at Forbes. As big as James, he looked colder and as dangerous as only desperate fear can make a man. Slowly, she repeated the conversation she'd overheard, doing her best to recall it word for word.

Forbes grew more and more anxious. So did the younger Kirkland warrior, who stood at Forbes's side.

"Bah!" Forbes kicked up a spray of dirt with the toe of his boot. "She lies!"

"Nay, Laird." She gave him a negative nod. "I've nothing to gain by lying. What I've repeated is what I heard, pure and simple."

"Her logic is valid, Forbes." Edgar waved his hand. "What would Catherine gain by lying?"

"She removes suspicion from Cameron. He is the guilty one."

Instinctively, Catie slapped the laird.

He stepped toward her.

James jerked her arm and pulled her behind him. "This once, I'll tolerate yer insult to me, Laird. We both know yer lying and spouting fear."

"The woman slapped me."

"Aye, she did. My angel's of a mind to be less forgiving. But if ye touch her, ye'll die."

"Ye dare to challenge me?" The Forbes laughed. "Ye? Alone with no clan?"

Feet shuffled and a wall of men shifted to stand beside and behind James. Catie tiptoed to peek over shoulders, but the men were too tall. She still couldn't see. James's grip on her wrist was firm and reassuring but, unwilling to hide behind him—these Scots would surely think she'd lied—she nudged at ribs until the men made room for her at James's side.

"Cameron doesna stand alone, Forbes."

The man saying that wore a MacPherson plaid. She scanned the group of them and located the laird. He winked at her. She smiled back.

The shuffling continued. MacFies, Fergusons, and even Kirklands joined James and the MacPhersons. Catie nearly cried. She didn't—to cry now would have told the clans that she was surprised by their support, that she considered it an unearned gift. But not crying was still damn difficult.

The men shouted angry words back and forth. Wedged between James and a Ferguson, Catie looked at Forbes. His composure was slipping.

"Enough." Edgar stepped between the two groups, then addressed Forbes. "Yer own clan stands against ye, Laird. Has that fact escaped yer notice?"

"Nay, Majesty."

"Yer guilty, eh?"

The Forbes seemed to crumple. "Aye, I betrayed ye."

"I would know why."

"Duty." Forbes lowered his gaze to study the dirt. "My mother was English."

"Ye've chosen yer fate." Edgar nodded to his personal guards. "Take him."

Catie tugged at James's arm to gain his attention. When he looked her way, she whispered, "Will Edgar kill the Forbes, James?"

"Aye," he said, not unkindly. "He's a traitor, lass."

"But—"

"He's lost the respect of his country and his people. He

will die, Catherine. If not by Edgar's hand, then by his own. If that happens, he'll be buried in shame on unconsecrated ground."

"So Edgar kills him not in anger, but in kindness?"

"A fair portion of both, I would say."

"And the Kirkland warrior, too?"

"Aye, him too."

"Catherine." King Edgar's deep voice boomed.

Catie trembled. "Aye, Majesty?"

"Ye've done yer duty."

She blinked. "Of course, Majesty."

James groaned. Catie backhanded his chest. "Well, Camerons do that—their duty, I mean."

Edgar laughed. "Aye, yer Cameron. *Aw frae the bein.*"

Jamie's words. Her heart wrenched. Was he well? Safe? Mourning her?

"James," Edgar said, rubbing his chin. "I apologize for doubting ye. It occurs to me that the Forbeses have no laird. And it occurs to me that ye have the allied support of the clans, but no clan of yer own. It also occurs to me that in ye beats the heart of a laird." He paused and looked at Catie. "A laird who will treat his people fairly. I'm of a mind to consider this matter."

Edgar then turned to Catie. She held her breath.

"I will allow ye to choose yer fate, Catherine. A reward for yer sound judgment." He took her hand. "I consider the Kirkland and James Cameron's claims to ye equal. Ye will choose which man shall have ye in his care." He raised a bushy brow in warning. "I would remind ye, lass, that the Kirkland is a man of wealth, a laird. James Cameron is a loyal and trusted subject much valued by me, but he is no a laird. I would be remiss in my royal duty to ye if I failed to remind ye that yer future with James will be less certain than it would be with the Kirkland."

Catie smiled at the king. He *was* a fair man. Nice, too. Feeling tender, she said, "Rich or poor makes no difference,

Majesty." She looked at the Kirkland. He knew her heart was Cameron, yet he wanted her anyway. "With my deepest respect, Laird, I would warn you against the flaw of greed. It makes a lonely companion and, if given free reign, it'll surely destroy your noble clan. I'm honored you want me but, because you're noble, you deserve a woman who takes you into her heart, and that I cannot do. So I'll be sparing you, Laird, for it would grieve me to dishonor you by giving you less than all you deserve."

He nodded, and she smiled at him, then turned back to Edgar. "In my heart, Majesty, I have no choice to make. I have belonged to James Cameron for a long time."

"Aye, I'm knowing, lass." Edgar smiled.

"Then why did you ask me to choose?"

" 'Tis yer fate. Wiser to allow ye to seal it, eh? James has a wicked temper, I'm told. Now ye canna blame me nor curse me for yer trials."

She laughed. "You're fair and wise, too, Majesty." She couldn't resist. "I'm pleased with you."

His eyes twinkled. "Of course."

James circled her waist with his arm. She looked at him and smiled. "Aye, my Jamie has a testy temper, but he is mine."

"You will wed now." Edgar looked to his left at a guard. "Summon MacDuff."

"Wed? Oh—" Catie began, but James's pressure on her shoulder shushed her.

"As a wedding gift, James, I'm making you laird of the Forbes clan."

Catherine Forbes's diary flashed through Catie's mind. She had to tell James, but Edgar was telling the MacDuff that they would have two ceremonies: one to make James laird; the second, a wedding. Good grief, now what did she do?

Before she could think, Edgar had dubbed James laird. James pledged his fealty and stood up, then turned to her.

"It is custom for a bride to reward her husband's successes, Catherine."

Because she had no choice, Catie tiptoed and planted a chaste kiss to his chin.

James laughed, lifted her, then covered her mouth with his. Stunned, she tried to pull back, but he held her head firmly and forced her to accept his kiss.

Jamie. . . . Jamie's kiss. She felt it and, fearing she'd never feel it again, she wound her arms around James's neck and kissed him back.

When he lifted his head, she became aware of the wolf whistles. The smell of cedar grew strong, then stronger. She looked deeply into his eyes. Clear green. Secrets as distorting as depression glass. She saw those secrets she'd gazed upon so often and her every instinct screamed he was Jamie. But that wasn't possible. He couldn't be, could he?

"We wed now," he whispered, his voice deep and husky.

"I-I can't."

"You must."

"No, you don't understand."

"Then explain."

She recounted the facts from Catherine's diary and from the records books, recalling that a Catherine had married James tonight. Fitting the facts together in her mind, she warned him. "I'll disappear tonight, James. I won't come back."

"Ye could stay, I'm thinking. Ye would learn to love me."

That darling Cameron arrogance. "It's not my decision, it's history. The records say I disappeared on our wedding night." She frowned. "At the festival in 1102, you'll wed Catherine Forbes."

"The faerie doctor!" His brows spiked up and he looked at her as if she'd lost her mind.

Catie smiled. "Aye, and you'll be happy with her, too, James. She loves you."

"She doesn't even know me."

"She will. And she'll love you fiercely." He looked so arrogant, she couldn't resist bringing him down a peg or two. "You'll love her, too."

"Impossible. Men don't love women, they own them."

"You'll love Catherine," Catie predicted in a singsong voice. "And you'll be a grand laird, James." Now was her chance. "You're very much admired in my time—for your devotion and compassion." Recalling what Jamie had said about James's ruthlessness being the reason his clan had survived, she quickly added, "And for your *judicious* ruthlessness."

"Of course." He lifted his chin. "But to remain laird of Cameron, I must wed ye first."

"I'll leave tonight and never return."

"Aye. Ye will leave. I'll stay here and lord the fine Clan Cameron and marry a faerie doctor. And ye'll return to yer Jamie and reveal the murderess." He hauled her to his side. "But first ye'll be marrying me."

She couldn't tell if he believed her or not, but they rejoined the group by the fire. MacDuff stood before them and, in short order, Catie married James Cameron.

When the ceremony was over, he kissed her again, gently. She smiled, wishing he were her Jamie and knowing he was wishing she were his Catherine. Aye, he'd believed her.

The crowd behind them cheered. Edgar wished them well. The Ferguson and the MacPherson did, too.

When Kirkland stepped forward, Catie caught her breath. James gave her arm a reassuring squeeze. So like Jamie, in tune with her emotional ebbs and flows. She had to keep reminding herself he wasn't her ally.

"I would ask that Kirklands and Camerons be allies," James said. "I've received the greater treasure, but I'll no leave my ally left with nothing."

James turned and faced Edgar. "I would rename Forbes Loch, Cameron Loch, Majesty."

"Aye." Edgar took a bite from a sharp-smelling wedge of

cheese, then washed it down with a healthy swig of ale. "MacDuff will see to the documents."

James nodded. "Kirkland, I gift ye with Cameron Loch."

"James, nay!" Catie groaned. What the spit was the man doing?

He held her to him. "As your ally, I ask that no dam ever be allowed on the loch—to symbolize the lack of barriers in our alliance. My stream and your loch shall always flow freely together."

He'd permitted the Kirkland to save face. Catie gave James a measuring look. He was supposed to be ruthless. But he didn't seem ruthless. He seemed compassionate and wise about human nature—just like Jamie.

The Kirkland nodded. "We accept yer gift and give ye our vow. No Kirkland will ever dam the loch."

James returned the nod, and then walked Catie back to the loch.

The mist curled thick from the ground up to their waists. Near the slope, James stopped. He clasped her hands in his and then gently squeezed them. "I'm thinking ye could stay with me, lass."

"My heart is there. My Jamie's in danger." She shrugged. "I don't belong here any more than you belong in my time."

He cupped her face in his big hands. "My namesake is blessed, I'm thinking."

She gave his hands a gentle squeeze of her own. "Jamie is lucky, too. He has a fine ancestor." Edgar hadn't given James Catherine Forbes. Catie frowned. "James, when you go back to the fire, you must tell Edgar the truth about me."

"He'll think I'm daft."

"Nay, he'll believe you," she countered. "And he'll give you a gift. One you must promise me you'll treasure."

"Aye, I promise. But no gift will have yer charm." He gently lifted a lock of her hair. "Nor such a lovely, white streak in her hair."

A white streak? He was teasing. How very darling. She

smiled, unhooked the chain from her medallion, then re-hooked it around James's neck. "If you're pleased with Edgar's gift, then wear this always and I will know you were happy."

"All right." His eyes turned somber. "Catherine, ye touched something inside me, lass, when ye came to me by the fire. I felt yer love for me down to the very marrow of me bones. I'm thinking it's changed me forever."

Her eyes felt hot and moist, her heart tender. "Aye, you have changed, James. You've known how it feels to be touched by love. Once you know the feeling, you can never be content feeling anything less."

"I'll be missing ye, Catie."

"I'll miss you, too." She hugged him, then drew back and laughed. "If you only had a beard."

"A beard?" He touched his jaw.

"Aye. You look so much like my Jamie, but he has the most beautiful beard."

"Mine will be thicker."

Arrogant. She smiled and kissed his cheek. He shook and pulled her close. She hugged him hard, and then patted his arm. Why was she so close to tears? "I have to go now."

"How will you leave?"

"I don't know. I just know that I will, but I have to go now."

She turned and walked into the thick mist, then sat down on the spot in the slope where she'd awakened. Something sharp dug into her hip. Her glasses. On touching them, a brilliant white flash temporarily blinded her. The mist rose, gathered on her face, her hair, as if it were a shroud. She was going home.

I'll be missing you, Catie.

Catie. Panic seized her stomach. He'd called her *Catie!*

And James's ballad. Dear God, it was the same song she and Jamie had danced to together the night of the Christmas Eve party.

She scrambled to her feet. *"Jamie!"*

The light snuffed out. Darkness surrounded her. She couldn't move. Her limbs went limp, devoid of strength. And she crumpled back onto the ground. *Oh God, please. Please, don't let me lose him again. Please!*

Nineteen

Groggy and stiff, Catie opened her eyes.

It was dark, and she lay sprawled on her side. The ground beneath her felt cool and damp and fine blades of dew-soaked grass pricked at her cheek. Her clothes felt sticky and smelled of . . . almonds?

A warning shiver zipped up her spine. Jamie's sheep had smelled of almonds. *Cyanide!*

Adrenaline surged through her veins and, in a flurry of motion, she stripped off the girdle, bliaut, and chemise, leaving only her camisole and lacy panties. The cool night air raised goose bumps on her exposed skin. Hugging herself, she darted a frantic gaze, looking for someone, hoping for help, but finding none.

Her gaze halted abruptly on the loch. It looked . . . clean. In the moonlight, it glistened sparkling clear. Was it clear because of the explosion? Or because, God help her, she was still in 1100?

Remembering what Jamie had said—that the ewe hadn't been affected until it was wet—she dried her hand on her bottom, snatched up her clothes, then ran toward the castle, her feet pounding on the uneven ground, jarring her teeth.

By the time she reached the castle's landing, her lungs threatened to burst. Letty's rocker. Oh, Letty's rocker. But had there been a rocker there in the past? Catie tried to recall, but couldn't remember for certain. She rushed inside.

Tile. The entry floor was tile. Weak with gratitude, she cried out, *"Jamie!"*

Glimpsing James's portrait on the wall, she came to a screeching halt. "Oh, my God."

As before, the man sat astride the reared beast, but now James was bearded . . . and wearing her medallion. Her heart wrenched. He'd been happy, aye, but had he also been her Jamie? Destined to be married to Catherine Forbes?

Annie screamed.

Catie nearly jumped out of her skin. Her hand flew to her chest and she wheeled toward the sound. Halfway up the stairs, Annie sagged against the banister, staring down at Catie as if she were a ghost.

"My God, we thought you were dead!" Annie rushed down and caught Catie in a crushing embrace. "Where have you been? Are you all right? Where are your clothes? Dear, Lord, Catherine, what's happened to your hair?"

Unable to keep up with the questions, Catie answered the last one with a question of her own. James had mentioned something amiss with her hair. "What's wrong with it?"

"It's streaked." Annie lifted a white lock. "Catherine, there's a white streak in your hair two inches wide."

Catie swallowed hard, tried to keep panic from her voice. "Where's Jamie, Annie?"

"Oh, you poor dear. Letty and I will put you to bed right away with a nice hot pot of tea." She patted Catie's shoulder. "Why are you running around in your underwear, dear?"

"It doesn't matter. Do you know where Jamie is, Annie?" Catie forced herself to be patient. Her godmother clearly was suffering shock.

"He stopped searching for you and came back to the castle some time ago." She clicked her tongue. "Mourning something awful, the darling man. He loves you, Catherine. There's no doubt—"

"Damn it, where is he!"

Annie gasped and backed away from her. "Catherine? What's happened to you?"

"Annie, please," Catie begged, softening her voice. "I'm sorry for yelling at you. Really, I am. But, truth is truth, and I have to see Jamie right away. It's urgent."

"He's at the feast, dear heart." She gave Catie a wary look. "Father MacDuff nearly had to drag him, but—"

Her heart soared. Jamie was here! Alive! "He wasn't injured?"

"No, he's fine. Can't recall a thing about the explosion, but otherwise, he's fine." Annie frowned. "He didn't want to go to the feast. But it's a laird's duty, you know. And with the Kirkland set on rebuilding the dam—"

"Rebuilding the dam?"

"Why, yes." Worry filled Annie's eyes. "Catherine, were you injured in the explosion? You're acting strangely, dear. And you still haven't told me where you've been."

Why was there a dam? There shouldn't be any dam. Kirkland had vowed there would *never* be a dam!

Wait. Wait. Edgar had said MacDuff would draw the documents. This Kirkland couldn't rebuild any dam, not if she could find the documents. But Jamie . . . Oh, what should she do? Jamie was fine. Annie said so. He was safe and fine, and he'd have her do what was most urgent—for his clan. Aye. She'd find the documents, then take them to Jamie.

"I'm not injured, Annie, but I am in a rush. I'll explain later. I have to get to Jamie." Catie kissed her godmother's cheek, then took the stairs two at a time.

"But the feast is that way." Annie pointed toward the front door.

"In a moment. I'm needing some clothes."

In the archives, Catie tore through the twelfth-century box until she found the folder of deeds. Flipping through it, she scanned the parchments until she came across the one containing the prohibition clause. No dam, it stated, clear and simple. "God bless you, MacDuff!" She kissed the parchment and blessed James, too, then left the archives.

Oh her way down the stairs, she stopped by her chamber, grabbed a bathrobe, tossed it on, then ran out to the battlefield.

Ignoring the strange looks coming her way, she made her way to the fire. Jamie stood with his back to her, talking with Duncan MacPherson. "Jamie!"

He stiffened, then slowly turned. "Catie."

His lips moved, but she heard no sound. Then he was running toward her, his cry splitting the night air. "Catie!"

Jamie scooped her up in his arms, jerked her close, crushing her to him. "Oh God, Catie." He buried his face at the cay in her neck. "Oh God. I thought I'd lost you forever."

She kissed him with rapid butterfly kisses, stroked his beard to reassure herself that it truly was him, and she cried. "Jamie." That was all she could manage.

The glistening in his eyes proved it more than enough. He cupped the back of her head in his hand and buried her face in his neck. She kissed the skin covering his pounding pulse and, from the corner of her eye saw Bronwyn and Iain, backing away from the fire and the clan. Iain was her accomplice? It fit. Poor Jamie would be devastated.

She reared back and pointed. "Stop them!"

Two Cameron men grabbed Iain. Colin Ferguson grabbed Bronwyn.

"Catie?"

She looked at Jamie. "Bronwyn committed the murders, Jamie. And, I'm afraid, Iain helped her."

"Do you have proof?"

Colin and the Cameron men brought Bronwyn and Iain back to the fire. Duncan MacPherson stepped closer, and Robert Kirkland stood at his side. Jamie set Catie down to the ground. "Bronwyn killed your grandfather, Jamie. She put cyanide in his milk."

"The milk wasn't tainted. I checked it myself."

Catie looked at Jamie.

"That's Elwin, the coroner."

"Iain was on his way to you with Harry's milk," Catie said. "Bronwyn met him on the way and she took the sample to your office. But before she did, she substituted the tainted milk with some not laced with cyanide. That's the milk she brought to you."

Deepening her voice to a whisper to soften the blow, Catie looked back at Jamie. "I suspect she killed your parents, too."

Bronwyn hotly denied it.

"I believe you did," Catie insisted. "I believe you dusted their clothes with cyanide, then forced them into the loch. When they got wet, the cyanide activated, and they died. That's why their skin was still pink." She looked at Jamie. "Just like she had your sheep dusted, Jamie. And my clothes."

"Is that why you're wearing a bathrobe?"

"Aye, I smelled the almonds."

He frowned. *"Had* my sheep dusted? Bronwyn didn't do that?"

"Nay, love." Catie looked at Iain. "A woman with the flock would have been noticed by the men. She didn't dust your sheep. Nor did she falsely accuse the MacPhersons of herding them from the water. That's where Bronwyn's accomplice made his mistake."

"What mistake?"

"A MacPherson wouldn't have herded the Cameron flock *away* from the loch, Jamie. Nor would they trespass onto Cameron land. And they certainly wouldn't sell tainted water in Edinburgh, either. Because it stinks."

"Damn right, Catie," Duncan MacPherson yelled out, then elbowed the Kirkland. "Grit. Aye, the woman's full of it."

"Iain?" Jamie looked at his second. "I would hear your accounting."

"I dusted the sheep. They weren't meant to die, though." Iain looked up at Jamie, regret in his eyes, and shrugged a bony shoulder. "I marked Catie with the thistle, and I attacked her in the archives, too."

"Why?"

Jamie's tone was ice cold, but she knew he was as hurt as he was angry. He'd trusted Iain. Catie squeezed Jamie's arm, offering silent comfort. "To keep you from marrying me," she said. "He wanted to be laird. Isn't that right, Iain?"

"Aye, though Bronwyn was attempting harm and I wasna. I only wanted you to ban Catie from Cameron. Bronwyn wanted Catie dead." He glared at Bronwyn. "I dinna kill Thomas, and I knew naught about the explosion either." He hiked his chin toward Bronwyn. "She did that all on her own."

"Which one of you attacked me?" Robert Kirkland grimaced.

"I did, Robert." Bronwyn smiled, but there was no warmth in it. "You and the Ferguson." She glared at Colin, still firmly grasping her arm. "Why did you give your flask to your man?"

Colin frowned, disappointment in his eyes. "He was thirsty."

"I had naught to do with that, either." Iain rushed to speak. "I'd no be killing a Scot."

"Yet you did mean to kill Catie in the archives," Jamie said, his muscles tensing under Catie's hands. Catie held him tighter.

Jamie locked gazes with Iain. "I'm no believing you didna mean Catie harm, Iain. You will tell me the truth."

Finally, Iain answered. "Aye, I did. I like Catie, but she's a Yank, James. It wouldna be right, her being a laird's wife."

"You did this, knowing she's my ally."

Iain narrowed his eyes. "She's no Scot, no Cameron neither, and never will be."

"You're wrong," Jamie corrected him. "She's Cameron *aw frae the bein.*"

Jamie turned to Bronwyn. "I would know why you have murdered my family."

She laughed, though there was no humor in it, and her eyes blazed hatred. "Camerons stripped Forbeses of everything, even their name, and you must ask me why? Christ, James. Your first laird even forced a Forbes to marry him. He took the only thing my clan had left to take: the will to cut out his black heart."

Catie stroked Jamie's arm. "If she believes James forced Catherine Forbes to marry him, Bronwyn is ill, love. He didn't."

"Catherine . . . *Forbes?*"

Catie nodded.

"James married Catherine . . . Forbes?"

Poor Jamie was stunned. "Aye, in 1102. But they loved each other, Jamie. He didn't force her to marry him."

"How do you know this?"

"It's in her diary."

"She had a diary, too?"

"Too?" Confused, Catie gave him a puzzled look.

"Never mind."

Father MacDuff stepped to Jamie's side. Letty held on to his arm, her expression as fiercely protective as a mother guarding her young.

"Laird," MacDuff said, not looking at all comfortable. "I have something to confess. Something I'm fearing I should have told you long ago. . . ."

Jamie waited.

"Go ahead, Gregor," Letty urged him. "James will be understanding of your reasons."

From the look in Letty's eyes, Jamie had best be understanding, or he'd be getting his ears scorched the rest of his days.

"My milk was being tainted, too." Gregor lowered his

gaze to the ground. "That's why I was feeling so poorly after Harry died. I knew it was one of my girls." He darted a glance at Celwyn. "I'm sorry, lass, but I couldna be certain which one." Then Gregor looked back to Jamie. "I knew you'd have no choice but to ban both Bronwyn and Celwyn, so I—"

"So you held your silence," Jamie said. He clasped the priest's shoulder. "I'm no approving, of course, but, aye, I'm understanding, Father."

"Oh God," Bronwyn let out an exasperated sigh. "I'm sick to death of this. Do what you will to me, just spare me from witnessing this nauseating scene."

Jamie nodded to his men. They led Iain and Bronwyn away from the fire then toward the village.

Catie breathed a relieved sigh. "What will happen to them, Jamie?"

"They'll be tried for their crimes."

"Will the court consider Bronwyn's illness?"

"Aye, lass." He wrapped his arm around her shoulder. "We're a compassionate people."

"Aye, we are that."

Jamie smiled. She'd converted, pure and simple.

"Jamie?"

"What, love?"

"Have you noticed how everyone is staring at us? Do we have dirty faces?"

"I'm thinking they're stunned. A lot has come to light here, I would remind you."

"Oh, I don't need reminding of that." She frowned up at him, then snuggled up against his side. "Where were you while I was gone? And how come you haven't asked me where I've been?"

"We've been a wee bit busy, lass."

Letty interrupted, hugging Catie. Her eyes were shiny and moist. "I would thank you, dear, for finding out the truth about my Harry."

"I'm so sorry it had to be like this."

"Me, too. But there's solace in knowing my Harry didn't die to get away from me."

Catie smiled, of a mind to put her questions to Jamie again about where he'd been and why he'd not asked where she'd been, but before she could get them out, Kirkland intervened, rocking back on his heels, his hand on his belt. "Well, James, it's been a hell of a festival, I'm saying."

"Aye, it has that."

Remembering the deed, Catie pressed it into Jamie's hand.

"What's this, love?"

"It says Kirkland can never dam the loch."

Jamie scanned the document, then looked at Robert. "It does say that."

"It won't be making no never mind." Robert scratched at his neck.

"The hell you say," Jamie countered.

"I've been talking with MacPherson and the Ferguson. We've pieced it together. Bronwyn substituted the water samples on all of us, James. I've talked to Daniel. She intercepted him on his way to Edinburgh both times. Though he dinna actually see her switch the water, I'm sure as certain she did."

"So you'll no be rebuilding the dam?" Jamie asked.

"Nay. But I will be making reparations to the villagers." Kirkland's face grew red. "And I suppose I ought to be telling ye I was the one selling the water in Edinburgh."

"Aye, I'm knowing," Jamie said softly. "Yer generosity with the villagers suits."

"Kirklands, generous?" Catie shrieked. "Since when?"

"Kirklands have been noted for being generous since James's time, Catie," Jamie said. "There's a legend that says an angel once warned the Kirkland laird against greed, and he took it to heart. Ever since, the clan has taken generosity into its creed."

"An angel, hmm?" So she was James's legendary angel,

and Kirkland's, too. Catie liked knowing that, and was grateful they'd not dubbed her a witch. With Scots, it could've gone either way. "I see."

"Not yet, darling," Jamie said. "But I'm thinking you're beginning to."

"That sounds like a promise."

"Aye, I said it."

"Oh." Arrogant. Darling, but arrogant.

"Oh?"

"Just, oh." She surely had her wifely work cut out for her with this charming barbaric beast.

Celwyn came up to Catie, wringing her hands. "Lud, Catie. I dinna know what to say. I'm so sorry."

"You haven't done anything." Catie stilled Celwyn's hands. "Stop."

Colin groaned. "James, where is Celwyn? Good God, she must be worried half out of her mind."

She stepped out from behind Jamie. "I'm right here."

"Ah, lass. I've been looking everywhere for ye." The young laird pulled her into his arms. "Dinna worry. Everything will be fine now. I'll be taking care of ye, and—"

"Nay, you'll not." Celwyn frowned up at him. "I'm not wanting to be in your care."

Colin frowned back down at her. "Why the hell not?"

"Can you believe the man, Catie? He chooses my sister as his festival bride, then wonders why I don't want to be in his care?" She glared at Colin. "I'm no rug you can walk all over when it pleases you, Colin Ferguson."

"A rug?" Jamie whispered close to Catie's ear. "Mmm, that has a familiar ring to it, I'm thinking."

Catie swatted at his arm. "Shh, listen."

Colin glared right back at Celwyn. "I'm knowing you're no rug, lass."

"You chose Bronwyn."

"She turned my head. It meant nothing. It was—"

"Wrong tactic. Think of this as war, man. Offense," Jamie whispered to Colin. "Ask her whose colors she wore."

"It was daft, is what it was, Colin Ferguson," Celwyn informed him. "I was there. I saw you claim her."

"And whose colors were you wearing? Oh, but you weren't a bride, now were you? That's right. Bronwyn told me ye'd be no man's festival bride. And why is that, I'm asking? You knew I wanted to claim you."

"I didn't know. How was I supposed to know? Did you bother to tell me?"

"Poorly put, Colin," Jamie whispered. "Logic will do you no good, man. Not in this battle. Use diplomacy, aye—and ask her whose colors she wore."

Colin crossed his chest with his arms. "I asked ye a question."

"What?" Celwyn shouted, her chest heaving.

"Whose colors were ye wearing?"

"It doesna matter since he didn't claim *me.*"

"Celwyn, you will stop shouting and answer me, lass."

"Fool that I am," she glared up at him, "I wore your colors, ye ungrateful, arrogant, sorry shepherd!"

"Ah, another familiar—"

"Jamie, hush." Catie elbowed him in the ribs.

"Mine?" Colin looked stunned.

"Aye." Celwyn's lip quivered and her anger faded. "A fool I surely am, but I'm loving you, Colin."

Jamie hauled Catie to his side. "Ah, peace within reach. Isn't it warming, Catie?"

"If he doesn't claim her, it'll be warming, all right," she told Jamie. "I'm going to scorch the man's ears."

"I'll beat him bloody."

"Jamie, you'll not. Celwyn would be furious."

"Furious? Why would the woman be furious, I'm asking?"

"For crying out loud, love, she'd have to wait for him to heal to cure her flaw."

"Ah, I'm seeing." He slung an arm around her shoulder and hauled her close to his side. "And I'm thinking you'll be bossing me until I'm planted on the ridge by Harry."

"True." Catie smiled up at him. "But I'll never let you suffer."

He chuckled under his breath. "All right, love. I'll help you scorch Colin's ears, then. But that's the last hexing I'm letting you get away with for a time. A woman has to learn her place, by damn."

"Oh, I know my place, Jamie." Catie smiled wickedly. "Especially when I'm feeling . . . soft."

He groaned.

Colin took off his jacket then walked over to Celwyn. "If I'd been knowing ye'd be among the brides, I would have claimed ye. I would claim ye now, love."

"Really?" She looked up at him through eyes that adored.

He smiled softly and draped his jacket over her shoulders. "You wear my colors, Celwyn Forbes."

Dewy-eyed, Celwyn smiled. "Aye, I do."

"Then I claim thee for my bride."

"Your festival bride," she corrected him.

"Aye. That, too." He kissed the tip of her nose. "I'm loving ye, Celwyn."

Jamie stretched and gave Father MacDuff's shoulder a nudge. "Hurry up and marry them, Father—before he forgets diplomacy and raises her hackles again."

MacDuff agreed with an enthusiastic nod, and hurried to his place by the fire.

Feeling warm and tender, under the crook of Jamie's arm, Catie leaned her head against his chest. The priest prayed in ancient Gaelic, saying the same prayer his predecessor had prayed to marry Catie and James. Catie decided to wait until they were alone to mention that fact—any of those facts. Jamie would be a lot less prone to scorching her ears if he was soft and she was soothing him.

When MacDuff finished, he asked all festival couples to step forward. Catie and Jamie joined the other eleven couples.

Father MacDuff smiled at them. "Which of you husbands are of a mind to marry your brides?"

Colin and two other men spoke up. Jamie didn't. Catie worried her lip. What was wrong with him? He'd given her the aquamarine.

MacDuff sidestepped a spray of sparks from the fire. "And which of you brides are of a mind to marry your husbands?"

Catie darted Jamie's profile a look that should knock him on his ass. Why hadn't the man spoken up?

MacDuff directed the non-marrying couples to withdraw. Jamie started to back up. Catie let go of his arm and turned to the priest. "Father, might I have a moment?"

"Sweet Mary." He crossed himself, then gave her his resigned approval.

That totally fouled her mood. She dragged Jamie a few steps away, out of easy earshot of the others, so long as they didn't raise their voices, then planted her hand on her hip. "Explain yourself, Jamie."

He gave her a puzzled look. "What are you wanting me to explain, love?"

"Don't you dare try to fool me with that darling innocent look. I'm livid with you."

"What the hell did I do?" He glanced over at MacDuff, whose frown proved he'd clearly heard the curse. "Sorry, Father."

"What *haven't* you done, would be a better question." She ticked the items off on her fingers. "First you make me your ally—without explaining what exactly an ally is, much less the duties that go along with the pleasures, I might add. Then you send me away—to a blasted, inferior Englishman. Then you let me spend six months thinking that you hate me—all the while, of course, you're knowing that I'm loving you with all my heart and missing you something awful."

"Catie, darl—"

"Nay!" she interrupted. "I'll have my say, Jamie."

His sigh heaved his shoulders. She didn't dare look at his face. "And as if all that weren't enough, I have to come home against your wishes—I am trying to be fair here and hold strictly to the truth, Jamie—and instead of telling me that you still love me, you again force me into an engagement with an inferior Englishman whose face is as bare as a bairn's arse! Then you claim me, put me through hell like I've never been put through it before—" She paused to look at MacDuff. "Sorry, Father." She returned her glare to Jamie. "And now, after all that, you won't marry me?"

Catie narrowed her eyes and poked her finger into his chest. "You said you'd be my friend." She gave him another jab. "You said you'd be my lover." A third poke followed the other two. "You said you loved me, Jamie. We even tried to make a bairn together. Now there's your infamous rub. You're a Cameron, right? Well, Camerons hold to tradition, honor, and duty, and they never lie. You said you'd marry me and you will, Jamie. You'll marry me right now—and that, as you're so fond of saying, is that."

"Aren't you forgetting something?"

"Most likely. You have a hell of a list of offenses."

He frowned thoroughly at that remark. "I'm meaning the wee matter of your engagement to Sir Andrew."

"The hell I am." She groaned and rolled her gaze to Mac-Duff. "Sorry, Father."

He gave her an understanding nod.

"You're not of a mind to be marrying the man?"

"I just said I wasn't. Damn it, James. Don't you listen when I'm talking to you?"

Jamie turned to MacDuff. "She's sorry, Father. I'm fearing the woman's needing a wee bit of soothing."

"Aye, a wee bit more than a wee bit, I would say." Mac-Duff nodded his solemn agreement.

"You never reunited with Sir Andrew," Jamie said. "You lied to me, Catherine."

"We're back to that again." She squeezed her eyes shut, and prayed for patience. "I did *not* lie. Would you kindly think, James Cameron? How the hel—heaven could I marry him, when I love you?"

Jamie went still.

Going beyond flustered and headlong into furious, Catie glowered at him. "I said, I love you, James. When your ally and bride says she loves you, it's your duty to acknowledge her feelings, in case you aren't knowing." She glanced at Letty who soundly confirmed Catie's assertion with a nod. So did Annie.

"Oh, I'm knowing."

"Well?" She shifted on her feet. "Don't you love me anymore?"

"Of course, I love you, woman. You're my ally."

"So will you marry me, then—willingly?"

"I said, I would, dinna I? Aye, by damn I know I did. And long before you came to Cameron," he reminded her. "Weren't *you* listening?"

"Aye, but—"

"All you had to do was ask."

"Me, ask?" God help her, it was another odd little Scottish tradition.

"Aye," Jamie said. "I offered, if you'll recall. It was up to you to accept."

"Well, hell." She slumped against his side and mumbled, "Sorry, Father."

" 'Tis clear as day you're needing soothing, lass. Shh." Jamie circled her shoulder with his arm, then turned her around until she faced the castle. "Look at me tower, love."

Catie looked up the honey-colored stone. At the top, three, and not two, flags unfurled in the wind. His Scots flag, the Cameron banner . . . and Old Glory.

"Oh, Jamie." Her eyes misted and filled with tears. "You do love me."

"Aye, lass." He turned her to him. "With all my heart."

She kissed him deeply, then smiled up at him, her eyes blurry. "Your tower's lacking."

"What?"

"Lacking. It's a slight, pure and simple."

"Catie darling, finding fault with me tower doesna raise affection in me Scots heart. I'm flying your damn flag. What more are ye wanting?"

"Insult. And I'm not taking it kindly," she warned him. "My flag's at half-mast. Yours isn't."

"Ah, I know what you're about. Yer thinking I'm saying Scots are superior, but yer thinking wrong. I was mourning ye, lass."

"Oh."

"Oh?"

"Well, if you were mourning me, your Scots flag, too, should be at half-mast."

"You've converted?"

She'd given her pledge to Edgar, but Jamie himself had told her she'd converted. He looked so tense for her answer, she didn't have the heart to remind him of that fact, though. She smiled instead. "Nay, I'm hexed."

Jamie laughed in her face, and hauled her to his side. "Go on, Father. Before she hexes all of Scotland, marry me to the witch."

"I'll take ye burden off yer hands, James." Duncan MacPherson grinned. "What are allies for?"

Jamie pretended to consider the offer. "Nay, I can't be asking that of ye, friend. The woman's a Yank, if you'll recall."

"But her heart's Scots." Pursing his lips, Duncan intently took her measure. "Aye, I'll take her. We MacPhersons never could resist a woman with grit."

"Nay, Duncan. She's mine." The teasing left Jamie's voice. "I'll no be losing her again."

"Jamie," Catie whispered. "You're never going to believe what happened to me after the explosion."

"Shh," he whispered. "I plan on hearing MacDuff. I'm thinking you might have hexed him into adding a few Yank vows."

"I wouldn't." She stepped closer to Jamie's side. "I know it's going to sound preposterous, but I went back in time, Jamie. To eleven hundred. And I met James—"

"Shh, darling. Later. It's over now."

"You're a wee bit blasé about this, Jamie."

"Will you hush, woman?"

"All right, damn it."

She and Jamie whispered in unison. "Sorry, Father."

He shot them a glare over the top of his glasses. "Do you, James, take Catherine Morgan as your wife?"

"Aye," Jamie snapped. "Could you hurry, Father? The woman's fixed on bending me ear."

"I'll take him, Father." She frowned at Jamie. "Satisfied?"

"You've got MacDuff crossing himself again, Catie. If the man's arthritis flares up, 'twill be your fault, I'm thinking."

"I won't accept full responsibility," she said. "You've done more than your fair share to set him to praying."

While she ranted on, Jamie turned to the priest. "Is it done, Father? Are we married?"

"Aye, 'tis done." He shouted to be heard over Catie. "Sweet Mary."

The woman did have a lusty temper. Darling, that. Grinning, Jamie scooped Catie up, pulled her flush against his chest, then kissed her quiet.

It took Catie a full minute of kissing to get her temper down, and another to forget her anger altogether. But then she curled her arms around Jamie's neck and kissed him back, putting her heart into the pleasure.

Something at his neck snagged her fingertips. Something . . . metal.

She rubbed the thin strip between her forefinger and thumb. A chain? She opened her eyes. Following its length with her fingers, she met with a round disc, and stilled. "My . . . medallion."

"Aye." His eyes twinkled.

Catie stared at him. Why didn't he say anything more? "Jamie?"

No answer.

Held high off the ground in his arms, she reared back and pivoted his face until she could see his hair in the light from the fire. Her heart started a slow, hard beat. "Jamie, you've got a white streak in your hair."

"Aye." The twinkle in her new husband's eyes warmed. "I'm loving you, Catie Cameron."

The awful man. "I should beat you bloody."

"Nay, darling, you're opposed to bloodletting." He caught her lower lip then gently raked it with his teeth. "And that's no way for you to be talking to an allied husband who's flying yer damn Yank flag from his tower, I'm saying."

"I've insulted you."

"Aye," he emphatically agreed. "And more than once."

She gave him her angel's smile. "I'll repay."

"Of course, darling." He rubbed their noses. "But first, you'll do your wifely duty and tell me you love me again— without your shouts." Reprimand laced his tone. "Aye, sounding sexy would be a lot more soothing, lass. I've a fondness for your soothing, and you have slighted me, taking so long to give me the words. Aye, definitely slighted me. I'm thinking maybe you should repay me twice. Tradition, for neglecting your wifely duty overly long."

She'd only been his wife a few minutes. But the idea of twice soothing Jamie appealed immensely, so she didn't toss him on his foolish elbow for that wee bit of blackmail. "More traditions." She feigned a sigh. "Now why doesn't that surprise me?"

"I'm waiting, Catie. Ye could be showing your husband a wee bit more respect. I'm a fierce laird, if you'll recall."

She recalled, all right. And knowing exactly how to soothe the temper right out of him, she stroked his wonderful beard. "Jamie, I'm of a mind to love you, darling." She gave him a slow blink. "Before, during, and after."

He smiled straight from the heart. "Aye, before, during, and after, love." And he kissed his beloved Yank to seal his vow.

Author's Note

"A lion in the world, a lamb by his own hearth."

That's a Scotsman—the spirit of the man—and the premise for this novel. My intent is neither to depict the modern Scottish political structure nor its royal hierarchy. My intent is to honor the Scotsman.

He's perceptive, imaginative, and fiercely loyal. He possesses enduring courage and deep pride. He's also ever-dutiful. To capture the essence of his ideals, of the devotion to family and to country etched in his Scots heart, I've portrayed the political structure and the role of royals as it was nearly a thousand years ago, for in all of my research, that is how both remain today—in the Scotsman's heart.

Some remote areas in the Highlands, the harsh and brutal and hauntingly beautiful, uppermost region of Scotland, seem untouched by time. It is one such region visited in *Festival*. One such region, and one such Scottish heart . . . in spirit.

Victoria Barrett
Fort Walton Beach, Florida